# ONE MORE TIME

To John,

**A NOVEL BY
MICHAEL DILWORTH**

I promise this book
will be better than
Bolton!

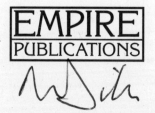

**EMPIRE
PUBLICATIONS**

First published in 2011

EMPIRE PUBLICATIONS
1 Newton Street, Manchester M1 1HW
© Michael Dilworth 2011

ISBN 1901746 801 – 9781901746808

Printed in Great Britain.

## ACKNOWLEDGMENTS

I want to dedicate the book to my late mum and dad, and also to Lisa, Chloe and Olivia for all their love and support with the book.

I would acknowledge the help and assistance of Paul Kennedy, to Ashley and Sadie and all at Empire Publications for their guidance, Martin Pearce and Sally Howard for their advice, and apologies to Pete Booth for not using his art work for the cover!!

# 2010

HAVE YOU EVER had a brilliant new chapter of your life begin only for something surprising from your past to re-appear? I did.

My name is Liam Kirk, I am 37 and as I got out of the taxi and went into The Sun Inn I reflected that I had a lot to celebrate. After several years of indifference towards my work in an insurance call centre I found myself with a book being published. I'm not instantly rich but I have myself a nice little advance on this book and on two future books. It means I can bin the head set and call scripts to work on my writing full time.

I have been keen on writing since childhood and in my late teens had started writing for football fanzines. My writing took a back seat once I got married and became a dad but when my wife and I separated I fancied a hobby and looked into some courses at a local adult college. The tutor was Marion, an inspiration, who told her class, "Most writers write about incidents from their own life. Look to your past for ideas."

With this advice in mind I wrote a few chapters loosely based around a relationship I had with a woman called Val in the 1990s when I was twenty-two, although I set it more up to date than that. Relationship was probably too strong a word for what really happened which I realised as I began to write my recollections down, so I bulled up what had really happened to make it more interesting. Marion liked what I had written and put me in touch with some literary agents to try to sell my work which is how I have ended up here.

My first novel - Who's Going To Drive You Home? – is out in all good bookshops, as they say, from Monday. The character that I based on me I gave the name Paul but as I did not really look too far ahead I did not change Val's name and we were too far down the publishing line before I thought it might be a problem...

I arrived at The Sun, a smart modern pub where a rough arse old one of the same name used to be, ahead of the time I had arranged to meet my former work colleagues for a celebratory drink and there is a reason for this; in a busy pub surrounded by people I find sweat forming on my brow very noticeably. The more polite people will not say anything but friends consider themselves helpful to point out, "are you sweating?" "No," I tell them, "it's just raining on me forehead." One day I will make the time to visit a doctor and get this sorted. One day, when my bloody writing work allows. I refuse to believe it is all just down to me being a fat bastard.

None of my old work mates were there yet but this was not a surprise as it was quarter past seven and we had all arranged to meet between quarter to eight and eight o' clock. It was a nice, late spring night, the sun was still shining, it was warm, people appeared to be out in shirt sleeves for the first time this year and there were a handful of people in. I noticed a couple, a man and a woman stood at the bar talking. He was tall and wiry framed wearing a check shirt, she was tall for a woman, a bit taller than me and was dressed in what I would describe as a bohemian style; a brown kaftan blouse and a flowery patterned skirt. As I neared the bar their gestures became aggressive although I only heard them as I got closer as there was some dirge of a Leonard Cohen track playing in there.

The woman spun round to face the man and snapped, "Oh, Barry, of course it fucking matters!" and then she clapped eyes on me, let her mouth fall open in shock but said no more. Barry left the pub muttering "bitch" under his breath as he passed me. I allowed myself a silly smile but the woman's jaw was still somewhere around her midriff.

"Bloody hell, Valerie Walters, it's been a long time," I exclaimed to which she never replied, just gawped. "Surprised you recognise me it's been so long." Looking at the figure of Barry disappearing through the door I laughed and asked, "Have I arrived at a bad time?"

"Didn't you always?" she replied. "So how have you been in the..." Val paused. "...however many years it is since I've seen you?"

"Thirteen years," I offered.

"I'd have said more like fifteen myself but you were always the memory man."

"Where do the years go, eh?" I asked her not expecting an answer and all I got was a barely interested shrug. Where did the years go? I was twenty-one when I first met her and twenty-four when I had last seen her. Still, despite only knowing her for a fraction of my life she must have made an impression, after all I'd written a book about her.

# WHO'S GOING TO DRIVE YOU HOME?

## A NOVEL BY LIAM KIRK

# INTRODUCTION

I T WAS A FRIDAY and it was raining, not altogether uncommon in Lancashire during the summer. Paul Stevenson, 23, was stood outside the local crematorium reading messages for his late mother on a number of wreaths. Somewhere nearby his two elder sisters - Cheryl, small, mousey haired and 'mumsy' looking, and Joanne, brunette, business like and taller - were comforting their father, who himself looked grey, pale and defeated. The girls themselves were being comforted by their respective husbands. Paul felt reflective and alone but after months of being ravaged by cancer felt that his Mum's death had been a blessing. Her suffering and illness gave him the chance to appear interested in her plight and it helped that his football team were having an indifferent season and weren't worth watching so he had more spare time on his hands than normal to be there for her. He tried to decide if the rain soaking his ill-fitting bought-from-ASDA-for-eighteen-pounds suit made the day more beautiful or made the day a sadder occasion and while he was weighing this information up an elderly lady approached him and smiled kindly, a smile which Paul returned. The lady looked at the wreaths for a moment.

"Are you all right Paul, love?" she asked finally, patting him on the arm.

"Yes, I'm okay, thanks," he confirmed as he needlessly brushed rain off the suit, last worn at his sister Joanne's wedding three years earlier. He smiled weakly at the woman who paused to take the information on board.

"Is there a do to go to anywhere afterwards?" the old lady asked in an upbeat manner with a vision of vol-au-vents and cocktail sausage rolls in her eyes.

"No, the family are going back to my Dad's but no, nothing else." The woman was disappointed but hid it and nodded to understand then held Paul's hand.

"Your mum was a lovely woman," Paul smiled at her kind comments, "but God help you with your father." The woman walked away. If nothing else his Mum's death had taught him that she was a lot more popular than his Dad. He was alone again with his thoughts until, from the throng of people around his Dad and sisters, came Nicky, a girl his sister Joanne had gone to school with and who Paul had always got on with, and fancied if truth be told, which is why he got on with her so well. She smiled sympathetically and then hugged Paul.

"How you doing, honey?" she asked untangling from the hug.

"Hanging in there, Nicky," he confirmed with a shrug. "Nothing more."

"No one with you?" she asked. "Not seeing anyone?" Paul shook his head.

"How does this happen, Paul? You are lovely, sweet and funny."

"I'd rather be handsome, boring and rich," Paul commented to which Nicky smiled again. "Why don't you go out with me if that's how you feel?" Paul asked her, chancing his arm but Nicky gave a hollow laugh.

"We're friends, Paul. It would be best to leave it at that, don't you think?" Nicky suggested as kindly as she could.

*No!*

"Take care," Nicky hugged Paul again and before Paul could return this sentiment she had blended away back into the mourners.

Later, back at his father's home, his middle sister Joanne patted him on the back as those gathered in the front room said very little but thought, mainly, as the vicar at the funeral service had put it, of their "wife, mother and friend".

"Come to the kitchen and help me put the kettle on, Paul," Joanne ordered.

"Okay," he said, and stood up to follow her. In the kitchen as they waited for the kettle to boil Joanne noticed some boxes and bags in the corner of the kitchen and looked at them in some confusion.

"What are these, Paul? Are they Mum's things? I thought me and Cheryl were going to see to that tomorrow,"

"No, Jo, they're my things, I'm moving out next week," Paul confirmed.

Joanne looked surprised, "You're moving out but what about Dad?"

"I think he's staying put." Joanne pulled a face at her younger brother as if to say 'not now, Paul, not with your silly jokes, not today.'

"You know what I mean, Paul," she said at last, "does he know about it?"

"He knows all about it, I told him the other week when we were watching the news after tea."

"And what did he say?"

"Nothing for three hours and then he fell asleep in the chair in front of the telly... again."

"Look, Paul, I know it's been tough for you here..."

"Do you? That's great Jo, but it's just been me here and it's been the toughest for me."

"I never said that it hadn't, Paul," Joanne snapped. Being two years older than Paul, their relationship had often been strained since childhood and whatever Paul had ever said on any subject he felt she always tried to turn it around so he sounded like a spoilt brat. Cheryl, being the oldest, always sided with Paul, as he was the youngest. Without another word Joanne left the kitchen and headed back to the front room looking upset.

"Jo, hold on, let me explain, Jo!" Paul called after her, but she carried on walking, causing Paul to throw the tea cup in his hand across the room. "Shit!"

After a few minutes Paul was joined in the kitchen by David, Cheryl's husband, and Tony, who was married to Joanne. They were in the process of putting on their jackets. If nothing else Paul thought this action meant they hadn't come to have a punch up with him.

"Lads?" he asked. "Is something the matter?"

"Come on, Paul, mate, we're going for a pint and a chat," Tony said. "You're the local, where do you suggest?"

"The Prince of Wales, it's a half decent pub in the town centre."

"Okay, then, let's go," David said.

At the Prince of Wales the lads headed in through the front door and the two 'out of towners' looked unsure at what to do for a moment, as if they had never been in a pub before. There was some good mood music playing in the background, something mellow from an Acid Jazz compilation or some such which clashed with the gloomy, miserable air that hung around the place.

"You two find a table and I'll get the drinks in," said David nodding in no real direction and he headed for the bar as Tony and Paul made for the tables in the window. Behind the bar was a man in his early twenties with long blond shaggy hair who looked more suited for surfing than pulling pints.

"Yes mate, what can I get you?" the barman asked amiably.

"Two pints of your best bitter and a coke, no ice, please," David said which prompted the barman to raise his eyebrows at the drinks being referred to as 'best bitter'. He clearly didn't think any of his bitters could be described as best.

"Right, coming up!" As the barman busied himself with the drinks a smart, friendly looking man who looked to be in his forties, came to the bar. He was wearing a denim shirt and black trousers and he soon fell into conversation with the barman.

"You all set up then, Jim?" the barman asked.

"Yeah, I know I don't start off for a couple of hours but I just wanted to get in and get everything sorted," Jim replied.

"Have you done any DJ-ing before?" the barman continued ignoring his customer.

"Yes, a few parties, not," Jim hesitated, "semi-professionally, shall we say."

Jim looked at David who was waiting for their drinks and nodded. David nodded back and then Jim looked around the pub to see who else was in at five o'clock on a Friday afternoon when he suddenly saw a face he knew.

"Hell's bells," Jim said to no one in particular, to neither the barman nor David, "there's a lad over there that I haven't seen for many a long while, I used to work with him. It's Paul, Paul Stevenson."

The comment made David raise his eyebrows; "Oh, you know Paul, then, do you?" he asked.

"Yeah, how do you know him?"

"He's my brother in law."

"Oh, right, I see," Jim hesitated and clocked that Paul, David and Tony were quite smartly dressed. "What's been the occasion today, then," he grabbed imaginary lapels on his shirt, "for the suits I mean?"

"His Mum's funeral unfortunately, cancer," David confirmed as quietly as the background music would allow, pulling a sympathetic face as he did.

"Oh, right, sorry, I haven't seen him for an age, I had no idea she was ill," Jim paused for a moment to reflect on the news and David shrugged.

"No problem."

"Here are your drinks," the barman said, "six-pounds, eighty, please." As David rummaged for change to pay a thought occurred to Jim.

"Can I go over to say hello to him and pay my respects?" he asked.

"Do you mind just giving us a minute, mate? We need to have a bit of a chat with him on a family matter first," David replied.

"Okay, no problem." David paid for the drinks, picked them up and with a friendly nod and a smile at Jim headed to join the other two.

"Bloody hell, Paul, the poor sod, his Mum's died. That's got to be hard on him."

At this point the landlord, Nigel, joined them, a tall, broad man, who looked like he might have occupied a rugby line out or two in his younger days and who was dressed as casually as his clientele in polo shirt and jeans, funeral parties notwithstanding.

"Blimey, you're keen, Jim," he said. "Glad we're not paying you by the hour."

Jim smiled, "Yeah, just wanted to know everything is all set and ready."

"Good, good. I was going to ask you something later but I'll mention it now," Jim turned to head back to the DJ stand and Nigel walked with him, "I'm thinking of setting up a quiz on a Monday night, how would you be fixed to run it and set it up for me, get the questions sorted and what have you?"

"Sure, no problem, great."

"Good lad, Jim, we'll see how tonight and tomorrow goes and we'll take it from there."

"Here we are then lads, here's your ale," David said, as he reached the table and put the drinks down.

"Cheers, Dave," said Tony, where as Paul didn't say a word but picked his pint up, took a big gulp and then looked out of the window at the world passing by. David nodded towards Paul and mouthed at

Tony, "Had a word, yet?" and Tony shook his head. David sat down.

"It's been a tough old time for you and your Dad recently, eh, Paul?" David said.

Paul nodded, "It's been no picnic, Dave, mate," he agreed.

"Paul, Jo told us you are thinking about moving out of the house," Tony began.

"Did she now?" Paul took a drink of his pint and the other two paused waiting for him to comment further. He sensed this after a moment so confirmed it. "Yeah, that's right, although I'm not just thinking about it, I'm doing it."

"Do you think it's wise so soon after what's happened?" Tony continued.

Paul shrugged and fought the anger he felt at being picked on or got at. "Look, I've been thinking about it for a while, lads, it's not as if I thought 'oh, God, my mum's died today, let me move out', I gave it a lot of thought." Paul shook his head to himself, in disbelief, and took another drink.

"Who are you moving in with, Paul?" David asked.

"Mate of mine, a lad called Martin. I went to school with him. He had a joint mortgage with a mate of his on a house and after his mate moved out and moved on he took the whole house on."

"Do you have to move in there right away?" David asked. "You'll be doing the girls and your Dad, and us two, a huge favour by stopping at home for a few months, and, you know, keeping an eye on him."

"I dunno about this, lads," said Paul. "He does me napper in, always has."

"Paul?" Tony said. David looked at him in a hopeful manner.

"Oh, sod it. Okay, I'll stay for a bit, keep an eye on the old bugger." The other two smiled at a job well done.

"Good lad, Paul," said David, patting him on the back. Paul stared into space and wondered, as the youngest of the three children, if he would ever get away from home. He felt duty bound to stay when his mum was ill to take some of the pressure off his dad to care for her. Now it appeared he had to do the same for his dad.

After a couple more pints for Paul and Tony with David sticking to the cokes the three of them stood up and made to leave the pub. Jim was at the DJ stand and seeing them leave he regretted not making it over to pass on his respects. As Paul and his brothers-in-law were leaving, a tall, attractive red haired woman of about Paul's age came towards the door from outside. Paul did not seem to take too much notice of her because as he led the way towards the door he was looking back at Tony and David who were grinning at each other for convincing him to stay. This made him feel worse, as if he had been conned into doing this and he felt the weight of the world on his shoulders. When he neared the door he noticed the woman approaching and he stood back to let her through first.

"Thank you very much, what a gentleman," she said in a cheery manner. Paul never commented back but walked on through the door. David looked at the woman as she carried on into the pub.

"American?" he asked, raising his eyebrows at Tony.

"Think so, is she lost? What's she doing here in this crap-hole?"

The woman was probably thinking that herself as she walked into a pub she had never been in before, and looked around for a moment before seeing who she was after. It was Jim. She headed over to join him and he looked surprised.

"Val, hi, thanks for coming down," he said.

Val stood there for a moment in front of him weighing up what she was going to say, "I'm not a hundred per cent behind you on this Jim and I think you should really have kept the job with the despatch company as well as doing this in the evenings, but I've thought of something that will make things easier for you."

"What's that?"

"I'll move in with you."

Jim smiled and Val was soon smiling too. Jim put his arms around her.

"Thanks," he said, then gave her a kiss, "I love you, Val."

## 2010

We had been stood next to each other for a few minutes and the conversation was not inspiring, leading me to rack my brains as to what to talk about.

"So, you're still teaching then are you, Val?" I asked her as I waved a ten pound note around suggesting I was trying to swat a fly when I was actually trying to get the barman's attention. His attention was drawn to leering at a blonde girl in a denim mini-skirt. To be honest I could not blame him. In the background the Smiths had replaced Leonard Cohen suggesting that sales of gin would be going through the roof tonight.

"Yeah, I've been in India doing it for these last three years"

"Aye, I know"

"How do you know?" she asked me with a surprised look. Yes, how did I know? Ah, Friends Reunited, I read her blurb, or blog, or whatever it is called but she never replied to the three messages I sent her, or was it four?

"Ian must have told me," I replied, hoping to save face. Ian was Val's boyfriend when I met her. In the book the character based on him is called Jim. Another name changed when I should really have changed hers.

"Oh, right, when did you last see him then, sometime recently down at the Prince of Wales?" she asked me.

"Yeah, here and there, out and about, you know?" I lied, actually thinking that the last time I saw him was about the last time I saw Val - thirteen years ago.

# CHAPTER ONE

I T WAS A SATURDAY NIGHT in May, the weather was getting warmer and the pubs were getting busier. Paul was on a night out and with him were Martin and Simon. Martin, the mate Paul was going to move in with after his Mum died, was still with the same girlfriend who had ultimately blocked this move at the time and he was on a rare night out. These would soon be rarer still as the girlfriend was expecting their first child. Simon was an old college friend of Paul's from when they were on day release from their respective jobs.

They made their way to the bar in the Red Lion pub with Martin pulling faces at how busy it was, as only a man who hardly ever goes out anymore can do, as the umpteenth teenager barged into him.

"Right, my shout, same again, lads?" Simon asked clapping his hands and then rubbing them together.

"Yeah," said Paul. "Nice one."

"Thanks," Martin added looking down his nose at his fellow customers.

Paul was looking to his left and laughed to himself at how the clientele were all getting a lot younger. Their dress sense made him think.

"Do you remember when we first started going out, Martin?" he said. "We had to wear trousers and a shirt with a collar to get into anywhere late on. In fact, to get into Liberty's back then we had to wear a tie!"

"I know, look at it now. Anyone not wearing a t-shirt looks like they are at a lumberjack convention," Paul laughed at Martin's comment. From Paul's right he felt someone tap his arm and he turned to face them and saw it was Nicky, Joanne's old school friend.

"Hello, Nicky love, how are you?" he asked. Nicky gave him a big hug.

"I'm fine thanks, Paul, and you?" Paul still fancied her and moved her away from the bar to get her out of earshot of Simon and Martin, which was a relief as the two of them were already making lewd gestures behind her back. Nicky looked as stunning as ever; she had a lovely smile that made you think she really cared for you. Her dark hair was styled in such a way to suggest hours and a small fortune had been spent on it. Her top was low cut, in such a way that made Paul struggle with eye contact.

"Have you been to the football today?" she asked.

"No, I watched it on Sky in the pub with the lads," Paul replied.

"You've got to be happy with that result, though, a two-two draw at Liverpool,"

"Yeah, I'd have taken that before the start."

"Still living at home?"

"Aye, I never moved out, still there," Paul confirmed.

"How are you coping with your Dad?" Nicky tilted her head sympathetically as she asked. Paul shrugged and gave a rueful laugh.

"Well, you know how that old bugger is, was and always will be."

At this point Nicky did something Paul never expected. In all the time they had known each other she had never done anything like this. She lunged forward and kissed him passionately, open mouths, tongues, hands on his face, everything. It was everything Paul had ever wanted from Nicky. When they stopped she kept her hands on his face.

"Paul, if you want, we can meet up for a drink in the week, for a chat, as friends,"

*As friends? What? After that?!*

"Sure," he said, finally regaining his composure, "how about meeting in the Crown at eight on Wednesday?"

Nicky smiled. "See you then." She gave him another quick kiss, wiped lipstick from his mouth with a girly giggle and went to re-join her friends, turning around on her way to smile, wink and wave at him. Paul walked back to join Martin and Simon who had watched the events unfold and were staring open mouthed in shock. So much in shock were they that the barman could not get their attention to pay for the drinks.

"Mate, hello? Excuse me, mate, eight pounds forty, please," he was saying to no one when Paul got there so he grabbed the tenner out of Simon's hand and gave it to the barman, "thank you," he said.

"Did you see the top she nearly had on?" said Martin, after a moment of silence. "Talk about a dead heat in a zeppelin race!"

"I'm meeting her for a drink in the week! Wednesday night, get in!" Paul told them.

"Good lad, well done," said Simon, patting Paul on the back.

"Yeah? Nice one! You've always liked her, hope it goes well, Paul son," Martin agreed.

On the night he was meeting Nicky, Paul took a call from Simon as he was getting ready and trying to steady his nerves.

"Are you still meeting 'Nicky Lovely' tonight, Paul?" he asked.

"Yeah, I am."

"Hope it goes well."

"Cheers, a little bit of me is disappointed that the footie is on tonight, UEFA Cup final."

"But, Paul, this is a gorgeous woman you are meeting tonight, one you have always wanted to go out with and, look, you don't support either team who are playing."

"Yeah, you're right, Simon."

"Yes, I am," Simon agreed and then paused. "Is she wearing that top again?"

Paul laughed, "I'm not sure, but I certainly hope so."

"Can I sit in the far corner of the pub and watch?"

"Simon, I'm going."

"I'll be quiet and discreet, you won't know I'm there," Simon pleaded as Paul hung up, laughing.

He got to The Crown early and it was not too busy. He noticed they had the football showing on a couple of TVs dotted around the pub and regardless of what top Nicky was wearing he might be looking upwards anyway, sneaking a glance at that. When she came into the pub just after eight o'clock she was dressed to the nines; black jacket over a black v-neck t-shirt and white three-quarter length trousers. So spectacular did she look that the old bloke sat in the corner with his whippet dropped his pint.

"Hi, Paul, not late am I?" she asked, with a big smile which would have made Paul forgive her for turning up ten hours late.

"No, don't worry, you're right on time. Can I get you a drink?"

A barman was stood nearby and Nicky asked him for a Bacardi and coke. Paul leant forward to kiss Nicky, intending it to be on the lips, Nicky saw him coming and tried to offer her cheek and the kiss ended up being a bit clumsy. Nicky laughed and Paul read this as her being part embarrassed for him and part mocking him.

When her drink arrived and Paul had paid for it Nicky said, "Let's go and sit down," and they headed to a table. Paul had his back to one of the TVs and couldn't see the other so resigned himself to watching the highlights when he got home, unless he got lucky and judging by the start to the evening he was not hopeful of that.

"I'm surprised you agreed to coming out tonight of all nights, Paul, what with the football final being on," Nicky said, almost reading his mind.

"Oh, right, yes, ha-ha, nice one! I'm not that one dimensional, Nicola."

*But not too far away.*

"I haven't heard from Jo for a while, is she all right?"

"Think so, not spoken to her for a bit," Paul replied, not since my Mum's funeral, he thought. "Dad stays in touch with her, and Cheryl." Nicky nodded and took a drink.

"And your Dad, is he okay?" Nicky asked.

"Yeah, he's fine," Paul replied.

*No, he's not.*

The conversation hit the buffers after that and Paul lamented that it took him several drinks to open up and be chatty with a woman, any woman, even one he had known for so long like Nicky. He was very nervous and wondered where the night might go. After a few minutes of drinking, silence and looking around the pub Paul suggested, "Shall we move on?"

Nicky nodded and downed her drink. "Sure, where shall we go?"

"The Prince of Wales?" Paul suggested.

"Okay, let's go then."

Once in the Prince of Wales they made their way to the bar and Nicky took the initiative with the drinks.

"I'll get these in, Paul" she said, while Paul hovered behind her looking around the pub. At the far end of the bar he noticed a man looking at his watch and also towards the front door, waiting for someone, Paul assumed, who was late. He was a man he once worked with called Jim and he thought about going over for a chat but Nicky approached with the drinks, "Here you go," she said and then Paul lunged again and got as far as kissing her on the lips when Nicky pushed him away.

"Woah! Hold on, sunshine," she said giving an indignant laugh, "what do you think you are doing?"

"Thought we'd carry on from where we left off on Saturday night," Paul replied, confused.

"Oh, right, I see. Paul, look, you're a lovely lad and I've known you since you were ten and you've grown up ever so well since then, so don't blow it now by acting like a stupid love sick little boy. I like you, but, as I said before so many times, as a friend, nothing else. Okay?"

Paul looked at his feet, "I feel really bloody stupid now," he finally said, glumly.

"Don't! Look, I should never have kissed you on Saturday. It was stupid of me, giving you the wrong impression like that. Now, come on, let's go and sit down and not let it spoil the evening."

Nicky smiled but for Paul it had already spoiled the evening. He sat opposite Nicky and really tried to make conversation but it just wasn't working. He was jabbering and talking nonsense as the events of the evening weighed on both of their minds. Paul excused himself to go to the toilet and while there he splashed water on his face to try and gee himself up a bit. His mobile phone beeped and when he took it out of his pocket he saw he had a text message from Simon.

HOW'S IT GOING WITH BUSTY BIRD?

So Paul replied.

SHITE

On his return to the table Nicky was deep in conversation with another man and they seemed to be enjoying each other's company with lots of smiles, hand touching and laughter. Nicky looked more upbeat than she had at any point so far in the evening. From her earlier comment the conversation seemed so adult, so grown up.

"Oh, Paul, hi there," she said in a break in the conversation, like she hadn't been out with Paul for the last hour and it was him just passing by. "This is Chris. His company supplies the computer equipment to my company."

"Hello, Chris," Paul said flatly. Chris got up from his chair and held out his hand to be shaken by Paul. "I don't think so, mate." Chris put his hand down by his side as it became clear Paul was not going to shake it and he sat down again. Nicky was aghast at Paul's rudeness.

"I am really sorry as I didn't know Nicky had a friend with her when I came in and saw her sat on her own," Chris said. "I came over to chat and keep her company and I was just about to ask her if she fancied going for a late supper somewhere."

"Oh, that would be lovely Chris, thanks, I'll go for that," Nicky said and both Chris and her got up from their chairs. "Have you tried that new Tapas bar in the town square?" She made to leave but stopped for a moment, "Nice to see you again, Paul, take care," and with a smile she kissed his forehead. Chris had a smug look of triumph on his face as they left which made Paul hate him even more. Paul was gobsmacked as he took in what had just happened and after a while made his way to the bar for a stiff drink shaking his head as he did.

"Yes, mate?" the barman asked him when he got there.

"A double, no, hold on, a treble Jack Daniels and coke, please, no ice," the barman nodded at Paul's request and went to get it for him. Paul ran his hand through his hair and shook his head again.

"Tough night, huh?" someone asked from Paul's right. Paul turned to see it was an attractive, smartly dressed, red haired woman about his age, looking at him with a look at once both sympathetic and saying 'so, what you going to do?' as she nursed a tall, cold drink. Paul just about detected an American accent.

Paul nodded, "Bloody hell, I'd say so, love," he agreed with a rueful laugh.

The woman was laughing to herself, "You don't know me at all and you call me love. After five years of living in England I still find that charming." The woman smiled at him.

Paul wondered for a minute if he was being chatted up. Should he smile back, ask her name, move down the bar and turn on the north Lancashire charm?

"You cared enough to ask me how my night was so you deserve it, and you wouldn't get this in the south of England, you know love, only the north."

The woman laughed again and then smiled at him. "So you people always tell me."

"Here's your drink," the barman said, "three fifty, please."

Paul handed him a fiver, "Keep the change, mate, cheers,"

"Thanks."

Paul looked into his drink, looked at the woman at the bar, raised his glass and then he smiled. He decided one beautiful woman rejecting him that night was one too many so downed his drink in one and put such nonsense of being chatted up out of his mind.

"Right, that'll do me," Paul announced to himself. He turned to face the woman, "nice to meet you, love," he said with a smile, "goodnight."

"Goodnight, take care, love!" the woman raised her drink back in salute and as Paul left the pub the woman was joined at the bar by her boyfriend who had been to the toilet while she was talking to Paul.

"I think I know him," the boyfriend said.

"Who?" she asked.

"The lad you were just talking to, did he say his name was Paul?"

"Never got that far, but the girl he came in here with tonight left with another man!" The woman raised her eyebrows and gasped in mock horror as if relating the latest plot line in a terrible daytime TV soap opera. "Oh my God, can you believe that?"

"The poor sod," her boyfriend offered. The woman took a drink and turned to face her boyfriend in dramatic fashion clutching the rail on the bar as if she would fall if she did not.

"So, James!" she said.

"Valerie?"

"Marriage."

"Oh, no, not this again."

"Yes, this again, when are we going to get married, Jim?"

Jim looked down at the bar and composed himself, "Look, Val, my last marriage."

"Went down the toilet, I know, I know, I know. God, you've told me this so many times! But why does this mean that our marriage would do the same?"

Jim hesitated before replying. "Look, isn't it enough that I love you, Val?"

Val shook her head, downed her drink, moved away from the bar and left the pub.

# 2010

"Do you still hear from Ian then Val?" I asked as she was swishing the ice around her glass looking a million miles away. She shrugged and allowed herself half a smile. As she had not looked surprised when I had lied that he had told me she was teaching in India I half guessed she did.

"Now and again, via e-mails and the like, bit less since I got married, but that is more my doing."

"Why's that?"

"Being a married woman in contact with my ex…it just didn't seem to be the done thing."

I nodded to understand and then said a name that I dared barely mention. "And what about Michelle, do you hear from her?"

Val downed her drink and put the glass down on the bar with some force. "No," she confirmed.

"No?"

Val shook her head. "No."

"Right,"

Michelle's name I also decided not to change in the book but I never put her surname in, mainly because the situation in the book never warranted naming her. When I told her there was a character based on her in my book she just laughed. When she reads how much it resembled her at the time she might not. The friend of Val's character in the book needed a name and Michelle being Val's friend at the time, well, it seemed obvious.

It was getting a little bit busier in the pub and Nick Cave was playing in the background now. Tonight really was going to be fun.

## CHAPTER TWO

IT WAS APPROACHING Christmas that year and Paul had been out with his work mates for their annual 'piss-up'. It was getting late and he found himself alone in a pub. He had decided it was probably best to go home and was heading towards the exit when a hand touched his arm and he heard a woman's voice say his name. Turning to face where the touch and voice had come from he saw it was Nicky. Initially he felt mad and considered leaving but he remembered that wasn't him.

"Hi," he finally said, "how are you?"

"Oh, you know, same old, same old," Nicky smiled weakly. They were both remembering the last time they had seen each other on their disastrous night out.

"So, how've you been?" Paul asked again to which Nicky smiled.

"Didn't you just ask me that but with different words?"

"Oh, yeah, I did, sorry, sorry," Paul looked embarrassed and Nicky put her hand on his arm.

"Don't worry. How's your Dad?"

"Great! Wide range of interests, always out and about, taking on every day full in the face," Paul replied.

*Huh, truth be told, he's terrible, losing loads of weight, never leaves the house and drinks a bit too much.*

"Last time we went out wasn't great was it?" Nicky finally offered and Paul shrugged.

"Do you think? The only reason I haven't rung for a second date is I've lost your number."

Nicky laughed and then leant forward, kissing Paul slowly and tenderly. "I'll come to your house tomorrow, we'll go somewhere for a bit of lunch and a proper chat, okay?"

"Yeah, look forward to it, best go now, I'm a bit wellied."

"Me too," Nicky admitted with a smile so Paul smiled and left, less excited about the second date than he had been about the first.

The next day, Sunday afternoon, Nicky found herself pulling her car up outside Paul's house. She felt very nervous when recalling their last night out again as she got out, went up the path and knocked on the door. After a few moments, just as she was thinking no one was in, Paul's Dad came to the door and Nicky could not contain a gasp. She last saw him at his wife's funeral and in the two years since he had lost a considerable amount of weight. The clothes he had on were far too big for his frame and were dirty. He was also unshaven and his hair unkempt. Nicky composed herself as he had not said anything at all after opening the door and gave no indication of recognising an old school friend of his second daughter.

"Hi, Mr Stevenson, it's me, Nicky," she began, forcing a smile.

"Oh," he replied, to suggest he still had no idea who she was.

"Is Paul in?"

"Yeah, he is, somewhere," Mr Stevenson turned from the door, walked into the lounge and sat down in front of the TV. The EastEnders omnibus was on and above the noise of cockneys shouting at each other Nicky called out.

"Can you get Paul, please, Mr Stevenson?" a request which he ignored leaving Nicky stood there feeling like a lemon. After a few moments Paul came down the hall and seemed surprised to see Nicky stood there.

"Oh, hello, didn't think you were going to show." he said with a smile.

"Well, I'm here now, shall we go somewhere quiet for some food and a natter?"

"Sure," Paul moved over to his Dad and placed a hand on each shoulder. "Just going out, Dad," to which there was no reply or outward sign of acknowledgement. Paul grabbed his keys and wallet from the side and moved to the front door.

"Where are we going?" Paul asked.

"I don't know, the Prince of Wales?" Nicky suggested.

"Sure."

Once at the Prince of Wales they ordered some drinks, both of them soft drinks as they were still light headed from the night before. They had not been very chatty and as they sat poring over the menu they glanced up at each other and laughed nervously about it. Nicky placed the menu on the table.

"Can I explain about the night out?" she began.

"Okay."

"Very early in the night I realised I was out with you for the wrong reason; I had kissed you for the wrong reason. You are a lovely lad and if I had to get married tomorrow it would be you I would marry."

Paul leant across the table, picked up Nicky's drink and smelt it.

"No, no Bacardi in there." They both laughed.

"I'm being serious here, Paul. Shall we start again, as a couple?"

"I'd love to." Nicky smiled and picked up her menu.

"Now, what are you ordering?"

Paul and Nicky had been an item for the last 3 weeks. They were taking things steady but it was going really well. Nicky bought him Christmas presents, the first time he had ever had a girlfriend long enough up to Christmas for this to happen. Blighting his copy book slightly he never got Nicky anything but she said she did not mind. His Dad had started having more good days than bad and Nicky would often call around for a brew and a chat with him if Paul was working and she wasn't, or if Paul was at the football.

For Paul this was the longest he had ever been out with anyone which was not surprising as the previous relationships usually only lasted no more than a couple of hours. He spent his days and nights wondering at what point did he get to say "I love you," to Nicky, which he really did, and then discuss moving in, engagements, marriage and children's names. When he mentioned it to Simon when they met in a pub for a pint after work just after Christmas he advised caution.

"No, Paul, you don't want to say that to her just yet," Simon had said, above the volume of Christmas hits of yesteryear and people getting too drunk too soon.

"I don't?" Paul replied.

"No, you'll only frighten her."

"You're not going to bloody suggest 'treat 'em mean, keep 'em keen' are you, you knob?"

"I wouldn't go that far, no, but don't spoil it, everything seems to be going so well."

"It is, I do love her."

"You really do?" Simon asked.

"Yeah."

"Wow, never thought I'd see the day, Paul."

Paul was worried that if he said "I love you" first Nicky might laugh, not say it back or dump him, possibly all three. How she behaved the night she went off with Chris still haunted Paul and while they had never mentioned it again, they were 'taking it steady' after all, the worry was still in Paul's mind. Simon's reaction led Paul to believe he would be best taking things easy.

Nicky was off work between Christmas and New Year but Paul wasn't and had a busy few days at the book warehouse he worked at. On the day before New Year's Eve Nicky had just got up and put on daytime TV when the phone rang.

"Hello?"

"Nic? It's me."

"Hi, babe! How's work?"

"Okay, I suppose. Look, do you remember Lee that I went to school with?"

"Yeah, he's the lad in the Navy, isn't he?"

"Aye, that's him, well he's home on leave and asked if I wanted to go for a few pints tonight. You don't mind, do you?"

"No! Not at all, we've just got Caroline and Gary's do to go to tomorrow night so don't make any plans for then."

"Of course, yeah, their New Year's Eve bash, no problem,"

"Go and enjoy yourself, Paul,"

"I will, I won't come to yours tonight, I'll stop at me Dad's in case it is a late and messy one."

"No problem, take care and see you tomorrow, love!"

"Will do, Nicky."

The next morning there was a knock on Nicky's door and she opened the door to Paul. He looked tired, ashen faced and downtrodden which Nicky took to be due to a hangover, so she gushed.

"Here he is! Here's my boyfriend!" she kissed him on the lips, a big, over the top smacker which she hoped might have cheered him up. "Come in! Come in! I want your opinion on something," Paul still stood there, "come in!" Nicky waved him in with her hand to which he wearily trudged into the hallway of the home.

"Now, I want your honest opinion, Paul! Which of these dresses should I wear tonight for the big New Year's Eve party?" Paul had followed her into the bedroom and sat on the end of the bed with a slump. "Blimey! Big hangover, mister?" she asked.

"Nicky, I need to tell you something," he finally said.

Nicky's face fell. "Has something happened to your Dad?" she asked.

"No, it's not about me Dad, please sit down, it's about last night."

The night before Paul, Lee and some of Lee's Navy mates had ended up in the Red Lion pub late on. They were still in there when the landlord rang the bell for time.

"Watch my pint, Lee, lad," Paul said, "I'm just going for a slash."

"Okay, will do," Lee said back.

On his way back to the bar Paul noticed an attractive blonde girl sat at a small, round table on her own. They made eye contact and Paul was going to just smile and move on to rejoin the lads when she summoned him.

"Here you are, pet, why don't you sit and join us?" she asked.

"Me?" Paul replied, pointing to his chest.

"Aye, I'm not asking anyone else, am I?" The girl patted the table with the flat of her hand so Paul sat opposite her. "You don't smoke do you, pet?" she asked him.

"No, I don't, er," Paul paused in reply as he did not know the girl's name and this pause confused her. "I don't know your name, love."

"Oh, I'm Michelle,"

"Paul"

"Do you know anyone who I could get a fag off for later?"

"I'll just go and ask me mates," Paul got up from the chair and went over to Lee and his mates at the bar.

"Are you in there, Paul?" Lee asked having seen everything.

"I don't know, mate, I might be. Can one of you give us a fag?"

"Didn't think you smoked, Paul," said Tom, one of the navy lads.

"No, I don't, it's for her. She's asked me to get her one."

While sat on her own waiting for Paul to return Michelle was tapping her hand in time to the song playing in the pub. Her friend Val, one of the group she had been out with that night, came over to see her.

"Okay, Michelle, we're heading off," Val said.

"Right, Val, I'll see you tomorrow,"

"You're not coming with us?"

"No," Michelle confirmed.

Val was surprised, "Sure? There's a chance we might get a lock in at the Prince of Wales,"

"Not if that perv of a landlord Nigel is in I'm not, he keeps grabbing me knockers, and he's a married man!"

"Shocking!" said Val. "If you didn't have your knockers displayed so prominently he might not try his luck."

"How I choose to display Mother Nature's gifts is no one else's business," Michelle said to end the discussion.

Val eyes were agog. "Anyway, as I said, I'm going now. I'll see you tomorrow, eight o' clock in the Prince of Wales, okay?"

"Righty-o, I'll just see how I get along with this lad here."

Val glanced towards the group of lads in front of her, "God help him. The poor bastard, you'll eat him for breakfast and spit him out in square bubbles!"

"I'm going to kill Jim for teaching you that saying, I'm not that bad!" Michelle laughed.

"Much as I want to stay and warn him, take care, sweetheart." Val patted Michelle on the shoulder and left just as Paul came back to the table.

Paul glanced at the woman leaving and then sat down opposite Michelle, "One fag as ordered, for later, in fact Tom gave me half a pack when he saw you." With no word of thanks Michelle put them in her bag.

"Do you think we could still get a drink here?" she asked him.

"Not sure, I think the landlord has called time," Paul replied.

"Will you try?" she pressed, so with a loud exhale of air Paul got up again, went to the bar and got the landlord's attention.

"I know you've called time, but any chance of a drink, mate?" he asked.

"You're joking, aren't you? I'm trying to get you bastards out!" the landlord replied with a throaty laugh.

"No problem, just thought I'd ask," Paul was about to leave the bar when the landlord grabbed his arm.

"Hold on, lad, I could sell you a couple of bottles but it would be as off sales only, so I cannot open them for you," he explained.

"Okay, nice one, two bottles of Becks, please," said Paul.

"Bacardi breezers!" Michelle shouted.

"Bacardi breezers, then," Paul said, rolling his eyes.

As the landlord got the drinks Lee came down the bar. "How's it going, Paul?"

"Hard to say," Paul confirmed.

"I've never seen you with a woman for so long!" Lee joked.

"Actually, I've been seeing someone for a few weeks now, Lee," Paul corrected him.

Whenever he was on leave Lee had always asked if Paul was seeing someone and as he never was it made going out on the pull together easier. This time Lee had not even bothered to ask.

"What? Who?" Lee asked.

"You remember Nicky, don't you?"

"Nicky Park? Nicky Park who went to school with your sister? Nicky Park who you have fancied since the beginning of time, Nicky Park?"

"Yeah, that's her," Paul confirmed proudly.

Lee, who was well over six foot tall, bent down and leant into Paul. "Then why are you messing around with that tart?" he asked angrily, nodding at Michelle.

"I'm not messing around with her, she's collared me to get some drinks, that's all," Paul reasoned.

"Here are your drinks, lad, five pounds, please," interrupted the landlord.

"If there is nothing going on there then leave me the drinks to take over to her and you run from the pub," Lee challenged Paul.

"Before anyone runs from this pub I hope one of you is going to bloody pay for these," said the landlord.

"Where's me chuffing drink?" Michelle whined. Paul took a fiver from his wallet and gave it to the landlord.

"Thanks, son," he said. Lee took the drinks and was staring at Paul. Without a word he opened them both with his teeth. His mates were stood behind him as they had finished their drinks and were ready to leave.

"Hope you know what you are doing, Paul," Lee said and left the pub. Paul took the drinks over to Michelle and sat down.

"Finally," she said, but with no thanks, again, and she took a big swig.

"Charming," said Paul.

"Here, you're not a poof, are you?" Michelle asked.

"No, why?"

"You just act like one, that's all."

*How?*

He shook his head and took a big drink. It was his first time drinking Bacardi Breezers and he knew it would be his last...

"So what brings you down to Lancashire from Geordie-land, then Michelle?" Paul asked. Michelle didn't reply as she was sinking the last of her drink and once done she slammed it onto the table.

"Education," she replied. "Come on, Paul, I think Liberty's is open tonight." Michelle headed for the exit while Paul tried to finish as much as the bottle as he could stand, gave up and left half of it.

Making their way through town Paul drunkenly threw his arms around Michelle at one point and with a laugh she threw them off her again.

"Behave your bloody self!" she shouted. Once they got to Liberty's they met disappointment as the place was closed.

"Oh, hell, it's closed," Michelle announced to acknowledge the fact. "I don't bloody believe it!"

"Yes, that is a surprise," said Paul.

"Ah, hey, if it's not open then I'm going home," and with that Michelle walked away.

"Any chance of a New Year's kiss, Michelle?" Paul shouted after her. Michelle sighed, turned and walked back to reluctantly give Paul a small kiss on the cheek.

"Happy New Year, Peter," she said over her shoulder as she walked off again.

"It's Paul, actually," he said to the uninterested retreating figure.

Paul had finished telling Nicky what had happened and waited for her to take it all in. He felt terrible but felt saying sorry would not appease her. Nicky's reaction shocked him; after a few seconds she smiled, shrugged and then she said, "For a moment there I thought you were going to say you slept with her. Oh, well, then, not to worry. Now, back to the frocks!"

"No, Nicky, wait. I never slept with her but why did I go off with her and buy her a drink? Why? What was I thinking? Why would I do this?"

Nicky began to cry as her bottled up emotions of the last five months finally exploded. She knew the reasons that she was with Paul were due to guilt about leaving him on their first date and sympathy about his mum and dad on her part and she had been lying to herself and Paul.

"You don't deserve me, or anyone else, treating you as badly as this, Nicky. I think we best give it up now." Paul stood up and made to leave the flat but as he headed down the hall Nicky caught him up and grabbed him.

"No, Paul, wait, you didn't do anything wrong, if it happened as you told me. You were honest enough to tell me what happened and I believe you and forgive you."

"Then why are you crying, Nicky? I'll tell you why; it's because I have let you down and a good man wouldn't have done that."

Paul left and headed for home through the sheeting rain and icy winds of winter. When he got back his Dad was sat in his armchair with a bottle of sherry in his lap.

"That was a short party," his Dad commented, then raised the bottle, "Happy New Year, son."

Paul leant against the wall and put his face in his hands, "Oh, Jesus."

---

# 2010

"Are you not going to check on..." I paused as I could not remember the name of the man Val had been arguing with when I came in as I only heard her yell it in his face, "what's-his-name?" I finally came out with pointing towards the door.

"Barry," she reminded me with a laugh and then rolled her eyes, "my darling husband."

"Husband?" I asked and Val nodded to confirm this. "Blimey."

"All he will be doing right now is marching up and down outside sulking and smoking."

"What was it all about, then, the row?" I asked.

"Well, I wanted to go and see Ian at the Prince of Wales tonight, just to say hello and see if anyone else was in that I knew, but Barry suddenly got jealous about me going to meet my ex."

"And by storming out of here he has left you with me."

Val looked at me with a slight look of confusion on her face, "You're not an ex of mine, Liam."

"I am as good as an ex though, surely?" I asked with some hurt pride.

"How do you figure that?"

"I should think so bearing in mind what happened with us." Val turned back to look behind the bar and looked to be taking on board what I had just said. The bar was getting even busier and I could not yet see any of my mates. I turned to face Val as she waved her empty glass at the barman with a smile. Unlike when I was waiting to be served he was over like a shot for her and she ordered a drink.

"Can I get you a pint of bitter, Liam?" Val asked and I nodded.

"Thanks." Val turned away from me to order and then waited for the drinks to arrive but turned back and looked intently at me.

"You're sweating," she told me but I let it pass without comment.

--

# CHAPTER THREE

## QUIZ NIGHT

"**D**AD, ARE YOU IN?" It was a Monday in late October and dusk was drawing in as Paul finally got home from work and entered his house by the back door. He took his Adidas jacket and baseball cap off and wrapped up the earphones on his I-pod.

"I'm in here, Paul," his Dad called from the lounge. Paul headed that way picking up the mail and putting it down again when he saw there was none for 'Mr P Stevenson'. He made a mental note to remind his Dad to open those letters which were addressed to him.

"I'm a bit late because the bus journey home has been a nightmare; no seats, women with prams and screaming kids and, to top it all, some junior 'chav' was thrown off by the driver for swearing and then spat at the driver, resulting in a scuffle. As the only other male adult," Paul continued, as he got to the lounge where his Dad put down his newspaper all the better to take in the story of woe and daring do unfolding around him, "people looked at me to intervene but I listened more intently to my I-pod and kept my head down. They glared at me for the remainder of the journey and even the driver muttered 'thanks for your help' as I got off."

Paul's Dad hesitated to make sure the story had finished. "Good God son, that sounds like hell on wheels!"

"It's about the norm now, Dad, it gets worse every day. I'd learn to drive but I wouldn't be able to afford a car, petrol and insurance if and when I passed me test."

"I could bung you some 'tatie' if you wanted help on that score, son,"

"No! Don't worry about it, Dad." Paul used his hand to wave the gesture away, but smiled as he did it. Any progress his Dad had made when Paul was seeing Nicky three years ago had gone. He still had good days but not as many as before. On the rare occasions Paul's sisters rang his Dad lied about how he was doing.

"Have you had anything to eat yet?" Paul asked.

"Just a snack at about half-three," his Dad confirmed.

Paul pulled a face, "A snack? Is that going to be enough for you, Dad?"

"Oh, yeah yeah, no problem. Some doctor told me that I should only eat when I am hungry and I never am nowadays."

"Which doctor was this, Dad?"

"I forget their name, but they write in the *Daily Express*."

"Right, I see."

Since his Mum died Paul's Dad had lost a total of six stone. He had been big previously but this was still a worry. Some days Paul worried that his Dad's skeletal frame would not be able to move even from bed to armchair and then back to bed again. Because of his Dad's health Paul had decided that living with him and keeping an eye on him was not the worst thing in the world and none of his mates ever gave him a hard time about it, like he thought they might have. Apart from the nights spent at Nicky's flat when they were together he never entertained the idea of moving out again. The book warehouse pay was okay rather than great and renting costs in the area, with a university nearby, were extortionate.

"I'm going to fix myself something to eat so holler if you want anything, okay?" Paul announced as he walked to the kitchen.

"Okay, son, but I should be all right, thanks."

On the way down the hall Paul's mobile rang, so he fished it from his jacket pocket and answered it.

"Hello?"

"Hi, Paul, Simon here, you okay?"

He thought about his Dad for a moment, then lied, "Yeah, good, thanks, just got in,"

"Fancy a pint?"

"Yeah, I'm up for that. Shall we go to the Prince of Wales?"

"Yeah, nice one, see you at half eight."

He ended the call and put the phone in his pocket and called back down the hall, "I'm out for a pint tonight, Dad, you going to be all right?"

"Yeah, no problem, son, there's some footie on later, I'll watch that."

Later on at the Prince of Wales, while the lads were at the bar Simon noticed there was a poster advertising that week's events, including the Monday night quiz.

"Do you fancy having a bash at this quiz tonight, Paul?" Simon asked pointing at it with his thumb.

"What do we win?" Paul asked.

"Dunno," said Simon, studying the poster for the answer.

"Ten pounds for the winners of the quiz and there's a pot of £75 tonight, carried over from last week, and you win it if you get all the questions right," the barman interrupted as he brought their drinks over. "Six pounds thirty for your drinks and if you want a quiz sheet see the DJ," he pointed at the stand, "pound per team to enter."

Simon made his way over to the DJ stand to get a quiz sheet from a man called Ken. His DJ-style was stuck in the 1980s and he kept reminding the customers that he was "standing in for Jim, who is on his hols," all night. The soundtrack to the evening suggested Ken had not bought a new CD since about 1993.

"How are things going with your Dad then Paul?" Simon asked him during a break in the quiz. Paul took a drink and looked thoughtful. After a while all he could do was shrug.

"I stay there to keep an eye on him but I wonder, most of the time, if I did ever move out would he notice?"

"Blimey, not good then?"

"Not really, some days are dreadful. Anyway, Simon, how are your family? We only ever discuss mine."

"To be fair you've had the worst of it family-wise all the time I have known you. Your mum was diagnosed with cancer when we were at college and we were all concerned about you."

"Thanks."

"It's only ever been me and me mum," Simon explained looking around the bar for 'student totty' as he termed it.

"I never knew that," Paul admitted with some guilt.

"I know you didn't. I never really knew my father as he left home when I was four. Only seen him once or twice since."

"I've lived in the same house as my Dad for 28 years and I don't think I really know him." Paul said at a poor attempt at humour. He had not spoken to Simon like this in all the time they had known each other.

"But he's there, Paul, and always has been, providing the roof over your head."

Paul nodded, "That's true enough."

The lads did well but were disappointed to lose the quiz on a tie-break to two other blokes, two student looking types.

"Shall we give this a bash again next week?" Simon asked, as they were leaving at the end of the night.

"Yeah, why not? It was fun, we had a few pints, and a big chat and, you never know, we might win next week," Paul agreed.

"Just wish there were more women here," Simon lamented, as they left the pub and headed for the nearest chippy.

## A WEEK LATER

"OKAY, PEOPLE, I make that five thirty, good work today, you can go." Valerie Walters, 31, originally from San Jose, California, sat at her desk in the college class room while her students filed out, full of happy chatter and the occasional "see you, Val," to which she looked up and smiled. She put on a pair of glasses and began marking some course work of the criminology class she took on a Thursday when she was aware of someone stood over her. It was Todd, a young man, the youngest in the class by some way, who sat alone at the back, wearing ill-matched clothing and gawped at her all through the lesson.

"Todd, can I help?" she asked with a knowing smile, knowing that he fancied her.

Todd rummaged in his file and produced some sheets of paper that were a bit ruffled in appearance, "I've done last week's coursework, Val," he replied, breathlessly. Val lowered her head, smiled some more and then looked over her reading glasses.

"And the week before's?" she asked.

"Not yet, Val. Look, this might be a bit off and out of the blue but would you like to go out for a drink?" Val was shocked, put her pen down and leant back in her chair.

"A drink?" she asked.

"Yes," Todd nodded but looked uneasy, "to discuss the coursework, and other things, of course."

"Todd, how old are you?" Val asked.

"Nineteen!" he replied brightly with a big smile.

"Do you know how old I am?"

He paused as he had never really given this much thought before and didn't want to get it very wrong, "Twenty-two?" he replied hopefully.

Val smiled. "I think we both know that is a tad ambitious, Todd,"

"If you want," said Todd, "bring the husband with you when we go for a drink," Val looked incredulous, threw her arms up and took off her glasses.

"Todd, just leave me the coursework, go home and grow up."

"Okay," Todd headed for the door, "sorry, but I like a challenge," he said as he left the room.

After Todd had left Michelle, Val's friend walked in. They had first met at the local university teaching college when Val was 22 and Michelle had been 19. Val had been and still was a confident, intelligent and educated young woman but at the time was still wary about being in a strange country, with wild weather and even wilder men. Michelle befriended her and showed her how to survive the north of England. Michelle herself was from the north east and the spirit of that region influenced her lifestyle and helped her get through life.

"Was that an admirer?" Michelle asked.

Val smiled, laughed and shook her head. "I think I scared him off. Have you had any joy on the job front recently?"

Michelle shook her head. Since graduating she had not taught permanently or had a full time job. Val humoured her and sympathised most of the time but privately considered her a bit idle and work-shy...

"Any plans for tonight, Valerie, I fancy pinning one on,"

And fond of a drink and lots of it.

"Jim's doing the quiz at the Prince of Wales tonight, so shall we go and do that and see him?"

"Yes, let's, I love Jim, and it'll be a giggle, and we might win!" Michelle gushed.

"All this time sleeping with the quiz master and I haven't won the quiz yet, but yes, we might." Jim Black was Val's boyfriend, although at 48 he was no boy. A divorced father of two originally from

Manchester he moved to the town with work ten years previously and had been seeing Val for seven years. He did the DJ work part-time a few nights a week and invested the rest of his time in other 'business', which Val didn't know a lot about and thought it best not to ask too much about.

"I just hope bloody Colin's not in there tonight being an ass, again," added Val.

Colin Little was a former work mate of Jim's who Val had been seeing on and off from when she moved to England and on one time when they were 'off' Jim asked Val out and they were away. It took a while for Colin to forgive them, if he ever had at all, even after all this time.

"I just hope that I meet a bloke tonight, any bloke," Michelle said, and then revealed her baser nature behind the university education. "It's been bloody ages since I've been given one!"

"Oooooh, Michelle, you old romantic!" Val said, disgusted, and began packing the coursework away. "I'll mark this lot tomorrow afternoon, when my stomach has settled." Michelle giggled with delight.

Paul and Simon had made it to the quiz again but while they waited at the bar for their drinks it was clear that all was not well.

"What the hell have you invited him for?" Paul asked Simon in disgust.

"Who?" Simon asked innocently.

"You know who, Fart-breath over there!"

"Look, please don't call him that," Paul and Simon both giggled about Simon's mate Alan Falstead, who Paul had re-christened 'Alan Fart-breath' on account of his on-going breath problems. "Go and get a quiz sheet, you great lummox, and I'll pay for these."

Paul looked in the direction of the music playing from the DJ stand and a look of recognition came over his face. Ken was not the DJ this week and as he had hinted at the week before Jim was now back from his 'hols'.

"Is that Jim Black over there?" Paul asked no one in particular.

"Yeah, that's him," confirmed the barman who was pulling pints near them.

"I worked with him at Manton's ten years ago!" Paul headed off to see Jim with a broad smile on his face at seeing an old pal.

"All right, Jim!" Paul said when he got there. Jim looked up from the laptop playing the music where he was lining up the next songs and his face broke into a smile.

"Paul! How are you?" they shook hands.

"Getting by, getting by," Paul told him.

"Sorry to hear about your mum, how long's it been?"

"Five years, now," Paul confirmed.

"Bloody hell, where's the time go, eh?"

Paul shrugged, "I know." The conversation stopped and they both thought what to talk about next.

"You still living with your Dad?" Jim asked finally.

"Yeah, I thought at the time that it was a good idea," Paul lied, "to keep an eye on him, you know. So, Jim, DJ-ing, eh?"

"Yeah!" Jim passed his right hand over the latest computer equipment in front of him which was playing something modern that Paul did not recognise.

"Do you do this full time, then?"

"I do this more than anything else. I have a mate who sells," Jim paused, "whatever he can get hold of and I help to fund his ventures and get a share of the profits." Jim hoped Paul would ask no more as it sounded very suspect how he just described it and he didn't know how to explain it any better.

Paul nodded as if to understand and a combination of good manners and confusion led him to ask no more. Instead he weighed up the computer equipment in front of Jim. "Have you not got anything on there from your era, Jim? Frankie Laine, Beverley Sisters? Where are your 78s?"

Jim laughed, "You cheeky sod!"

"I've actually come over for a quiz sheet, as well as for a natter, obviously, my friends and I thought we'd give it a go," Paul said.

"Great!" Jim passed him a quiz sheet, "pound a team."

"Two of us were here last week and we heard you were on your hols, a lot," Paul commented.

"Yeah, that would have been Ken, standing in for me," confirmed Jim.

"Where did you get to?" Paul asked as he fished a pound out of his pocket. Jim looked past Paul and waved at someone at the bar.

"Me girlfriend's here, now," Jim told him, seeming to not hear Paul's last question.

"Oh, right, I'll leave you to it. Here's the pound, good to see you again, Jim, I'll be back over again for a chat later."

"Okay, Paul, nice one, good to see you again, also," and the men shook hands again.

"Get us a vodka and lemonade, Michelle, will you and I'll just go and see Jim," Val said at the bar.

"Aye, okay. Er, have you got any money, pet?" Michelle asked. Val rolled her eyes but before she could get her purse out the barman spoke up;

"We'll put them on Jim's tab, he's not drinking tonight as he said he's going to drive home from here."

"Oh, great," Val sighed, "he'll be Mr Boring-and-sober later." The barman and Michelle both laughed. "Bring the drinks over when you get them, Michelle, I'd best go and say hello."

"Okay, pet, will do."

As Val approached the DJ stand she noticed a man walking away. She gave Jim a kiss on the cheek and turned to look at the retreating figure.

"You two were very chatty," she said looking in Paul's direction. "Friend of yours, is he?"

"Yeah, he's called Paul, Paul Stevenson. I used to work with him years ago. He's a good lad is Paul."

"Notice he was getting a quiz sheet when he was here. Will he beat me and Michelle?"

"Oh, is Michelle here?" Jim asked, and noticed she was heading over.

"Ho, Jimmy, how are you, darling?" Michelle squealed running over and with an over the top greeting threw her arms around Jim and gave him a quick kiss on the lips. Jim always laughed when she greeted him like this and laughed away now, but Val hated it and tapped Michelle quite hard on the shoulder to bring the embrace to an end.

"I think we'll leave you to it, go and sit down and let you start, Jim," Val said firmly walking away.

As they walked away from the DJ-stand Michelle spotted Paul,

Simon and Alan sat at a table.

"Let's sit near them men over there, Val, they're new!"

"Cor! Look at the blonde heading over this way!" Alan breathed. Simon spun around quickly to have a look. "Not so keen, man, not so keen!" Alan whispered.

"My God, she's fit," Simon said. "Her mate's not bad either, the red head. What do you think, Paul?" Paul had been quietly mulling over the quiz sheet and raised his head.

"Eh?" he looked towards Val and Michelle just as they were sitting down. Val glanced his way and smiled, knowing that he was Jim's friend, and then she turned back to Michelle. Paul had smiled back briefly at Val but had not clocked her as she was stood at the bar when Jim had mentioned his girlfriend was in and didn't know her from Adam.

"Yeah, nice," he commented, turning away, suggesting indifference.

"Nice?!" Alan spat, loud enough that the women and two shaven headed men on the table behind them heard and turned around. "Nice?" he whispered this time, "Weather can be nice, jumpers can be nice, but women? Nice? We need new nouns for you, Paul."

"Adjectives," Simon corrected.

"Oh," said Alan. "Are they?" Simon nodded and Alan shrugged to suggest he wasn't really bothered either way.

Paul picked up a pen and began to write on the quiz sheet. "Team name," he said to himself, "Vocabulary for the Mad."

"Did you see them, Val?" Michelle simpered. Val had been filling in their team name on the quiz sheet and suggested she hadn't seen anything.

"See who?" Val asked.

"Them! Men!" Michelle pointed in what she believed to be a discreet fashion but was actually similar to a jab in boxing accompanied by a stage whisper. Alan and Simon turned around as if they had heard something but were unsure from which direction it was coming.

"Oh, sure, yeah I saw them, you gonna go over and talk to them?"

"Hell, no!" Michelle said. "Few more voddies needed for that."

"Okay, everyone," Jim announced into a microphone as the music he was playing faded, "it's time for tonight's quiz. Ten pounds for the winners, with eighty three pounds in the pot…"

"Wooooooooooooh!" shouted the teams.

"…If you get them all right. Okay, question number one;"

"Think, lads, think!!" ordered Alan.

"Sssssh," said Paul, ducking under Alan's breath.

"What is the state capital of California?" Jim winked at Val. Every week at the quiz there was a question, usually the first one, linked to the USA. Val smiled at this act. On the next table Alan looked at Simon, who shrugged and looked confused so they both looked at Paul.

"Haven't got a clue," he confirmed, "have you?" and the other two shook their heads.

The quiz reached the half way stage and time for getting some more drinks so Val headed to the bar.

"Hi, Stuart," said Val to the barman, "vodka and lemonades for me and my unemployed and penniless friend, please. Is Jim's tab still open?"

"As long as I'm here, yeah," Stuart the barman confirmed.

"Great, bless you!"

As she waited Val noticed that Michelle had left their table and was deep in conversation with two of the three men at the next table. The conversation was animated; giggling and arm waving on Michelle's part, grinning and nudges from the two men. The third man, Jim's friend Paul, was dividing his time between finishing his drink and checking their answers. This was the man she had smiled at as she sat down and the fact he wasn't leering over Michelle, like his mates, intrigued her. With his drink finally finished he got to his feet, did a hand gesture to his mates behind Michelle's head which after many years in the north of England Val knew meant 'do you want a drink?' and was not a rude gesture as she had thought when she first saw it and after they nodded to confirm he headed for the bar.

Val's drinks had arrived, "Thanks, Stu," and she decided to stay there at the bar for a moment to see if the man came and stood anywhere near her to engage her in conversation, but he did not. There was a clear ten yards of bar space between them. Val wondered for a moment if this suggested shyness or ignorance, hoped it was the former as she found it sweet then shrugged and went to chat to Jim, giving Michelle her vodka on the way,

"Cheers, pet." Michelle said. "Are you two lads local?" Michelle asked Alan and Simon as Val wandered over to the DJ stand and Jim.

"I am," Alan confirmed.

"I'm from Carlisle originally," said Simon.

"What do you do for a living?" Michelle continued, thinly veiled as "how much do you earn?"

"I own my own record shop," Alan replied.

"And you, Simon?" Michelle asked quickly, hoping for better news there.

"Three pints of bitter, please, mate," Paul asked the barman. He noticed the woman who had smiled at him as she sat down earlier walking away from the bar. She was about his age, a little taller, classy looking, smartly dressed but not too smart for the pub. After giving a drink to her friend she made her way over to the DJ stand and he assumed this was Jim's girlfriend. She was a nice looking woman, he thought. When they worked together Paul knew that Jim was living apart from his wife and had not seen him recently enough to know who he was seeing now.

After getting the drinks Paul headed back to the table. The other girl, who had said she was called Michelle, was still holding court.

"Me fella dumped us, you know, the bastard," she was saying, as Alan and Simon were lapping it all up. She went on to explain "I went to Ayia Napa with a mate of mine," not Jim's girl, it would appear, unless her name was 'Holly the Virgin', "and once I was there I slept with a lad called Steve, who was Notts County's left back at the time, and a male stripper called Enrique." On her return home all the good teaching jobs had gone and her fella, "wanker Gavin", to give him his full name, had dumped her when he saw her holiday photos, "surrounded by blokes, I was, and no bikini top on." It became apparent to Paul that this had happened some years ago.

"Okay, ladies and jelly-spoons, back to the quiz," Jim announced. Paul noticed that Jim's girlfriend had sneaked back to her and Michelle's table and he still did not know her name, unless it was Holly. "Question number sixteen, what was the name of the Royal family prior to it becoming Windsor?"

"Know it," Alan said, "pen, please, Paul."

Val didn't hold out much hope of them winning the quiz. A lot of the questions made no sense to her American roots; how would she know where the Marylebone Cricket Club was based, or who they were for that matter? After talking to the two lads at half-time Michelle was no help and was wittering.

"Alan has breath issues and is a bit fat, but has some original 45s by the Clash!" Michelle gushed.

"Great!" Val gushed back, wrestling to recall the capital of Peru which the three lads seemed to know.

"Simon, the tall, dark one," Michelle continued, "ooh, he's a bit nice, lovely smile, works as an architect in Leeds and Manchester. Might ask for his number, bit forward, like, I know, but I feel like I must move on from Gavin now."

"Yeah, you do that, five years is long enough,"Val said. She glanced at the three lads and noticing that Paul was nodding agreement to an answer made her wonder why Michelle had not mentioned him.

"Six and a half years actually,Valerie," said Michelle correcting her Gavin linked faux pas.

"Sorry," Val whispered. "What about the third one, what's he like?"

"Third one?" Michelle asked. Val pointed her pen towards the three lads. "Oh, him, he never said a word when I was over there, so I've no idea, gay, probably."

"Just because he wasn't slobbering all over you, like the other two, doesn't automatically mean he is gay, Michelle."

"S'pose not,Val," Michelle agreed.

Val was weighing Paul up, "He looks a bit familiar, though. As he is a mate of Jim's perhaps I have met him before in here once and just forgotten him. I'm not sure."

The quiz came to an end, Jim had finished the marking and was ready to reveal the results, "The bad news is that no one got all the answers right," he announced.

"Bollocks!" shouted Big Doug, a pub regular, from the bar to everyone's amusement.

"So no one," continued Jim, "wins the jackpot, but the winners, with 27 out of 30, are 'Vocabulary for the Mad'! Come and get your tenner, lads."

"Hey, we won!" Alan cheered. "Simon, we won." Simon was deep in conversation with Michelle and waved Alan away. "Fiver each then, Paul?"

"Yeah, okay, then," Paul stood up and rooted in his pockets. "Here's a fiver, I'll get it on the way out. Shall we come down here next week?"

"Yeah, sure," Alan replied with a smile and a thumbs-up, picked up his drink and joined Simon and Michelle. Paul made his way to the DJ stand where Jim had been joined by the woman who Paul assumed to be his girlfriend and they were chatting.

"That'll be us, Jim, by some miracle," Paul said. Jim laughed and handed him a ten pound note.

"Well done, Paul. Are you lads coming down next week?" Jim asked. Paul glanced in Simon and Alan's direction.

"Think so, my friends appear to like the entertainment," he replied, put the tenner in his wallet and as he made to leave Jim said, almost as an afterthought. "Paul, sorry, I never introduced you earlier, this is my girlfriend, Val," Val rolled her eyes at being forgotten.

"Hi, Val, lovely to meet you," Paul said giving her outstretched hand a gentle shake and she responded with a friendly and quite sexy smile.

"And you, Paul, well done tonight,"

"Thanks, Val, cheers. Paul clocked her accent immediately and with a daft grin said, "Bet you knew the capital of California question," to which Val pulled a face and turned to Jim.

"I think we've been busted," she said and Jim roared with laughter. "How did you know I was from California?"

"Oh, are you? I didn't know, it was just a lucky guess, I just heard your accent and, you know, I put two and two together."

"I put a question in like that every week for Val," Jim confirmed, "about the States, but keep it under your hat."

"Otherwise, if he didn't, all of the questions about sport and the UK would swamp me," Val said.

"Ah, I see, I will keep that to myself, then. From listening to Michelle's story I'm just glad you're not 'Holly the Virgin'."

Val and Jim laughed, "No, I'm not 'Holly the Virgin' and to be fair I know Holly and neither is she."

"Great," Paul said for no reason he could think of. "Well, I'll see you both next week, then." With that Paul turned and left.

Later that night, as Jim was talking to Nigel, the pub's landlord, after Paul had gone home and Michelle had also left with Paul's two friends tagging along behind like two rather obedient puppies, Val felt like a spare part stood at the DJ stand. She didn't know Paul at all but for the sake of someone to talk to she wished he had stayed a bit longer. He seemed charming enough and friendly. At the back of her mind was a burning question; he looked so familiar, where did she know him from?

"Only me, Dad, you'll never guess what? We only went and won the quiz at the Prince of Wales," Paul called out as he entered his home. As the lights were on he thought it meant his Dad was still up but then he then noticed his Dad snoring and asleep in the armchair with Sky Sports still playing. Paul went and fetched a duvet and put it over him.

"Night, Dad." he whispered.

As Jim drove home later on, and with no conversation, Val was startled when he suddenly announced "Great to see Paul again, he's a good lad."

"I'm sorry?" Val asked, stunned and sat up straight as she had sunk into the seat and had been letting her mind wander towards Paul again and what they could have talked about if he had stayed.

"Paul, the lad whose team won the quiz tonight, he's a good lad." Jim added to confirm. Val saw her chance to dig for a bit of information.

"Is he married, or living with someone?" she asked.

"Not now, don't know if he ever was. He lives with his Dad, keeps an eye on him after his mum died," Jim replied.

"Was it sudden, her death?"
*Where the hell did that come from?*
Jim shrugged, "I didn't work with him then so I don't know. I've only seen him on and off in the last ten years. Hard worker, good lad, he would help anyone."

"What's he do for a living now?" Val probed further as they stopped at some traffic lights and the red light streaked the rain on the windscreen that the blades could not reach.

"He works in a warehouse," Jim confirmed, and Val could not contain her astonishment.

"He wins quizzes against me, with a degree, a masters and a PhD and he works in a warehouse?! Something has gone wrong somewhere."

Jim laughed, "To be fair to you he's English and a keen sports fan so he probably knows who the MCC are."

"True," she said nodding as the lights changed and Jim drove on. "There is something about him, though," Val continued.

"What, you mean you fancy him? Should I pack me bags when I get home?" Jim laughed.

"No! Not that I fancy him. I mean, he's not Big Doug ugly. There is something about him, but there is also this thing that he could just walk into any bar or pub in the world unnoticed. I wouldn't have taken any notice of him today if I hadn't seen him talking to you or if my sex crazed Geordie friend wasn't cooing over one of his mates."

"Yeah, she's a game old girl is Michelle," Jim agreed, clunking a gear change slightly, "whoops!"

"And if she doesn't stop that over the top greeting with you I'll be having some words with her!" Val glared at Jim who noticed this and laughed.

"It's not my doing!" he protested but Val wasn't sure and looked away without another word.

"He looks familiar does Paul, have I met him before when you've been working at the pub?" Val asked. Jim thought for a moment.

"It's a while since I've seen him. The day I started at the Prince of Wales he was in with his brothers in law after his mum's funeral,"

"Irish type wake, was it?" Val asked. "Banjos, violins, drinking, laughing, that sort of thing?" to which Jim shook his head.

"They seemed to be discussing something serious that day, didn't stop long." Jim paused. "I never spoke to him but wanted to which I regret not doing. So, I'm not sure when I last spoke to him actually." Jim paused and then recalled something else from a few years previously. "There was a time when me and you were in the Prince of Wales having a drink," he paused again remembering how this particular night had ended, with Val leaving him to stop with Michelle for three nights after yet another marriage discussion had fallen apart, "and you had been chatting to him at the bar and he left just as I came back from the loo."

"I was talking to Paul?" Val asked. If nothing else this could be where she recalled him from.

"Yeah, something about his girlfriend left with another bloke."

"Oh, God, I can't remember that."

"Really?"

"Not at all."

Jim shrugged, "You're right, then, he can sneak into any bar or pub unnoticed, can't he?"

"I guess so," Val agreed. Jim smiled but was a little bit relieved that his fear that Val was attracted to Paul was unfounded.

THE LADS WERE waiting expectantly in the Prince of Wales a week later for Michelle to arrive. Paul was struggling to breathe among the overpowering aroma of after shave and strong mints coming from Fart-breath.

"Here she is again! My God, she's even fitter than I remember her," Simon drooled with a look of triumph as Michelle entered the pub.

"Did you not bang her last week then?" Alan asked to which Paul shook his head slowly and smiled in a mixture of disgust and amusement as the conversation unfolded without him.

"No! Course not. I've got a feeling she's a real looney tune, she's a Geordie for a start, so not doing that in the maiden innings," Simon replied.

"Good lad, good call." Alan offered. Michelle came to the table where the three lads were sat via the bar but with no drink.

"Hi, lads! Here, one of yers get us a drink, will yers, I'm parched!" Paul and Alan looked at Simon. Alan even nodded towards the bar to assist him.

"Oh, right, that's me then," said Simon in realisation and got up from his chair.

"And a pint each for us!" Alan shouted after him. Michelle smiled and followed Simon.

"I'll get a quiz sheet," said Paul getting up from his chair.

"Oh, are we even going to bother?" Alan asked, nodding in the direction of Simon and Michelle.

"Yeah, I want something to distract me from having to watch Turner and Hooch over there going at it." Paul said and headed towards the DJ stand, where Jim was excelling himself with some forgotten 80s pop classic playing from his laptop.

"Hello, James, here we go again!" he said. Jim smiled and shook Paul's hand.

"Going to win again, Paul, lad?" Jim asked, taking Paul's pound entry fee and handing him a quiz sheet.

"We'll give it our best shot," Paul said. Jim tapped his laptop to set up the next section of music and Paul thought about what to say next. Seeing Michelle and Simon getting re-acquainted at the bar gave him the idea to ask where Val was but before he could a man joined them on the stand.

"Colin, are you well?" Jim asked the man in a serious tone.

"Yes," Colin replied, and then there was silence, so Paul kept his head down and pretended to study the quiz sheet, which was hard, as it was blank save for 'team name' some lines and numbers one to thirty. He decided to wait until the two men had finished their chat to ask where Val was.

"Doing the quiz?" Jim asked Colin after a few moments of struggling to think of what to say next.

"I don't think so," Colin laughed disdainfully. There was silence again and Paul had stayed too long to just wander off at this point back to his chair and hoped neither Colin or Jim thought he had stayed just to be nosey. He stole a glance at the two men, neither of whom was looking in his direction, and they were staring at each other. It looked as if one might punch the other. More than likely Colin, as he looked mean but Jim was as white as a sheet.

"Is Valerie not in tonight?" asked Colin, which at least saved Paul the job of asking where she was.

"Er, no, no she isn't, she's got a meeting at work," Jim confirmed. It answered Paul's question but he still could not move away.

"Meeting at work, Jim?" Colin repeated and gave an ironic laugh, "I remember a few of them when I used to see her."

"Now listen, Col," Jim began, "you could never make your mind up about…"

"Oh, this was before you, Jim," Colin cut in to interrupt, "she screwed me over and she'll do the same to you given half a chance."

The two men paused and Paul continued to study his sheet wishing he had stayed in to watch telly with his Dad.

"Please leave," said Jim finally and Colin left. Paul looked up from the sheet after a moment and breathed out.

"Right, Jim, I'll get ready for the quiz and speak to you later," he said, in a voice an octave or three higher than normal. He patted Jim on the shoulder and went to join the others, looking back on the way to check on Jim's mental state. Jim had his head bowed and looked ill. After Paul had sat down at the table Michelle leaned across.

"Were things a bit tense over there then?" she asked. This was the first time she had spoken directly to Paul since he had started coming to the quiz.

"No, not really" he lied. "Why do you ask?"

"That was Colin," Michelle started to explain. "He was shagging my mate Valerie, who was here last week," Michelle put the back of her right hand to her left cheek, and whispered, "and me on the side," with a giggle, "until Val dumped him for Jim. Shocking, Jim and him had been big mates, an' all."

"Is Jim shagging you on the side now as well?" Alan asked, checking for patterns developing should Simon get lucky.

"Not yet," Michelle replied, which Paul thought was an odd answer. He thought, "No! Certainly not. I'm not the common tart you obviously think I am," might have been more appropriate.

"Right," Jim said into the microphone, in a subdued manner, "question one..."

It was the end of the quiz and the marking was complete; "Again, no one has got all the answers right," Jim announced.

"Bollocks!" shouted Big Doug again.

"So the ninety-seven pounds rolls over to next week. This week's winner, with 23 out of 30..."

"That's low," said Alan, and the others nodded to agree.

"Big Doug!"

"Yes! Get in!" Big Doug shouted and headed to collect his winnings. Looking at Doug's table Paul noticed he appeared to have got some help from Colin.

"Right, I'm heading off," Paul said, getting up from his chair, "same time next week, everyone?" There were murmurs from the other three but not positive ones to suggest any of them would be there. "Okay, then." Paul put on his jacket and headed for the exit, on the way he held up his hand to bid Jim farewell who returned the gesture.

Val pulled into the car park at the rear of the pub and turned off the engine. The meeting had been hard work and her pounding head suggested bringing the car and not drinking had been a great idea. Also, if Jim had had a few lagers he might not be Mr Boring-and-sober tonight. She got out of the car and headed for the pub.

"You're cutting it fine for his tab tonight," Stuart the barman said when Val reached the bar. "I've just called last orders."

"I'll just have a mineral water with a slice of lemon, please, Stuart," she replied.

"Oh," said Stuart, but no more.

"Val! You made it!" Michelle came over and hugged her, a little the worse for wear.

"Just about, yeah, you lot had fun?" Val asked, noticing Alan and Simon hovering, but no sign of Paul who she had wanted to get to know better. Of the three men he seemed the only one with any soul. Not in his record collection she thought, but certainly in his personality.

"Aye, not so bad, but we did nowt in the quiz so we're off to Liberty's for a late one, aren't we lads?" The lads nodded wearing stupid, love-sick puppy grins again.

"Do you want to join us?" Simon asked.

"No. Thanks, but late finish tonight, early start tomorrow," Val replied. Michelle hugged her and the two lads headed for the exit.

"I'll call you, okay?" Michelle whispered and smiled. She then turned to catch up with the others at the door. Val took her drink to the DJ stand where Jim was packing up. He looked up and smiled as she approached but carried on busying himself.

"How did the meeting go, Val, did you get finished okay?" he asked after a while.

"Yeah, dragged on forever and ever, of course," she confirmed. Jim seemed quiet and Val noticed that he appeared to be packing away at a furious pace. "Who won the quiz?"

"Big Doug," Jim confirmed and Val looked shocked.

"No!" she gasped, to which Jim nodded to confirm and carried on packing. "How is that possible?"

"He had help," said Jim. Val took a sip of her drink and with no further information forthcoming from Jim she had to ask him.

"Who from?"

"Colin," said Jim, not looking up.

"Oh," Val took another drink and really wished it was something stronger, bad head and early start or no bad head and early start. "Was your friend Paul in tonight?"

"Yeah, but he left before his mates did. They were sat with Michelle." Jim had finished packing up. "Come on, Val, let's go."

## CHAPTER FOUR

IT WAS MONDAY evening after work and Paul had been surprised; his Dad had played a blinder. For tea, for them both, he had produced chips, fried egg, bacon, sausage, black pudding and beans. When his mum had been alive this was what she called their 'Monday night tea' but they had not had it since and his Dad wolfed down the lot. It was one of his good days.

"Cheers Dad, that was great!" Paul said clearing the plates from the table. "I'll wash up for you, least I could do after that." His Dad glanced at the clock on the wall.

"Time's getting on, son, are you not going to go to your quiz tonight?" his Dad asked. Paul had clean forgotten about it, so pleased had he been by his Dad's efforts.

"Right, the quiz, I forgot! Simon hasn't rung me to say he's going down there yet but, you wouldn't mind if I do go, will you?" His Dad shook his head.

"No, I won't mind, there is some footie about to start on Sky, West Brom versus Derby, I'll watch that."

"Blimey, Dad, don't tempt me to join you in your crazy life!" Paul stopped as the comment had seemed so tactless but his Dad laughed.

"Go on, Paul, life is for living, go and live a bit, I'll be fine," his Dad said. Paul smiled and headed to his room to get ready, ringing Simon's mobile on the way, but it went straight to voice mail.

"That's odd," he thought, pulling a face, throwing the mobile on the bed and opening the wardrobe to choose a shirt.

Paul had made it to the Prince of Wales with just enough time to spare before the quiz started and he headed for the bar. He looked around the pub to see if Simon and Alan were in but they were not.

"Yes, mate, what can I get you?" asked Nigel the landlord, doing a rare stint behind the bar.

"Bottle of Bud, please," Paul replied, as his mobile started to ring. He read the display; SIMON. "Hello, Si, mate! I'm at the quiz, you coming down?"

"Not exactly, no," he replied.

"Not exactly? Are you not well?" Paul asked, concerned, then his face fell, "Oh, no, don't tell me Fart-breath is coming down on his own!!"

"I very much doubt it. Look, I went to Michelle's last week after the quiz."

"Did you? Bloody hell, you dirty old bastard!" Paul exclaimed, quite loudly, so loud that people turned around, including Jim and Val at the DJ stand, some twenty yards away and over the volume of Lady Ga-Ga pumping out of the laptop. "Sorry!" he said to everyone around him, holding his free hand up.

"Alan went too," Simon continued.

"Blimey, it's not you who is the dirty old bastard, then," Paul commented.

"No, she's a game old girl, all right, but things never went according to plan, sexually. I'll, er, call you later in the week." Simon hung up. Paul's Bud arrived so he paid for it and headed over to Jim and Val at the DJ stand. Val had a sneaking feeling that Paul had been on his mobile to Simon as Michelle wasn't out in case Simon turned up, although, strangely for her, she had not elaborated. "Ring me if he is not at the quiz and I'll come down," Michelle had said.

"Hi, Paul, doing the quiz?" Jim asked as Val greeted his arrival with a smile.

"Yeah, I'll give it a go," Paul replied and paid his pound for the quiz sheet.

"Are you on your own, Paul?" Val asked.

"Yeah," he confirmed, "bit sad doing it on me own, but I'm here now so may as well give it a bash."

As Jim handed Paul a quiz sheet he nodded at Val and suggested, "Why don't you and Val team up?"

"Yes! We'll do great!" Val said with a big smile and lots of enthusiasm, grabbing Paul's hands.

"Sure," said Paul, "but is your friend, er, Michelle, is it? Is she…" Paul hesitated and was trying not to laugh.

"Don't ask!" Val said. Jim was laughing, "And you don't breathe a word!!" she said, kissing Jim on the cheek. "See you later, Jim, I'm going quizzing," and Jim smiled.

Val and Paul sat at the table that Val and Michelle normally sat at for the quiz. Val took a pen out of her bag, "What's our team name going to be tonight then, Paul?" she asked.

"How about, 'The team that friends forgot'?" Paul suggested.

Val smiled, "Good one. Talking of which, I must send Michelle a text to tell her your friend, or friends," she winked, "aren't here." Paul laughed.

Between questions Val got to find out a bit more about Paul, some of it she knew from what Jim had told her, but she wanted to hear it from Paul himself, to open him up a bit. He wasn't very chatty, which she soon learnt was down to shyness but Val was and off she went.

"So, I know nothing about you, Paul and here's my chance to be out in the open and all American on you." This made Paul laugh. "So, here we go, brace yourself; have you ever been married, Paul, engaged, lived with anyone, any secret children?"

"No, none of that," he confirmed.

"Oh, right, I see."

"I still live at home, with me Dad."

"Not your Mum and Dad?" she didn't want it to appear that Jim had been talking about him or she had been asking about him.

"She died of cancer, five years ago."

"I'm so sorry about that."

"After that I thought it was best to stay put and keep an eye on me Dad," Paul had nearly convinced himself that this was the truth, that it had been his idea, he had said it enough times, "not that he would kill himself, of course, just remind him to breathe in, breathe out, eat, wash and change clothes now and again."

"What about work?"

Paul pulled a face and shrugged, "What about it?"

"What do you do?"

"I work in a book warehouse."

"Some sort of manager or supervisor, I bet, intelligent man like you,"

"Intelligent? Me? No, I just get given a list of books to pick from the warehouse, parcel them up and get the post office to collect them."

Val looked gobsmacked. "That's all you do?" she asked and Paul nodded. "How about studying or re-training? I could bring you some leaflets from my work about it if you like, for you to have a look through."

"Oh, where do you work, Val?"

"Adult college."

"Right."

"I'm a tutor."

Paul smiled, "I wouldn't have thought you emptied the bins, Val, love!"

Val smiled and they each took a drink and a break in the conversation. Paul looked around the pub as the other teams came in, bought drinks and sat down, all at their usual tables, and Val finished sending a text to Michelle.

"Do you have any interests while you are waiting for the right girl and job to come along?"

"Football and a few pints with me mates, when they are not all out and about with their women."

"Of course."

Val liked Paul; he was a straight up, honest, no nonsense sort of a guy. Beer and football at the weekend seemed his main interests, only interests it would seem, which might explain the 'no current girlfriend' bit, but he was still a likeable person.

"That concludes the answers to tonight's quiz," Jim announced later after running through the answers, "with the £104 rolling over to next week as no one got all the answers right, tonight's winner, with a score of 24, is Big Doug!"

"Yeeeeeee-eeeeeeeeeessss!" Big Doug roared.

"He's won again?!" Paul asked in disbelief. Val was laughing, it was the sort of quiz where Paul, who worked in a warehouse, and Big Doug, who did work on the bins, can beat a highly educated woman like Val, and she found it funny. She stopped laughing when she saw who had been helping Doug. Colin, again.

"Colin! What's that bastard doing here?" Val asked angrily.

"I heard the tail end of a very heated discussion last week with him and Jim at the DJ stand," said Paul, who pulled a sympathetic face, which Val liked him even more for.

"Oh, look, Michelle's here."

---

# 2010

As the barman got our drinks together we had fallen quiet and Val was looking at him and also towards the door wondering, I imagined, if Barry was going to come back in soon.

"I've seen Michelle recently," I found myself saying in between discreet wipes of my moist brow with a tissue.

Val turned to face me with a look on her face to suggest she was trying to be interested, "Really?"

"Her profile turned up on Facebook as a mutual friend, so I put a request in, got accepted and shortly after that I, er, bumped into her one night, in a pub in town."

"Right," said Val as the barman arrived with the drinks. "Surprised she remembered you as you were never really that close as friends, were you?"

"I know, but there you are. I must have made some impression. She probably still has nightmares about all the times you and Ian tried to fix us up."

"You'd have been better than some of the blokes I used to see her with, but she wasn't for you."

I had been a bit economical with the truth; I had looked Michelle's profile up after failing to find one for Val hoping I might find Val among her friends. I had to put a friend request in as this information was not on view. Once she had remembered me, it took some explaining, she accepted me, we got chatting and Michelle had suggested going out for a drink.

# CHAPTER FIVE

ICHELLE APPROACHED the table in a fairly angry stomp and with a face like thunder. "Hi, babe," said Val. "Glad you've made it." Michelle remained stood over them both.

"Do you want a vodka and lemonade, Michelle?" Paul asked. Michelle glared at him.

"Oh, you'd love that, wouldn't you?" she replied.

"I'm sorry?"

"Paul only asked if you wanted a drink, Michelle," said Val. Michelle shrugged like a spoilt child not getting their own way.

"Are your two friends not here tonight, then?" Michelle spat at Paul.

"No, apparently not," he confirmed and sensing some mischief he asked. "Do you know why that might be?" Val lowered her head to try not to laugh.

"I'm going to the bar," Michelle snapped sharply and marched off.

"Well," said Val, "angry she might be but at least she's buying her own drinks, finally." Val and Paul laughed, as Jim approached the table, having left his laptop entertaining the clientele with the Mamma Mia soundtrack.

"Good effort tonight, second again, Paul." Jim told him, to which Paul nodded. Jim leant forward, "Are you going out with anyone?" he asked. Val was open mouthed at how direct he was being.

"Jim," Paul began, "we've been through this, we've been out before, it was messy and anyway you're with Val now." Val and Jim laughed.

"Not for me, you fool," Jim came back with, "why don't you ask Michelle out?" Paul looked past Jim to the bar where Michelle was flirting her way to free drinks from Nigel.

"Er, well, I, blimey, I don't know," Paul stammered and laughed nervously recalling his earlier call with Simon. Paul thought Michelle was attractive but doubted she would go out with him or that he actually wanted to go out with her.

"Do you think that is a good idea, Jim?" Val asked, looking worried.

"You mean so soon after 'wanker Gavin' binned her? You're right, seven years, the wounds can't have healed!!" Jim laughed, but Val looked serious.

"You know what I mean," she said, raising her eyebrows, which Paul didn't know what she meant by it.

"Think about it, Paul," Jim suggested, then left to go back to the DJ stand.

Paul did think about it; Michelle was blonde, attractive, smart – sometimes – and funny, and, unlike Val, was not going out with one of his mates, or anybody for that matter, in the conventional sense. She also appeared to be a terrible flirt with some questionable bedroom related hobbies.

"Val, can I link up with you at the quiz from now on? Seems like the lads have been frightened off."

Val smiled, "Sure, no problem."

"That's if Michelle doesn't mind." Paul added.

"Why would she? And it seems match maker Jim over there has some plans for you both." Paul smiled, stood up and put on his jacket.

"Night Val, see you next week."

"Night, Paul."

Paul raised his hand to wave goodnight to Jim and then left.

Later that night Val was lying in bed reading as Jim was sorting himself out in the bathroom. After a while he came in and got ready for bed.

"I hope Paul and Michelle get it together," he said, out of nowhere. Val turned to face him.

"Do you really?" she asked.

"And you don't?" Jim asked, to which Val shrugged.

"Not bothered, really. She's my friend but a menace to men everywhere and he is such a sweet guy they just seem all wrong."

"Right," Jim said. "I dunno, I thought it would be good to go out with them on double dates, a couple of couples, if you will."

Val sunk into the bed sheets some more while Jim got in and cuddled up to her. Val smiled.

"Night, love you, Val," he said quietly after a few minutes.

"Night, love you, Jim." Val said back and as she lay there she shuddered at the thought of Paul linking up with Michelle and having his heart torn apart by her.

---

## 2010

My mobile started ringing and there was a number on the display I did not immediately recognise. On answering it the caller was revealed as Damien, a lad I had worked with in the call centre.

"Where are you?" he asked.

"I'm at The Sun." I confirmed. "Why?"

"The Sun, I thought we were meeting in the Penny Bank?"

"Nah, I said The Sun, didn't I?"

"Ah, right, we'll wait here for you, okay?"

Val was stroking her cheek with her hand and looking at the floor, pretending, I imagine, not to be eavesdropping. "Okay, I'll, er, be there by nine, or so." With that I ended the call and when I turned to face Val she was looking at the clock above the bar.

"By nine, and what, Mr Kirk, will you be doing for the next hour and five minutes?" I smiled weakly and laughed as I really didn't know why I had said that. Val smiled and shrugged, "Do you still go and watch the football, freckle?" Val had used the West Yorkshire nickname that she used to call me by, almost like a pet name and it made me smile. I had written that the Val in the book was from California but the real Val was not. She was also a brunette, not a red head like the Val in the book. I'm still not really sure why I changed those details about her and not her bloody name. Oh, well, too late to change it now.

"Now and again," I confirmed about the football, "but not as much as I once did."

# CHAPTER SIX

PAUL FOLLOWED BLACKBURN ROVERS and when he attended their games he met up with a mate of his called Dan. Dan was Paul's age and went in for logical plain speaking, as they conducted their conversations in the back room of a pub near the ground. The chatter of expectant fans and Sky Sports didn't interrupt them although trips to the bar to purchase the next round did.

"How've you been, Paul, everything okay with work and your Dad?" Dan asked him as they took their seats at their usual table.

"Yeah, fine, as well as can be expected, both of them," Paul confirmed, taking a drink of his pre-match pint, or one of five or six of his pre-match pints.

"Terrible, then," Dan suggested.

Paul laughed, "Yeah, pretty much!" he agreed.

"And socially, any recent mad nights out?"

"None really, but I've been going to a local pub quiz in town."

"Wow! Calm down, son."

"Okay, it's not wild, but I went with a mate to begin with and after that I teamed up with two women who are regulars there."

"Two women? Is this going to be a bit we-hey!?"

"No, not yet."

"Something promising, then?" Dan probed, to which Paul shrugged.

"Probably not, Dan, no."

"Great, I'm really happy for you, Paul."

Paul laughed, "It's a bit strange but one of them is going out with an old work colleague of mine, he does the quiz, and he is trying to fix me up with the other one and she's a bit mad. Of the two I get on better with my mate's girlfriend. It's odd as I've never had a close friend who was a woman before, but we really get on."

"Hey, lad, talk about growth!"

"What do you mean?"

"It's like the wheel being invented, son, you've got a friend who is a woman and you are not attracted to her. Are you?"

"Well, she is attractive, but a friend's a friend, because I know and like Jim, her old man, never looked at her that way," except he had, and was, right now. Thinking about holding Val, kissing Val, removing Val's clothing and...

*Thank you, Dan, for putting that thought back in my mind.*

"Good lad, we all get this one day, when we meet a woman who we are just friends with and nothing's going to happen. If a bloke messes her around and she's crying all the time then around to her place you go with bottles of wine and chocolate. If your girlfriend leaves you for a rugby player she finds you in the pub with your mates, buys you a pint, kisses your cheek and tells you what a great guy you are."

Paul recalled how this was a little bit of what Nicky used to be for him until he messed that up.

"I had such a woman friend, just after I left college and we got on really well," Dan continued after a moment's pause.

"I see. Are you still in contact with her, Dan?"

"You could say that, I married her."

"Oh, good one, well done." Paul was confused about Dan's argument on why having Val as a friend when she is a woman was a good idea – he married his Val.

# CHAPTER SEVEN

## THE FOLLOWING MONDAY

PAUL HAD LEFT work early and while walking through the centre of town got his mobile out to ring and update his Dad as to why.

"Hi, Dad, Paul here. You haven't started making tea have you?" he asked him.

"I'm not hungry," his Dad replied wearily.

"Right, I see. Well, I'm off to the dentist, I've got chronic toothache, think I'll get them to just pull the chuffer out! I'll see you later."

"Okay, son, see you later."

Reluctantly the dentist did indeed 'pull the chuffer out' and prescribed Paul some painkillers. These made him drowsy and at home he was nodding off in front of the telly when the six o'clock news was starting.

"I'm turning in, Dad, I'm practically falling asleep here," Paul said getting out of the armchair in an unsteady manner.

"Giving the quiz a miss, then?" his Dad asked.

Paul nodded, "Best had."

"I'll let the lads know if they ring to ask, son."

Paul nodded and headed for his room. He was so tired that when he woke the next morning he could not remember going to bed.

"Welcome to tonight's quiz, everybody," Jim announced. "Question number one;" Val checked her watch and wondered where Paul was as Michelle sat with pen poised. When they reached the half time break Val wandered over to see Jim.

"Did Paul ring to say he wasn't coming down tonight?" she asked.

"Don't think he knows my number," Jim replied. "Why would he ring?"

"Just with you wanting to fix him up with Michelle and me inviting him to join us on our team, I just thought he might have rung you or the pub to let us know if he couldn't make it."

Jim shook his head and shrugged his shoulders a bit too passively then busied himself with the laptop to which Val was aghast.

"Jim, I thought you two were big mates," Val pressed a bit too much and Jim reacted aggressively.

"We were work mates once, Val. I like Paul and he's a good laugh, but there's twenty or so years age difference between us and we didn't hang out." Val fixed Jim with a stare.

"There is nearly twenty or so years between us, Jim, but we hang out. Or we at least did until this pub's DJ job became your be all and end all." With that Val went back to the table to join Michelle and got stuck into her vodka and lemonade with gusto.

"Shame Paul couldn't make it," Val said after a while.

"Who?" Michelle asked, while looking around the pub for men.

"Paul," Val repeated. Michelle looked blank. "I did the quiz with him last week."

"Oh, right, him." Val wasn't convinced that Michelle had any idea who Paul was or could recall him.

"He got some questions right last week, sport, 80s pop music, might be worth having him on the team to try to win the jackpot." Val commented for a reaction from Michelle.

"Okay, steady on, professional quizzer Val, I only do this thing for a bit of a laugh, you know," Michelle said, with a laugh.

"Right."

"Here," Michelle looked worried, "he won't be wanting any of the money if we do win the jackpot, will he? I mean I don't know him. He could just be a big perv after bagging me. I'll buy him a pint as a thank you, but he's having nowt else."

Val was gobsmacked, "He's doing well, the first time you met him you thought he was gay as he did not want anything to do with you and now he is a 'big perv'."

The penny dropped; "Oh, you mean him! Why didn't you say so? Here, if we want to win the jackpot that bad, why don't we ask Big Doug and Colin along? They've won the quiz the last two weeks." Michelle giggled and Val, appalled at her friend's tactlessness, took a large gulp of her drink.

The next day Val only had one lesson and had finished by eleven-thirty. Jim was meeting up with her as they had arranged for him to pick her up behind the market in the town centre at eleven-forty five and go for lunch. Val got soaked during the relatively short walk to the market from college, even with an umbrella for cover, as the typical Lancashire weather did its worst. She stood shivering sheltered by the umbrella and the market wall.

"Bloody, fuckety, British bloody weather, take me home!" she muttered to herself.

Still feeling rough with his tooth, or lack of it, Paul had rung in sick and decided a trawl through the town's bookshops and sport biography departments might be in order. Walking around the back of the market he saw Val under her brolly. Although soaked she looked stunning and a part of him wished she was free and it was the ample-breasted Geordie pisshead who was living with his mate. As he approached she cursed.

"First sign of madness, that is," he said, "talking to yourself in public." Her reaction surprised him.

"Paul!" Val yelped, hugging him. "Are you okay? Where were you last night?"

"I was being a bit of a wuss, I'm afraid," he explained, still thrown by her greeting, "I had a tooth out, got some painkillers and was knocked out." Val looked a bit intense which threw him some more.

"You ring the pub the next time you can't make it, okay? I was really worried."

Paul was a bit shocked, "Okay, will do," he smiled nervously.

"Better still, here, give me your mobile and I will give you my number," Paul handed the phone over and Val punched the number into the contacts. After doing that, Val caught herself on and realised how she must have sounded and so became more composed.

"Off work today?" she asked, coolly.

"Yeah, I took a sickie."

"What are you up to?"

"Buying books."

"Oh," said Val. "Man of reading, are we?"

"It's not War and Peace, Val, football biographies, mainly."

Val nodded, "Well at least you've heard of War and Peace, Paul, it's a start."

"Have you finished for the day?"

"Yes, I only have a morning class on a Tuesday."

Their conversation stopped and Paul stared at Val, her face framed by the red hair, her blue eyes sparkling and her warm, friendly smile.

*Ask her for a drink, now,* he thought, *Jim's not that much of a mate, ASK HER!*

"Was Michelle at the quiz last night?" Paul finally asked, and Val's face fell.

"Oh, you are interested in her then, are you?" Val asked.

"No! Well, yeah, possibly. I mean, not really. No, I asked as," he paused, "I'd have felt bad if because I hadn't turned up you'd have been on you own." Val smiled a warm smile that remained warm despite the Lancashire rain and cold. There was the sound of a car horn and a shout of, "Val! Over here!" that signalled Jim had arrived.

"Gotta go," said Val.

"Oh, right, is that Jim?" Paul asked.

"Yeah, we're spending time together this afternoon," Val put her brolly down and made towards the car. She stopped halfway and came back at Paul holding his gaze and said sharply, "he's my boyfriend, after all," which confused Paul, as he, of course, knew that.

Val got in the car. "Hi, love, was that Paul?" Jim asked.

"Just drive, Jim," Val snapped.

Paul made his way to one of the town's bookshops, one of only a handful of shoppers in there, and as he was weighing up his potential purchases he was surprised to see Michelle pass by.

"Michelle!" he called. She stopped in her tracks and gave Paul a puzzled look. "How did you do in the quiz last night?"

*Christ! Weak as piss that one, Paul lad.*

"Won the tenner but not the jackpot," Michelle replied.

"Great," said Paul. "Val asked me to join you but I had a medical mishap so couldn't make it."

"Oh, you're that Paul, right!" Michelle realised who it was now. Paul felt foolish that she had not remembered him, which was odd as they had been in each other's company but away from the quiz perhaps he had not registered with her and looked for something to say.

"Do you fancy going out with me some time, for a drink, or something?" he blurted out. Michelle barely contained a laugh.

"Er, no!"

"Oh, right, not to worry," Paul said.

"You seem surprised I said no."

"Well, Jim seemed to think that," he paused and made hand gestures to signal he was confused and didn't really know what to say, "you know," Paul shrugged and felt embarrassed and stupid.

"Jim seemed to think what, Paul? You're his mate so go out with his girlfriend's mate? Get a life, will yer?" She walked away but after a few yards came back. "I'll see you at the quiz next Monday. Val said you know a bit and it's going to be a £123 jackpot next week and I could do with half of that."

"A third, Michelle, there'll be three of us, so you'll get a third,"

Michelle looked agitated, "Jesus wept! Okay, a fucking third, then," and stormed off. The other people in the shop turned around at the sound of the profanity and then went back to browsing for their books. Paul paused for a moment and headed for the 'sport' department.

*That went well.*

## CHAPTER EIGHT

AFTER WORK PAUL had finished off the 'Monday' tea his Dad had made, then afterwards showered and changed. He walked through the lounge and intended to bid his Dad farewell as he left at the front door but just short of the door he stopped.

"Off out?" his Dad asked.

"Yes," Paul replied after a short pause, still frozen to the spot.

"Quiz, again?"

"Yes, Dad," Paul confirmed, but still he was not moving.

"You'll be late standing there all night if you get there at all, lad."

Paul thought of his conversations the previous Tuesday with both Val and Michelle. Was going to the quiz really such a good idea? Did either of them really want him there? What did Val mean with the "he's my boyfriend" comment. He sat on the sofa and his Dad looked at him quizzically.

"Paul?"

"Give us a minute," Paul said.

His Dad laughed, "Okay, son, I will. If you need a minute I will give you a minute." His Dad picked up the paper to read it but carried on talking. "Do you still go to the quiz with Simon and Fart-breath, when you ever get there?"

"No, they are staying away from it at the moment."

"Why?" his Dad asked.

"Er, it's complicated. No, I've chummed up with the girlfriend of a friend of mine who goes there." His Dad lowered the paper and looked at him for a moment.

"What?" His Dad laughed again, "Be careful there, son."

At the quiz an anxious looking Val could not disguise her glances at the door and her watch too well and Michelle noticed.

"Well, Valerie," Michelle began, "doesn't look like 'wonder boy' is turning up, does it?" Val looked aghast.

"My God, you hate him, don't you?" Val asked. "Jim was quite keen to set you up with him."

Michelle sighed. "All right, he's not that bad a bloke, but I had a feeling one of you was plotting something and I just hate being set up, that's all. It's awkward for both parties. I ran into him in town last Tuesday."

"Did you?"

"Yeah, in a bookshop, and when he asked me out I was a bit hard on him."

"Paul asked you out?"

"Don't be surprised, wasn't that part of Jim's masterplan?" Michelle asked, almost mockingly. Val was very surprised at this information, both that Paul had asked Michelle out and that Michelle was in a bookshop.

"You were in a bookshop? How long have some of them contained bars?"

Michelle gasped. "Eee, you cheeky beggar, Val!"

Just a few minutes later Paul came to the table with a pint in his hand. "Evening, girls, sorry I'm cutting it fine," he said.

"That's okay," said Val. "How are you?"

"Fine, thanks, fine. JIM!" Paul bellowed with his arm raised, over the music towards the DJ stand, and Jim waved back. "Right, let's win this baby!!"

Val stood up, "Just getting a drink, same again, Michelle?"

"Yes, thanks." As soon as Val was out of earshot Michelle leant towards Paul and took the chance to explain a few things to him. "Look, can I apologise, I was a bit harsh when I saw you the other day. I had an inkling Jim and Val were planning something with you and me getting together, so..."

"Don't worry, Michelle," Paul said, interrupting. Michelle shook her head and continued.

"Maybe as I get to know you better you might turn out to be the sort of bloke I will end up going out with. You're not a bad lad but I just don't like being fixed up." Val had returned.

"Michelle, Nigel's just asked me to tell you he's in," she said.

"Did he? Right, okay," said Michelle, "I'll just go and have a word with him." After Michelle had gone Val smiled and put her hand on Paul's.

"Paul, I'm sorry, last Tuesday was a tough day; work, Jim, the weather, jammy rag week,"

"Jammy rag week?!" Paul exclaimed loudly, shocked.

"My period," Val confirmed.

"Yeah, I know what it means, I just never expected a graceful, foreign national to utter such an expression."

Val looked towards Michelle at the bar, "I lived with a borderline, alcoholic Geordie for four years and even as a graceful, foreign national – bless you, Paul - you pick things up," Val continued. "I think you got the brunt of it last Tuesday and I'm really sorry about that."

Paul held up the hand that did not have Val's hand on it, "No problem," he said, "and you've both apologised to me tonight." As Paul took a drink Val looked surprised.

"Oh, that's rare for Michelle,"

"I asked her out, silly of me, didn't really want to but you know, you and Jim put the idea in my head. She said no, she's attractive, could have the pick of any bloke she wanted so would never go for me in a million years."

"I'm sure some attractive woman would, Paul. Don't be so harsh on yourself, you are a great guy,"

"Thanks, Val, but I'm no George Clooney in the looks department, am I?"

"I bet even George Clooney doesn't think he's George Clooney in the looks department," Paul looked confused, "you know what I mean," Val added. Paul laughed, finished his pint and then got up from his seat.

"I'm going to get another pint before Jim starts." Paul made his way to the bar and ordered a pint from Stuart. While he waited for it he noticed Nigel and Michelle heading out of the back door. Curious, he sneaked that way himself and looked out of the window. In the far corner of the car park they clambered into the back seat of a car. Michelle was just unbuttoning her blouse when…

"Here's your pint, mate," Stuart called, and Paul went to collect it. "Six weeks I have worked here and that happens every Monday at some point in the evening," he said gesturing toward the back door.

"Oh, I see," said Paul, fishing for change in his jean's pocket.

"While the boss is away, mate, this one is on me," said Stuart.

"Great, cheers!"

At the half way stage of the quiz Val and Paul were running through the answers so far. Michelle came back to the table with drinks for all.

"Here we are," she said cheerfully. "Dig in guys."

"Thank you," said Val, picking up her vodka.

"Compliments of Nigel are they?" Paul asked cheerfully, causing Val to nearly choke on her drink.

"What do you mean by that, like?" Michelle asked, clearly offended.

Thinking quickly Paul explained, "Well, you are always skint and you went to see him before."

"Oh, right, no I got them this time."

"I'm going to see Jim," said Paul, before he got into anymore bother. After he left Val said to Michelle, "Bit longer this week?"

"Yes, he was!" giggled Michelle. Val put her hand to her face.

"My God! Where's his poor unsuspecting wife tonight, then?"

"No idea, don't care, doubt he does either," Michelle replied.

Paul and Jim were in deep discussion about the Michelle situation, whispering in shouts as best they could over 'Sam's Town' by the Killers.

"So I asked her out, and she said no," Paul began.

"Too soon, Paul, too soon," said Jim, shaking his head.

"And I felt like a prick, but she explained tonight that one day she might know me well enough to go out with me," Paul continued.

"Promising," Jim commented.

"There is the little matter of her being banged by the landlord in the car park every week."

Jim pulled a face, "You know about that?" he asked.

Paul nodded, "Not sure that's the sort of thing I want to follow, or share."

"Fair enough," said Jim.

Later, at the end of the quiz, with Big Doug triumphing again, Paul sensed Val was getting tired so decided to leave.

"I'll be off now," he announced, standing up and putting his jacket on.

"Can I drive you home?" Val asked.

"Yeah, that would be great thanks, as long as you don't mind and it's no trouble. Where's Michelle? You won't be leaving her in the lurch, will you?"

"She's busy," Val rolled her eyes.

"Landlord?" Paul asked. Val looked shocked. "Saw everything, well, nearly everything, just before when I was getting a pint. Made me put things a lot more in perspective about her."

"Right, I'll just let Jim know we are going," Val walked over to the DJ stand to tell Jim and as she approached Jim was handing some money to a young man of about nineteen who scurried away. Momentarily, he looked shocked to see Val approach but pulled himself together to smile.

"Who was that?" Val asked.

"Some lad who comes in at the weekend," Jim replied.

"Why were you giving him money?"

"He's getting us something for the business to sell on."

Val took this information in, "Okay, okay, well, I'm going and I'm giving Paul a lift home."

"Right, love, I'll see you at home then." Val walked away and halfway back towards where Paul was waiting with his jacket on. She turned back to look at Jim who smiled and waved.

"All set, Val?" Paul asked.

Val paused for a moment. "Yeah, come on, let's go."

After they left, the lad came back to see Jim. "That was close," he said.

"She doesn't know that I get you this shit to sell then?" the lad asked.

"No, she does not, and that is how it will remain."

On the drive home the little exchange Val had seen troubled her and while she did not want to dump her worries all over Paul, as she did not know him that well, she thought he might have some answers having known Jim a long time. She was quiet and looked worried.

"You okay, Val?" Paul asked. "You seem miles away. Something on your mind, is there?" Val pulled a face. "Can I help?" Paul smiled.

"Do you?" she began and then stopped to try and start again. "That chav-like boy in the," she paused again, "do you know what

Jim does for a living, other than the DJ work?"

"No," Paul replied. "I've no idea."

Val changed gears aggressively. "Neither do I and it is starting to worry me a bit."

## CHAPTER NINE

ON THE FOLLOWING MONDAY Paul approached the DJ stand once again, "Good to see you Paul, quizzing I take it?" Jim asked.

"Yeah, here's me pound."

Jim handed over a quiz sheet and took the pound noticing behind Paul that Michelle and Val had just arrived.

"The girls have just come in, are you going to chance your arm with Michelle tonight?"

Paul sighed, "Have I really got any chance at all, Jim?"

"I think so and you won't know until you try."

Paul headed over to the table they always sat at and on the way Val noticed him and smiled to which he nodded back. Once sat at the table he weighed the two of them up and after a while Val headed over to the table while Michelle headed off to see Nigel.

"Hi, sweetie, you okay?" Val asked sitting down.

"Yeah, and you?"

"Okay," Val took a drink and looked around the pub to check out the opposition. She then looked at Paul and he looked nervous. "Sure you're okay, Paul?"

"Jim asked me if I was going to ask Michelle out tonight."

"Oh?"

Paul took a drink, "I don't know, she is attractive and that but, you know, carrying on with the landlord, puts me off." Michelle appeared back in the bar and was heading over. "Oh, hell, she's coming over, what do I do?"

"Be yourself, Paul, if it's meant to be, it's meant to be," Val advised.

Michelle plonked herself down on a stool and took a drink. She never acknowledged Paul.

"Hi, Michelle," Paul said.

"Mm," was all she said in reply.

"You okay?" Paul tried again. Michelle just shrugged. Paul leant forward and whispered to Val, "Going well, then." Val smiled.

"Welcome to tonight's quiz," Jim announced. "Question number one."

"Good luck, Michelle," Paul said with a big daft smile giving her arm a playful little punch. Michelle rolled her eyes and lowered her head over the quiz sheet. The quiz was not won but neither was the jackpot.

A couple of weeks later on another Monday evening Paul was in his room making a phone call.

"Simon? It's Paul, where are you?" he asked.

"Dewsbury," Simon replied.

"Ah, well, as it's nearly seven o' clock that'll be a no to you coming to the quiz tonight, then?"

Simon laughed, "If that loony tune Michelle still goes to it I'll give it a very wide berth forever, Paul, son."

"What even happened with you two that night?"

"Jesus, Paul, nearly crashed the car, then. I'll ring you for a pint later in the week, okay?"

"Okay, Si." Paul smiled and threw his mobile onto the bed to start getting ready. "What a lad!"

Paul went to the quiz and teamed up with the girls and as Jim was finishing marking and about to give the answers Val went to the DJ stand.

"Did we win?" she asked. Jim shook his head.

"No, second, again," he replied. "No one's won the jackpot, though, so it will be £201 next week."

"Christmas week as well."

"Right," said Jim, picking up the microphone, "this week's winner," he announced, "with 27 out of 30, Big Doug."

"Yeeeeeeee-eeeeeeeeeeeessssss!" Big Doug yelled, as he came to collect his tenner winnings. Once he had left Val nudged Jim.

"What?" he asked.

"Look!" she replied, pointing.

Paul and Michelle were walking, deep in conversation, towards the fruit machine.

"I noticed Nigel wasn't in tonight," said Val.

"Fell downstairs and broke his leg, the big fat bastard," Jim confirmed. Val drained her drink.

"I'm going to get another drink, and eavesdrop," she said with a smile, heading to stand as near as she could to Paul and Michelle at the bar. Michelle was pressing a lot of buttons and bending and bobbing down to look for nudges on the machine which amused Paul.

"You seem to know what you're doing here, Michelle," he said.

"Aye, I do," Michelle confirmed.

"Part of your degree course was it?"

Michelle smiled. "Me Dad taught me, he could treble his wages from the colliery most weeks."

"Impressive," gasped Paul.

"That, and Big Doug pumped about £70 into it earlier today so at some point it is bound to-" she paused as there was a clunk-clink-clunk of coins leaving the machine, "-pay out!!"

"Well done!" said Paul.

"Thanks. I can finally buy you back a pint for all the drinks you have bought me over the weeks."

"Michelle, you don't have to, but thanks," Michelle put a hand on his shoulder.

"I insist, Paul. Every week when I am skint you're kind enough to stand me a round."

They stood at the bar and Val turned to Jim with a daft grin on her face and he returned it with a thumbs-up. Val headed for the table they sat at during the quiz while Paul and Michelle waited for their drinks to arrive.

*Shall I ask her out?* thought Paul. *Why not, you're getting on well tonight, give it a go.*

"Michelle," he began, and she turned to face him with a warm smile, "if you remember a few weeks ago you said," Michelle's face lit up like a child being handed a huge birthday present but she was ignoring Paul and looking over his shoulder.

"Oooooooh, who are these!?" she gushed. At this point a group of men had entered the bar, all wearing matching blazers, ties and grey trousers. They were brash, loud, shouting 'in jokes' at each other and singing snatches of raucous songs. This was Michelle's kind of birthday present...

"Rugby team!" Michelle moved down the bar to be among them and the busty blonde instantly became their new mascot.

"Here's your drinks, Paul," said Stuart, "Seven-forty, please, mate." Paul suddenly realised he would now have to pay for them after all.

"Oh, right, okay, Stuart," said Paul and went to get his wallet from his pocket.

"Paul, I'll have mine here," Michelle said slapping the bar twice as a prop forward ogled her cleavage.

"Breaks your heart, every bloody week," Stuart said and Paul nodded.

"Just a bit," he admitted with a rueful laugh. Val had seen everything happen and watched Paul trudge over and wearily sit down next to her and let out a big sigh.

"Paul, I am so sorry," she began.

Paul shrugged, "Don't worry about it Val, it's not your fault."

"You were getting on so well tonight," added Val and Paul shrugged again and sighed. He suddenly felt tired and had a headache. "She has warmed a bit towards you, when we first met you here she thought you were gay, you've made progress."

"Hold on!" said Paul, suddenly, "That's it, she's that Michelle."

"Which Michelle?" Val asked, confused.

"Day before New Year's Eve, about three years or so ago, I was in the Red Lion in town and this girl was sat at a table on her own and got me to join her by slapping the table twice," Paul copied it now, "just like she has done at the bar for her drink just now. She got me to buy her a drink and cadge a fag from a mate of mine then asked me if I was gay."

Val rolled her eyes, "That does sound like one of her old tricks and she was a regular at the Red Lion." Val went white and felt ill as she remembered she had been in the Red Lion that night and had left as Michelle was waiting for a man to join her from the bar.

Paul nodded but looked crushed. "Can I drive you home, Paul?" Val offered.

He nodded, "Thanks, Val, you're very kind, at least."

"I'll just go and let Jim know." Val wandered over to the DJ stand and Jim was surveying the shambles at the bar. Michelle was in the middle of a hastily arranged rugby scrum.

"What a cow!" said Jim.

"I know," Val agreed. "Listen, Paul is in a bit of a state so I offered to drive him home again."

"Okay, good one. The poor bloke, heartbroken. Again."

"Again?" Val asked.

"Yeah, I heard a few New Years ago that he finished with his girlfriend after he was feeling guilty about chatting to a girl in a pub in town. Absolute love of his life was the girlfriend, apparently."

"Oh, God," said Val feeling sick. Back at the table Paul was looking discreetly over towards the DJ stand and noticed Val occasionally look his way with a kind and sympathetic expression on her face. He really liked Val and now considered her as much of a friend as Jim was, in some ways more so.

Conversation was nil on the relatively short drive to Paul's except for Val asking him "Are you okay?" a lot. Paul would then say, "Yeah, no problem," in reply far too often. When they pulled up outside Paul's house Val turned off the car engine and began a pep talk.

"It will seem empty now, Paul, but you are better than her and you can do better than her. And you will!" This comment of Val's struck Paul as being odd as this was her friend she was talking about.

"Cheers, Val, and thanks for the lift." Val had her left hand on the gear stick and Paul patted it as a thank you and then placed it on there. They held each other's gaze and gave each other comforting looks.

*Could I kiss her?*

It looked possible. He wanted to and there was a look in her eyes that suggested she wanted him to. But she was Jim's girlfriend and he had to remember that, so he gulped back his emotions and pulled himself together with a smile.

"Right, night, Val," Paul laughed nervously.

"Night, Paul. Take care." Val said quickly as Paul got out of the car. She watched him open the door with his key and wave as he entered the house. She smiled and waved back, then allowed herself a sigh and a shake of the head,

"What am I doing? What am I thinking? Focus, Val, focus."

With that she started the engine and headed for home.

Val was in bed later that night when Jim finally got home and he came straight upstairs to bed. "Everything all right?" she asked as he got into bed alongside her.

"Yeah," he replied. "How was Paul?"

"A bit better by the time I dropped him off, I think."

"Good, I'm glad, poor sod."

"And Michelle?"

Jim looked angry. "Last I saw she was being carried shoulder high by the front row of that rugger team," Jim thawed a bit, turned off the bed side lamp, kissed Val and snuggled in. He let out a big sigh as he dozed.

"Night," he whispered, dozily, after a few minutes, "love you, Val." Val smiled to herself as Jim began to doze and appreciated his sentiment, as she always did.

"Night," Val whispered back after a few moments, "love you, Paul."

*Paul!* She thought. *Had Jim heard that?*

She sat upright in bed, turned on her bedside lamp and saw, luckily, that Jim had fallen asleep, so she headed for the bathroom and threw water on her face. It didn't help.

"I love Paul? Oh no! I do, I love Paul," she whispered and then began to sob, "how could I let this happen?"

---

# 2010

I had excused myself to go to the loo and on the way back my heart stopped to see that Val was not at the bar. If she had gone I was disappointed that we had not swapped telephone numbers to stay in touch after all this time. After a moment I told myself she could also have gone to the loo but then I noticed that she was outside talking to Barry. His head was bowed and he looked apologetic and Val had her arms folded and looked angry, but she was silent and listening to him. I headed towards the bar and kept myself to myself waiting for something to happen. Glancing up at the clock above the bar I noticed it was ten past eight and I still had plenty of time before nine when I had rearranged to meet my friends. I had more of a chance to make my mind up when Val would be back in the bar so sat tight and waited with the occasional glance towards the door.

So many things that had happened between Val and I were racing through my mind and I couldn't wait for her to come back in. I wondered if she had ever thought about me in the years we had not seen each other. She had often occupied my thoughts. Did she ever think about what happened between us? I certainly did.

# CHAPTER TEN

## Within the next few days

VAL WAS AT COLLEGE marking some coursework after a lesson had finished when her colleague Geraldine knocked on the open door of the class room.

"Got a minute, Val?" she asked.

"Sure, come in," she said cheerfully, having put recent events to the back of her mind. Geraldine came in and closed the door. She looked serious and Val was worried. "Is something wrong?"

"Katie McBride," Geraldine announced sharply.

"What about her," Katie was in the Tuesday criminology class Val took.

"I have just had her in my class and she made a comment about something you did in yesterday's lesson."

"Oh? What did she say?"

"She said you snapped at her for talking," Val put her pen down and leant back in her chair with tears welling in her eyes.

"I did," she admitted.

"We are not teaching children here, Val, these are young adults. This is not like you; all your students love you for how you are in your lessons, what's wrong?"

"I've fallen in love with Paul."

"Paul? I thought you were living with someone called Jim?"

"I am, that's the problem."

"Oh, I see, now this makes sense," said Geraldine, and as Val began to cry Geraldine made her way to the desk to comfort her friend.

Paul came home from another day of hell at work followed by a nightmare, hour long bus journey home, made worse by leaving his MP3 at work and having to listen to all the inane chatter of the chavs and WAG wannabes, to find his Dad on the phone talking away, laughing occasionally and appearing quite bright and cheery which pleased him and also confused him.

"Ok, love," he was saying, "great, can't wait. I'll see you next week!" He put the phone back on the stand, "Hi, Paul, that was Cheryl."

"Oh," said Paul, surprised his elder sister had rung.

"She's had a chat with our Joanne and they have decided I'll be spending Christmas with Cheryl and David then a few days later Joanne and Tony will come and collect me for New Year."

"That's great, Dad," said Paul, "a break from these four walls will be good for you." His Dad looked glum, "what's up?"

"I didn't include you in all this, Paul, lad. I didn't know what you were working over Christmas and New Year and I figured you'd have your mates to hang out with."

"No problem at all, Dad, I'll be fine," he lied, "you go and enjoy yourself and pin one on."

"Are you sure?"

"No, honestly, I'll give you your presents to take with you"

His Dad looked surprised, "Presents? You shouldn't have bothered, son."

"It's Christmas and you're me Dad, what should I have done? Now go on, go and pack."

Val was sat at a table in the quietest corner of a pub in the town centre and was staring into space as Geraldine came back from the bar. It was getting busier, a mixture of students, workers and Christmas shoppers all fighting to be heard above Noddy Holder screeching from somewhere in the background.

"White wine, okay?"

"Thanks, Geraldine," Val picked up the glass, took a large drink, put it back down and looked into space again. Geraldine was looking at Val weighing her up.

"This isn't like you, Val. This is what I'd expect from a teenager."

Val laughed, "I was never really a teenager. I sometimes think I was born a mature twenty-two year old."

"Does he have good prospects, this Paul?"

"You sound like my Dad!"

"Sorry," said Geraldine, "what's he like, is he nice? Is he attractive?"

Val looked at her wine glass in a thoughtful manner and weighed up her thoughts on him, other than the fact she had fallen in love with him. "He is twenty-eight and works in a book warehouse, he likes soccer, or football as I have to call it over here and drinking, but he has a lot of knowledge, wins quizzes, reads biographies and has a lovely spirit on his good days."

"And is he attractive?" Geraldine pressed again.

Val laughed, "He's not Brad Pitt but he's not ugly or retarded."

"What about Jim? Does he know or suspect anything?"

"No, but I blurted out Paul's name when I went to say I loved Jim in bed the other night."

"Oh, good God, Val!"

"I know, but he was asleep, thankfully."

"How are things going with Jim? Any sign of him popping the question?" Geraldine took a sip and looked at Val waiting for her reply.

Val rolled her eyes and sighed. "After what sometimes seems like a billion years together I still haven't even met his kids. We never have nights out together or trips or holidays. We're practically a corpse."

Val took a drink of her wine and Geraldine took another sip of hers.

"Something will happen that will sort this all out, Val, but if I was you of the two I'd go for this Paul, he's your age, it will be a chance to live a little, be the teenager you never were."

"At thirty-one?!" said Val, and they both laughed.

## CHAPTER ELEVEN

### Monday, Christmas week

AT THE NEXT QUIZ NIGHT Paul went to the DJ stand after he arrived and filled Val and Jim in on what had happened with his Dad. Val listened to the plans of Paul's Dad's trip and her feelings for Paul were raging, especially after confiding in someone about him. Just being near him was leaving her confused and a little bit light-headed. She had never felt this way about anyone, not Jim or any of the other men she had been out with.

"I am glad he's going away, glad for him, obviously, for a number of reasons," he told them, "the Christmases since Mum died have been lousy and it'll be great for my sisters to step up to the plate for a change."

"So what will you do at Christmas?" Jim asked.

"On the day itself, I dunno; get up, have breakfast, see if there's anything worth watching on TV and if not bang on a DVD."

"Oh, God, Paul, that's awful," said Val with much concern and Paul nodded then shrugged to confirm how lousy his lot was. If truth be known he was glad he would be on his own for a while and have some time off from worrying about his Dad. His last comment had made Val want to reach out and hold him even more than she did anyway. She really felt for him.

"And Christmas Eve, are you out with your mates?" Jim pressed further.

"No, most of me mates are coupled up and either out with their other halves or stopping in with their kids. Simon is in New York with some work mates, he asked me along, but cost wise it was beyond me."

"Well, this couple you know aren't out together," said Val pointing at Jim and her, "Jim's working here and I'll be sat at home on my own. The prospect of being in here watching Jim being slobbered over by drunk, teenage girls does not appeal to me."

"Bet it does to you, Jim, any chance I can get in on some of that action?" said Paul, and all three of them laughed. "Is Michelle not out?"

"Yeah, but not around here, back home in Gateshead," Val waved an arm in the general direction of the north-east of England, "or somewhere up that way, does it every year."

Paul took a drink and looked thoughtful, "Well, if this is all right with you Jim why don't me and you go out for the night, Val?" he asked. Val's eyes were momentarily agog but she recovered her composure and kept her racing emotions in check. She stole a glance at Jim who seemed unfazed by the suggestion. When Jim had suggested they team up to do the quiz she had been really enthusiastic but did not love Paul then. Now, she loved Paul and because of this his idea seemed like the worst idea in the world.

"Okay," said Val, hesitantly, "well, that's an option, but I don't think it would be a good idea."

"Sure, why not, Val? Go on, go out with Paul and have a few drinks and a laugh," said Jim.

"Really?" asked Val hoping Jim might change his mind.

"Yeah, there'll be nothing on TV, you'll be bored, you like Paul and get on with him, go for it!"

"Great! Cheers, Jim. Shall I get a round in before the quiz starts?" Paul left the DJ-stand wearing a big smile and Jim was also smiling broadly as he went back to his laptop. Val, however, felt like she was the victim of an elaborate practical joke. Part of her had really, really wanted Jim to say 'no', it would be too weird and he did not want Val to go on a night out with Paul.

"Jim," she began, "are you absolutely sure on this?" Val's emotions and feelings for Paul almost begged for an excuse to get her out of it and she wondered how she would keep herself under control on the night, not get carried away and tell Paul everything.

"If anyone else, any other bloke I know in the world had suggested it, I would have said no," Jim confirmed, "I wouldn't have trusted them, but Paul, nothing to worry about there; he's one of life's good guys. I trust him."

"Right," said Val. In a daze and wondering if she trusted herself she headed over to their table to sit and wait for the quiz. Paul came over with the drinks and a big smile still on his face.

"What a man Jim is, can't wait, Val, we'll have a blast!" he said patting her on the shoulder with a big smile and a cheeky laugh. Val looked at him in bewilderment and at that moment Michelle arrived.

"Hello, all," she said sitting down, "and who's having a blast, now?" she asked.

"Me and Val," Paul replied, "I had a word with Jim and we are having a bit of a 'sesh' on Christmas Eve while he works here."

"Are you now? Well, that sounds like fun, shame I'm up in the north-east and missing it all," said Michelle, smiling as if sharing Jim and Paul's private joke. Val rolled her eyes and her mind raced away with how her thoughts for Paul could impact and ruin their night out. He was no longer Paul, the man her boyfriend once worked with, who she was friendly with from the quiz. He was now Paul, the man she was in love with.

"Paul, if it's going to be strange for you don't worry, we don't have to," Val began.

"What? Going out for a few drinks with someone I consider a friend? I think we'll be fine, Val." Paul smiled and filled in their quiz team name. Val couldn't help but love him even more and wanted to grab him, hold him and kiss him, right there.

Later on the quiz results had been announced; Val, Michelle and Paul had won the quiz but not the jackpot and Paul went to collect the tenner winnings.

"Hard luck, Paul, just one wrong," Jim said, handing over the money.

"Are you sure on that Christmas number one of 1986?" Paul asked, "I'm sure it was Jackie Wilson."

"I always use the Guinness book of hit singles as a reference and that says it was The Housemartins," Jim confirmed.

"Fair enough," said Paul. He looked around the pub and was prompted to say something by seeing Val who at that moment looked downcast. "Is Val okay, Jim?" he asked.

Jim looked up from his laptop, "I think so," he replied. "Why?"

"She's not looked well all night, and I was just concerned, that's all," Paul commented with a shrug.

"For a week," Jim corrected, "she's not looked well all week."

"A week?" asked Paul. Jim nodded.

"I think going on a night out with you will do her the power of good, give her a boost and cheer her up a little bit."

Paul saw his chance, "And you're all right about it, Jim? Honestly?"

Jim nodded and smiled, "Yeah, no problem."

"It's just that Val kept asking me if I was all right going on a night out with her and I am, but it seemed a big deal, like she didn't really want to go and that you would object,"

"No problem with me, Paul, I'm fine about it."

Michelle approached the DJ stand.

"I'm off lads, early dart for the north east in the morning," she threw her arms around Jim in an over the top manner, which he returned, and she kissed him on the lips. For Paul she put her hands on his shoulders, squeezed them and kissed his cheek. "Take care, Paul, love," she said.

"And you Michelle, and have a merry Christmas," Paul returned.

After she left Jim leant forward and asked Paul, "You get any further with her, Paul?"

"After discovering the landlord affair and witnessing the rugby team debacle, James, let's not go there!"

Paul went over to see Val who still looked a bit queasy. He was concerned as to what might be up and wondered how best to approach the subject. He sat next to her and looked at her kindly.

"Are you sure you are all right, Val?" he asked. "You're looking a bit peaky, love."

"No, but it'll pass hopefully. I'm giving Jim a lift home so if you want one you'll have to hang around till closing."

"I won't, Val, but thanks. Give us a ring about Christmas Eve, okay?" Val nodded and Paul stood up to put his jacket on. "Wish we'd bagged 'the biggie' tonight, Val, two hundred pounds, bloody hell, could've done with that." He leant forward and hugged Val, a gesture out of nowhere which threw her a bit and he stood up straight wearing a lopsided smile. "See you soon," Paul said and left, waving at Jim as he did.

"Bye," Val whispered after he had gone.

---

# 2010

Val came back into the bar and stood alongside me. She did not look angry, sad or happy. She just looked impassive and deep in thought as she leant on the bar with her chin cupped in her hands. I wondered for a moment if I should reveal I knew where she had just been and decided to do just that.

"I saw on my way back to the bar that you were talking to Barry outside," I began, pulling a sympathetic face. "How did it go? Is he coming back in? Do you want me to go and leave you two to it?"

Val looked at me, smiled and then placed her hands on my face and we began kissing, softly, teasingly.

*Blimey, I had good memories of this!*

"I bloody well hope he's not coming back," she told me when we had stopped, "and I would prefer it if you stayed put."

# CHAPTER TWELVE

## Christmas Eve

IN A RARE SHOW OF GRATITUDE the book warehouse bosses decided to let the staff leave at 12 midday every Christmas Eve, just in time for the pubs' opening. With his Dad on the way to Warwickshire, Paul decided to have a few hours with the lads, all either too old or too young to knock about with him, then head home to get ready for his night out with Val. They found their way to a pub that was soon filling up with other workers all finishing early.

"So who are you out with tonight, Paul? It didn't make any sense when you told me before," asked Keith, the one man who was Paul's age, but was married with a child. The two of them were sat on the end of a long table that the lads from work had commandeered.

"It's a woman called Val. She's an American and a girlfriend of a mate of mine. I go to a quiz with her, we get on really well, my mate's working tonight so I suggested we go out for a drink or two," Paul replied, "so we weren't sat at home on our own." Keith took a drink of his pint.

"Is she fit?" he asked.

Paul laughed. "She is. She's tall, slim, red head, educated."

"Pity," said Keith, "she sounded all right until the last one because if she wasn't educated you might have had a chance. So why are you not banging her again?"

"She's going out with a mate of mine."

"So?"

"What do you mean, 'so'?" asked Paul.

"Do you like her?" Keith asked back.

"Yeah, she's great."

"Great," said Keith. "I'm not getting a lot of warmth from 'great'. It's bound to go all wrong when you're out tonight, Paul, mate."

"Eh? What? Why? How? How is it going to go wrong tonight? What's going to go wrong, exactly?"

"Me and me family are having Christmas lunch at that carvery place at 1 o' clock tomorrow, we have a spare place as Uncle Stan died last week, poor sod, I'll come and collect you, take your mind off the disaster of the night before!" Keith laughed, not a nasty laugh, but a matey laugh, and slapped Paul on his back.

"It won't be a disaster, it will be okay. A few drinks, a good chat, a few laughs and then I'll wake up in the morning with my face in…" Keith raised his eyebrows, "…a pizza!"

Keith sighed and shook his head, "Ever the optimist, Paul."

"Well, you're the one who thinks it will be a disaster!"

"It will be a disaster and I'll collect you half twelve tomorrow to hear all about it." At which point Keith patted Paul on the shoulder and winked at him.

At home an hour or so later Paul was setting up the Sky Plus box when the phone rang.

"Hello?" he answered.

"Hi, Paul." It was Val.

"You okay?" he asked.

"Yeah, absolutely, can't wait for tonight,"

"Great, it's just you looked a bit Jimmy Hill the other night."

"A bit what?" Val asked.

"A bit ill," Paul corrected his slang.

"Oh, I'm fine, don't worry."

Paul did think from the tone of her voice that Val sounded back to her normal self but felt it best to mention her state of mind.

"If any part of tonight is weird for you then please jib, Val, I won't be offended,"

"I'll do no such thing, Paul. I'm looking forward to it. See you in the Red Lion at eight." Paul was looking forward to it as he got on well with Val and liked her. It did worry him why she had looked so ill and tense the other day. Also, meeting in the Red Lion, scene of his nightmare meeting with Michelle all those years ago, brought a shudder over him and made him feel a bit queasy, especially so close to New Year's Eve.

Val replaced the receiver just as Jim came into the front room.

"Was that Paul?" he asked.

"Yeah, yeah it was."

"Is he still out with you tonight?"

"Oh, yes, Red Lion at eight o' clock. I can't wait!" Val smiled, and punched the air to signify some enthusiasm.

"Right, I'm heading off now, setting up early at the pub,"

"Okay, we'll pop by during the night to say hello."

"Make sure you come back later, for the lock in!" said Jim with a smile. "Right, off we go, love you," then he left. As she heard the car door close and the engine start Val began to sob again. She had fallen in love with Paul and her mind and stomach were doing somersaults of nervous excitement just thinking about the night ahead.

Not far from the pub Jim saw the 'chav' that had been in the pub at the quiz who Val had seen and he flagged Jim down.

"How did that go, Jim? Did you sell any?" he asked.

"Yes, but I don't like it much, so keep it under your hat."

Paul had been on many nights out and many Christmas Eve nights out before, so why, he wondered, did he feel sick to his stomach as he made his way to the Red Lion for this one? He had only had three pints after work, they had done a bacon butty run in the morning and he had made himself a fairly hefty tea. So why did he feel so odd? He dismissed nerves as the cause as he had been out many times before with Val.

He tried to get there before eight so Val wouldn't have to sit on her own being leered at by desperate, drunken, north of England men but she was already there and had survived, despite the leering.

"Hi, Paul!" she greeted him with a huge smile. She had butterflies herself but she knew why that was. She gave him a hug, "let me buy you a pint." After she ordered Val turned to face him and her eyes were drawn to a plastic bag in Paul's hand.

"What's with the bag?" she asked.

"Oh, yes, the bag, something to get us all Christmassy!" he pulled from the bag a Santa hat, which he held in his left hand and a set of antlers and a red sponge nose, which he held in his right. "Who do you want to be; Santa or Rudolph?"

Val was laughing, "Oh, God, I'll be Santa, please!" and she grabbed the Santa hat while Paul put on the antlers and the nose. Once they were on he looked at Val with a serious face, nudged the antlers slightly to the left as she cracked up some more. "That makes it worse,

Paul!"

His pint had arrived, "Cheers, Val, oh, hell, this could be a problem," as the sponge nose was getting close to the bitter. Val was in tears but of laughter for a change. Within minutes Paul had made her feel so much better.

"Perhaps bottles of beer from now on, Paul," she suggested.

"No, I've got an idea," he said, and then leant over the bar, "can I have a straw, please, mate?" he asked the barman.

"God, this hat's making my hair itch, I can't wear it," Val said.

"I'll wear that as well then, give me it."

When the straw arrived the sight of Paul wearing the red nose, antlers and the Santa hat, which Val had abandoned, drinking his pint of bitter through it made Val laugh even more.

"Oh, Paul, you do make me laugh," she finally said. She placed her hand on his shoulder and smiled. Paul looked at her hand and also smiled, delighted to make such a beautiful woman so happy.

*There was a moment there,* Val thought.

*Was there a moment there?* Paul thought to himself.

"Thanks, Val, thanks ever so much, this has cheered me up."

"And me, Paul." They both sensed the other really meant it and smiled and laughed some more.

Jim was at the Prince of Wales, pumping out all the Abba, Grease and Christmas songs the clientele could handle, when Val came dashing up to the DJ stand wearing a big smile. Jim was so pleased she looked happy at last, he didn't care who or what had caused it.

"Wait till you see Paul!" she said, "he's getting us all a drink." Jim's booming laugh told Val that Paul was on his way over and the Christmas package had made an impression.

"Merry Christmas, James," Paul announced, "I've got you a pint."

"Cheers, Rudolph," said Jim.

"And this get up is not all," Paul continued, producing from his pocket the straw from the Red Lion, putting it in his pint and drinking through it. Jim and Val laughed at the faces he pulled while drinking, "this is knackering up my sinuses" he confirmed stopping for a moment as Big Doug approached.

"You sad, sad man," he shouted in Paul's face spraying crisps and beer in the process and then walked off, shaking his head. While he let this comment wash over him two drunken, late-teenage girls came over and grabbed him by the arms.

"Come on, Rudolph, come for a boogie!" they squealed.

"All right, then," said Paul as he put his pint down and was dragged away.

Val looked on confused and worried. "I hope he comes back," she said, while Jim just laughed, then Val also laughed at Paul's daft dancing. While she had strong feelings for him, loved him even; if she was being really honest with herself, she had never seen him in such good form. How often in his life did he get the chance to enjoy himself like this? Val took a little bit of the credit and also thought that her own good mood tonight was down to Paul's actions and her feelings for him.

After a few minutes he was off the dance floor, with the girls looking disappointed and back with Jim and Val. He leant on a ledge and panted in an exaggerated manner.

"Christ, I'm shagged!" he declared and Val laughed.

"Lock in here later, Paul, lad," Jim told him, "be back in here by eleven." Jim backed this information up with a wink.

"I'll be here, great," Paul said, "you stopping out, Val?" Val nodded.

"Of course," she replied. Paul was finishing his pint, quickly, in one, through his straw and then gave the sides of his nose a rub as the cold beer took its toll.

"Right," he said, "Rudolph's had a boogie and he's had a pint, next pub Valerie?"

"Yes, certainly, Rudolph, wait by the door, I'll just be a moment." After Paul had left Val turned to Jim, "You still okay with me and him being out together?"

Jim smiled, "Are you kidding me? Of course I am. He'll probably cop off by the end of the night at the rate he is going." Jim noticed an impatient yet smiling Paul/Rudolph waving from the door of the pub while disco dancing and smiled some more.

"Rudolph awaits!" he said and gave Val a kiss. "Love you."

Val smiled and headed over to Paul and as she walked away Colin appeared from the crowd on the dance floor, pint in hand and came to the DJ-stand.

"Colin," said Jim, and he warily held out his hand, "Merry Christmas." Colin shook it, looked towards Valerie leaving the pub and smiled.

"That's brave of you," Colin said, "letting her out with another man."

"Not Paul, he doesn't have any inclination that way, he prefers her mate," Jim replied, hoping he was right.

"I see," said Colin, and taking a drink from his pint disappeared back into the crowd.

Paul and Val were in the next pub, The Crown, and were sat at a table. The conversation had stopped but being close friends there seemed no need to chatter all the time, although the occasional smile was swapped. Val broke the silence.

"I still can't believe you are dressed like that," she laughed, as Paul took a drink, "and drinking pints of bitter through a straw!"

"It's Christmas!" Paul said, in as festive a manner as he could muster. His glass was empty, if nothing else the straw speeded up the downing of pints. "That's that one finished," he looked at his watch, "I reckon we can sneak in another pub before we need to be back at the Prince of Wales for the lock in."

"Okay, great," said Val, and they stood up to leave. As they headed for the exit a pretty, dark haired girl came in and appeared to be looking for friends.

"Lydia," said Paul, "hi, how are you?" Lydia laughed at Paul's outfit.

"Hi, Paul, are you out with Fart-breath and his gang tonight?" she asked.

Paul shook his head, "No, and I cannot believe you call your own brother that!" They both laughed as Val was hovering with eyes agog at being left out while Paul talked to a younger woman. She even allowed herself a pretend cough to get their attention.

"Oh, yeah, sorry, Val, this is Lydia. The first night I met you at the quiz one of the lads who was with me, Alan, the record shop owner, this is his sister." Val held out her hand which Lydia shook.

"I cannot remember him, but, great to meet you, Lydia and Merry Christmas," Val said.

"Merry Christmas, Val and I'm surprised you don't remember him," said Lydia, "his breath is rank!"

"Oh, God, him?" Val pulled a face and the other two laughed.

"Do you know of anywhere open late tonight, Paul?" Lydia asked doing a little boogie as she did, "I was a bit last minute as I was going to go out with my boyfriend, Carl, but instead I binned him, the useless fat bastard, so I don't have a ticket for anywhere."

"Liberty's will be the best bet, get in before eleven," Paul replied, not wanting to let the lock-in at the Prince of Wales cat out of the bag.

"Great! Cheers for that, Paul, I'm just going to meet up with some friends, have a good night."

"And you!" Paul made to leave with Val, when Lydia asked teasingly, "Do I not get a Christmas kiss?" and grabbed Paul's arm and with her head tilted to one side, in a cheeky manner, especially as she had no idea whether Val was Paul's girlfriend or not.

"Okay!" said Paul, to suggest it was going to be a chore and kissed her on the lips, lingered a moment. "Have a good 'un, Lydia." And with a big smile on his face he left the pub with Val, and Lydia, giggling, went into the pub to meet up with her friends wearing a big smile too.

Val and Paul made their way to the Victoria pub through the sleet and wind of the Lancashire winter and Val looked at Paul, weighing up how he looked for a moment.

"Oh, will you at least just lose the nose?" she asked, with a laugh.

"Okay, okay," said Paul, removing it and throwing it over his shoulder. Val smiled and linked arms with him, in friendship and also to try to warm herself against the bitterly cold weather.

"She was pretty," Val said to try to prompt a reaction. Paul looked confused for a moment and Val nodded back towards the Crown, "Lydia."

"Yes, nice girl with it as well, you'd not believe she came from the same gene pool as Alan Fart-breath."

Val smiled again, loving Paul even more for the funny things he said. They walked a few more steps and then she asked, "When do you think I'll get my Christmas kiss from you tonight, Paul?" squeezing and stroking his arm as she spoke.

"Er, oh, ha! Er, I dunno," Paul was nervous and uncertain about this, although he had imagined he might get a hug and a peck on the cheek from Val to celebrate Christmas later on he immediately thought of something else and his mind raced away thinking Val might be thinking along the same lines as well, although he never thought any beautiful woman ever would, "Midnight?" he suggested with a non-committal shrug of his shoulders.

"She got a kiss," said Val, "and a lingering one on the lips, not a peck on the cheek like you might do with a female friend."

Paul laughed nervously as this was Jim's girlfriend and she was acting a bit strange, as well as seeming to read his mind. Although he had been with and been out with a number of women in the past he had no previous experience of this sort of behaviour from any woman towards him, especially one living with a mate of his. And Val was a female friend of his or at least she had been up until now...

"Oh, look here we are, at the Vic," Paul said, laughing nervously as they reached the door, hoping this line of questioning might stop now.

Paul got the drinks in and Val stood around the corner of the bar next to where the empty glasses were collected. Her heart was beating so much she thought it might come bursting through her chest. Enough was enough, she didn't care if she was with Jim, Paul needed to know how she felt about him and tonight was the night to tell him so he could decide what to do about it. When Paul brought the drinks over, Val started on him all over again.

"Well, am I gonna get a Christmas kiss from you like she did, Paul?"

"Here we go again," Paul muttered, taking a drink, straw free for the first time that night.

"Yes! Here we go again. She got one," Val continued. Paul glanced at himself in the mirror behind the bar; his eyes were starting to get bloodshot, with bags and dark rings underneath them from too many sleepless nights, he was wearing antlers and a Santa hat, and had red fluff on his nose from the discarded red sponge version he had been wearing until recently.

*Who'd want to kiss me?*

"Who'd want to kiss me?" he said out loud to himself seeking clarification.

"She did, I do, and it's Christmas," Val argued. Paul sensed Val was not teasing him here, that she really wanted to kiss him, like it was a big deal that Lydia had kissed him and she hadn't. He began to worry a little of her mental health. "I want a Christmas kiss, Paul. Not at

94

midnight, not at the Prince of Wales, that Lydia got a Christmas kiss from you, why not me?" she was almost whining like a spoilt child and Paul was just glad the music in the pub was loud enough to drown it out and they did not have an audience listening in. The pub was busy, but not packed. Finally, he relented.

"Okay," he said, for the second time that night making the act of kissing a beautiful woman sound like it was a chore.

*What is wrong with me?*

Taking a moment he paused and composed himself. As Val was a close friend he was very fond of as well as a beautiful woman he wanted it to be meaningful and significant. Val wore a smile, not of triumph, but one of someone getting something they really wanted, almost a grateful smile. He reached and held her hands, "Merry Christmas, Val," he whispered.

"Merry Christmas, Paul," she whispered back.

They moved closer, their lips met, they lingered, longer, Paul thought, than the kiss with Lydia, which he thought at the time was Val making a point then he pulled slowly away. After a few seconds pause Val moved towards him and kissed him back, lingering again, longer now. She pulled away but came back again, lips parted this time. It was probably only a few seconds yet it felt like minutes, their tongues touched, slightly, teasingly, sending tingles down Paul's spine. During this last kiss Paul's mind was racing.

*Wow! This is great, but, this is also my mate's girlfriend. I shouldn't be doing this, but she is an intelligent woman, she's been to university, she must know what she is doing. When we stop we'll probably start laughing at how silly it all is. Is she drunk?*

When they stopped Paul smiled but Val didn't and looked serious. He was aware that the Santa hat and antlers had stayed in place the whole time which kind of spoilt things. Val sighed, a big, long sigh.

"Paul, I've wanted to do that for weeks, now," she said finally, "I've fallen in love with you."

Paul would always remember the song playing in the background at this point; 'Stop the Cavalry' by Jonah Louie. There was a pause as Val let him take in the information and he kept smiling as he tried to make sense of what he had just heard as if he was waiting for a punch line of a joke he didn't get. The smile became a bit forced after a while.

"I'm sorry," Paul said, confused, "what?!" but inside he thought, *Whaaaaaaaaaaaaaaaaaaaaaaaaaat?!*

## CHAPTER THIRTEEN

"**Y**OU'RE IN LOVE WITH ME?" I asked her, and she nodded, "But how?"

"I can't help it, I'm in love with you. What are we going to do?" Val asked.

*We? What are we going to do?*

"You can't be in love with me," Paul said, "I'm ugly." He glanced up and removed the Santa hat and antlers thinking that this was too serious for them to still be worn. He had also sobered up very quickly but was unable to think straight through the fog of his mind.

*Average looking women he knew never came up and said they were in love with him, why would such a gorgeous foreign national like Val say it? What was happening?*

"You're not ugly, Paul," said Val, "and I've fallen for you, the person. Your spirit, your kindness. You." As she said "you," she gently thumped Paul's chest with her fist to make the point.

"What about Jim, Val? Does he know, have you told him or anything?"

"Not a thing, no. This has been so hard, Paul. I was cuddling him one night a few weeks ago and realised I wished it was you. I even blurted out your name." Paul's eyebrows shot up and his heart stopped. "He was asleep," Val confirmed.

"Thank Christ for that!"

There was silence as Paul rolled it through his mind. No woman had ever fallen for him like this before. On top of that Val was stunning; she was funny; she was bright. She was of course living with his mate who had recently been trying to fix him up with Michelle.

*What a pickle!*

"What are we going to do, Paul?" Val asked again. This question suggested joint responsibility but Paul mainly heard it that it was down to him to make a decision. He took a drink and thought about it and just then the pub's glass collector came near them, a girl Paul knew, to say hello to, but not by name.

"How you doing, how you doing?" asked Paul, "Merry Christmas, here," he adorned her with the hat and antlers, "have these."

"Thanks," she smiled and then wandered off.

"Shit!" exclaimed Val, "Colin's over there!" Paul turned and saw that Val's ex was indeed in the pub.

"Oh, bloody hell, did he see us kissing?" asked Paul.

"I doubt it, knowing him if he had he would have been over here making a big deal of it." Val downed her vodka. "Finish your drink, Paul. Let's go to the Prince of Wales, now."

"Okay," he said. This sounded like the best thing to do, even though it would put them both in the same building as Jim. As they walked to the pub they were linked arm in arm again. Val looked at Paul and sighed.

"Bit of a pickle this, Val," said Paul, then he gave a nervous laugh, "and we are about to have a lock-in with your boyfriend."

Val sighed again, "Oh, God!" Paul stopped in his tracks.

"What's up?" Val asked him.

"In case I never do it again," he said, and then kissed Val, quickly, passionately. Then they started walking, again.

"If nothing else, Mr Stevenson, you are a damn good kisser," said Val. Paul laughed his nervous laugh again.

"Oh, no," he said. "That is the nicest and most tragic thing I have ever heard."

"We need to discuss what happened tonight, Paul," Val said. Paul looked thoughtful.

"We will, but we are about to meet up with your boyfriend and tomorrow is Christmas Day so we will have to bide our time a little."

Once at the Prince of Wales Paul and Val ordered a couple of shorts, each, Jack Daniels and coke for him, vodka, neat, for her. They found a table, sat down and looked wearily at each other. Neither of them spoke, there was the occasional forced smile, a sigh here and there. Eventually Jim joined them.

"Merry Christmas! You two had fun?" he asked in all innocence.

"Yeah," said Val wearily, "bit tired, now."

"Champion, great," said Paul in a daze.

"Hi, Jim, mate, how you doing? Merry Christmas!" a man, older than Paul and Val but younger than Jim, came to the table. Jim shook his hand.

"Ken, mate, how are you?" Jim asked. Paul suddenly realised it was Ken who had been the DJ when he first went to the quiz.

"Seem pleased to see each other, this one hasn't been out with you, then?" Paul whispered to Val. She tried not to smile and smacked him, playfully.

"You remember Val, don't you, Ken?"

"Hi, Ken," said Val.

"Hello, Val, still with him then? Not fallen for a younger model, yet!" Ken and Jim laughed and started chatting.

"Astute man," commented Paul.

"Also, world's most boring man," remarked Val.

"Even so, with vision and foresight like that, does he know next week's lottery numbers?" Val looked at Paul wearily and let his last comment pass.

"This lad here is a former work mate of mine. This is Paul, a great lad," added Jim.

"Ken," said Paul, leaning forward and shaking Ken's hand.

"Likewise," Ken said back.

"Ken's a fellow DJ, Paul," said Jim, forgetting himself that Paul had been in the pub when Ken did the quiz, "and Paul and Val have been on a 'sesh' tonight, which is why they both look so wankered!" Ken and Jim laughed again and then talked DJ stuff, "Talking of DJ-ing, Ken, you might be able to do me a favour."

After a few moments of silence on their side of the table Paul whispered, "Val?"

"Yes, Paul," she whispered back.

"Is that your foot rubbing up and down my calf?"

"Yes, it is, Paul," she confirmed. Paul took a drink.

"I'm a little glad it is not one of them," he said, nodding at Jim and Ken. Val gave him a sexy, 'I want you' smile.

Jim and Ken had talked for a good two hours, mainly about DJ-ing but Paul and Val had drunk little in that time and said hardly anything, either to each other or to the other two, each playing over the night's events in their mind with the occasional sideways glance at each other. If they caught each other's eye Val would smile and it would break Paul's heart a bit among the confusion he was feeling.

"Jim, I'm tired, when are we going home?" Val asked so Jim drained his pint.

"No problem, I'll get Stuart to order us a taxi now," he replied and stood to try to get his attention.

"I can give you both a lift," Ken suggested, "I've drunk orange juice all night."

"I should also add," Val whispered to Paul, "Ken is 41 and his wife, Molly, is 19."

"Dirty bugger!" Paul butted in but Val shook her head.

"Molly is 19 and also being serviced by our erstwhile landlord."

"Nigel? As well as Michelle? Holy Christ, how does he do it, now he is ugly!" Val laughed at this comment as Jim handed her coat to her.

"Paul, are you on my way? Can I drop you off home, as well?" Ken asked. Paul fancied staying to drink himself daft as his way of either making sense of or forgetting what had happened that evening.

"He is on the way," Jim confirmed, "Val drives him home after the quiz most weeks, don't you, petal?"

"Yeah," Val confirmed in a weary voice. Soon they had left the pub, got in Ken's car and were on their way.

"Any further plans for tomorrow, Paul?" Jim asked during the short journey, "your Dad's away, isn't he?" Despite her love for him Val thought, Oh no, please God, Jim, don't invite him around! And was relieved when Paul replied,

"I'm out with a work mate and his family, a bit of a last minute job." Paul confirmed. They were quite near his street, "Anywhere on the left here will do, cheers, Ken," he said. After Ken had stopped the car Paul clambered out with handshakes for the men and a quick peck followed by a meaningful stare, or what he hoped was one, into Val's eyes. "Merry Christmas," he whispered.

"Merry Christmas, Paul," she whispered back, looking glum.

"Hurry up, man, getting cold with the door open," shouted Jim. Paul got out and shut the door, and as the car pulled away Val mouthed the words,

"I love you," at him. It was raining hard but Paul stood rooted to the spot for nearly a minute.

"Oh, sweet Jesus Christ almighty," he muttered, before realising he was getting soaked and headed home.

Once home Jim opened the front door and Val dashed straight upstairs to be violently sick in the bathroom. It went on for some time and Jim came upstairs after locking up downstairs.

"Everything okay?" he asked cheerily, thinking it was only drink causing it.

Val shook her head, "No."

"Can I get you a glass of water?" Val started being ill again. "How much did you have to drink? Paul seemed quite sober at the end of the night."

Once she stopped Val whispered, "No idea."

"I'll get you some water, back soon."

Val pulled away from the toilet bowl, wiped her mouth and face and began to cry.

Paul made it as far as the front room and was stood in the middle of it, just staring into space.

"What the bloody hell has just happened tonight?" he said to himself. He put his head in his hands and shook his head slowly. "Unbelievable. I need to tell some chuffer." He dug his mobile phone out of his jacket pocket and rang Simon's number.

"Hello?" a voice said, "Paul? Merry Christmas!"

"Yeah, and you, I need to talk, Simon."

"Bit busy at the mo'," Simon said. In the background Paul could hear women giggling, "We'll catch up when I get back." Simon hung up.

"Great," said Paul. He hung up. "Great, might be too bloody late by then. What do I do?"

---

# 2010

I took in the kiss that had just stopped and tried to gather my thoughts. This was when a funny thought struck me and I began to laugh.

"Kissing in pubs when you are seeing someone else, we've been here before, haven't we Val,"

"Yes, I know," she agreed, which pleased me that at least she was finally seeming to acknowledge my part in her past.

"After all these years we are still naughty, aren't we?" She giggled then took a drink and looked a bit more thoughtful.

"So are you not seeing anyone at the moment?" I hesitated to wonder if this was her fishing for information to take up where we, well, where we never really left off.

"I'm separated," I replied casually, as if Val had asked me when I last cut my toenails or something else really everyday or humdrum.

Val looked shocked, "You were married?" I nodded to confirm this was indeed how these things normally worked and Val smiled. "Wow!"

"It has been thirteen years since I've last seen you, Val. I could have fitted a lot of things in during that time,"

Val nodded to agree, "Any kids?"

"A son, called Sean. He's five now."

"Blimey," Val shook her head. "So when I leave you for thirteen years this is what you get up to?" We both laughed and as I took a drink I sneaked a look at the clock to check the time. Twenty past eight. I wondered what to do; stay here with Val or meet up with the others.

"So is Barry coming back, then?" I asked.

"Nah, freckle, it's just you and me tonight," and then she smiled, "unless you want to go and meet up with your friends."

"No," and I smiled, then I remembered something. I had half invited Michelle to meet up with me and my friends tonight, just a casual 'if you've got nothing else on' throwaway invitation. Had I told her the wrong pub or the right pub? I just hoped it was the wrong one as I don't think Val and Michelle were ready to meet up just yet.

"I only hope you are not still working in that book warehouse you worked in when I last knew you," Val said and I shook my head to confirm I did not "That's good, so what do you do for a living now, then?"

I am writing for a living, I've just had a book published, with Valerie Walters in it. Oh, shit. "Liam?" she pressed me with a kind smile. "What do you do for a living now?"

# CHAPTER FOURTEEN

## Christmas Day

IT WAS CHRISTMAS MORNING. Paul had woken up with hangovers before, even on Christmas morning; he had woken up not remembering who he was or where he was before. On this Christmas morning he awoke, lying in bed on his back and remembered instantly the night before.

"Val said she loved me."

He was frozen with shock, to such an extent he could not move, not even to turn his head and see what time it was on his bedside clock. After a while the phone rang and after six rings it stopped ringing and then beeped, which meant the answer machine had picked up the call. Still he laid there and did not move, Val said she loved me, he thought to himself, but why? No other woman has.

Sometime later the phone rang again and still he could not move, so the answer machine again picked up the call.

Some time later he forced himself to move, fearing if he did not then he never would. "Oh, Jesus," he said reading his clock, 12:01, and remembering Keith had said he was picking him up at half-past. He grabbed some clean clothes, as last night's were soaked with rain and screwed up on the floor and made his way downstairs. Once in the kitchen he pressed the button on the answer machine.

"Hi, Paul, Dad here, Merry Christmas! Cheryl sends her love. I take it you are sleeping off a massive hangover, I'll call later."

His Dad's message had been left at 10:01. The machine beeped and the next message started.

"Paul, it's Val," she whispered. There was a pause and a deep sigh, "God I wish I was with you today. Jim's loading the car with his kid's presents. Please call me back later. We both think the world of you. Merry Christmas, love you."

Paul was shocked that the second message was left at 11:34, over an hour and a half after his Dad's message. It hadn't seemed that long, lying there. Paul picked up the phone and dialled.

"Hi, Cheryl, it's Paul, Merry Christmas," he began.

"Hi, Paul! Merry Christmas!" she wished back.

"How's Dad?"

"Fine, enjoying himself,"

Paul nodded, "Oh, good, good, I'm really glad he's enjoying himself. David okay?"

"Yeah, already drinking!"

"Good, are Marjorie and Phillip there as well?" these were Cheryl's in-laws.

"Yeah, full house,"

"Great! Does Dad want a word?"

Cheryl shouted "Paul's on the phone,"

His Dad shouted back, "Merry Christmas, son!"

Paul laughed. "I'm off out soon so let him know I'll call again later, love to all."

"And you, bro', take care."

Paul replaced the phone and then picked it up and dialled Jim and Val's number, hanging up before he finished.

"Later," he said to himself, "much later."

Keith led the way and Paul followed into the pub which was just getting busy with drinkers seemingly keen to escape their homes at Christmas. "Everyone, this is Paul, I work with him," Keith announced to his family sat around the table in the carvery section.

"Hi, Paul," everyone chorused back and Paul forced a smile among his despair.

"Hello," he said raising his hand, by which point everyone had turned back to the table.

"Here, Paul," said an attractive woman with dark hair, who he had not noticed until then, "you can sit here, next to me." With which she smiled and patted the chair next to him.

"Paul, this is Jodie," said Keith by way of introduction, "my cousin."

"Oh, right, hello Jodie," said Paul. Keith put a hand on Paul's shoulder as he made to sit.

"How did it go last night then?" Keith asked with eyebrows raised and wearing a look of apprehension.

Paul made a deflating noise, shrugged and began to say, "Well, you know."

"Oh, Jesus, it was a disaster, then, just as I thought," said Keith. Paul nodded and Keith went to sit with his wife. Paul was left with Jodie, who was forcing a smile, wondering what to say.

"Are you local, Jodie?" he asked finally.

"Originally, yes. I live near Derby, now," she explained.

"Oh, right, what do you do?"

"Radiographer."

"Right, nice one," although he wasn't too sure what one was.

"You're not with your family today then, Paul?" Jodie asked.

"No, there's only me Dad round here and he's gone to stop with my sisters over Christmas and New Year."

"No girlfriend?" Jodie pressed. Paul winced. "Blimey, I've hit a nerve with 'girlfriend', haven't I?"

*Just a bit, but not for the reasons you think.*

"No, no. No girlfriend," Paul confirmed.

"Something's amiss, though, what is it?"

Paul shook his head, "Oh, God,"

"Come on, tell me. Problem shared!" Jodie smiled sweetly. Paul looked around the pub; somewhere a pint glass was knocked over and smashed leading to a cheer and a bit of arguing over whose pint it was. Members of staff looked around trying to find out where it came from. In this environment a complete stranger was about to have Paul's heart poured out.

"Oh, God," Paul said again, took a drink of his pint, composed himself and began. "I went out last night with the girlfriend of a mate of mine. She's a friend of mine, also, which is why we went out, he was working, you see. Recently this mate of mine has been trying to fix me up with one of his girlfriend's mates but it's been a mess and now I am not interested. Last night his girlfriend kissed me and said she loved me," Paul took a drink and Jodie's jaw almost dropped to the table, "and I woke up this morning to a message from her on my answer phone asking me to ring her, so, no, Jodie, no girlfriend, no. What about you? Married, are you?"

"Right now, after hearing that, I can't remember."

Paul got in from the carvery at three; "Just in time for the Queen's speech," he said to himself, "doubtful." The house was colder than normal and all around was darkness where he wanted light. Once in the kitchen he noticed the light was flashing on the answer machine, "Oh, God, please be Dad, or Simon, even Fart-breath." Paul pressed the button to play.

"Paul. Val, again. I convinced Jim to grab a shower before lunch and hoped to catch you, please, please call me."

"Oh, bollocks," said Paul. He picked up the phone and dialled Val's number thinking it was time to get it done and over with.

"Hello?" a man had answered. Jim.

"Jim! Of course, Jim, why would you not answer? I've rung your house after all." Paul gabbled.

"Merry Christmas, Paul," said Jim, laughing.

"And you, mate, right back at you!" Paul tried to be his normal self but could not remember what it was.

"Have we been drinking, sir?"

"Ha, well, you know,"

Jim laughed. "Do you want a word with your new best mate, 'drunky-drunkyson'?"

"I wasn't that bad!" Val shouted in the background.

"Here she comes, Paul."

"Paul, hi, Merry Christmas," Val said assuredly, as if this was just her boyfriend's mate she was addressing and the last night had been some dream or elaborate hoax.

"And to you, Val, love, you okay? Got any nice presents?" Paul asked. There was a deep sigh.

"Oh, God, Paul," Val whispered, with a choking sob in her voice, "no, I'm not okay. What are we going to do? We need to talk and sort this out."

Paul suddenly felt sick, "Val, where's Jim gone?"

"Kitchen, why?"

"For an awful moment I thought he was still sat next to you."

"When can we meet up, Paul?" Val pressed.

"Well, tomorrow I'm off to the football but the day after that I'm free."

"Do you have no other hobbies and interests apart from drinking and football?" Val spat the last word out finding something within herself.

"I know, shocking, isn't it? I'm nearly thirty and I need the love of a good woman!" There was a pause and Paul suddenly realised his last comment was a touch tactless.

"Okay, Paul, meeting up the day after tomorrow, that'll work," said Val changing the subject. "Jim's going to Manchester to see his kids. They're in their teens now and after all this time they still don't know I exist."

"We'll meet then, come here for lunchtime and we'll, er, think of something then."

"Okay, Paul."

"And Val, try to keep it together, you must."

"Love you Paul, I really do."

"See you the day after tomorrow." Paul put the hand set back.

*Oh good God*

Val sat reflecting on the call after she had hung up, wiped her tears and tried to get herself together as Paul had suggested.

"Can I tempt you with a glass of wine, yet, Val?" Jim shouted from the kitchen. Val got up quickly and headed upstairs to throw up again. Jim headed through from the kitchen and followed the noise and commotion to the bottom of the stairs. "I'll take that as a no then, love."


The next day Paul met up with his mate Dan at the football. As Dan lived out of town he had never been to the quiz. He was an outsider, so to speak, and Paul toyed all day with the idea of dumping his problems on him. They met in the pub beforehand and Dan got the drinks in. The pub was getting busier as kick-off approached and on good days, like this, gave the impression its walls might burst and send the punters inside flying in all directions.

"Cheers, Paul," he said.

"All the best, Dan, cheers," and they each took a man size swig.

"How's your Christmas been?" Dan asked.

Paul laughed ruefully and let it go, "Oh, God, Dan, mate, shocking, absolutely shocking, like you wouldn't believe."

"Oh, Christ, not your Dad, again?"

"No, Dan, he's fine, he's stopping with me sisters, right as ninepence. No, there's this woman, you might remember I mentioned her, from the quiz,"

"Of course, yes," said Dan, who had forgotten what the deal was but hoped Paul might remind him in the next few minutes.

"She's going out with a mate and I'm friends with this woman, also," Paul said by way of a reminder, knowing his friend would have forgotten what it was all about. "Last night we went out for a drink."

"All three of you?" asked Dan.

"No, just me and her. Anyway, I agreed to give her a Christmas kiss, it got a bit passionate,"

"Wahey!"

"No, no, Dan, please, not wahey, and she told me she loved me."

"Crumbs! Just a little bit 'wahey', though. Where did all this happen, Paul?"

"In the Victoria pub."

"In the pub? With witnesses and things?" Paul nodded. "Where was her old man?"

"In another pub, DJ-ing."

"Does he know?"

"Christ, Dan, I hope not!"

"Right, right." Dan thoughtfully took another man size swig and Paul paused for a moment waiting for a big dollop of wisdom to come his way. Elsewhere in the pub a chant was starting and Paul would normally have joined in but waited. Fearing no wisdom was forthcoming Paul carried on.

"She wants to meet up and 'talk'," he added.

Dan paused some more and then spoke, "Okay, Paul, do you love her?" he asked.

"No, I mean I like her, as a friend, a lot, she's great, attractive and I can't believe she thinks like this about me."

Dan looked thoughtful, again, "I don't think she does, you know."

"What, you mean she's made all this up?"

Dan shrugged, "When you go for a talk don't commit yourself, let her do the talking. She might give something away."

"Right, good," said Paul. Another man size swig and Dan finished his pint. Paul still had most of his left and was letting Dan's advice sink in.

"Want another?" Dan asked.

"Yeah, great, go on," replied Paul. Dan stood up from the table and paused before heading to the bar.

"Listen, Paul, if you get too involved here you're heading for a parcel of trouble." Dan then headed through the hordes to the bar.

"Probably," Paul agreed.

The next morning Paul shaved and showered to try to gee himself up. He got dressed relatively smartly and waited in the lounge in silence. The butterflies in his stomach were going crazy and he felt like he wanted to be sick. Shortly before midday there was a knock on the front door and when he opened it Val was stood there and she did not look at all well.

"Oh, God, Val, how are you?" Paul asked with concern.

"Get in the car, Paul, there's been a change of plan. I haven't got as long as I had hoped for." They got in the car and Val started the engine. "Where shall I go?"

"Just drive," Paul said, realising he had not given this part of the day any thought whatsoever. Then, he had an idea, "Seahurst, we'll go to Seahurst. I know a quiet pub there on the main street."

"I've never been to Seahurst before, what's it like there?" Val asked.

"Not good, I used to live there, the natives still point at planes." Val allowed herself a smile at Paul's comment.

"Michelle rang before I left."

"How is she?" Paul found himself asking but thinking he couldn't care less and didn't know why he asked.

"Sounds okay, but she's back in town and I said I would go and see her, which is why this is tricky. Jim was still at home when she rang so I left straightaway."

"Right, I see. Do you think we'll have enough time to talk?"

"No, Paul, I don't, but I am running out of nerve ends worrying." Her voice squeaked a bit as if she was going to cry, again.

"Look, Val, what we don't resolve today we will soon, trust me," said Paul, bearing in mind Dan's advice not to give too much of himself.

After ten minutes of driving they arrived in Seahurst town centre which, in the pouring rain and the howling wind looked completely unwelcoming, as litter flew through the air with a hint of celebration.

"God, what a hole," muttered Val. "It's like the town at the end of the world."

"That's because it is," Paul replied, and cursed himself for coming so far out of town to a place no one would know either of them. It would have been easier to have gone to the Red Lion or the Prince of Wales. "The pub's down this street, here, and the car park is at the back."

"Okay," Val acknowledged. Once they had parked up and gone into the pub Val said, "Grab a table, do you want a pint?"

"Yes, Val, thanks," Paul replied and went to sit at a table away from the other customers. He looked at Val at the bar, an American woman, attractive, smart in so many ways, trying to sort her mess of a life out in a grotty back street north of England ale house. Paul bet she wished she was anywhere else right now, especially back home in the States. As Val came over with the drinks, bitter for Paul, vodka and orange for her, he quickly tried to change the subject and assess Val's mindset. Coincidentally, bearing in mind Paul's last thought, 'Born in the USA' by Bruce Springsteen was just finishing on the jukebox, which looked like it had not had any records changed since the mid-1980s. The records inside were still vinyl.

"Here you go," she said, sitting down. Several leering eyes had followed her to her chair and she was possibly the first woman to come into the pub for some time.

"Cheers, Val. Did your family have a nice Christmas?" Paul asked. Val looked surprised, as Paul had never asked anything like this before.

"Yes, Paul, they did," she confirmed.

"I know so little about them, where do they live?" Paul continued in a cheery manner to distract them from the important matter in hand. Perhaps he was taking Dan's advice on board too literally and was changing the subject before it came up.

"My Mum lives in Portland, Oregon, and Dad in San Jose,"

Paul nodded to take the information in, "Are they divorced or is that just a bloody big house?"

Val laughed. "Oh, Paul, of course they are divorced," Paul was away now and it was like being back at the Carvery and as if he was with Jodie.

"What do they do for a living?" he asked.

"Dad's a teacher and Mum is a psychiatrist," Val replied, thinking they could do with her Mum's help now, professionally. Val put her left hand over Paul's mouth to stop him asking so many questions, sighed and rested her chin on her right hand, "What are we going to do, Paul? This needs sorting."

"I know, I know," he said and looked thoughtful to buy himself some time. A man was stood near them pumping coins into the jukebox. As he walked away the first choice came on; 'Last Christmas', by Wham. The man was about 22 stone and covered in tattoos. Paul looked at him and couldn't help himself. "Did you really mean to put this one on, mate?" he asked.

"What do you mean?" the man fired back, looking puzzled.

"It just seems like an odd choice for you, that's all."

"I love this bloody song," the man confirmed angrily.

"Paul, Paul, focus, now," said Val.

"Right, Val, sorry, it's just, how did he know?" Val nodded and then reached to hold Paul's hands. They fell silent for a while, Val wanting Paul to take the initiative and Paul, taking heed of Dan's advice, waiting for Val to talk.

"I love you, okay? I can't help it, I can't help who I fall in love with and I've fallen for you, Paul. I love you." Val said.

"Thanks, Val," said Paul. "I'm not sure what else I can say, but thanks." Paul paused as the last few notes of Messrs Ridgeley and Michael's love lament faded.

"Shall we elope?" Val suggested laughing nervously. Paul also laughed, but was not really sure what 'elope' meant. After their laughter stopped they were silent for a time.

"The thing is Paul I cannot imagine my life now without you." The jukebox started playing the man's next choice; 'Without You' the original by Nilsson, not Mariah Carey's version. This combined with Val's tiredness caused by recent lack of sleep led to some problems as she searched for the right thing to say. "I can't live, Paul, if my life is living without you, oh Christ, I'm just repeating these lyrics!" Val turned to the landlord, "Can you turn this off?" she shouted.

"I paid a quid for these!" tattoo man complained. Val opened her purse and threw him a pound coin. "Here," she said, the barman flicked a switch and Nilsson stopped.

Val sighed, "Finally!" and the next song started; 'Two Out of Three

Ain't Bad' by Meat Loaf. Paul decided to take the initiative, despite what Dan had advised.

"Look, Val, we can talk all night," he paused, "but that ain't getting us nowhere, oh, God, I'm starting now!" Val laughed. "How does tattoo man know?" Paul asked. Val steadied herself.

"Paul, I want you, I need you, and yes, these are the lyrics, and I don't know how tattoo man knows, but this is it, take it or leave it. I love you, get used to it, deal with it." Val paused. "Do you want me to leave Jim?"

Paul was shocked at the suggestion but it would be the next step if they were going to see each other. He leant back in his chair, "You've thought about it, then?" he asked.

"As soon as I knew for sure how I felt about you," Val confirmed. Paul recalled she had left Colin, who was Jim's mate, to go out with Jim.

She's got form if nothing else.

"I can't decide what to do right now," Paul started, "but you've put your cards on the table, I know how you feel, so I'll mull it over." Val smiled. "And," Paul continued, "if that jukebox plays 'Valerie' by Amy Winehouse, I'll...." Val laughed and they both waited with baited breath for the next song. Then it came on; 'It Started With a Kiss', by Hot Chocolate.

"Think I'd have preferred 'Valerie'," said Paul.

"Let's go," said Val, "I have to meet Michelle." Once in the car they closed the doors and faced each other in silence for a few seconds, then kissed. After they had stopped they put their seat belts on and Paul sensed someone in the car next to them looking at him. He looked around and it was Stuart, the barman from the Princes of Wales. Val had started the car and was reversing.

"Oh, shit," said Paul.

"What?" asked Val. Paul thought for a moment and decided they had enough problems.

"Er, nothing, nothing, drive on."

They drove in near silence for a time both mulling over the last few day's events, and for Paul the nightmare bonus of being witnessed in the act, just once, he hoped, as Colin more than likely did not see them on Christmas Eve.

"Where shall I drop you off?" asked Val.

"How about I come with you? We can just tell Michelle you saw me in town and you are giving me a lift home."

"Okay,"

When they got to Michelle's her face betrayed her bemusement at Paul being there and the conversation on the journey home was strained.

"Did you have a nice Christmas, Michelle?" Paul asked after many minutes of silence.

"Not bad, not bad." she replied.

Val dropped Paul at his house and then she and Michelle drove on to Val and Jim's. As they pulled away from Paul's Michelle exploded.

"What the hell was he really doing with you, Valerie?" Val sensed that Michelle was angry as she used her full name, her 'Sunday name', as the English called it.

"Oh, God, Michelle, what am I going to do? I kissed him on Christmas Eve on our night out."

"So? I kissed loads of blokes up in Gateshead, and shagged one but I'm not giving them a lift here, there and every bloody where."

"Have you spent the last few weeks falling in love with any of these men?"

"Er, no, and what are you talking about? Falling in love?"

"I've fallen in love with Paul," Val began to cry. "What am I going to do?"

"Oh, bloody hell, Val."

---

## 2010

Val had gone quiet and had a look of disbelief on her face after taking in the information about my new career and then she laughed.

"You've had a book published? Oh, my God, that is brilliant, Liam, well done!!" she moved nearer to me and gave me a hug, sticking a big kiss on my cheek accompanied by a girly little giggle.

"Thanks."

"They do say everyone has a book inside them,"

"That's where it should stay with some people," I offered in the way of humour to which she smiled.

"Did you even write when we used to hang out? I can't even remember, last time I saw you was about the time you were doing a Psychology GCSE at college." I felt sad that it had really been that long since I last saw Val and so much of each other's lives had been missed out on. The congratulations had made me go shy and coy and Val was looking at me to suggest I tell her a bit more about the book and my writing in general.

"I used to write for football fanzines after leaving school and then years later I had it in mind to write my drinking memoirs."

"Drinking memoirs?" she nudged in. "That would have been a big book with lots of pages bearing in mind how you used to be!"

"Yeah, I did used to cane it."

"I'd say, me and Ian used to worry about your drinking, you did so much."

I was touched by this, "Surely no more than anyone else?" I asked.

"I don't know about that, back then you used to drink Special Brew in the bath when you were getting ready for a night out," this was a kick in the guts, I forgot I used to do that. Val took a drink. "So back to the book."

"Yeah, I tried to get the drinking memoirs published but after a few years of publishing indifference I decided a college course might help and it took off from there."

"Well done, Liam, this is great, I must read this book," Val told me. Oh, shit, I thought, fancy meeting her now of all times. "Drinking memoirs? That would have been interesting to read. Am I in any of these books, ha, ha, ha!" Val laughed.

*Oh, shit. Oh, shit!*

"Why don't you buy it and see?" I chirruped in a squeak of a voice. I composed myself a little and gave her a bit more information. "It's out on Monday and it's called 'Who's Going to Drive You Home?'."

"Who's Going to Drive You Home?" Val nodded and gave a little laugh. "I'll be on Waterstone's doorstep first thing Monday morning to buy it!"

*That's what I was afraid of.*

"Great!" I lied. At that moment the music system was playing 'Valerie' by The Zutons. Val pointed upwards in the general direction of the speakers.

"They're playing my song!" she said in a strange, strangled cockney like voice and laughed.

"Yes they are!" I said back, at least it wasn't Nilsson, Wham! or Meat Loaf.

# CHAPTER FIFTEEN

## It's All Gone Horribly Wrong

IT WAS ONE OF THOSE HORRIBLE, dull days between Christmas and New Year when you are glad to be off work but are bored senseless and need to have the lights on all day because it's so dark and miserable outside and inside. Paul was watching a DVD of one of his favourite shows, 'Auf Wiedersehen, Pet', hoping that tales of Geordie bricklayers in Germany would distract him from Val. It did not, especially when she rang in the middle of it.

"Hello?" Paul was stood in the hallway when he answered.

"Oh, God, Paul, it's Val, it's all gone horribly wrong!" Val yelped.

"Oh, Christ, Jim knows?" Paul asked clutching his head with his free hand and sliding down the nearest wall to the floor.

"No, worse," replied Val.

Paul pulled a face and sat up a bit, "Worse?"

*What could be worse?*

"Michelle knows."

"How did she find out about this and how is this worse?"

"I told her," Val confirmed. "And believe me, when she's finished with us Jim knowing might be better."

"Oh, Jesus!" Paul felt sick and was in a panic trying to think what to say next.

There was a small moment of silence as the information washed over them both. "Look, Paul, this is all your fault."

Paul was confused, "What do you mean this is all my fault?"

"She saw through the 'just picked up Paul' story the other day and just after I left home she had rung here looking for me and it doesn't take an hour and ten minutes from our house to hers."

Paul covered his eyes and felt worse, "Oh, God. Will she tell Jim?"

Val paused and sighed, "She stopped here one night after we had a lock in at the Prince of Wales. I was a tad delicate the next morning and in my fragile state I walked slowly around our house and I heard Jim and Michelle."

"Shagging?" asked Paul.

"No, flirting, you dirty little Englishman, you. Although it might have got that far if I had not walked into the lounge when I did."

"So do you think Michelle will use this to bag Jim?"

"Only as a notch on her bed post. Either way, Paul, we still have things to resolve, when do we talk properly? When do you decide our future?"

"Wow! That's a lot of responsibility just for me." Paul was still confused as to why it was going to be all down to him.

"It's your call, Paul."

"Why is it my call and not yours, or ours?" he finally asked.

"I am with Jim and if I have to stay with him, well, there are worse men to be with and we've been together for so long that I won't have to break stride. With you..." Val paused.

Paul paused for a moment also to think and take on board the most enormous thing he had ever had to deal with in his life, greater than the death of his mother.

"Is Jim doing the quiz tomorrow?" he finally asked.

"Yes, he is," Val confirmed a little confused but letting Paul explain where he was going with all this.

"Come here and pick me up first and I'll have decided by then. No matter what we decide we'll go to the quiz, in a big black cloud of gloom, as either way nothing can happen too soon."

"Okay," Val agreed.

"Is Michelle at the quiz?" Paul asked, "That might be awkward for us."

"No, it was only a whistle stop trip back here from Gateshead, for clean knickers."

"Ye, Gods, the mind boggles!"

"I know," they both laughed. "I love you, Paul." Val said to him again, as if he had forgotten.

"Thanks again, Val. No matter what happens I'm fond of you, at least know that."

Paul replaced the phone and thought about it again and again. If he decided to make a go of it when would Val tell Jim? What would she tell Jim? Would she mention him? Would they see each other as boyfriend and girlfriend and take things slowly or move in straight away together? Paul had never lived with anyone or gone out with anyone much longer than a few nights out, apart from Nicky where all was not as it seemed, so this was all new to him.

The phone rang, "Oh, God, not again," he thought to himself and reached for the phone. "Hello?" he answered a bit snappily.

"Is that Paul?" a female voice asked quietly.

"Yes,"

"This is Jodie, Keith's cousin from the carvery on Christmas Day."

"Oh, right, yes, hi, Jodie! What a lovely surprise!" Paul moved into the lounge to sit on the sofa.

"I hope you don't mind me ringing you out of the blue, I'm stopping with Keith and Sally, and the little one, until New Year and Keith mentioned you go to a quiz on a Monday, is it on tomorrow?"

"Er, yes, yes, it is."

"Don't mind if me and Keith tag along do you and have a go?" Jodie was grinning as she chatted and playing with her hair lying on Keith's spare bed.

"No, not at all, more the merrier," Paul replied.

"Good! I wanted to see you again to check you were all right, after the Christmas you had, and Keith fancies a go at the quiz. It's at the Prince of Wales, isn't it?"

"Yeah, that's right,"

"What time will you be there for?"

"I'm usually there by eight-thirty,"

"Great! See you then, Paul."

"Cheers Jodie, great, looking forward to it."

"Bye, Paul," Jodie was bursting with joy and rolled onto her stomach.

"Bye," Paul was smiling when he hung up as it would be great to see Jodie again but then he recalled his pre-quiz chat lined up with Val, "oh, big hairy bollocks, I forgot about Val!" and put his head in his hands.

*Shit!*

## CHAPTER SIXTEEN

"RIGHT, VAL, I'M off to the pub," said Jim. Val was reading a magazine and did not look up. Her mind was elsewhere of course thinking of the chat with Paul to come.

"Okay," Val said.

Jim remained stood in the doorway and Val finally sensed this and looked up at him, "Are you not coming?" he asked.

"You know I'm not coming now, Jim, I'm coming down later, with Paul."

"You always used to come down with me when you were off college before, so why's he so special all of a sudden?" Jim snapped, which shocked Val.

"Hold on, Jim, is there a problem with me hanging around with Paul, now? I thought you were his friend?"

"There's something," Jim hesitated and said no more, clearly thinking better of it, and instead swayed in the doorway.

"Something? Something what, Jim?" Val asked.

Jim shook his head and then headed out of the front door, "see you down there," he shouted over his shoulder and slammed it on the way.

"Shit!" cursed Val and threw her magazine across the room.

Within the hour a knock at Paul's front door told him the moment had arrived and Val was here for their chat. When he opened the door she looked tense.

"Val, come in," said Paul, and tried to smile.

"Jim has just played hell," she began as she came into the house, "wanted to know why I am coming down later with you and not earlier with him." Val sat on the sofa, "why am I going down later with you, Paul? What are we going to do?" The fight with Jim had given Val a harder edge that was scary. Her frightened and confused state of the last few days had gone.

"Right," said Paul, to compose himself taking a seat on the sofa next to Val, "this decision isn't easy. I'm very fond of you, Val, I've weighed up all the options, even considered that Jim isn't that close a friend, but he doesn't deserve what I thought of doing."

Paul paused, closed his eyes and sighed, "Anytime you and Jim split up I'm interested, very interested. You're smart, attractive, funny, not English, so different to any woman I've ever met and what's more, you've fallen in love with me." Val smiled. "But Jim's a good bloke, one of the best, and I cannot do this to him."

After a short while Val stood up. "Paul, you are truly one of the good guys and I understand your thinking. It just adds to how I cannot understand why you are single. Now, come on, let's see if we can beat Big Doug for a change."

Paul smiled. They headed for the door and went to Val's car. On the short drive to the pub they didn't speak much but Paul thought about what he said and a thought struck him; Val never suggested tonight that she would leave Jim, give it a short while, then see how Paul and she did. He had thought of it and he wasn't the one who had fallen in love. He glanced at Val as he thought this through but all she did was turn and give Paul a lovely smile which he struggled to return.

Another nightmare visited Paul as he got in the pub, Stuart. "Val, I'll get the drinks, go and see Jim," Paul said quickly patting her on the back in the direction of the DJ stand.

"Okay," said Val a little confused at the sudden haste on Paul's part as she headed towards Jim. There was no one waiting and Stuart had finished serving when Paul got to the bar.

"Hello, Stuart, lad," he started with as much determination as he could. "Pint of bitter and a vodka and orange, please," Paul ordered.

"You dirty bastard!" Stuart said laughing, as he began pouring the drinks.

"I'm sorry?" Paul asked playing dumb.

"Don't be coy, I saw you in Seahurst the other day."

Paul was rumbled and he guiltily bowed his head, "You did, didn't you?"

"Who was she, then?" Stuart asked cheerily.

"Eh?"

"The girl, who was she? Never saw her, just your ugly mug."
*Saved!*

"No one you know."

Paul walked away from the bar with the drinks, nodding and smiling at Jim as Val walked from the DJ stand.

"How is he?" Paul asked when Val was in Jim's view so he could not lip read.

"Oh, fine now." Val confirmed.

"And you?" Val just smiled.

"Paul! Over here, mate!" Keith called from a table, nowhere near where Paul and Val would normally sit. Paul smiled at Keith and Jodie, who gave a little wave.

"Ah," said Paul quietly, "I forgot about them."

"Them? Who are they?" Val asked as Paul walked towards them. "Paul?"

Once at the table Paul put their drinks down.

"Val, this is Keith, who I work with, and his cousin, Jodie." Val's face had been like thunder on the walk to the table but thawed slightly to smile as she sat.

"Charmed," she said.

"Paul goes on about this quiz at work all the time so I thought I'd give it a go," Keith explained, "and I brought Jodie along, who is stopping with us for a few days." Val was taking her jacket off and sitting back down. Out of her sight Keith nodded at her and pulled approving faces.

Jodie smiled, "Did you enjoy the rest of Christmas Day, Paul?" she asked.

Val's eyes shot almost out of her head. "Yeah, okay, thanks," said Paul. Val was fidgeting and looked edgy.

"Paul, before the quiz starts, can I have a quiet word?" she asked, then got up from her stool and walked off. Paul followed, pulling a face and holding his hands out at Keith and Jodie as if to ask 'what could this be all about' and once out of ear shot, in the entrance to the pub, she asked, "When did you invite them?"

"Yesterday," he confirmed.

"Yesterday?" Val shouted at which point Big Doug was wandering into the pub and sang, "All my troubles seemed so far away!" which to Paul seemed apt. Val glared at Big Doug as he walked towards the bar and then she continued.

"Before or after we had agreed to have a chat first?"

"After," Paul admitted. Val gave an indignant laugh.

"So, whatever you decided to do with our futures tonight you were going to meet up with them afterwards? You already knew you were going to turn me down, didn't you?" as Val said 'knew' she shoved Paul in the chest with some venom which shocked him. Keith and Jodie were watching events unfold.

"Aye, aye," Keith muttered, as Val shoved Paul in the chest. "I know a domestic when I see one. "Jodie just smiled but was concerned for Paul's safety and well being.

"Shall we intervene?" she asked Keith.

"Are you kidding?" he replied. "I'm enjoying this, it's better than EastEnders."

"Really, Val," Paul continued, "I was still thinking it all through, weighing up the pros and cons, up until an hour or so before you arrived."

"Oh, God," Val was shaking her head and looking at the floor, "I can't even look at you right now. I'm going to the bathroom." Val stormed off pushing Paul in the chest as she did and Paul crept sheepishly back to join a smiling Keith and Jodie.

"Blimey, mate," Keith said laughing, "not even me and Sally argue like that and we're married! I'm getting a pint."

After Keith went to the bar Jodie leant towards Paul.

"Is that the Christmas Eve girl?" she asked.

Paul nodded. "And tonight I told her I didn't want her to jeopardise her relationship for me."

Jodie looked at Jim, "that must be your mate and her boyfriend over there, then. He's a bit old, isn't he?"

"Forty-eight,"

"Good God!"

Paul's mobile beeped with a text and it was Val's name on the screen.

BACK BAR, NOW!

"Won't be a moment, Jodie," he said, stood up and left.

Val was sat in the back bar area and looked a little worried as Paul came over and sat opposite her. "I'm sorry," she began, "I was out of order." Paul shrugged and waved a hand at her.

"Don't worry, it's been a difficult night," he said.

"I might be a bit quiet tonight and don't think ill of me if I leave early, will you?"

"Of course not."

Val smiled at Paul's reply, but tears were welling in her eyes, "Bathroom, again! I'll see you back at the table." After she left, Paul stood up and was shocked that Stuart was stood at the bar behind him in the glass collection area and had taken all this in.

"It was her," Stuart said, "the girl in the car you were kissing, it was her." He looked disgusted.

"Keep it under your hat, Stu," Paul said, "the last few days have been a bloody nightmare. I didn't look for this, I'm not proud."

Stuart got on with emptying the glass washer, "You're no better that that fat bastard upstairs," he said referring to Nigel. At his lowest ebb Paul had to think to himself the man had a point.

After the quiz, another narrow victory for Big Doug, Jim came over to the table with a big smile on his face.

"Paul, Val, I've just had a thought, why don't you two do on New Year's Eve what you did on Christmas Eve?"

Jodie almost choked on her drink and Val's stomach and brain did somersaults.

"What's that?" Paul asked, managing to regain his composure.

"Go out drinking, you fools! I'm working again and you seemed to enjoy yourselves last time." Under the table Jodie elbowed Paul while wearing a silly grin. "I wouldn't want either of you in on New Year's Eve when you could be out together enjoying yourselves." Jim continued.

"And are you still okay about this, Jim?" Val asked, raising an eyebrow to try to remind Jim of his mood from earlier in the evening.

"Oh, are you two out on New Year's Eve, or any of your other mates, Paul?"

"Don't think Sally would be keen on me being out," Keith said. "Talking of whom, we best get back, Jodie."

"Okay," she agreed, rising from her chair and Paul did from his, being the northern gentleman. Jodie put her hand on Paul's shoulder and with a hint of mischief said, "lovely to see you again, Paul, and *great* to meet you, Val."

"Yes, he's a dark horse this one," Keith added, smiling at Paul then leaving with Jodie. Jim left to go back to the DJ stand and Paul sat back down with a smile, a shake of his head and sighed.

"Oh, dear me," he said. Val was deep in thought.

"She knew what happened with us on Christmas Eve," said Val.

"Yeah, I told her on Christmas Day," Paul confirmed, to which Val's eyes almost bulged out of her head. "I'd never met her before, never thought I'd see her again, she just said one thing, a door was opened and – bang! – I was away." Val was silent, letting his explanation sink in.

"Well, I confided in Michelle, you needed someone as well," she smiled, patted Paul on the back and picked her drink up, adding, with a laugh, "as long as it was just the one!"

"Two, actually."

"Jesus Christ, Paul!" Val cursed. "Who was the other one? Keith? Was that what he meant by the 'dark horse' line?"

"No, it wasn't Keith, and I am not really sure what he meant by the 'dark horse' line. I met up with my mate at the football on Boxing Day, lad called Dan. He doesn't live around here, he's not a problem."

Val paused for a moment. "If truth be told, Paul, I confided in a second person, also. A lady from work called Geraldine, head of psychology." Val tapped the side of her forehead. "She suggested I go for you."

"Oh? Is that what swayed you?"

"Yes," Val finished her drink, got up and walked over to Jim. The chat did not last long and she was soon back. "Can I drive you home?"

"Yeah, thanks," Paul got up, leaving his drink and waved at Jim on his way, who responded with a big smile and a thumbs up. On the way home they were silent for a time. As Paul had said earlier in the evening it had been a big night and they were both tired.

"How's Jim been, other than being angry this evening? Does he suspect anything?" Paul asked. Val shook her head.

"He just thinks I've had a hangover."

"For four days?"

"Or a cold, I don't know. He sensed something was amiss, he asked if it was because Michelle was away."

The conversation stopped until they got to Paul's house and there were butterflies in his stomach, again.

"Thanks for the lift, Val love."

"No problem."

They were quiet again.

"New Year's Eve, then, eight o'clock at the Red Lion?"

"Sure, Paul, looking forward to it," Val smiled that lovely smile of hers, again.

"Thanks again, Val, night."

"Night, Paul."

Resisting the temptation to give Val any kind of kiss even a friendly kiss on the cheek Paul got out of the car and waved after Val as she drove off. Not only did he think their friendship was doomed, because of all that had gone before, there was also not a hope in hell that should Jim and Val split up she would have anything to do with him, as a couple. It was just a feeling he had in the pit of his stomach, that sort of thing never happened to him and the only time it did, with Nicky, it ended in disaster. Once he was in the house he slumped on the settee and sat there in silence for hours. Again.

## CHAPTER SEVENTEEN

### New Year's Eve

"AND YOU ARE ALL right with this, Dad?" Paul asked down the phone.

"Yeah, no problem, not as if I have work and a job to come back for," Dad replied. He had just let Paul know that he was staying with his sisters until the end of January. "The change has done me the power of good, the waistband on me kecks is getting tight with all I've eaten!"

"That's great, Dad!"

His Dad paused for a moment and then asked, "Do you want me to come back, Paul, is that the problem? Are you looking after yourself?"

"Yeah, I'm fine, don't worry, crack on with it. I'm having a whale of a time," Paul lied.

"Great son, I'm glad, you know I worry, don't you? Well, Happy

New Year,"

"Happy New Year!" the early party guests shouted in the background.

"And to you all" Paul shouted. Putting the phone back on the stand he went to get ready for his night out.

Paul made sure he got to the Red Lion first that night and Val smiled warmly when she came into the pub, getting ogled by desperate old northern men as normal.

"Paul, hi, how are you?" she gave his arm a pat and a loving squeeze.

"Fine, thanks, vodka and orange okay?" he asked, a little tersely, which Val noticed.

"Please," she replied, letting the comment, or at least how it was said, pass, for now. Paul ordered the drink from the nearest barman and as he got it ready there was a pause as Paul and Val each recalled the last week's events and their situation. Paul avoided eye contact and smiled weakly when Val finally got him to look at her.

"Jim okay?" Paul asked.

"Okay, Paul! Stop that, right now!" Val snapped.

"Stop what?" he asked, confused.

"Every time we meet up you mention Jim."

"He is your boyfriend and my mate."

"I know, but it's like you don't want me to forget him, Paul."

"Look, Val, this is still hard for me to take in."

"How do you think I feel walking around thinking about you like I do and knowing I can't have you?" Val asked.

"It's not that you can't have me, it's that you have Jim. Look, I think life would be easier if we didn't go out tonight and carrying on knocking around together might not be the best idea either." Paul got off his bar stool at this point and Val held her hands up, making a pleading like face to protest.

"Here are your drinks," said the barman, looking at Paul and Val in some confusion.

"At least stop for one," Val said. After paying for the drinks they left the bar to sit at a table, oblivious to the New Year's Eve merriment around them. "If nothing else, Paul, I love you as a friend and I want you in my life, as a friend."

"And to keep an eye on me."

"I'm sorry?"

"What if I turn up at the quiz one night with a girlfriend, how would you react?"

Val mulled the scenario over in her head and tried to pull a positive face, "I'd hope to be happy for you. Jim and I are happy," Paul raised an eyebrow, "most of the time, and as long as we were when you and your mythical girlfriend turned up, I'll be fine and happy for you. I was in love with one great man then I fell in love with another. I couldn't help it."

Paul took a drink and weighed up the party goers around them, "I bet you were judging Jodie the other night."

"I was not!" Paul pulled a silly face with eyes wide open to suggest he did not believe her. "All right, but my last kiss on Christmas Eve was probably still on your lips when you met her."

Paul smiled, "I got home from that meal on Christmas Day and noticed traces of your lipstick still around my mouth."

Val gasped and put her hand over her mouth, "Oh, no!" Paul nodded and they both laughed. When they stopped Paul looked serious.

"Any other set of circumstances in your life, if you were not still with Jim, I would be with you like a shot."

"Thanks, Paul, that means a lot," Val held Paul's hands in hers and smiled back.

Later, at midnight, back at the Prince of Wales, Paul was in the gents as the clock struck midnight and when he came out the first person he saw was Jim who was on a short break, as people stopped dancing to gather their thoughts, kiss or fight, sometimes all three.

"Happy New Year, Jim" said Paul, and they shook hands, "all the bloody best."

"And to you, Paul, and many of them. Val was looking for you."

"Was she?"

"Probably wondered where the straw and antlers were!"

"Yeah," Jim walked away from him, laughing. "Nice one." Paul made his way to the back bar and found Stuart stood there. "Happy New Year, Stuart," he said, with hand outstretched. Stuart shook it.

"And to you, Paul, I was a bit out of order the other night."

"Don't worry about it, Stuart. I'd have done the same in your position. I'm not proud of what I did but it kind of happened around me."

"I was talking to Colin, you see, and I never said anything to him about the two of you, but he mentioned Val. Looks like she has a bit of form, fill yer boots, son! Oh, eh, up, she's coming, I'm off." With which he went back behind the bar.

"Paul!" Val announced, she threw her arms around him to give him a big hug and a kiss on the cheek then placed her hands on his shoulders to look into his eyes. "If nothing else, can we keep our friendship?"

"Of course," Paul replied with a smile. Val gave him a big, daft kiss on the lips, accompanied by a 'mwah!' sound. She then picked up a random drink at the bar and downed it at which point Paul noticed Stuart nodding at Val and winking at Paul with a daft look on his face. Paul shook his head and waved his hand as if to say, "Leave it".

"Can't drive you home tonight, Paul, I'm 'mullered' as you English say. I'm going to find Jim." As she walked off Paul decided that was enough for the night and left the pub for the lonely, cold and wet walk home. Very soon he was soaked. Along the way he sighed a huge sigh and began to sing to himself, quietly:

"Can't live, if living is without you, I can't live, I can't give anymore..." and he began laughing to himself.

---

# 2010

I am stood at the bar wondering what the impact of Val reading the book will be and also that I never thought I would see her again. When I had put her name in the work I did at college it never looked like it was ever going to be a problem. The tutor had asked us to write a few chapters so I wrote about me and Val kissing at Christmas and the fall out from that and I changed my name. The tutor seemed impressed and as a separate project asked me to write a few more chapters, they made their way to a literary agent and here I am.

"Can I have your phone number, Liam?" Val asked with her head tilted to one side.

"Sure, no problem," I replied, and with that we had our mobiles out putting our numbers in each other's phone. Val was a bit more competent and quicker getting my number in hers as I had to look at a card from my wallet to remember mine!

"Great! I'll buy your book, have a read and call you to slag it off!"

"Thanks, I can't wait, and if you are going to be in the area for some time we'll meet up for a proper drink and a yarn." With that, Val hugged me, gave me a quick kiss and left. I sighed and glanced up at the clock showing it was five past nine. I was not sure where my friends would be now and didn't really care. This seemed like a good time to finish my drink and get the hell out of there. I just wanted to go home and try to wrap my head around it all. What a strange night it had been. But before I had finished my pint something else happened to stop me in my tracks again.

"Hi, Liam!"

I turned to face Michelle, "Hi, you made it then?" Thank Christ Val left when she did, they must have missed each other by seconds.

"Yeah, sorry I'm late. Is it just us?" she asked, looking around me for other people.

"Now it is, yeah, here," I handed her a tenner, "get a round in, I'm just off for a slash."

"Okay!"

Once in the toilet after I had been I washed my hands, splashed water on my face and stared in the mirror. "Bloody hell, that was close." I said out loud. Then there was a flush of a toilet and a bloke came out of one of the 'traps'.

"You all right?" he asked after looking at me for a long time.

"Yeah, just had a fright, that's all," I told him. He nodded and left. Shortly after I did the same and joined a smiling Michelle at the bar.

"Pint of bitter okay for you, Liam?"

"Yeah, no problem," I took a drink. "Came to an even tenner, did it, the round of drinks?" I asked.

Michelle smiled, "I'll put the change towards the next one."

## CHAPTER EIGHTEEN

IT WAS EARLY ON A Sunday morning in the New Year when Paul woke and he let his eyes adjust to the greyish daylight creeping through the curtains. His head was pounding, his mouth was dry and his throat was sore, which meant he must have had a good night the night before. He looked at the floor where his going out clothes had been scattered in the early hours. To his right was the naked back of a woman who, sensing he was awake and moving, rolled over to face him. As her own eyes blinked and got used to the light she smiled.

"Morning," she said.

"Morning, Jodie."

Jodie leant into Paul to kiss him and then cuddled up to him. "Was it a surprise me ringing you like I did?"

"I'd say. I didn't think you were interested in me like that."

"Yeah, first Val, then me," Jodie paused and kissed Paul's chest, "nothing happening there now, is there?"

"No, God, no, she's staying with Jim."

Jodie smiled, "I'm glad, otherwise you would not have been here with me for the last two weekends. Is no one wondering where you are? Did you bring your mobile this weekend?" Paul decided not to mention the 17 missed calls from Val on his mobile when he got home the previous Tuesday morning. He had not spoken to her since he left the pub on New Year's Day.

Paul just shrugged. "No, no-one is wondering where I am, as long as I ring me Dad when I get home all is okay."

Jodie nodded then bowed her head and bit her lip as if she had done something naughty and was being found out.

"Can I put my cards on the table?"

"Okay," said Paul. "I'm a little scared, now."

Jodie smiled, "I'm also seeing someone. Mark, he's a doctor, he'll be in Africa till March."

"Oh, right," Paul felt a little disappointed but tried to be as casual about this as Jodie clearly was and hoped his face did not show how he really felt. Paul didn't think he was a 'casual' kind of man when it came to women and had hoped he might have made more of a go of it with Jodie. Was she just a rebound from Val, he wondered?

"When I met you I thought you were a lovely bloke and I decided to cheer you up!" Jodie gave Paul a big kiss on the lips. "Did I help?"

"Hard to say."

Jim wandered into the lounge and found Val sat in one of the arm chairs with her back to him and with her mobile to her ear. As she was facing away from him he could not see her anxious face.

"Calling Paul, again?" he asked. Val jumped out of her skin.

"Oh, you know, worried about him, not at the quiz, not answering his phone, no one home when I popped around," she replied. Jim nodded but was surprised to hear she had called at the house. He knew about the calls but not the house visit and hid his wonderment well.

"Do you think he's gone to see his Dad? Isn't he somewhere down south at the moment?" Jim asked.

"I dunno, I just think it's odd that he hasn't rung after the last time I was worried about where he was."

Jim smiled, "Steady on Val, love, you're not his mum!"

Val smiled wearily. "I'll send him a text, his phone's off at the moment, I haven't done that yet."

Paul got back from Derby late Sunday evening and turned his mobile on. Twenty three missed calls from Val, and a text;

MISSING IN ACTION; QUIZ EXPERT, ANSWERS TO NAME PAUL. IF SPOTTED DO NOT APPROACH, HE IS DANGEROUS. QUIZ MONDAY? 210 POUNDS, VAL X

Paul stared at the message and wondered what to do.

"Please stop this, Val," he said towards the phone. "I don't know what to do with you."

"Coming to the quiz tonight, Val?" Jim asked. Val was staring at the TV but not taking any of it in, as even after all these years in England the local news made no sense to her.

Where was Thornton Cleveleys, anyway? she thought to herself.

"I don't know. I haven't heard from Michelle all weekend and *God* knows where Paul is,"

"Oh, still no news on what he's been up to?" At this point the land line phone rang, "I'll get it," Jim said as he was stood next to it, and Val's heart skipped a beat wondering if this was Paul. "Hello? Hi, yeah, she's here, hang on," Val smiled as Jim held out the phone, "Michelle," he said, and she struggled to hide her disappointment.

"Hi, babe," she said.

"Off to the quiz tonight?" Michelle asked.

"Sure, if you want to, why not?"

"Don't sound too enthusiastic, pet."

"I'm sorry about that, Michelle, I'm a bit tired, just getting back into the swing of things at work, you know? I'd love to go and we can catch up."

"Oh, for a moment I thought you and Jim had had a row."

"No, we haven't, we're fine."

"Is Paul going to be there?" Michelle asked with a giggle.

"I don't know, I've not seen him since New Year's Eve."

"Really?! Perhaps your little love tryst has forced him to go and join the French Foreign Legion," Michelle laughed. Val bit her lip.

"Here's hoping! I'll see you at the quiz, Michelle. Usual time, usual table," said Val ending the call.

Val and Michelle were at the quiz at the usual table, Val busied herself filling their name in on the quiz sheet and Michelle scanned the pub for men as usual. Jim was at the DJ stand playing something for the young people who were not in the pub on a Monday evening.

"Did he shag you?" Michelle asked suddenly and quite loudly.

"I'm sorry?" Val asked back, alarmed.

"Paul! Did he shag you? You know, give you one?"

"No, he did not. And," Val nodded in Jim's direction, "keep your voice down. We kissed, once. Well, twice actually, that's all."

*Three times if truth be told or was it four?*

"Was he a good kisser?" Michelle asked further.

Val smiled at the memory of it all, "He was, yeah."

"Better than Jim?" Val didn't reply, just stared at Michelle. "Oh, here he is now, Paul!" Michelle called out with a wave and a big smile.

Paul was stood at the bar getting served and waved back, smiling.

Val had a million and one things to ask, or so she thought, but where to start?

*Where had he been? Was he okay? How was his Dad? How was work? Why didn't you call me? Did you not see my messages? Have you lost your mobile? She also wanted to say; I've missed you, I still love you, Jim's doing my head in, Michelle is mental, why didn't you tell me to leave him? Why are we not together?*

Paul came to the table with drinks for all three of them, "Hi, how is everyone tonight?"

"Paul," Val acknowledged, coolly. She was prepared to ask some of the questions and give him a really hard time about it but then Michelle stole her thunder.

"Hi, Paul," she patted the stool next to her. "Sit here! How've you been?"

"Okay,"

"We've missed yer, haven't we Val? Weren't we just saying how much we've missed Paul? You quiz legend you!"

Val noticed Michelle had bizarrely linked her arm into Paul's after he sat down. "Yes, we have," Val confirmed.

"Ooooh, I love yer jacket, Paul, is it suede?" Michelle ploughed on.

"Er, yes, I think so."

Michelle giggled and turned to take a drink. Paul looked at Val and nodded quickly at Michelle with a quizzical look, as if to ask, "What's her game?" Stuart approached the table.

"Michelle," he said, "Nigel's in."

"Not tonight he's not!" Michelle said, causing Stuart to leave, confused. Val rested her chin on her cupped hand, rolled her eyes and looked glum. Paul smiled but remained very confused.

At the halfway stage of the quiz Val and Paul went to the bar to get some drinks in, "My God, I cannot believe her!" Val exclaimed on the way.

"Who?" Paul asked.

"Michelle!" she replied sharply.

"Why?"

"Why? What do you mean why? You're on the end of it." Stuart approached them and before he asked them what they wanted Val said sharply "Usual."

131

"On the end of what?"

"How naïve are you, Paul? On the end of her flirting!"

"Oh," Paul said, smiling as if remembering a private joke.

"She's only doing it because I've told her about us."

"Why? What did you say?"

"That I thought you were a good kisser."

"Oh. Thanks, Val. Am I?"

Val nodded.

"Here are your drinks, seven pounds-eighty, please," said Stuart. Val paid and after Stuart had gone to the till Paul commented.

"I sometimes think it would've been better for us all if it had been Michelle that had kissed me on Christmas Eve."

Val looked at Paul disgusted, "Thanks a lot, buddy." For a moment Paul feared he was going to be wearing Val's drink as he realised what he said.

"Oh, right, no, hold on, when I say that," he began to explain, digging even further, "well, what I mean is," Val walked off, "Val! Hold up! I need to tell you what I meant." Val stormed to the table, put the drinks down in front of a confused looking Michelle and then stormed past Paul.

"Outside," she said out of the corner of her mouth. Paul followed and when he got outside it was clear Val was fuming.

"Okay then, Paul, tell me why kissing Michelle would have been better than kissing me? Did the fact I put myself out on a limb for you all over Christmas and New Year mean nothing? Falling in love with the wrong man is no freaking walk in the park, I can tell you!"

"The only reason being," he began, "is that she is single and not going out with my mate. That is all. Not that I love her or think better of her or find her more attractive than you, certainly not that."

"You don't prefer her because she is blonde, busty and English, and probably understands soccer and cricket and knows who Blackburn Rovers is? Are?"

Paul shook his head, "No, I really don't."

Val shivered in the cold, north-west night, "Fair enough," she whispered, and put her hand on Paul's chin and pulled him towards her, giving him a quick kiss, "thanks." They smiled at each other for a while.

"Why, people," Michelle called from the door, "the quiz is about to start again!" Without another word they filed back in. The storm had been quelled but they still felt no better being in other people's company together.

For a short while the atmosphere around the table was flat and Michelle's chippiness and flirting hit a brick wall. As the night carried on they all eventually got a bit more talkative and were doing well in the quiz. The second to last question Jim asked was...

"What is the capital of New Zealand?"

"Auckland," Paul said confidently.

"Oh, is it really? I was going to put Wellington," challenged Michelle.

"No, it's Auckland."

"Guys, I dunno," Val said with a little laugh, raising both hands, "it's your empire!"

"I'm sure it's Auckland. Yes, it is, they play most of the cricket and rugby there, it's Auckland," Paul had said it but now wasn't convinced.

"Not Wellington, Paul?" Michelle asked. "Sure?" Val and Michelle stared at Paul intently.

"No," Paul paused as he was uncertain now, "it's Auckland, put Auckland down." He gestured with a pointed finger that was shaking with nerves.

"Okay, then, answer to question 29, Auckland," said Val, writing it down, "sure?"

Paul nodded, nervously rubbed his thighs and looked away. Michelle shrugged and took a drink.

Later on when Jim revealed the answers they were excited to discover they had them all right, and were on course for the jackpot, until...

"Question 29," Jim announced, "the capital of New Zealand is," he paused, "Wellington! Question number 30..."

"Shit!" cursed Paul, and the girls looked momentarily crushed. "Sorry, ladies,"

"Don't worry, it's all right," said Val, despite being disappointed and consoled him with a pat on the back.

"All right!? It's not bloody all right, Val. This prick has just cost me my share of two hundred and ten quid!" Michelle spat.

"Steady on," said Paul, as other quiz teams nearby heard the raised voices and were looking over.

"No, I bloody won't. I only agreed to you coming on the quiz team 'cause 'yer bird' here said we'd win with you on the team. Well, three months on and we haven't won. In fact, we've won shag all! Why don't you just sling yer bloody hook?"

All was silent. Around the table, everyone in the pub, even Jim who had finished the answers and was looking over in confusion. The only noise was a Lily Allen song playing quietly in the background. Jim brought himself back to the job in hand.

"All right! The winners of tonight's quiz, who win a tenner as no one got them all right, with 28 out of 30, it is Michelle, Val and Paul."

"Twenty eight out of thirty?" said Val in confusion.

"Oh, we must have got the last one wrong, an' all," said Michelle, looking slightly embarrassed.

"All yours, Michelle, spend it wisely," Paul said, rising from his chair, putting his coat on and leaving the pub. Michelle opened her mouth to say something but nothing came out.

"You bitch," Val said to Michelle, before getting up and going after Paul.

She caught up with him crossing the car park which was no easy task as she was walking briskly with her arms folded. "Paul! Wait, can I at least drive you home?"

"No, don't worry about it, go and see your mate," he shouted back over his shoulder.

"I've just called her a bitch, which she can be sometimes. Christ! It's cold out here," she said, almost just to her self, "my nipples will be tearing my blouse in a minute. Paul! Wait a minute!"

Paul stopped and turned to face her, "Go back in, Val. Jim and Michelle need you more than me," he then turned, and set off, quickening his pace to almost a jog leaving Val behind.

"PAUL!" she shouted after him, but when he walked on she returned to the pub. Jim met her near the bar.

"How's Paul? Is he okay?" Jim asked. Val shook her head.

"You're freezing, Val, here," he hugged her which she couldn't return as she was frozen. She saw over Jim's shoulder Michelle flirting with Nigel at the bar and a tear rolled down her cheek.

# 2010

It was the Monday morning after meeting Val again for the first time in ages and also the day my book hit the bookshops up and down the country.

Michelle and I had a good chat after she appeared in the pub, I had told her Val had been in there earlier but did not say they had missed each other by seconds, then we chatted about the book and Val and hers part in it. She took it all rather well when I told her that the character reflected the wilder side of her nature back then. There was an invitation to go back to hers at last orders in The Sun but I feigned a bad head and a sudden interest in a donner kebab so I headed for home. God knows what would have happened there, probably nothing I imagine.

Back to the Monday morning; I woke a little after nine o'clock to wearily drag myself out of bed, head downstairs and make myself a bowl of cereal. Once finished I then made my way to my desk, turning on Sky Sports news on the way, and between mouthfuls flipped open an A4 pad with 'next book' written at the top of the page and allowed myself a sigh.

"Fuck knows," I said to myself putting the pen down and shaking my head. I figured I would finish breakfast, get dressed and flower my ego with a trip to WH Smiths to see my book on the shelves. Just then my mobile started to ring and when I picked it up I saw 'VAL' on the screen and for a moment forgot what she would have been reading today. I even allowed myself a smile at her ringing.

"Well hello, Miss Walters, oh, no, it isn't now, is it, what do I call you?" I blabbered.

"You bastard!" she bellowed down the phone. Ah, there was the reminder. Valerie Walters, the leading lady in my book and my life, still the same old charmer she always was. .

# CHAPTER NINETEEN

"SO ARE YOU EVER coming back, then, Dad?" Paul had just been hit by a bombshell; his Dad was moving permanently to be near his two sisters.

"Now and again, like, yes. It's just while I have been down here I've been going on days out with Audrey, Tony's Mum, she's widowed, you know, and we've hit it off, so I'm stopping down here, moving in with Audrey and seeing how we go."

"Oh, right," said Paul, who then went quiet.

"Are you upset? Is it because of your Mum and everything?" his Dad asked.

"No Dad, really, it's fine. We've had a tough time but this is great, I just want you happy, that's all that matters. It's just a bit sudden,"

"There'll be no problem with the house, the mortgage is all paid off and direct debit pays the bills so as long as you don't go daft you'll be fine." It wasn't how he expected it to happen but Paul suddenly had a place of his own.

"Thanks, Dad. Visit my house any time you want."

His Dad laughed, "Take care, son."

Paul had not been to the quiz for a few weeks, since the Auckland/ Wellington/prick debacle. Val had not tried to ring or text him, but taking this decision was hard for her as she missed him. Work kept her busy and she had resigned herself to never seeing him. Paul had a night out with Simon, still went to the football now and again and had a few curious texts from Jodie, which he ignored. Val and Michelle had gone to the quiz each week and not won but were barely on speaking terms while there. Michelle wisely did not mention Paul's name fearing she might hit a nerve and felt guilty about how she had acted when they were last together.

Towards the end of February it was Paul's birthday and he had booked the afternoon off work, a Friday, with no specific plans to do anything, just that he did not want to be at work all day on his birthday. He arrived home to find the postman had put a card through the door saying he had tried to deliver a parcel and that it could be collected from the main Post Office. With nothing else to do he walked into town to collect it. It was from his Dad and looked like a DVD box set. As he walked away from the post office, wondering what it could be, he saw Val.

"Val! Hi, love, how've you been?" he said cheerily.

She looked rather taken aback but as gorgeous as ever. After a moment she smiled warmly at him.

"Okay, I suppose, I've missed you, Paul," she playfully slapped his arm and he smiled at her kind words as she carried on, "I haven't spoken to Michelle hardly since, you know, what happened at the quiz with the capital of New Zealand and everything." Paul nodded solemnly and Val looked at his hands.

"What's with the parcel, Paul?"

"I'm not sure, I've just collected it from the Post Office, birthday present from me Dad, I think." Val gasped.

"When's your birthday?"

"Today."

"Happy birthday!" she leant forward and kissed him, clumsily, just off the lips on the cheek, then rubbed away some lipstick with a lovely smile and a giggle. "Better get rid of that!"

"Thanks!"

"Any plans?"

"For what?"

"Your birthday, silly! Perhaps a night out with your friends, with a meal and drinks, or something along those lines?"

"Nope! None at all."

"None? On your birthday? That's sad," Val paused, "and I mean that in the truest sense."

Paul shrugged, "I know, but what can I do? Everyone is busy or partnered up, except me."

"You could get yourself a partner," Val suggested.

"Of course, it's that easy," they both laughed and thought of the lunacy that they could have been partners themselves if things had worked out differently in the last few weeks.

"Did you say this parcel was from your Dad?"

"Yeah, he lives near my sister's now. The randy bugger pulled at Christmas!"

"Good for him!" Val looked a bit nervous. "Say no if you want but why don't I go out for a drink with you tonight on your birthday? Nothing fancy, just to the Prince of Wales for a chat and a laugh."

"Will Jim not mind?" Paul asked, wondering if there had been any further developments there and hoped Val would say, "No, we've split up, I'm all yours, big lad," but doubted it very much.

"He's working there tonight and keeps asking me if I have heard from you or rung you, so I'm sure he won't mind"

"So you decided not to ring me?" Paul asked.

"Thought you were mad with me," Val confirmed. "And you never rung me, it's a two way street, buddy."

"Mad with you? I'm not mad with you," I love you, he almost added, something which surprised him a little and made his stomach leap in excitement but made him feel a bit sick as if he was getting off a roller coaster ride. "I'd love to meet you for a drink, Val, eight o' clock?"

"Sure? Now, can I drive you home?"

"No, it's all right Val, it's not far and the walk will do me good. See you at eight." Paul walked off and Val smiled glad to have seen him again and then sighed, thinking of the feelings she still had for him that would not go away.

Val arrived home, opened the front door, and called out, "Only me, I'm home!"

Jim was on a call on his mobile. "Val's home, I'll call you back," he said to end it and then he called out, "you okay?" Jim was sat at the desk in the office area under the stairs. Val smiled, came over to where he was sat, gave him a hug and kissed him on the head.

"I saw Paul today."

"Great! How is he?"

"Okay, his Dad has moved down south."

"Really? Blimey, so he's rattling around that big house all on his own?"

"So it would appear, and today is his birthday, so I suggested that him and me go to the Prince of Wales for a drink."

"Oh, right, did he say yes?"

"Yeah, we'll be there at eight," Val paused, "is that okay?"

"Sure!"

"Is it really? It's not odd that I am in there with another guy while you are working?"

"No, it was not a problem at Christmas, New Year and all the quizzes and it's Paul! He's a great lad." Jim smiled and then turned to face his computer and started typing.

"Okay, then," said Val, and walked off heading upstairs. "Just going to have a bath," she called back. After she had left Jim stopped typing and sunk back in his chair, shaking his head.

*I'll be watching him like a hawk, though…*

The night went well; Val and Paul sat at a table in a quiet corner and had a few laughs while out of sight Jim played the latest hits to bring the youngsters in and then confuse them with traditional floor fillers for the oldies – Abba, the Grease soundtrack and, bizarrely, the theme from Rawhide.

"Oh, look, Val, there's me mate over there, Simon. Do you remember him? He came to the quiz a couple of times. SIMON!" Paul shouted to get his mate's attention and he came over to their table.

"Hi, Paul, how are you?" Simon was with a girl. "This is Helen," not the same one Paul last saw him with.

"You remember Val," said Paul.

"Yeah," Simon replied, slowly, "I do, how you doing, Val?"

"Fine, Simon. Not seen you at the quiz for a while."

"No, that's true. Special occasion you being out, Paul," said Simon changing the subject.

"Birthday."

"God, yes, of course, here," Simon rummaged in his pocket and passed Paul seven pounds 37 pence in change, "I'm off to The Crown so the next round's on me. See you both."

"Bye, Simon, nice to meet you, Helen," Paul said as they headed for the exit and Helen gave a little wave.

"He changed the subject of the quiz very quickly, didn't he?" Val asked.

"Yeah, something happened with him and Michelle and I am not sure what."

"Surprisingly, Michelle never mentioned anything about it either, the most indiscreet woman in the western world and nothing." Val smiled.

Jim came to join them at the table with the pub in a frenzy boogeying on down to 'Dancing Queen' and the Mamma Mia soundtrack playing in his absence.

"Happy birthday, Paul, can I buy you a pint?" he asked.

"Cheers, Jim, very kind." When he returned he sat opposite Paul and Val.

"Do you work here every Friday?" Paul asked Jim.

"Nah, I usually do Saturday but Ken's doing that tomorrow for me."

"Something planned for tomorrow, then?"

"Jim's off to see his kids tomorrow," Val confirmed in a stern voice rolling her eyes. Paul raised his eyebrows.

"Oh? Are you not going, Val?"

"No, never do," she confirmed and glared at Jim.

"I took my girlfriend before Val to meet them once and they freaked out," Jim explained, "don't think their mother helped matters, stirring up trouble."

Val put her drink down hard on the table.

"They're teenagers now, Jim, not babies like they were then," she snapped.

"I know, I know. Have a nice night, Paul, back to the music." Jim raised from his chair and headed back to the DJ stand.

After he left Val said, "That really pisses me off, why I can't meet them?"

"Are you the maternal type, Val?" Paul asked.

"Not really but it would just be nice to meet them. They are Jim's kids after all and as such are a part of him."

Jim had put some 1990s disco song on which made Paul pull a face of despair.

"Christ, I remember dancing to this when I was leathered in my youth."

"Focus, Paul," said Val.

"Sorry."

"With Jim away tomorrow you could do me a favour," Val said with a smile.

Paul's mind ran amok for a second at what the favour might be, "Oh, what's that?"

"I'm off back to the States next week, my Dad's birthday, and he's a keen sports fan – you'd like him. He likes books on sport like you do; baseball, basketball, hockey."

"Ice hockey," Paul corrected.

"Right, yes. Football…"

"…American football," he corrected again, "in our version they actually use their feet."

"Whatever, anyway, I thought I could take him back an English sports book, something he won't get in the States. Shall we go into town and sort something out?"

"Sure, Val, happy to help out, it would be great to spend some time with you again," Paul smiled.

"So you are not at a football match tomorrow, then?"

"No, we have a free weekend. Coventry City knocked us out of the FA Cup last month,"

"Right. I've absolutely no idea what that means."

"Well, you wouldn't, would you?"

They smiled at each other and Val clinked Paul's glass as he raised it to take a drink. "Happy birthday, Paul," to which he smiled.

They remained quiet for a moment as every woman on the dance floor sang along tunelessly to 'Summer Loving' from Grease which led them both to pull a face.

"Valentine's Day last week, Paul," Val said suddenly out of nowhere.

"Yes, I assume you got a sack full of cards delivered by the post man from a battalion of adoring men the world over?"

"Oh, yeah, one card from Jim and some flowers from the gas station"

"Ouch, sorry."

Val took a drink "Did you get anything?"

Paul looked into his drink mournfully and then smiled "No. No card, no admirers."

"Except me," Val said seriously.

"Oh, right, of course, I forgot. Part of me did expect one from you."

"I did think about sending you one but my emotions were confused. Do I send it as a friend, with love, or as someone who is in love with you?"

"Someone who is 'in love' with me?'" Paul repeated back confused "present tense?"

"I can't help it, Paul, I still love you," Val paused and held Paul's gaze, "I could kiss you right now." Paul felt the butterflies form in his stomach again. Part of him had hoped this had passed due to the aggro and grief it caused and yet part of him was very flattered that a beautiful woman felt this way about him.

"A birthday kiss, you could do that," he said. Val leant forward slowly and kissed him gently on the lips, with a hand on his cheek, lingered a little, then pulled away.

"Happy birthday, Paul," Val whispered. Paul smiled and as he went to pick his drink up he glanced at his watch and noticed it was getting late.

"Thanks for the drink, Val," he said, standing up. Val looked bemused.

"You're going already? Why?" she asked.

"I don't want to be too bleary eyed when we meet up tomorrow."

"Oh, right, no problem," Val smiled, "I can't drive you home as I've had a drink but if you leave it until one Jim would, I'm sure."

"Best not, I'll grab a taxi,"

"I'll come out with you," Val said.

Outside the pub the freezing February air caught their breath, Val's more than Paul's as being Californian this weather was still a shock, even after all the time she had lived here. Even Paul put his jacket on quickly and Val folded her arms and rubbed them as she did, in a useless attempt to get warm.

"Will you pick me up in the morning or shall we meet in town?" Paul asked. Val lunged forward and gave him a passionate kiss. Paul was aware that Val was Jim's girlfriend, as she had been at Christmas when they kissed in public, but unlike last time this was happening outside the pub in which Jim worked. Paul still enjoyed it though, although he should not have done. Val finally stopped and fixed him with a smouldering look, her lips were parted, her ice blue eyes framed by her flame red hair.

"I'll meet you outside Waterstone's at one," she said finally and went back into the pub. Paul walked over to the taxi rank and with no queue of people waiting fell into the cab at the front.

"Crompton Avenue please, mate, near the chippy," he said to the driver.

"Righty-o," the driver acknowledged, and left the rank. Paul was in a daze and did not make any chatter. "Did you have a good night, mate?" the driver asked.

"Yes, and no," Paul replied.

"Oh?"

"I got something I wanted but really didn't need,"

"Oh, right," the driver said, confused, and drove on. "FA Cup tomorrow, who do you fancy to win it this year?"

Paul slept fitfully and woke several times thinking over the evening's events. He finally got out of bed at eight o' clock and two and half hours later felt a bit better. Two paracetemols for his headache caused more by guilt than drinking, and a glass of fresh orange juice worked a bit. Paul picked up the phone and rang Val as much to test the water than anything else.

"How does it feel to be 29 and one day?" she asked him.

"You'd know, you are older than me,"

"Ouch," Val laughed a hollow laugh, "you funny little English bastard," to which Paul laughed also.

"Still want to meet up?" Paul asked.

"Of course," she replied in a tone suggesting there were no reasons why they should not. "I have a book to buy and you're going to help."

"Shall we meet for lunch before or go for lunch afterwards?" he suggested, looking for a chance to discuss what happened the previous night.

"No," said Val, "I can't eat much at that hour of the day, we'll sort something later."

Just after one o' clock Paul was stood in the 'sport' section of Waterstone's weighing up the shelves in front of him, much like other people considered art in a gallery. Val was stood beside him and loved him for the passion he was showing in the books which made her want to laugh.

"How much do you love being in this section?" she asked.

"I could seriously take home every book in front of me, right now," Paul replied.

"Do you just read sports biographies?"

"Mostly, some entertainment, film, music, TV."

"Never novels?"

Paul shook his head, "Not that many now, hardly any, some contemporary novels mostly, but funnily enough it was novels that got me into reading on this scale."

Val leant on the middle shelf of the rack, "How come?"

"I hardly read books as a child, or at school, but I went to stop with my aunt and uncle just after leaving school and my uncle had a load of Mickey Spillane books. I read most of them when I was there."

Val pulled a face, "They're dreadful!"

Paul laughed, "It's a long time since I've read them now but still, I came home and I was away, reading some biographies my Dad had lying around."

"Working in a book warehouse must be heaven for you," Val commented.

"Not really. My first day there I got a book and found a quiet corner in my lunch hour and began reading it, only to be discovered and threatened with the sack."

"God, that's awful."

Paul shrugged, "They had a point, I suppose, it's a bit like working in a clothes shop and taking the stock home to wear on a night out, then taking it back."

"I suppose," agreed Val. Paul paused then turned to the book shelves again. Val looked at the books.

*Was he thinking as much about her as the books? What did he think of her kissing him like that again? Was he playing it cool or did he not really care? Was his stomach as full of butterflies as hers was?*

"Paul," she began, "about last night, do you feel…"

"Here, this is what we need," Paul interrupted as she began talking, getting a book down from the shelf and passing it to Val who looked at it, weighing it all up. It was baked gold in colour and the same shape as a house brick.

"And this is?" she asked.

"Wisden, the bible of cricket."

"Cricket; an insect," Val said smiling.

"Cricket; like baseball, but better," Paul corrected.

"I saw cricket on the TV once, it lasted for days," said Val, flicking through the pages, the text of which made no sense to her American eyes.

"It can."

"And still no one had won at the end of it all,"

"That can also happen. Buy it for your Dad, Val. It'll be interesting for him, like me reading about baseball."

"Do you own this book?" she asked.

"I'd love to but it costs forty pounds, it's a lot to shell out."

"Forty pounds for a sports book?" Val spat the last two words out. Some members of staff turned around to look their way as Val's outburst disturbed the library like atmosphere. Paul laughed but with a shrug Val took a second copy from the shelf.

"I'll buy you one as well," she said, "as a thank you for choosing it for my Dad and also as a belated birthday present."

"No, Val, you don't have to, it's forty quid! What would Jim say?"

"Screw him, it's my cash." Val headed for the counter to pay so Paul followed and when he got there Val had handed the books over to a member of staff.

"How are you today?" the man at the till asked Val as Paul caught up with her.

"I'm fine, and you?"

"Good." The man noticed Val's accent. "Visiting these shores?"

"No, we live here," Paul replied abruptly.

"Oh, well you at least sound like you're local," the man commented, then leant towards Val and whispered, "You do realise you've picked up the same book twice?"

"Yeah, I do it all the time!"

The man smiled and then turned to Paul, "Where did you get her from, mate? She's fantastic!"

Val rolled her eyes, while stood there holding out her credit card in a desperate attempt to pay.

"Hot-American-redheads-dot-com," Paul replied. The man smiled and took Val's card.

"Good one!" he said, then after he placed the card in the machine asked, "Is that a real site?"

"Did you not used to need a degree to work here?" Paul asked. The man looked embarrassed and hurried through the sale to get rid of them.

Once outside the shop the change from the warmth inside and the bitter Lancashire cold outside cleared Paul's brain and he wanted to try and clarify where he and Val were again, other than outside a bookshop, obviously. Val had wanted to discuss matters in the shop but really did not know where to start.

"Shall we get some lunch now..." he asked, "and chat?" he added with a smile. "There's loads I want and need to talk to you about, Val. Don't you agree?"

Val was looking down the street and pulled a face at Paul's suggestion, "Later on, maybe," she replied, "I need to sort something out. Come on," she linked her arm in his, "I'll drive you home." Once at Paul's he invited Val in 'for a drink' and she accepted. As they got in the house he put his copy of Wisden on the sideboard and turned to face Val.

"Tea or coffee?" he asked, to which Val grabbed him and kissed him, more passionately than before, as if hungry for something and kissing Paul would be the only thing to stop the hunger. Paul knew they were behind closed doors for the first time together and no one could see them but still feeling guilty he kissed her back and let his hands and arms discover her body like never before. Pausing after a while Val looked longingly into his eyes and Paul, he imagined, looked stunned, because he was and was gasping for breath.

"Val," he said after a moment, "please, can we talk so I can just clarify something?"

Without a word Val made her way past Paul, paused at the bottom of the stairs and pointed up them.

"Bedrooms?" she asked, to which Paul hesitated, as this was still Jim's girl and then hating himself a little nodded to confirm it. Val climbed the stairs almost in a sprint.

"Come on, Paul," she called back down behind her, "I don't know which one is yours." Paul sighed, shook his head and made his way upstairs.

Afterwards they lay in bed and were quiet as neither knew what to say next. The wind and the hail of the Lancashire winter battered the glass of Paul's bedroom window, which had, until recently, been his father's bedroom, with a little bit of sunshine trying to get through. Val looked towards it and wondered how she had got herself there.

"Blimey," Paul said after a while with a small laugh which was all he could manage. Val rolled onto her side to face him.

"I'll really miss you when I'm in the States," she told him and moved to kiss him. Paul smiled at her.

"Wish I was coming with you," he offered, hoping there was some way Val might suggest this could happen.

"I know. My Dad will be surprised Jim's not with me, so you turning up would be a big surprise."

"Has Jim been over there before then?" Val shook her head at Paul's question.

"No, my father came over here and they met then. We took him to the Lake District."

"You haven't mentioned your mum," Paul pressed, "will you see her?" Val shook her head. "Any reason why not?"

Val shrugged, "Don't get on."

"Oh," Paul put his arms around Val who cuddled in. "Why does this feel like the best and worst moment of my life?" he asked her.

"I'm right with you there, honey," she replied.

---

# 2010

I gave it an hour or so of trying to stop myself smiling and giggling in a silly way and then I rang Val back. It rang for a while and I fully expected it to go to voice mail but after a while she answered.

"What?!" she barked at me.

"How much of it have you read so far?" I asked.

There was silence to begin with and while I waited I typed 'the next great novel' onto the PC then deleted it, shaking my head.

"When I called you before I had just read the back and saw my name in the description," she explained.

"Right, I see."

"Liam, how fucking could you?" she sounded angry, upset, let down, but strangely amused by it, all at once. "And why am I an American with ginger hair?"

"I cannot remember what made me choose that, possibly to be different from you, I think, but read it, Val, just read it. You might have a surprise at how the character based on me, Paul, how he-" I paused. "Just read it and let me know what you think, okay?"

Silence again, and then, "Okay, I owe you that at least." Then silence, yet again until a thought struck me.

"What is your married name, Val?"

"For work I am still Ms Walters but officially Mrs Endean, why?"

"Just curious, that's all. Are you still with him?" Silence once more. "Let us know what you think about the book."

"Will do," I went to end the call and then I heard her shout out. "Oh, Liam, I've got something funny to tell you." She sounded upbeat which I hoped was her thawing to me slightly.

"What's that?" I asked.

"In the pub after I left the other night I got outside and realised I had left my bag on the bar stool, so I went back in to get it, you were nowhere to be seen but Michelle was sat on the bar stool I had just been sat on? What a coincidence!"

*Oh, blimey.*

"Yeah, wow! Did you talk?"

"No, too soon for that, I sneaked the bag off the stool and left, but someone spotted me and thought I had nicked Michelle's handbag so they followed me, grabbed me in a head lock — thought I was being mugged — and flagged down a passing police car to have me arrested. Just glad I had my driving licence still in my purse to prove it was mine."

"Yeah, good job, and your Dad being a copper an'all."

"Blimey, you remember that?"

"Yeah, I helped you purchase a present for him once."

The pause on the end of the phone was the sound of Val thinking although I initially thought she had lost her signal, "You did?"

"Yeah, a gold-plated tie pin."

*How do I remember all this and she doesn't?*

"Oh, God, yes, I remember it now. He wore it earlier this year for his retirement do and when I said it was nice and asked where he got it from he looked at me like I was mad and told me I bought it for him, but could not remember when." Then, there was silence again, but this had been great, like old times. I was about to share this thought with her when she said, "I'll read the book and let you know what I think." And the call ended.

# CHAPTER TWENTY

I T WAS LATE ON A FRIDAY EVENING and Paul had not been out, instead he put himself at the mercy of the best Friday night TV could offer. It had not worked; his mind was still an emotional swamp. All his thoughts were of Val, the gorgeous American redhead who was his friend's girlfriend, then his friend and now his secret lover. It excited him and scared him in equal measure. He had even taken the last three days off work ill. He felt sick but never was physically sick, them damn butterflies again.

He began to get tidied up before bed, the half drunk beer poured down the sink and the half eaten pizza thrown in the wheelie bin on top of the half eaten curry from the night before. One day, he thought, he will feel like eating properly again.

*One day.*

The phone rang and as it was late it worried him initially and he thought of ignoring it but he thought better of it and picked up the receiver.

"Hello?"

After a pause a woman's voice said, "Paul?"

"Hi," he hesitated as his heart skipped, stopped, did somersaults, "how are you?"

"Great! I'm at my Dad's now. I'm going to the top of the daughter's league table, he loves the book! My twin sister," twin sister, Paul thought, there are two of them; "only bought him a jumper! He's been sat flicking through the book for hours. He's heard of the book, which made it even better and cricket as well!"

"Great! And how have you been?" Paul asked taking a seat at the kitchen table.

"I'm having a great time, I've been seeing some old friends and some of my family, been out a few times and…"

"Leave Jim, Val," Paul suddenly said out of nowhere. It surprised him but he wanted to say it, needed to say it.

"Sorry Paul, bad line I think, I didn't quite catch that, what did you just say?"

"When you come back home leave Jim and move in here with me."

"No, Paul! What are you saying?"

"Look, we love each other, Val, we are great together, we're the same age, we get on and we've even had sex. It all makes sense." Paul's voice was shaking but he was determined to say these things.

"None of this makes sense, Paul, where was all this at Christmas when I poured my broken heart out to you in some crappy little pub in the north of England?"

"Not seeing you for these last few days, especially after what has happened, has given me focus. I know it is wrong on so many levels but in every way it is right. Come home now and leave him. Come and live with me."

"Paul, look, I can't talk about this right now." And she hung up.

"Val? Hello? Are you still there?" Paul got up from the table, dug out the telephone directory and flicked frantically through the pages at the front for the international directory enquiries. After finding it he rang.

"Good evening, international enquiries?"

"Yeah, hello, number in San Jose, California, USA, please, name of Walters."

"Do you have an address, sir?" the operator asked.

"Sorry, no, I don't have an address," Paul replied.

"Or a first initial, sir?"

"No, how many are there?"

"Six hundred and twelve," the operator confirmed.

"Six hundred and twelve? It's not that common a surname. No problem, thanks for your help." Paul slammed the phone down and leant on the work top in the kitchen.

"Bollocks!"

Blackburn's game that weekend had been moved to a Sunday, Paul feared the worst and then it happened. Rovers lost. He went to the pub afterwards to mull over the game and recent events. With him again was his mate, Dan, and among all the other disappointed fans in there they found a table.

"Well, at least we shouldn't get relegated this season," Dan said, looking for a silver lining.

"This is true," Paul agreed and they both took a man size swig of their pints.

"We could still be in Europe in September," said Dan trying again.

"If there's a war!" Paul suggested before they took another man size swig. "How much do you want to cry right now?" Paul asked to which they both laughed. "I'm glad I don't care about them as much as I used to, this time ten years ago I would have been looking for a bridge to throw myself off."

"It also helps if you have things other than the club to care about," Dan said. He was hinting at his marriage.

"I suppose so," Paul agreed which led him to think of Val and then more drinking of their pints.

"Did anything further happen with that girl from Christmas?" Dan asked. Paul finished a swig of ale and nodded.

"Last Saturday we had sex," Paul confirmed, matter-of-factly, as if describing a trip to the shops, which bizarrely was how it all started.

"Wahey!" said Dan.

"No, Dan, not wahey, quite the opposite, she's still with my mate."

"Oh, bloody hell."

"And when she rang me on Friday I asked her to leave him and move in with me and she went mental." Dan took a big swig and looked thoughtful.

"Well, Paul, all I can say on your behalf is," Dan paused, "good old Coventry City!"

"I beg your pardon?"

"If they hadn't knocked us out of the cup you'd have been at a match last weekend and you wouldn't have jumped the bones of, of..." Dan did a rolling gesture with his hand to signify he had no idea what this woman was called and looked at Paul for help.

"Valerie," Paul said helping him, "I wouldn't have jumped the bones of Valerie."

"Valerie?" Dan asked, confused, "Valerie? What is she, a school dinner-lady?"

"No, why?"

"I thought only school dinner-ladies were called Valerie."

"You cheeky sod! No, Valerie is not a school dinner lady, she is

American,"

"American? Blimey, that's exotic, exciting."

"Yes, she's American. She is also a red head, a college tutor, gorgeous, bright, she's funny and, right now Valerie is stood at the bar! Jesus Christ, Dan, she is stood at the bar! What's she doing here? She was in San Jo-bloody-se on Friday night!"

Val was indeed stood at the bar among blue and white half shirted drinkers of all shapes and sizes, many of whom were now leering at her.

"San Jose? My God, she is some well travelled school dinner-lady!"

"Will you leave it with the school dinner lady-bit, Dan? Christ, she's coming over, I forbid you from speaking to her." Paul stood up to greet Val but wasn't sure how to now after all that happened.

"Val, hi, how are you?" he asked with a smile. Val had a face like thunder while Dan wore a daft grin and tried not to laugh.

"Paul, can your friend leave, please?" She asked and Dan downed the rest of his pint.

"See you in two weeks, kidder," he said to Paul, nodded at Val, got up and left. Val then sat where Dan had just been and glared at Paul.

"Do you know how many God forsaken pubs I have had to go into in this hell hole to find you?" she asked.

"But you did, thanks."

Something told him that Val's gesture was not one of love and them getting together. The signs were not good, her mood and temper were as fiery as her hair. But then, as she spoke some more, what was Val trying to tell him?

"Jim doesn't know I'm back in the UK; after your call I booked the next flight to this country that I could and thirteen hours later I arrive, in freaking Glasgow. So I booked a hire car with built in sat-nav, tapped in Blackburn, Lancashire – thank you, the Beatles - headed south and now I am here."

Paul smiled as he was amused by the fact that 'A Day in the Life' by the Beatles, from Sergeant Pepper's Lonely Hearts Club Band had led Val to his football pub.

"Now you're here."

"I even had the sports radio on to tell me if you would be out of the game by the time I arrived," she allowed herself a smile, "heard you lost, again." Paul shrugged. "I take it you came here on the train, Paul? Come on, I'll drive you home."

They began the journey in silence with only some 'hits' type compilation CD filling the silence. Paul was still amused that Val had driven to Blackburn to come to find him but only wished it was in happier circumstances.

"I'm sorry I asked you to leave Jim," Paul began. Val stole a glance at him. "After saying at Christmas I didn't think it was a good idea it was unforgivable. But you tell me on my birthday you want to kiss me, then you do, and tell me that you still love me and then you throw yourself at me in my own home and let me tub you."

"Tub me?" Val asked, stealing another glance.

"You know, 'tub'."

"Oh, right, that. I'm sorry, I can't blame you for being confused, Paul, I was out of order." They drove home in more silence for a while as Pixie Lott did her best out of the CD player. Paul's mind was racing, the old Paul, the Paul that didn't have a gorgeous American in love with him and fell over the right words to say to make women interested and was to all intents and purposes a gentleman.

"So Jim doesn't know you're home yet?" he asked.

"No," Val confirmed again.

"I've got a couple of spare rooms if you wanted to, you know, avoid going home just yet and stay over,"

"Yes, I'll stop at your house tonight, Paul, but I'm not going in any spare room." Paul let the information wash over him. "You understand?"

"Right, I do, yes. Champion," he said.

Paul was awoken the next morning by the radio alarm advising of road works going into town. He turned it off and decided that he had better make an effort of going back into work today. There was a set of car keys on the pillow next to him and he realised he was alone now but hadn't been the night before.

"Okay, then, that was that," he said to himself, getting out of bed to get dressed. A few minutes later as he headed downstairs there was a knock at his front door and he opened it to a smart man of his own age in a suit.

"Hire car company," the man said, "come for the car, we were told you had the keys."

"Right, here you are," Paul handed the keys to the man who took them and smiled.

"Thank you, sir, I hoped you enjoyed it," and he left.

"Yeah," said Paul, then as he shut the door.

*And the car.*

## CHAPTER TWENTY-ONE

"HELLO?" It was a horrible, wet, miserable Wednesday evening after work, there was nothing on TV, he was skint and Paul had answered his phone with little enthusiasm.

"Paul? Jim here."

*Oh, hell!*

"All right, James?" he asked, wondering if a certain woman of their acquaintance had taken leave of her senses and blurted a few things out.

"Yeah, you've not been to the quiz for ages and we are all missing you. How have you been?"

*All right I suppose in the last three and half weeks since I tubbed your missus.*

"All right, I suppose," Paul said.

"Any plans for tonight?"

"Tonight's Wednesday, right? I'll check my diary. Ah, big problem,"

"Oh, what's that?" Jim asked.

"Well, I don't have a diary and if I did every day would be empty."

"Hell! Well, do you know Rossi's restaurant?"

"Yeah, not been there for a while but yeah I know it."

"Get some decent clobber on and meet us there at eight."

"Us?" Paul asked with a hint of terror in his voice.

"Just be there," Jim said firmly, "see you later." Jim put the phone down on its stand and turned to Val who had waited with baited breath for the call to finish and had wondered how Paul had been.

"He's coming," he said.

"Did he sound all right?" Val asked not sure of the reply.

"Said he was," Jim confirmed with a nod.

Val looked surprised, "Right, great, I'll go and get ready, then," she said, and got out of the arm chair. Jim grabbed her as she passed him on the sofa and hugged her.

"Are you happy?" he asked with a satisfied smile.

"Really happy," she replied and smiled also. As they hugged closer she allowed her face to drop in misery to reflect how she really felt.

Paul walked rather tentatively into Rossi's wondering what this was all about and what he would find when he got in there and as he did a waiter approached.

"Table for one, sir?" he asked.

"No, actually I'm with a party you might possibly have booked in, in the name of Black?"

"Si!" the waiter exclaimed. "Signor Black, he has booked, yes, take a seat, you're first to arrive, can I get you a drink?"

"Pint of Peroni, please," Paul took a seat to wait and after a while the waiter had came over with the drink. "Thanks, mate, any ideas what the occasion is Mr Black's booked this for?"

The waiter shook his head, "No idea, sir, sorry."

Paul took a drink and wondered where everyone else was and when they might arrive. Then a horrible thought came over him. "Meet us" Jim had said. Had Val told him what had happened and then scarpered, or been murdered, before she could warn Paul, and Jim had rounded up a posse like they did in the wild West to do him in? A bead of sweat rolled down his back but at that very moment in walked Michelle and Paul put such nonsense to the back of his mind, unless she was one of the posse members Jim had got together. Being a Geordie Paul thought she might be useful in a punch-up.

"Hello, Paul!" she greeted him in a friendly manner with a smile and a little wave.

"Hi," Paul could not offer much more as he recalled the word 'prick' being spat in his direction the last time they were in each other's company, but as the waiter approached them he remembered his manners and stood up.

"Another for Mr Black's party?" he asked. Michelle shrugged and Paul nodded.

"So it would appear," she replied.

"A drink while you wait, Miss?"

"Glass of white wine," Michelle confirmed and sat on the sofa next to the armchair Paul was sat back in. She smiled at him again and he responded with a tight lipped smile of his own and a slight nod. He wished he was somewhere else but did wonder why he had been invited and what was happening.

"Any idea what this is all about?" she asked.

"Not a clue, not a clue," Paul confirmed.

"So has Val not mentioned anything to you about what it could be?"

"No, I haven't seen her for a while."

"Oh, right," Michelle looked surprised and Paul pulled a face back at Michelle as if to ask why this might be a surprise.

"Ah, they're here," Paul announced, noticing Jim and Val. Jim chatted to the waiter, who was on his way with Michelle's drink, while Val came to chat to Michelle and Paul.

"Hi, Val, love your top!" Michelle gushed, whereas Paul loved what was in the top. Well, love might be too strong, he thought.

*Incredibly fond of, big fan.*

"Thanks, Michelle, how are you keeping?" Val asked back, giving Michelle a kiss on the cheek and grabbing her hands to hold them.

*She's all right, Val, she hasn't secretly slept with her partner's mate, only because she hasn't got a partner, then you'd no doubt both be in the same boat.*

"Fine, fine, I was back up Gateshead at the weekend,"

*God help Gateshead.*

"Is everyone okay up there?" Val asked further.

*See, even an outsider from the States is now concerned of the welfare of the north-east of England.*

Paul's mind was racing at a million miles an hour.

"Aye, blinding."

"Great!" Val let go of Michelle's hands and turned to face Paul, her smile getting warmer, Paul thought, meaning she cared more for him more than she did for her oldest English friend.

"Hey, you!" she gave Paul a hug.

"Hello, Valerie, how are you, how've you been?" he asked carefully. Michelle got stuck into her drink with several millilitres disappearing down her throat.

"Eeee, that's hit the spot," Michelle said to no one in particular.

"Good, I'm good," Val replied to Paul's query.

"Yeah? Are you really?" he asked a bit too forcefully as if he didn't believe it.

"Of course, Paul," Val confirmed firmly, the smile freezing. Jim approached the trio, all smiles.

"Right, chaps, table ready, come on," he said, grabbing Val's hand and following the waiter.

"Oh, is it just the four of us?" Michelle asked, and set off after them. On the way Paul had a thought of what the night might be all about and tapped Michelle's arm lightly.

"What?" she asked.

"If this is a ploy to get us fixed up," he began, "forget the ups and downs we have had, I'll leave in disgust first."

"Ok, thanks," said Michelle, who then smiled knowingly, "not doing that to get into our Valerie, are you?"

"No, not at all, never crossed my mind," he lied. At the table the waiter had left them with menus and once they had all ordered brought them wine and a jug of water, then left them to it.

"Right," said Jim, clapping his hands together, which made Paul jump a bit. "Big announcement time. On Monday after the quiz, which, Paul, you are still welcome to come back to and take part in again whenever you like." Everyone smiled.

"Thanks, Jim, mate," said Paul.

"I decided enough was enough. I asked Val to marry me and she said yes!" Michelle gasped and then glanced at Paul who, without missing a heartbeat, rose from his chair.

"Congratulations to you both!" he said, shaking Jim's hand patting his shoulder and then giving Val a kiss on the cheek accompanied with a smile and a whispered "well done," Michelle was hugging her at the time.

"You lucky man, Jim, you deserve it," Paul added.

"Cheers, Paul," they re-took their seats and tried to compose themselves as the waiter brought over some champagne.

"Is that the ring there?" Michelle asked as Val held out her hand. "Eee, it's smashing that!" Val smiled and simpered in equal measure and seemed to be revelling in her moment but kept looking at Paul to gauge his reaction. Paul was smiling every time she looked at him and his eyes gave nothing away. On occasion he raised his glass and mouthed "well done" and hoped he meant it.

"Any plans on when you're going to get wed?" Michelle continued, "or where? How's about Mauritius?" Val's eyes were wide at Michelle's enthusiasm.

"I can hear my bank manager sobbing," Jim quipped, a comment which made Paul laugh.

"What about the States?" Paul suggested sensibly which made everyone thoughtful and led Val to make a positive noise.

"Would your Dad pay, Val?" Michelle asked, picking up the baton.

"I don't know," Val replied. Michelle went off and outlined to Jim her various wedding ideas and plans, ignoring the fact she had no current man. Val tapped Paul's hand.

"Paul," she said, "let me get you a drink," and rose from her chair nodding towards the bar.

"It's okay, Val," Paul replied, "I'll have the wine and the champagne for now."

"No, I want to get you a beer, come on," and she headed to the bar. With Michelle and Jim still embroiled in a discussion about a naked wedding idea she had, Paul got up and followed Val. When he caught up with her Val was stood at the far end of the bar facing Paul with her arms behind her on the rail that ran the length of it. She looked worried and a little frightened.

"What do you think of the news, then?" she asked leading Paul to give a snort and then a nervous laugh.

"With everything that happened when I last saw you, what do you expect me to think?" he asked back. Behind the bar was one of the waiters who hadn't noticed them there until they began to talk.

"Drinks?" he asked.

"Not yet, mate, maybe in a minute," Paul replied and the waiter left them to it.

"Are you happy?" he asked her. She sighed and gave a shrug suddenly aware of tears forming in her eyes.

"Not really, but Jim is a good man."

"And I am not? No, don't answer that, with what we've done I know I am not."

"It was not what I meant, Paul. You are a good man. Jim is the here and now. We've been together so long it feels like the next natural step and I'm too tired to sit down and work out how you and I could ever work it out to get together."

"So I shouldn't expect you back at my door any time soon? Just so I know where I stand."

"Probably best not to expect me back there ever again," Val advised, "just to be on the safe side."

Paul held out his hand, "Congratulations, Val, and I mean that." They shook hands very formally.

"Thanks, Paul," she whispered, both of them suddenly looked miserable and felt it too. They both felt sick to their stomach and had lost their appetites. Paul let go of Val's hand and turned to walk back to the table. His head was pounding and he felt dizzy and light headed. Val shook her head, fought back tears and, thanking her stars it was an emotional night to explain them away, made her way back to the table a few steps behind him.

The night as Paul saw it had been a complete shambles and he could not wait for it to end, but not everyone seemed to think this, "Well, it was great of you both to come tonight, guys," Jim began at the end of the meal, "Michelle as Val's oldest friend in England and Paul is someone we are both fond of," Paul smiled and he glanced at Val who looked very ill, as if she was about to throw up. The plates had been cleared and a waiter had brought the bill over in a leather wallet on a plate with some mints. The girls grabbed the mints in a playful manner, both laughing, although Michelle with more conviction than Val. "I'll just go and pay this," Jim said, leaving the table with the wallet.

Paul had been subdued all evening since his chat with Val and remained quiet, Michelle was a bit quiet as she had drunk quite a lot and Val was reflective about the decision she had made and from her earlier chat with Paul. At least Jim seemed pleased.

"Are you giving Paul a lift home, Val?" Michelle asked. Before Val answered Paul chipped in,

"Oh, don't worry about it, Michelle, it's their night, I'll hop in a taxi. They don't want a beered up lout in their car, ruining things." Michelle smiled and Val leant forwards towards Paul.

"It won't be a problem, Paul, we don't mind," said Val.

"Don't worry, Val," he said, waving his hand.

"I'll run you home, pet," said Michelle, to which Paul and Val turned to face her.

"Run me over more like with what she has had to drink," Paul whispered. Jim had returned, "Don't worry, Michelle, you live at the other end of town to me, I'll be miles out of your way,"

"How do you know where Michelle lives?" Jim asked. Paul tried to think how he did know where Michelle lived and remembered his little trip out with Val at Christmas.

"Val knows how," Michelle said, giggling.

"And how much have you had to drink?" Val asked. Jim looked confused.

"How does Val know?" he asked.

"Lift home once, after the quiz," Val whispered and lied.

"Oh," said Jim to understand.

"Liar!" Michelle mouthed at Val.

"Michelle, leave your car, we'll share a taxi and drop you off first," Paul suggested.

"Do you not fancy coming in so I can get a bit of your action?" Michelle said, saying the last word in a deep voice, more slurred than the intended sexy. Paul weighed up the offer but then stood up.

"I'm off, congrats again," he said towards Val and Jim and then left quickly. Val looked longingly after him.

"He's been in a right off mood all night, he has," said Michelle.

"Hasn't he just," Jim agreed, sternly.

Despite the light hearted invite from Jim during the meal Paul did not go back to the quiz by the time March turned into April. He had not rung or been rung by Val or Jim in that time. He continued to go to the football with Dan and before the latest match they were sat at their favourite table intending to put the world to rights.

"So how are you and the school dinner-lady getting on, then?" Dan asked. Paul laughed.

"I've only seen her once in the month or so since she turned up here," Paul confirmed.

"Oh,"

"That night that she came here we went back to mine and slept together but she sneaked out in the morning before I woke up."

"She didn't rob your house, did she? Naughty dinner-lady!"

"No she never robbed my house, Dan. But three weeks later her boyfriend…"

"Your mate?" Dan asked to confirm.

"Yeah, that's him, my mate Jim, rang and invited me out for a meal and when I turned up Val was there and her mate..."

"The one they wanted to fix you up with?"

"Yeah, that's her, and Jim and Val announced they had got engaged."

"Blimey!"

"And I haven't been in touch since. I haven't rung them, they haven't rung me. On their part it might be because I acted like a top drawer twat on that night out, it certainly is on my part!" Paul laughed.

"Right, okay," Dan looked thoughtful, paused and took a drink of his pint, "three points today, then Paul?"

"I think so Dan, yes."

The following Monday Paul had just got in from work and was contemplating what to have for tea when the phone rang.

"Hello?"

"Hi, Paul, how are you?"

He allowed himself a cheeky smile, "Good thanks, and you, the soon to be Mrs Black!"

"Yes, I suppose I will be, Mrs Val Black, one day. I'm good thanks."

"Unless you keep your 'stage name' when you get wed and remain Valerie Walters, international woman of mystery." Hearing Paul say her name sent a shiver up her spine. "Is Jim okay," it was something Paul always did when he was alone with Val or talking to her on the phone, he asked how Jim was, almost as if he was trying to forgive himself and make him seem a better person than he felt he was.

"He is, yes. Listen, I'm ringing for two reasons; one, the quiz jackpot is up to £525 tonight,"

"Hell! That's worth winning!"

"Of course and the last two weeks Big Doug and Colin have won the tenner, getting 29 out of 30 each time. We need you down there with us, Paul."

"Could you just not ask them to join you?" Paul said it with good intentions but realised how tactless the statement appeared as soon as he said it.

"Michelle suggested that once, but no, we cannot, and you know damn well why not!"

"I see, yes, sorry," he said, getting away with it, just.

"It would be nice to see you again as well,"

"Thanks, Val, that's kind of you." He opened the fridge hoping for some inspiration for tea but there was none.

"Look, I always said I never wanted to lose your friendship, no matter what, and I still don't. Second thing, it's my birthday this Sunday..."

"Is it Val? I had no idea, you doing anything nice?"

"Jim and I are off to Paris at the weekend."

"Marvellous."

"But as he is working Friday, DJ-ing, I'd love someone to come out with me for a few drinks,"

"What about Michelle?" Paul asked, seeing only banana skins up ahead going off their previous record of nights out together.

"She's back home as it is Easter Weekend."

"Oh, God, I forgot it was Easter, yeah, no problem, I'll see you at the quiz, normal time?"

"Yes it is, see you then, Paul." Paul put the phone back on its stand and continued rummaging in the cupboards for something to eat. Val put the phone down at her home and Jim came into the living room from the kitchen where some 'Spag Bol' was being made.

"Was that Paul you were ringing?" he asked sharply.

"Yeah, I somehow talked him into coming to the quiz," Val replied brightly.

"Good. I'll be having a word with him, then." Val turned to look at Jim as he walked back into the kitchen, amazed that he sounded like a Mancunian Clint Eastwood, albeit one with an apron on and brandishing a wooden spoon.

When Paul reached the Prince of Wales all was as it normally was, Val and Michelle were at the bar getting some drinks from Stuart.

"Here's Paul now, Val. Hi, Paul!" Michelle said brightly. Val smiled at him, that warm smile of hers that Paul so loved and had missed these last few weeks.

"Hey, Paul, do you want a pint?" she asked.

"Love one, thanks. Shall I get the quiz sheet from Jim?"

"Aye, Paul, if you could, pet, we've only just got here," Michelle replied. He made his way to the DJ stand, dug out a pound from his pocket and braced himself.

"Hello, Jim, how are you? Quiz sheet please, mate," Jim turned to grab a quiz sheet, gave it to Paul and hadn't smiled or spoken, which threw Paul, but then,

"I'm disappointed in you, Paul, mate," Paul's heart jumped.

"Why?"

"The meal out, you left rather abruptly."

"Sorry, did you want me to pay my share? How much was it?" Paul hoped that was all Jim was mad about and rummaged for his wallet until Jim grabbed his arm.

"The meal was on me, Paul, but you disappearing after being moody all evening didn't make it a good night. Val cried all the way home," Paul felt massively guilty there as it was more than likely not all about his behaviour on the night that had caused Val to be like that, "and Michelle hoyed up in the car."

"Oh, Christ, I'm sorry. I knew it hadn't gone down well that's why I have stayed away from here. After the previous run-in with Michelle then how she was on the night, I think she's bi-polar, or something. Are you okay with me being here tonight to help the girls? What about being out with Val on Friday for her birthday drink?" Jim fixed him a stare and it struck Paul that Val might not have mentioned the birthday drink yet.

"I'm going to have to be okay then, aren't I? Good luck with the quiz."

Paul turned without another word and walked slowly to the table they always sat at and waited for the girls to come over with the drinks. While waiting he mulled over Jim's comments.

*What must be going through his mind? Why would he think that the news of their engagement would cause a former work mate to be so moody and then this lead to his fiancée to cry all night? It was all over the place as far as Paul was concerned and he toyed with the idea of being a coward and leaving. Or was it doing the right thing and leaving?*

Paul brightened a bit by the time the quiz started and chipped in with some answers, which pleased Val and Michelle.

"Have you been up to anything recently, Paul?" Val asked between questions.

"Nothing much, football, a few nights out, couple of new books and I went to see my Dad down in Warwickshire."

"Okay, is he?"

"Happy as Larry, thanks."

"Have you been seeing any girls, Paul?" Michelle asked with a giggle, thinking it wound up Val, when it was worse, like a block of ice through her heart.

"No, none for a while."

"None since our Valerie here!" Val and Paul glared at her. "Come on, I know what happened, don't I? It's massive! How do you ignore it?"

"It's nothing," said Val.

"I just plough on," Paul added.

"Nothing, really," Val said again.

"It was nothing, no, tiny, not massive, wee."

"Okay, guys, I get the idea!"

Later, as Jim began to go through the answers, Paul and Val were at the bar getting the next round of drinks. Paul was stood close to Val and had held this woman passionately and made love to her but tried not to think about it too much. When he did it sent him a little bit mental.

"I wish she hadn't said those things," said Val as they waited for the drinks to arrive.

Paul raised his eyebrows. "But she did and here we both are still hanging around with her," Val shrugged. "On your birthday can I ring you to wish you a happy birthday? Will you have your mobile?"

Val smiled. "Of course you can, Paul, I'd love you to." They took the drinks over to where Michelle was sat and by now Jim had finished reading the answers out. Michelle looked bewildered.

"I don't believe this, guys," Michelle said.

"What?" asked Paul.

"We haven't got a single question wrong!"

Paul sat down, "Bollocks! Pull the other one."

"No, it's true, I tell you!"

"It is impossible to win this quiz," said Val, "and I sleep with the man who sets and asks the questions."

"Which means," Jim announced, "winning the jackpot of £525 and the tenner, is Val, Michelle and Paul!"

"YESSSSSSSSSSSSSSSS!" screamed Michelle.

"Finally, we've won!" shouted Val. Paul sat there with a daft grin on his face, shaking his head in disbelief, as the two girls hugged each other. Seeing Paul still sat down both girls hugged him.

"Cheers, Paul, thank you, thank you, we love you!" Michelle screamed in his face. Val sneaked a hug and a kiss on the cheek.

"Couldn't have won it without you," she whispered in his ear and smiled.

"Thanks, Val," he whispered back.

"Five hundred and twenty five pounds, I make that one hundred and seventy five pounds each," Michelle said, then winked at Paul after her previous outburst of leaving him out, to which he gave her a thumbs up.

"There's the tenner as well," said Val.

"I've got plans for that," Michelle said, which left Paul and Val wondering what it could be. After a while Nigel came over with the money for them.

"I've only got the extra tenner in pound coins, sorry," he told them.

"No bother, pet, give us them here," said Michelle and she walked off. Paul and Val looked confused.

"What's she doing?" Val asked. Paul smiled as it dawned on him what she was doing.

"Fruit machine," he said, and by the time they had got there it was clunk-clunking out some winnings.

"There's an extra £20 each," Michelle said, and Val laughed shaking her head.

"Cheers, Michelle, nice one, but you can have no more of our cash after this," said Paul.

"Spoilsport," Michelle smiled back.

"I'd love to drive you home but I appear to have celebrated our win a bit too much," Val said later in the evening, clutching a bottle of wine. The table in front of them was full of bottles and pint glasses.

Michelle had already left the pub and she had gone with Nigel to Liberty's for "some action".

"No problem," said Paul. Jim came over to join them at their table.

"Taxi's on the way, Val," he said.

"Right, I'll just nip to the bathroom." Paul was left with Jim.

"I'll apologise now for being a knob, if you want," Jim said. Paul shook his head.

"Don't, you were about on the money, my behaviour when we went out was shocking and I've no excuse or explanation for it. Hopefully I've made up for it tonight as far as the girls are concerned." Jim smiled and Paul downed his pint.

"Say goodnight to Val for me, Jim, and unless any different I'll meet her in the Red Lion at eight on Friday."

"Okay, Paul."

---

# 2010

I was toying with the idea of making my second novel a historical one and was thinking about what era I could set it in; second world war, Roman times, ice age. Inspiration wasn't coming easily so I put the pen I was scribbling with onto the desk, shook my head and muttered, "I don't know." Then my mobile rang again and it was Val's name on the display. This made me smile as I answered.

"Hello, Mrs Endean," I greeted her, which was met with a disappointed sigh, suggesting all was not well.

"I can't believe you put in about us winning the quiz, what relevance does that bloody have?" she asked.

"Have you read what happened next?"

"Not yet, no."

"Can you remember what happened next?" I asked, and there was the sound of what I imagine was Val thinking, dredging up her past.

"No, I really can't." The rest of this book is going to be a shock for her.

"Well, carry on and by Christ, you are reading this quick, are you taking all this in?"

"Oh, yes, the memories are all flooding back."

"Good memories or bad memories?" It was worth asking and she paused to gather her thoughts.

"Bit of both, but mostly good, I think." I swear I could tell she was smiling on the other end of the phone but thought she might not be when she next called.

## CHAPTER TWENTY-TWO

IT WAS THURSDAY and Paul was at home after work looking at the TV guide in disbelief as there was nothing on that he would want to watch when the phone rang.

"Hello?"

"Hi, Paul, it's me, change of plan for tomorrow."

"You can't make it?" he asked, somewhat in hope he found, which surprised him, possibly based on recent disasters.

"No, I can, no problem, but we'll have a third person with us."

Paul was filled with horror, "Jim?"

"No, he's still working."

"Michelle?"

"No, still in the north east."

Paul was stumped, "Big Doug?"

Val laughed, "I wish! No, it's Molly."

"Oh. And Molly is?"

"Ken's wife," Val confirmed.

"Ah, right. And Ken is?"

"Jim's mate, he gave you a lift home on Christmas Eve." They both paused at the significance of that date for them.

"Of course, boring Ken. Isn't Molly about twelve?" Paul asked.

Val laughed, "Paul! She's not that young,"

"Will she get served in any of the pubs? Do they have enough lemonade in?"

"Paul! Stop it! I feel bad about this, the only time we went out she threw up everywhere and she kept crying."

"Sounds fun, why have we not been out with her before?"

"That was one hell of a hen night."

"You two were on the same hen night?" Paul asked.

"Her hen night!"

"Oh, God!"

"It was Jim's idea that she joined us tomorrow," Val added. It all seemed to make sense now to Paul. Perhaps Jim was onto them and this was his idea of a joke. Or perhaps he no longer trusted Paul with

Val. "Ken's working tomorrow night, as well."

"Well, if we have to have her with us, we have to, I'll see you tomorrow."

## CHAPTER TWENTY-THREE

PAUL MADE HIS WAY TO THE RED LION for eight on Friday. He was not nervous or worried about the night ahead, even with the presence of the unknown Molly. He felt that perhaps with Jim and Val now engaged that his relationship with Val would now calm down and their friendship could continue on an even keel. Val was already there, perched on a bar stool.

"Hello, Val, happy early birthday," he said and gave her a kiss on the cheek and a big hug. Val smiled.

"Thanks."

"I got you a little something," from behind his back Paul produced, "the world's biggest Easter egg!"

"Thanks, I'll dump this in Jim's car at the Prince of Wales." Paul ordered a bottle of Bud from a passing barman instead of a pint, thinking he best keep his wits about him as best he can.

"Looking forward to your trip?"

"Yes! I really am, never been to Paris before, lots planned for when we get there. Oh, Molly is here," Val gave a wave and Molly approached. On hearing a 19 year old was joining them Paul let his imagination get the better of him as to what she might look like. What arrived was a small, skinny girl with straight black hair and no make up.

"Molly, hi, this is Paul," said Val.

"Hi, Molly, pleased to meet you, can I get you a drink?" offered Paul in a friendly manner.

Molly paused for a moment. "Val led me to believe you were a good looking man," she said.

"Nice," said Paul, raising his eyebrows. Val put her hand to her forehead and rolled her eyes in despair.

"No! What I meant was George Clooney or Brad Pitt attractive, not..." Molly waved her arm up and down in front of Paul and it was apparent she did not think him attractive, "...you type attractive," she concluded with no conviction. "Pint of cider, I'll have."

"Cider! Oh, Jesus," said Paul.

As the barman poured the drink he patted Paul's shoulder. "Good luck, lad," he said. When Molly got her pint she tapped it on the top of Paul's bottle leading to beer going everywhere, as Paul desperately tried to put his mouth over the end. Molly giggled and shouted a "WOOOHH!" to show she was partying. After drinking all the beer he could Paul whispered, "I hate that," to Val and she shook her head.

It was a dreadful night and to his shame Paul took every excuse to leave Molly to Val. They stayed in the Prince of Wales for several hours and for most of it Paul was in the company of Stuart, Jim and even Big Doug.

"I'm glad Molly's married to Ken, Jim," Paul said.

Jim looked puzzled. "Why?" he asked.

"It stops you trying to fix me up with another loony tune!" Jim laughed and then said.

"Oh, God, she's coming!" Molly was indeed careering towards the DJ stand.

"Hey, Jimmy! How's it hanging?" she yelled, throwing herself at him and almost knocking him off his feet.

"Fine, thanks, Moll."

"Here, how old are you?"

"Old enough."

"Too bloody old if you ask me. Anyway, come on Paul, you ugly get, we're all off to Liberty's – woo-ooh!"

"Jim, trade lives with me, immediately!" said Paul. Jim smiled, shook his head and free of the clutches of Molly he picked up his microphone.

"That was the Red Hot Chilli Peppers," he announced. Paul tried to avoid following Molly but seeing Val at the door waiting he thought he owed it to her and headed that way. Once in Liberty's, the first time Paul had been in for some five or so years, Molly draped herself over the first bouncer she saw.

"Hiya, gorgeous, you having a good night?" she shouted at him, then planted a big kiss on his lips

"Just going to check our coats, Molly," Val said in her ear, above the din of drum and bass. Getting no reply, as Molly was kissing the bouncer, she grabbed Paul's arm.

"Now's our chance, let's get out of here!"

"What?! I've just paid twelve pounds to get us all in," Paul protested.

"Small price to pay to dump psycho bitch from hell," Val said, "come on, back to the Prince of Wales." Once back there they got a drink, found a quiet corner away from the majority of drinkers and dancers in the back bar, sat at a table and both sighed. Then they laughed.

"Happy birthday, Val," said Paul clinking her glass, then leaning forward gave her a kiss on the cheek and winked. Val smiled.

"My God, she was a pain!" Paul added and then Val's face dropped.

"Oh, God, she's found us, she's back in here!" Molly made her way over to the table and sat down facing them.

"Have I done something wrong?" she asked, and then began crying, big, heartbroken sobs. People on other tables were looking over and Paul had his head in his hands, shaking his head. Val tried to think quickly.

"I had to leave you, Molly, Paul here was plotting to steal you from Ken," she said.

"What?" Molly asked damply between sobs.

"What?" Paul asked in disbelief, suddenly sat up straight.

"I knew it!" Molly said in triumph, suddenly stopping her tears. Val saw a window of opportunity to carry on in a similar vein.

"He also once tried to steal me from Jim!" Val smiled in a bizarre sense of sisterhood and Paul gave her a look which said, 'what the fuck are you doing?!'

"Is that why you two have been acting so weird towards each other since Christmas?" Val and Paul found a sudden common bond to glare at Molly in confusion.

"You've only met me tonight, how do you know how I have, or haven't, been acting since Christmas?" Paul asked.

"Ken told me," Molly confirmed.

"And how does he know?" Paul asked, although more to Val than Molly.

"Jim told him that before Christmas you two were really chatty and friendly with each other but now when you meet up you tend to whisper a lot away from other people and look glum."

If Jim had said that to Ken then perhaps he had an idea that something was, or had been, going on.

"What's up with you, Paul?" Val began, picking the sisterhood baton up once more. "Why can you not get a girlfriend of your own?"

"Yeah, you big fat ugly hairy-arsed poof!" Molly spat, leaving Paul to wonder how she knew he had a hairy arse.

"Poof!" Val added, shouting it right in his face.

"What the fuck are you doing, Val?" he now asked quietly, almost pleading.

"What's the matter, hit a nerve have I, gay-boy!" Val wore a mad grin to suggest that she was actually enjoying this. Paul looked distraught.

"Give him hell, Val, only bloody language they understand, the bast-urh, oh, no, NO!" Molly threw up, luckily onto the floor on the other side of the table.

"Lovely," said Paul, lifting his feet and looking under the table to make sure she had missed them, "bloody lovely." There was cheering from other people sat and stood nearby as Molly continued. Paul gave an ironic little smile and Val finally pulled herself together and woke up to the fact she had gone too far.

"Paul, look, I'm sorry, it's been a crappy night," she began, and was going to tell Paul she was sorry for the things she had just said until Paul stopped her in her tracks

"I'm telling Jim, Val," Paul said suddenly. "He deserves to know and the longer these things carry on the more it is doing my head in and making you act like this."

"Paul, wait," Val continued with alarm as Paul had appeared not to realise what she meant, "I was about to say I was sorry that I went too far tonight and it was my fault as I allowed Molly to get to me."

"Fine, if that's what you want me to think, but I don't believe you and I'm still telling him,"

At which point he stood up, stepped over the prone and still puking Molly and headed for the exit. Val put her head in her hands and wondered how her life could end up like this. Upsetting a man she was in love with and loved as a friend while a stupid 'child' threw up next to her.

Paul hardly slept and felt rough at the pre-match pint with Dan. With the usual hubbub of football talk and drinking in the background he filled him in on the latest.

"And then I said I'm going to tell Jim, and stormed out," he concluded.

"Blimey, that school dinner lady can give it out as she sees fit," said Dan. "What are you going to do? Are you going to tell Jim?"

"God, no!" Paul said. Dan let the information sink in.

"I said back at Christmas I didn't think she loved you."

"Bloody hell, yeah, you did," Paul recalled.

"You've just called her bluff. Every time something happens like this she pushes you away. She's slept with you twice, kissed you God only knows how many times but every time a chance comes up to take it further she pulls back, seems offended." The penny finally dropped with Paul.

"You're right, Dan, you're bloody right,"

Dan took a drink of his pint, "Don't reveal you've figured this out just yet, I think it will peter out soon, anyway. Before you know it you'll never hear from her ever again."

"Right," said Paul. "Good call."

Paul wasn't sure that never hearing from Val again was something he wanted. Was it fate that brought her to him and by going against this was he turning down the only chance of true love he was ever likely to get?

---

# 2010

It was Tuesday morning and Val had not rung back since reading the bit about the quiz. I was not going to ring her but instead I was going to leave her to read on. I was curious to know what she was thinking.

At the time I had no indication that this was effectively the end of our close friendship. If I could have my time again I would have tried to laugh off what happened. If I had my time again perhaps I would have told her to have gone for it at Christmas. If that happened I might not have met and gone out with Fiona, we would not have married each other and had Sean. Or perhaps Val and I could have gone out for a short while and it turned out to be a complete disaster and then my life would have gone back on track as it turned out.

I had written the book and how Val told me she loved me near enough exactly how it happened. Since I wrote it and sent it for publication I often looked back on what happened and allowed myself a smile. There were things I recall that I often think of more objectively.

## 1994

Val and I were sat in my mum and dad's kitchen and we were both ashen faced mulling over what had happened in the week before. She had told me she had fallen in love with me, I had opened my heart to my mates at the football about it, Val and I had then had a heart to heart in a pub but it was still not resolved.

"One thing puzzles me, Val," I began. "No one else has ever told me they had fallen in love with me. You are seeing a great bloke and you are an attractive woman. You didn't need to fall in love with me but you have."

Val forced a smile, "I know, sad, isn't it?" which we both managed to laugh at. "Surely someone must have felt like this about you, freckle, you're a lovely lad."

I shook my head, "No, no they hadn't."

Val shrugged and took the information on board, "How sad that the only woman who thinks this way about you is going out with your mate."

## 1986

I was thirteen years old and it was New Year's Eve. At that age I was too old for a babysitter but too young to be left on my own at home until the early hours so my mum and dad put their heads together and had an idea.

"We're going to the pub on New Year's Eve with your uncle," Mum reminded me, "both your brothers will be at the disco in the back room, you can go along with them as long as you sit in the corner."

"And bloody behave yourself," Dad helpfully added.

So I was in the back room disco and did indeed 'bloody behave' myself, I drank coke all night and only spoke when I was spoken to. The back room of the pub was like an overgrown youth club/school disco; some of the people in there were only a school year older than me. It was an advantage to living in a village in the middle of nowhere, miles from the nearest passing police car.

One of the fourteen / fifteen year olds in there was our Neil's mate, Taggy, and he was getting completely smashed on Holsten Pils.

While this was going on, his girlfriend Karen must have been bored. She made her way over to where I was sat in the corner and sat on my knee. She was fifteen and while I knew who she was I had never spoken to her before. Somehow I must have made an impression.

"You're Steve and Neil's brother Liam, aren't you?" she asked me from her new vantage point. I nodded to confirm this, "aren't you cute?" she kissed me on the cheek, "Happy New Year!" All I could do was laugh shyly. She stayed there for most of the rest of the night other than to pacify Taggy who kept coming over every half hour or so to shout, "What's my bird doing sat on your knee?"

When it got to midnight people mingled to shake hands and swap kisses to welcome in the New Year. Both my brothers passed by to shake hands with me and their respective girlfriends gave me big kisses on the lips as they passed and also commented that I was cute. Karen had disappeared, possibly to see Taggy, and when she came back to sit on my knee – she had a very bony bum, I recall – she kissed my cheek again.

"How about a kiss on the lips for a change?" I suggested and she smiled.

"Okay," we snogged, my first ever, for about ten seconds and I caught sight of Steve and his girlfriend smiling like lunatics at me from across the table. We snogged some more and I enjoyed it and from the bony bum movements I think Karen was enjoying it too, it was great, until I heard...

"I'M GOING TO FUCKING KILL YOU!"

Taggy had rumbled us. As he tipped over tables sending drinks in all directions I was moved out of his way and through a side door into the back of the pub. I made my way upstairs for safety and following a dim light found myself in the front room of the pub's accommodation catching the landlord's wife and the head cook shagging. They caught sight of me, gasped and stopped. I was stuck for something to say to them and there was a very awkward silence.

"Happy New Year," I finally said.

# 1991

I was at my mate Richie's place watching Rangers play in the European Cup when Richie brought me a beer from the kitchen and bizarrely did not think to offer Andrea, his girlfriend, a drink of any kind when he did this.

"C'mon the Rangers tonight, Liam, eh?" Richie said in a matey manner.

"Nah," Richie looked shock.

"Why?"

"Well they're Scottish for a start."

"British, man, British, you can't be cheering for the frogs tonight, please," he insisted.

"And I'm called Liam Kirk, I cannot support Rangers, can I?" highlighting my Irish Catholic heritage contrasting with the Protestant support Rangers enjoy. This seemed to upset Richie and he went quiet but Andrea stifled a laugh. The game was exciting and Rangers came back from two goals down to equalise at two each. When their second goal went in Richie jumped up from his chair and ruffled my hair.

"Fuck off, Liam!" he yelled causing Andrea to go into a low orbit.

"For God's sake, Richie, he has been sat there barely saying a word all night, just watching the game, you don't even support Rangers, what's your problem?" at this Richie threw his can towards Andrea which hit her on the shoulder covering her in lager.

"And you can fuck off and live somewhere else if that's how you are going to talk to me," he shouted at her before storming from the flat. I headed to follow him but when I reached the bathroom door I went in there, grabbed a hand towel and brought it into the lounge to give to Andrea to dry herself.

"Here you are, I'm sorry," I offered and she took the towel between sobs.

"Thanks, s'not your fault,"

I shook my head and looked in the direction Richie had just left, "What a tit!" I spat as Andrea dabbed her lager stained jumper and smiled.

"Sometimes I wish he was half as nice as you, Liam," she told me. I turned to face her and say thanks but before I spoke something made me stop. It was a look on Andrea's face that I couldn't read but the only thing I could do was kiss her, slowly at first, then quickly, passionately. When we stopped we looked at each other to suggest we should have been doing this all the time and then at the same time we both came to our senses.

"Think I best go, Andrea," I said getting up from the chair and putting my coat on.

"Yeah, right, I'll, er, I'll see you, okay?"

"Yeah, night, then," and I left the flat bloody quickly. Earlier in the evening we had all been discussing me moving in with them into their spare room but a few days later I took a phone call at work.

"Liam, it's Richie," it was the first time we had spoken since he stormed out of the flat.

"Now then..."

"Look, sorry about this, but me and Andrea have been talking and we don't think you moving in will be a good idea. Sorry, lad."

I didn't hear from him for another few months and when I did he seemed happy but did tell me very early in the conversation that he had finished with Andrea. I never saw Andrea again.

# CHAPTER TWENTY-FOUR

IT WAS SUNDAY LUNCHTIME And Paul, with a combination of no sleep, what seemed like a million pints and the hangover from hell, avoided Dan's advice and made good his promise to call Val on her birthday. It was only a few days previously, but after what had happened and been said on Friday night, that promise seemed now as if it had been made in a simpler, happier time. He pressed call next to Val's number in his phone and waited as it rang.

"Hello?"

"Happy birthday to you, happy birthday to you," he began to sing in a drunken growl.

"Paul, stop! Enough is enough. If anyone is telling Jim it is me that will have to do it. I've brought this shit on myself and I'm telling him this evening."

"Oh, smart move, Valerie, and then what happens?" he asked. "Hello? Val? Are you there? And then what?" She had either hung up or lost her signal so Paul rang again but the call went to voice mail.

*Shit a bloody brick!*

---

## 2010

It was the following Tuesday afternoon and I got a text from Val;

REMEMBER THAT ARGUMENT WHEN I RANG YOU FROM MY FOLKS PLACE IN LEEDS AND SAID I WAS GOING TO TELL IAN?!

I thought the exclamation marks gave the message a humorous feel that did not reflect how it was at the time, but it was fifteen years ago, we are all a lot older, so I sent in reply;

MY MUM WAS IN THE KITCHEN WHILE WE ARGUED!!

And I felt happy enough to do the same. I hoped this was us getting close to being as friendly again as we once were.

# CHAPTER TWENTY-FIVE

O**N MONDAY EVENING** Paul went into the Prince of Wales at half eight but did not know why. Did he imagine all would be right with the world again, if it had ever been? Had Val told Jim all about what had happened? On the walk there he felt the adrenaline building up inside him, excitement and nerves.

*What am I doing? What am I thinking?*

When he got to the Prince of Wales no music was playing and no one was in, no bar staff, no customers. This felt eerie; had he dreamt it all? Just then Stuart appeared behind the bar,

"Hi, Paul," and then Nigel walked past with a poster.

"Now then, Paul, you okay? How's my money?"

"Evening, lads, I've spent it. No quiz tonight?"

"No," Stuart confirmed.

"Oh, right, is that because Jim is in Paris?" Stuart and Nigel gave each other a knowing look.

"No," Nigel began to explain, "last week, when you won the jackpot, there were only three teams taking part. As the same teams kept winning no one was interested any more."

"I see," Paul stood there figuring that no more quiz meant that he had no outlet to meet up with Val anymore. For a moment he figured this was the answer to all his problems and as Dan had mentioned this would mean he would never see her again but such was his state of mind he did wonder if she was in on all this.

"From next week, on Mondays we'll be doing something a bit different," Stuart said and nodded at Nigel who was putting up the poster.

"Karaoke!" Nigel said proudly. "You pay a pound, sing a song, enter as many times as you like, then everyone in the pub votes for the best singer. Then the winner, or winners, take the pot."

"How's your singing voice, Paul?" Stuart asked.

"Oh, beautiful, Stuart, beautiful."

He left the pub in some confusion immediately and on the way home a wicked thought entered his head as he looked back over the last six months with Val and considered the Prince of Wales's new entertainment. He was still grinning about it when he reached home and the phone was ringing.

"Hello?"

The caller did not speak at first but Paul heard a sniff and knew someone was there.

"Hello? Who is this?" he asked quietly.

"Paul, it's Cheryl. Dad's had a massive heart attack while we were out this afternoon and has died!"

Paul sunk to the floor, "Oh, God, oh good God, no." There was more sobbing at the other end of the line.

"Can you come down and help us out?" Cheryl asked.

Paul fought to pull himself together, "No worries, Cheryl, I'll get a bag packed and be down as soon as I can."

"Thanks, little bro', it will be appreciated."

"No problem, I'll get there as quick as I can. Take care, Cheryl, see you soon."

*Just when I have enough on my plate this happens.*

A week later and Paul was stood, alone, in his sister Cheryl's front room, among a small band of mourners. They had just returned from the crematorium where a vicar who did not know their Dad talked about him like they were old pals. His sister Joanne kept looking at him as she sat crying in an armchair and Paul could not figure out if this was due to concern for him or blaming Paul for what had happened. His other sister Cheryl came up, putting aside her own grief and gave Paul a hug. She knew what he had been through with their Dad until he had moved down there.

"You okay, little bro'?" she asked, to which Paul managed a nod. "Joanne and I have a favour to ask you. Can you take Dad's ashes and scatter them somewhere scenic back home?"

"Yeah, sure, no problem."

"David's got the car ready and will run you home whenever you want." Paul looked at his watch.

"Can he take me now? I know it's sudden but," he shrugged as explaining why he felt he had to go right this minute now, having just had the suggestion put to him, would just confuse matters.

"No, don't worry, I'll go and tell him." Cheryl departed to ask David to get ready and Paul figured that he had just enough time.

On the journey north conversation was limited, but Cheryl had marked David's card about Paul's state of mind and so David asked him occasionally, "Sure you're all right, Paul?" and he nodded to say he was, despite the box with his Dad's remains in them being between his feet. "Cheryl said that you haven't been ringing your Dad so much in the last two months, is that bothering you now?" David asked.

Paul shrugged. "Not really, I've been busy and did not have the time. Also, thanks to yours and Tony's little pep talk six years ago I had enough time in his company, thanks very much." He glared at David as he finished saying this and this led David to feel guilty. If Paul was having troubles in his life now, could it all be traced back to Tony and he talking him into staying with his Dad after his Mum had died?

"You won't feel ill of me if I make a call on me mobile, would you, David?" Paul asked part way into the journey.

"No, go ahead." Paul dialled a number and David listened to Paul's side of the call.

"Hi, Simon, it's Paul."

"Hi, mate, sorry about your Dad, read it in the paper."

"Right, cheers, that's kind of you, mate."

"When are you having the funeral?"

"It was today in Warwickshire, I'm just heading home. Do you fancy meeting for a pint at the Prince of Wales tonight?"

"Sure, is it still a quiz there on Mondays?"

"No, not anymore, they're doing a karaoke!"

"Karaoke?"

"Yeah, should be a grin."

"Will that mad Geordie bird be there?" Simon asked concerned.

"I don't know if Michelle will be there, no. I'm not in contact with her and her mate now."

"Oh, really? Right. Okay, Paul, I'll go."

"Nice one, good lad, I'll see you then." As he turned the phone off David weighed him up for a second.

"Grief's a funny business, Paul," he said.

"Isn't it just? Listen can you drop me in town after I've quickly put me bag-" he tapped the box on the floor, "-and Dad of course, in the house?"

"Sure," he paused for a moment and then asked, "is there any reason you didn't have your Dad's funeral in the north-west?"

Paul shrugged, "We were his only close remaining family, most of his old workmates have already died and he didn't talk to the neighbours after mum passed away, so it just seemed a bit of a waste of time."

"Fair enough, Cheryl never really gave me a clue. Sometimes those closest to you don't really know you."

Paul allowed himself a hollow laugh, "Wise words, Dave."

---

# 2010

"Claudius," I typed, "made his way to the forum." Then I stopped as it was bollocks...

I was just thinking what I could base my next book on when my mobile rang and it was Val.

"Hiya," I greeted her and there was a pause.

"Have your parents died?" she finally asked solemnly.

"My Dad did in 2002, heart attack," I explained by way of an update. Then there was another pause.

"I'm sorry. How's your mum?"

*This could be tricky, what could I say.*

"Bet she's proud you have this book published, she was a lovely woman to me when I used to pop round to see you."

*My Mum is ravaged by Alzheimer's.*

"On her good days I like to think she is, yes." I didn't see fit to tell her too much more and if nothing else it showed it was a bloody long time since we had last seen each other; people getting married, people being born, people dying, people getting ill. So many things happen when you don't see each other for years.

# CHAPTER TWENTY-SIX

## Just a Bit of Fun

SHORTLY AFTER EIGHT O' CLOCK that evening – "Welcome, ladies and gentleman," Jim announced, "to something a little bit different, the Prince of Wales' first karaoke night!"

"Woo-ooh!" the drinkers, who numbered about thirty or so, greeted this announcement.

"I've left pens and paper around the pub, I've got the latest music programme on the laptop, so tell me your favourite song, pay a pound and if you get voted the best we'll give you the contents of the pot!"

"Woo-ooh!"

A muscular, tattooed arm held out a piece of paper towards the DJ stand.

"Is this the first song?" Jim asked, expectantly and then unfolded the paper. "Big Doug, you cannot sing 'Albatross' by Fleetwood Mac, it's an instrumental!"

"Oh, bollocks, go on, let me!"

"Jim!" Michelle squealed, dragging Val by the arm, "we'll sing for you!" and handed over a piece of paper. At this moment Paul entered the pub at the far end of the bar, still dressed in a black suit, white shirt and black tie. He allowed himself a smile at the girls getting ready to sing and while he was waiting he was approached by Stuart.

"Hi, Paul, don't tell me, Blues Brothers! I'm right, aren't I, eh? Eh?"

"No, my Dad's funeral, actually." Paul corrected him.

"Oh, shit, sorry." Stuart suddenly looked ill.

"Don't worry, you weren't to know. Double scotch, please." Paul looked at the dance floor area next to the DJ stand to see Michelle and Val ploughing their way through 'Waterloo' by Abba. Simon came over having spotted Paul at the bar.

"Here, Paul," said Stuart handing him a glass, "it's a treble, on me."

"Sorry again about your Dad, Paul," said Simon, patting him on the back.

"Thanks, mate."

"It said 'died suddenly' in the paper, what happened?"

"Heart attack."

"Really?"

Paul nodded, "Ironic after losing all that weight, he must have been living the high life too much in the last few months."

"Are you having a go at this tonight?" Simon asked nodding towards the dance floor where Val was still singing with Michelle. A thought struck Paul to say, 'already have done and look where it's got me' but instead he downed his scotch, picked up a pen and paper and wearing a big grin started writing.

"I think I will, it should be fun," he said. As he finished writing Val and Michelle had finished their song to warm applause, wolf whistles and cheers.

"Never easy going first," Jim said into the microphone, "so well done girls." Val was smiling as she had enjoyed it more than she thought she would but it faded when she saw Paul. As she left the dance floor and Jim was asking for anyone else to have a go, Val grabbed Michelle's arm.

"Paul's in," she said.

"Really?" said Michelle in reply. "Oh, hell, good job you never told Jim after all. Do you think he'll say owt to Jim tonight? Do you think that is why he is here?"

"I don't know, but I hope not," Val continued to look his way. "He's a bit over dressed for in here. I wonder why he's got a suit on?"

"Job interview perhaps?" Michelle suggested.

"Yes, I suppose it could be," said Val.

Paul had finished his drink and what he was writing, "Simon, hand this in for me, will you? I'll get you a drink for going," said Paul, handing Simon the piece of paper.

"Yeah, no problem," Simon replied and innocently headed for the DJ stand. Jim took the piece of paper and Simon retreated quickly in case anyone thought it was him who would be singing next.

"Right, we have our next song," Jim announced, "can they top the girl's effort?" Jim opened the piece of paper and looked puzzled but then laughed as he typed into the computer. "Well, it is April, it was Easter last week and it's raining, but to sing 'Last Christmas' by

Wham! is our quiz legend Paul!" This announcement was met by a mixture of cheers, laughter and abuse.

"Oh, shit!" said Val, as Paul dashed to the dance floor, waved to the other drinkers and grabbed the microphone from Jim.

"James! Nice trip the other week?" he asked.

"Yes, yes thanks, Paul, it was great," he looked at Paul's suit, "bit over smart for a Monday night, aren't you?"

"Yeah, I know," Paul agreed with a shrug but said no more as the opening bars of the song began. Most of those gathered were giggling as Paul began to sway and wave his arms in time to the music wearing a daft grin.

"Last Christmas," Paul sang out of key, "I slept with your tart," much laughter "but on her birthday, she said I was gay," more laughter and cheers except from Val who put her head in her hands.

"Hey, he's good, isn't he?" said Michelle, much to Val's horror and disbelief.

Paul completed the rest of the song with the correct lyrics after the start and left the dance floor to cheers and applause but mostly laughter and good natured banter. He rejoined Simon at the bar who looked bewildered.

"Good effort, Paul," he said.

"Thanks, I enjoyed it," Paul leant over the bar. "Stuart, another scotch, please, mate."

"Blimey, another scotch, is this grief?"

"Not sure, yet," Paul was scribbling again, "take this one up for us Simon and I'll get you a pint."

"Okay, then, but after your next song I really think we need to chat."

Jim, unfolding another piece of paper, read the song written down and shook his head.

"Big Doug, if you can find any lyrics in 'Stranger on the Shore' by Acker Bilk you can sing them!" Simon had reached the DJ stand, handed over the piece of paper and dashed off again.

"Where do I know him from?" Michelle asked Val as Simon retreated.

"No idea, never seen him before," she lied.

"Here we go again," Jim announced. "What's this one?" he paused to laugh and began tapping into his laptop. "He's back, our quiz and, who knows, possibly karaoke champion, it's Paul!" More cheers from the drinkers.

"Oh, Christ, no, what now?" Val asked herself. As Paul grabbed the microphone from Jim it became apparent that the next song was 'Without You'. Val shook her head and felt trapped in a nightmare. Paul made big, exaggerated piano playing actions as the music began and the singing was worse and even more off key than the last effort. Mixed in with the cheers and laughter was some booing and someone, possibly Big Doug, shouted, "You're shite!" towards the end. Michelle was swaying with the music and seemed to be enjoying it all.

"Shall we do another one?" she asked Val, who looked aghast at the suggestion.

"Seriously?"

Back at the bar after he had finished Paul ordered another scotch and Simon was trying to think what to say. "Paul, I know it was your Dad's funeral today, but I don't think this is just due to the grief what you are doing tonight. Are you ready to talk, yet?"

"Talk? No, I'm just having a laugh! Everyone thinks I am miserable and moody but I am showing them tonight, just wish I still had my antlers and santa hat to wear, eh, lads?" Paul looked at both Stuart and Simon but neither of them knew what he was getting at. Paul took a drink and looked thoughtful for a moment but then with a big daft grin said, "Here, I've thought of another one."

After he scribbled the note he passed it to Simon to take to the DJ stand and once there he decided to take action.

"It's Jim, isn't it?" he asked.

"Yeah, that's right, you're Paul's mate, aren't you?"

"Simon, yeah, I've got another one here for him."

"Great!" Jim enthused.

"No, it's not great, Jim, something's wrong,"

"I dunno, he's just having a laugh, isn't he?"

Simon handed the paper to Jim. "It was his Dad's funeral today," he told him.

"Oh, God, I didn't even know he had died. Has it hit him hard?" Jim opened the request and on reading it started looking for the next song on his laptop.

"Hard to say, he insists this behaviour tonight is nothing to do with that, but I'm not sure."

Simon returned to the bar and noticed that Paul was thankfully drinking orange juice and just hoped there was no vodka in there.

"Orange juice, Paul?" he asked, to make sure.

"Yeah, Stuart's idea," Paul explained, "and I agree, Vitamin C does you good."

There was a song finishing and Jim took the microphone to address the drinkers when their applause stopped.

"Thanks to Big Doug for finding a song with lyrics in them, finally, and I am sure even Christina Aguilera would agree that Big Doug is, indeed, beautiful, in every single way. Right! Next one, it's Paul, again"

"NO!" shouted the drinkers.

"No!" whimpered Val. Paul was there like a shot, grabbing the microphone,

"Thank you, thank you," he said, as the opening bars of Meat Loaf's 'Two Out of Three Ain't Bad' began.

"Baby we can talk all night," he growled, then raised both his arms to the drinkers,

"BUT THAT AIN'T GETTING US NO-WHERE!" the drinkers shouted. The song continued with no mishap, apart from extra emphasis on the 'she kept on telling me' part for which Paul drifted towards where Val was sat but did not look her way. When he finished singing the booing had been replaced by some respectful applause. Before going back to the bar he wrote another song on a piece of paper and handed it to Jim. Once back at the bar Paul took a drink of his orange juice and as he was sweating he removed his tie to mop his brow.

"Paul," Simon began, "I'm here if you do need to talk, about your Dad, or anything else that's clearly bothering you." Paul shook his head.

"Nothing bothering me, I'm just having a grin, Si'," he said.

"Right, okay, as long as that is all." As they stood there letting the events of the evening sink in Simon suddenly straightened up. "Aye, aye, here we go. Hello, Val!" he said. Paul spun around.

"Valerie!" he exclaimed. "My God, you're looking as gorgeous as ever! How was your trip? Did you have a nice birthday?" Paul opened his arms wide to hug Val but it was clear this would not be returned as Val glared at him with her arms folded. Val hesitated before replying and looked sad.

"Paul, what are you doing? What is this all about?"

"I'm trying to enjoy myself and make people happy," he replied, and leant forward to whisper in her ear, "you saw how successful I was doing that at Christmas," Paul smiled but Val looked shocked. "I should have done this years ago!"

At this moment Jim appeared with a piece of paper in his hands. "Paul, oh, hi, Val. Paul, I've scanned my programme but I cannot find 'It Started With a Kiss' on there'," behind the bar Stuart dropped a glass.

"Oh, good God," Val whispered, turning away from Jim and looking like she might royally throw up.

"Do you want to choose another one?" Jim asked.

Paul smiled broadly. "Sure!" as he walked off after Jim towards the DJ stand he patted Val on the bum and smiled. "Back soon," he whispered. Simon weighed up the situation for a moment.

"Has something happened between you two?" he asked.

Val looked at him with her eyelids getting tired and heavy. "You've figured it out then?"

Simon took a drink. "At first I thought the only reason he was acting like this tonight was because it was his Dad's funeral today, but now I don't know, it could be down to you as well."

Val looked stunned and gasped. "His Dad died?" she asked.

Simon nodded. "Last Monday afternoon it happened, he had a heart attack. Did you not know?"

Val shook her head and looked at the dance floor at Paul, with his suit on, daft grin, microphone in hand and ready to start another song.

"The poor bastard," she said, with a sad look on her face. "What must he be going through? He must feel like the loneliest man on earth."

"So what has happened with you two then?" Simon asked with a smile. "You did seem to be spending an awful lot of time together."

Val sighed, "I'd rather not say, Simon."

"Right, people, brace yourself, he's back!" Jim announced, to which a cheer went up. "We didn't have his first choice of song,"

"Thank Christ for that!" shouted Big Doug.

"But here to sing 'Valerie' by Amy Winehouse, it's Paul!"

"Oh my good God, no," said Val, "not this."

"Oh, blimey," said Simon, stifling a laugh.

"The poor sod, no matter what he's having next, sod the orange juice, I'm going to have a scotch," said Stuart. The three of them stared towards the dance floor and waited with some apprehension as to what was coming next. Part of the way into the song it go too much for Val, possibly the mention of the 'I miss your ginger hair' line, and she stormed out of the pub.

"Oh, night, Val," said Simon in confusion to the retreating figure. "Thanks for dropping in."

Paul had spotted her but Jim had not, so Paul passed the microphone to him.

"Back in a mo', Jim," he said, and dashed after her. "Valerie! VALERIE!" he called, still following the lyrics.

Once outside, "Val! Hold on," the rain was lashing down in the car park as Val headed towards her car, "Val! We need to talk, please come back, did you tell Jim anything?"

"Paul, go back in the pub, or go home, one of the two, either way just leave me alone! You're in no state to talk," Val shouted back.

"No, I can't, I need answers, VALERIE! What am I to you?" He had caught up with her, grabbed her shoulder and spun her around. "Val!"

"No, don't hit me, Paul!" Val screamed.

"Do us a favour, Val, whatever I am or whatever I might be I'm certainly not that sort of person, and you know it!"

Val composed herself. "I know you aren't Paul," she said. The rain was hammering down and they were getting soaked.

"What was I to you? A bit on the side? A bit of fun? Did you love me? Do you love me? Was that all bollocks? What was I to you, Val?" Val began to cry but as the rain was lashing down it did not matter.

"Paul, you weren't anything to me," she wailed between the sobs.

"I wasn't anything to you? What's that meant to mean? Something only people who have been to uni-bloody-versity would grasp?"

Val wiped her eyes and then folded her arms but did not answer.

"Is this where you say 'it's not me, it's you', I mean, 'it's not you, it's me' and I'm meant to feel a whole lot bloody better and you still come out of it all as the good guy, Val?"

She shook her head, "Paul, it's nothing like that," she replied.

"Then what was I, Val? The last six months don't make any sense."

"I know, it must be confusing for you," Val paused, "but when I say you were not anything to me it isn't a bad thing."

Fed up of the rain Val headed to her car and got in, then opened the passenger door, so Paul got in.

"Where are we going?" he asked her, as he closed the door.

"Nowhere, in more ways than one!" Val replied. "It's drier in here and I don't want to go back into the pub," she wiped the tears and rain from her face, "not just yet."

"Val? You said I wasn't anything to you, please explain what it all means."

"The thing is, Paul, I'd been with two men in England since I came over, Colin and Jim. Colin is a lot older than me, as is Jim, obviously. You came along and you're my age. We have a laugh and you're a lovely guy. I was happy to be your friend. Still am. I told you I had no maternal instinct but there almost was when I saw how crushed you were when Michelle rejected you. Before I knew it this had turned into love, I was in love with you and I could not help it." She paused and Paul could not think what to say in reply so there was silence.

"As well as loving you I got a glimpse of what my life could have been like on Christmas Eve," Val continued, "the silly hats, the antics, the daft jokes and dancing. I decided to grab the bull by the horns and tell you how I felt without really thinking about what I was doing. I knew I loved you before that night but it confirmed for me that I had fallen in love with you. I'm with Jim and the best thing would have been to have hidden those feelings but right then, I wanted you so much. How no one would want to go out with you, Paul, I'll never know." She smiled. "I've always acted older than I am, even at UCLA my boyfriend was my forty-four year old tutor."

"Good God!"

"I know, huh? What a stupid cliché I was. If you'd have agreed to me leaving Jim then I would have. By the time you decided you wanted me too, I had already resigned myself to my lot with Jim and stayed."

"But we slept together before and after then," Paul reminded her.

"And that was the only time in my life I was the stupid, impulsive teenager."

"A thirty-two-year-old teenager?"

"Thanks, Paul, that makes me feel even more wonderful," they allowed themselves a laugh despite the gravity of what they were discussing but then Val looked serious.

"Sorry about your Dad, you should have rung me," she put her hand on his. "How are you doing, sweetheart? Do you want to talk about it?"

"I wouldn't know where to begin to talk about him. Spending these last few months with you has pushed him to the back of mind. To be fair it was a blessed relief to see the back of him after being alone with him for so many years."

Paul smiled at Val's kind words but then a thought struck him so he had to change the subject.

"Hang on a minute, were you resigned to your lot when you agreed to marry Jim?"

Val sighed. "I was. That moment in the restaurant at the bar – that was your second chance. That was your window to get me out of there. If you'd have said 'leave him and come and live with me' then I would have done."

Paul looked at the rain continuing to lash down, "Oh, Jesus, I wish I had now, I wanted to as well."

"I could tell," Val put Paul's right hand in both of hers and turned to face him. She tilted her head and looked lovingly into his eyes.

*Is this a third chance?*

They allowed themselves a smile.

"And he doesn't suspect anything about us, still?"

Val shrugged, "He suspects something about why you keep disappearing but if anything he thinks it is you falling for me not me falling for you."

"I see. Let's be fair, it would make more sense, you are gorgeous."

Val smiled again but then sighed. "There was another reason for all this, Paul. Even if I hadn't fallen for you a thought struck me that I would have done all this to bull up your confidence for one good reason."

"What's that?" he asked.

"Michelle. Oh Christ, she's not the girl for you, Paul. You're a lovely man. Never end up with someone like her, promise me, she's a nightmare,"Val's eyes were pleading with him. Paul smiled.

"Okay, but if you are staying with Jim to do that there is only one thing for it then, Val."

"What's that?" she asked.

"Get your twin sister over here, set us up!"Val laughed but she was shocked and she playfully hit him.

"She's married!"

"And?" Val playfully smacked him again and shook her head. "Being with someone never stopped you." They laughed at how ridiculous the suggestion was but then they were quiet. The rain continued to bash the car.

"I best go," Paul said. "I don't know why, or where, but go I must."

"Okay Paul."

He went to grab the door but then he stopped and turned to face Val with a confused look on his face.

"Paul? What is it?"

"No, hold on a minute, Val, this still doesn't add up," he said.

"What's that?"

"This whole 'you'd have done it because of Michelle'. That's why you did it, isn't it?"

"No, it really isn't, Paul,"

"You've messed me around to see if you really did love Jim. You hadn't fallen in love with me, had you? You've messed me up good and proper, haven't you?"

"I did love you, Paul, if anything I still do."

"Bollocks!"

"I've been here once all ready over here, haven't I? That's why I left Colin,"Val argued.

"Really?"

Val rested her head on her hands which were on the steering wheel but before she could answer back any more Paul had got out of the car and she began to cry.

"Paul, I didn't make all this up, I really did love you and I still do, think what I am going through here. Please come back, Paul!"

Paul carried on walking and got lashed by the rain again.

"What a mug," he muttered to himself as he walked away and then slapped his forehead, "what a bloody mug!"

---

# 2010

"The bit with Paul and Val in the car park," Val began.

"Yes?"

"Was that how you interpreted what I was doing when I was telling you I had fallen in love with you?"

I paused and smiled, "So you do remember saying that to me?"

Val nodded, "Of course I do. I would never deny that."

"With you being so coy and evasive afterwards whenever I mentioned it or brought it up I started looking at other options as to why you might have said it. It seemed too good to be true that such a beautiful woman would have felt like that about me."

"Would you say that all these years since it happened, since I last saw you, that you still hold a torch for me?"

"Yes, I do."

"Me too."

This conversation was not taking place over the mobile phone network but in my bath with a bottle of white wine and two glasses next to us. I put my arms around Val and kissed her neck.

"I'm so glad you rang me and came around."

"Me too," she agreed with a smile.

This time I never asked about Barry.

# CHAPTER TWENTY-SEVEN

## A MONTH LATER

VAL HAD FINISHED HER LAST CLASS of the week and dismissed her students who, when they filed out, left with a cheery, "Night, Val," while others chorused, "Have a nice weekend," to which she smiled. When the last student had left she went to tidy up her books and papers but found herself sobbing. The last month since Paul had left her crying in her car had been hell, with her and Jim deciding to split up. She blamed Jim for how she felt about Paul and that she could not have him even though she knew this was unreasonable. She had tried to ring Paul but got no reply on either mobile or landline, until one day she got a 'number not recognised' tone for the landline and on ringing directory enquiries she had been told the number had been changed and was now ex-directory. She had called around to visit as time allowed but no one ever seemed to be in.

Back in the class room Val dried her eyes and gathered her things together. She now decided that action was needed for her own good.

"Enough, now, Val," she said to herself, "come on, you've cried enough."

She left the class room and headed along the corridor, up the stairs and steadied herself as she stood outside the principal's office before knocking on the door and walking in.

"Bill, can I have a word?" she asked.

Bill Anderson, the principal, a man in his early sixties, rose slightly from his chair, as a gentleman would, then beckoned at the chair opposite.

"Of course, Valerie," Val sat down and once settled paused, composed herself and began.

"With some regret, Bill... No. Let me start again... With much regret I won't be back to teach here in September." Val stopped and bit her lip.

Bill looked shocked. "Oh?"

"I love the job but I am heading home to the States. Do you need this confirmed in writing to keep it official?"

"No need for that, I'll let the governors know. You'll be missed, Valerie. You're popular with the staff and the students."

Val smiled, "Thanks, Bill, that means a lot."

"Any particular reason you're leaving, Val? Home sickness, perhaps?" Bill asked, hoping for a chance to be able to make her want to stay.

"No, I've lived here long enough to be used to it by now, the reason I am leaving is English men," Val rose from her chair and made to leave the office, pausing to comment, "no offence, Bill."

"None taken, Valerie, I was born in Dundee."

Val smiled again as if to understand and said, for a reason she did not understand, "Good," and headed for the door.

Later on that same month Paul was putting a few books away at work when Keith approached.

"Hi, Keith."

"Paul, mate, any chance of a word in my office?" Keith asked him.

"Sure."

He put the books down, followed Keith and once took a seat. Keith sighed.

"No easy way to say this, mate," he paused and rubbed his head, looking very tired, "but head office has decided that redundancies will have to be made and you're one of them."

"Oh," said Paul, but he could not immediately think of anything else to say. Keith shrugged and shook his head, allowing Paul to soak up the news.

"You may recall this was speculated to be the next course of action in the last monthly memo..." Paul didn't read the monthly memos.

"Yes, I remember," he lied. Keith nodded and leant forward onto his desk.

"We managed to get you half your take home annual pay as redundancy," a quick sum told Paul that this would be about £6500.

"Okay," he said.

"Look, Paul, you're young enough to go to college and retrain or study. Some of the other blokes here will die in service."

"Stanley did," Paul interrupted.

"And I've apologised and apologised for that," Keith carried on. "You've been here that long that the next job upwards you could go for is mine and I ain't going anywhere!" Keith laughed. "Hang on, I had just better check that," he grabbed a sheet of paper with a list of names on it, "no, I'm safe! The cheque's here, Paul" Keith opened a draw on his desk and passed an envelope to Paul. "We'll send on your P45 and if you want to go today, now, go. I weighed up your options, you live in a house with no mortgage and you said the bills were being paid from your Dad's account, even after he died. Life's for living, Paul, go and live a bit, while you can." Paul picked up the envelope and thought things over for a moment. Right then Keith's words had made him remember his Dad for the first time in a while. He looked out of the window but the late spring sunshine coming in made him bow his head to shield his eyes.

"Cheers, Keith, it's a shock but it might be something to, you know," Paul made a pushing motion and Keith nodded. Paul got out of the chair and made to leave the office.

"Jodie still asks after you," Keith said with a wink and a cheeky grin.

"Good, good for her," said Paul and with that he left the office to get his things together and prepare to leave for the last time.

As he began to walk from the book warehouse towards town he noticed the adult college and a light came on in his head. He headed towards it and followed the signs for reception.

"Hello, can I help?" a woman asked.

"Yeah, I just wondered if there were any details on courses for this September."

"You're in luck, the new booklet is out today!" she replied, handing it to Paul.

"Great! Can I take a seat and have a read through?" he asked and the woman nodded. Paul took a seat next to the entrance to the reception and before starting to read he put his MP3 player on. Val was passing near the reception and raised a hand and smiled at the lady on reception.

"Heard you are leaving, it's so sad," the lady called.

"Thanks," Val glanced at her watch, "I'll come in and chat tomorrow, okay?" and the lady smiled back. As she left the building Paul stood up, took his ear pieces out and headed to the reception desk.

"Found something you like?" the lady asked.

At Jim's at the beginning of July, Val left the house for one last time as an International removal company's van pulled away. Jim followed her down the path and they exchanged forced smiles, still barely believing it had come to this. Val pulled at her engagement ring to try and remove it and give it back to Jim but he held up his hand.

"Keep it," he said, "something to remember me by."

Val pulled a sympathetic face and then smiled, warmly and genuinely this time. "Oh, come on, I won't need a ring to remember you by, but thanks," Val came forward and hugged him. "Take care, Jim." After she had stopped hugging him Jim took his chance to ask.

"Was it something I did? Or something I didn't do? I know it's too late but I'd love to know, that's all."

"No, it was something I did and I'm sorry." Val confirmed and Jim smiled, relieved that he could have done no more.

"Can I ask you, the little runt in the hooded top, you were buying something from him and selling it on. What was it? I had my suspicions but whatever you say I'll believe you," Val fixed Jim with a stare.

"Hooded tops," Jim replied.

"Really, is that all?"

"Yeah, I wasn't sure where he got them from so I didn't want to tell you."

With that Val smiled, walked down the path to the waiting taxi and got in.

And that will remain the official party line, thought Jim.

"Manchester Airport isn't it, love?" the taxi driver asked as Val got into the back of his cab. Val smiled wondering if this would be the last time a man from the north of England would call her "love".

"Yeah," Val confirmed and then she had an idea. "Actually, can we go via an address in town?"

"No problem, love," said the driver, "the fare's fixed, but don't be too long, you might miss your flight!" Val directed the driver to Paul's house for one last time and on the way tried to think of what she would say to him if he was in when she got there. How about he came with her? Could he come now and try to get a flight? Would she have enough time to convince him that she meant every word, that she did love him and that it wasn't some crazy plan to keep him away from Michelle as he had been somehow led to believe?

As they neared Paul's house there was a man hammering a 'For Sale' sign into the front garden and watching him were Paul and Simon. Val decided that she really did not know what to say to Paul and Simon being there would not have made it any easier. She panicked.

"Never mind," she told the driver, "airport now, please."

"Okay, love."

"Can't see why you are selling this, Paul," said Simon. Paul turned away from watching the man hammer the sign into the ground and faced him. "It would be a real pulling palace when you are at college, if you did it up. All the girls will choose you ahead of the spotty lads living in a grotty bed-sit."

"It's a family home," Paul said, "and an absolute bastard to clean and hoover on me own. As soon as it's sold am I still okay to move in with you, then?" Paul was still unsure after his other mate Martin had let him down on allowing him to rent a room around the time his mum had died.

"Sure, the garage is all converted to a 'Granny' flat and it's all yours. Don't worry too much rent wise, unless you go crackers with the hot water and electric."

"I won't."

"Well, I have to say, going to college and still living here, that would have been something." At which point Simon headed towards his car, got in and drove off. The man had finished hammering in the sign.

"All done," he announced, at which point the sign fell over. The man sighed and wiped his sweating brow. "I'll try again, then."

It was a nervous Paul Stevenson who entered full time education for the first time since he was sixteen the following September. As he checked the notice board for where his lessons would be he had butterflies when he saw the name VALERIE WALTERS crossed out as the tutor on some of the courses. He had forgotten she taught there and for a moment he wondered why her name had been crossed off. The butterflies soon passed and after a few weeks he gave up expecting to walk into her at any time simply because he hadn't.

## CHAPTER TWENTY-EIGHT

### Two Years Later

PAUL TOOK TO STUDYING AGAIN at the local adult college and with encouragement from one of his tutors looked to do a degree course at the local university. After looking through their prospectus he had applied for a sports psychology degree also studying for diplomas in journalism and American studies. He was delighted to be accepted but on his first day he was nervous again, feeling very much his 31 years surrounded by 18 year olds.

As he headed to his first lecture he became aware of someone in the doorway of the next room looking at him so turned to face them.

"Michelle!?" he exclaimed, "Bloody hell, you're in full time employment?"

"You cheeky sod!" she smiled as she came over to give him a hug. "I'm lecturing in English."

"Great, nice one."

"Well, there is only so long you can watch the Jeremy Kyle show and Loose Women in bed."

"True enough," then Paul looked puzzled. "Where's your Geordie accent?"

"It's still there but I thought it best to tone it down a touch when teaching Shakespeare," Michelle explained.

"Fair point" Michelle considered the bag on Paul's shoulder.

"You're here to study?"

"Yes, journalism, sports psychology and American studies," Paul confirmed.

"Wow! That's a lot of work," Michelle moved forward to whisper, "at least you have a bit of experience of studying Americans!" and then she giggled.

"Ah, Michelle, you're back!" said Paul, to which they both laughed.

"How is Val?" they both asked at the same time leaving them both feeling confused and clumsy.

"You're not in touch with her?" they both asked each other again at the same time.

"Last I heard she moved back to the States just over two years ago," Michelle reported by way of an update.

"Ah, right, that will explain why when I was at the adult college her name had been crossed off a list of tutors on some of the timetables," Paul said as much for his benefit as Michelle's. She looked confused.

"Right, so she hasn't been in touch with you recently then?"

Paul shook his head, "Last time I saw her was the night of my karaoke debacle at the Prince of Wales."

Michelle pulled a face, "What was that?" she asked leaning against the wall to get out of the way of passing students.

"Do you not remember? You were there, I sang, very badly, a selection of hits and standards of the day and…"

"Excuse me, but are you Paul Stevenson?" he was interrupted by a voice behind him and turned to see a serious looking man in his fifties wearing a tweed jacket.

"Yes, that's me."

"Good! Journalism, we're looking to make a start when you are ready." The man raised his eyebrows at Paul and went back into the class room.

"Right."

"I'll see you later, Paul," Michelle said patting his arm, "still can't remember that karaoke night, though." But as she turned to enter her own lecture room a knowing smirk came over her face.

A few weeks later and thinking everything was going well with her relatively new job Michelle got a message to see Brian Flanagan, the head of the English faculty at the university. She began to worry about what it could be about but when she arrived at his office Brian seemed in good form. He was a tall, stocky Irishman with a greying beard and dancing, happy eyes.

"Michelle, Michelle, come in, come in, take a seat," he boomed gesturing to the afore-mentioned seat onto which Michelle quickly scurried. "How you settling in then, mmm, is it going okay?"

"Yes, think so," she replied with a nervous smile. "Is anything wrong?"

"No! Not at all, not at all. Why? should it be?" he asked raising an eyebrow. "No, I called you in because I received an e-mail from UCLA, then a phone call from there, also. I went there, you know."

"To UCLA? Really?" Michelle was impressed.

"Yes, 1969 to 1972, golden years," he paused and had turned his chair around to be looking out of the window, "better than stuffy old Oxford." He paused again and his mind seemed to be wandering until he came back. "So! UCLA, they e-mailed, then they phoned, their English department has a few students interested in coming here to take up positions with our teacher training department, which I believe you went to and want to bring them over to have a look around."

"I see."

Brian grabbed his computer mouse and looked at the screen, "The tutor over there also went to our teacher training college when you were there."

"Did they?"

"You might know her."

"It's possible."

"Her name's on this e-mail somewhere. Hold on a minute," Michelle thought with a chill down her spine. It can't be, can it?

"American girl," Brian added, not lessening the suspense any, "ring any bells?"

"Valerie Walters?" Michelle offered in a shaky voice which surprised her.

Brian shook his head, "No, that's not her."

"Oh," Michelle felt a touch relieved.

"No, hang on, wrong e-mail, Valerie Walters, that's her. Is that the name you said? Did you know her then?"

"Just to say hello to," Michelle lied.

She left the office to head to her lecture room and as she got there Paul was leaving the one next door full of happy chatter and laughter with a girl a dozen years younger than him. He still spotted her, "Hi, Michelle," he called out but she did not reply. Instead she was stood frozen to the spot with her hand on the door handle. Paul came over,

"You okay? You look like you've seen a ghost." Michelle fixed him with a stare so they were eye to eye.

"Not yet we haven't," she told him, which left Paul confused.

"We?" he asked and Michelle nodded to confirm information Paul did not really know. "Okay," he said with no conviction and walked away.

Michelle felt bad as Val's visit got closer. She had not left things with her on good terms and consequently Val had not told her she was leaving. She couldn't really remember exactly what the deal was between Paul and Val when she went back to the States and every time she tried to warn Paul about it she failed to find the words. Typically, one day she saw Paul walk past the car park as she was getting out of her Ford Focus. "Paul," she called to him.

"Oh, hi, Michelle," he said with a smile and headed over to see her.

"Paul?"

"Yes, Michelle?"

"How's the course going?" she asked, cursing herself inwardly for failing to tell him again.

"Great! I'm trying to get a work experience placement with the local rag for the journalism and the other courses I'm really taking too, everyone is so friendly."

"That's great, Paul!" They smiled and Paul headed off towards his next lecture.

*Think, Michelle, think!*

"Fancy a drink one night?" she called after him, to which Paul stopped and turned to face her.

"Sure," he replied with a smile and carried on walking. Michelle just hoped that Paul was somehow on his placement when Val was over and missed seeing her.

The best laid plans of mice, men and cowardly Geordie university lecturers – Michelle was struck down with a chest infection and had only been back at work for three days when Val and her group of students arrived. In her absence Paul had not given the invitation for a drink any more thought and was just getting on with his life. He had also not been on his journalist placement with the local paper.

On the day in question Val and her students arrived in a mini bus and Brian Flanagan headed out to meet them. "Valerie isn't it?" he asked offering a hand, "pleasure to meet you. Please come in, all of you, out of this vile, Lancashire weather."

"At least that has not changed since I've been away," she smiled and led her students into the entrance hall. Once indoors Brian stood before them and smiled.

"Welcome all of you to North Lancashire University. What I propose doing is to spend a few hours at the teacher training college, then show you the English department and then we can have a wander around wherever you fancy, okay?"

"Fine," Val agreed with a smile.

"Right, this way, then," and with that Brian led the way and Val caught up to walk alongside him. After a few yards Brian stopped to recall something.

"Actually, Valerie, we have a member of your alumni here, teaching."

"Michelle?" Val shrieked in disbelief as she suddenly appeared in front of her.

"Hi, Val," Michelle said quietly. Val came forward and gave her a hug.

"You're teaching here? The one thing you vowed never to do!" Michelle laughed weakly and loosely shrugged her shoulders.

"Well, you know, bills to pay."

"How've you been?" Val asked her grabbing her hands.

Michelle smiled and nodded, "Okay, I guess."

"Great!"

"You look well. At least in LA you're getting some sunshine and daylight." They both laughed at this but Brian and the students were fidgeting and getting bored. "Listen, Val, I think there's something I should tell you."

"Okay," said Val. "I'm listening."

"Sorry to break this party up, ladies, but I think we had better get on," Brian interrupted.

"Of course, we'll catch up later, Michelle, okay?"

"Okay, Val," and with a smile they went their separate ways.

They met up later in the staff room and Val grabbed a coffee and came to sit next to Michelle and gave her another hug and smiled.

Michelle looked at her warily but did smile back.

"So Michelle, what's your gossip, then?"

"Nothing much, except I've just had a chest infection," Michelle replied. Val pulled a face disappointed this was all her gossipy best friend could come up with.

"Are you better now?"

"Oh, yeah, yeah, great thanks," Michelle took a drink.

"Any man in your life? Or men?"

"Valerie!" Michelle was shocked and looked around the room but Val just laughed.

"Come on! You were a bit wild when I left you."

"I know, but really!! I have been work driven these last few years, not really been looking for anything like that,"Val shrugged.

"I see,"Val smiled again.

"I only found out you had gone back to the States when I went to the Prince of Wales and Jim told me. I couldn't believe you had done that without telling me."

Val took a drink and looked around the room, "I'm really sorry but I had to make very quick changes in my life and could not hang about. If I had stayed here a moment longer I would have gone mental. Have you seen much of Jim recently?" she asked, concerned Michelle might have added Jim to the bedstead as a notch.

"I haven't seen Jim since to be honest. I've been avoiding pubs like that. So, nothing you see while you are over here will make you want to stop?" Michelle asked, knowing her little secret might influence things. Val drained her coffee.

"No, nothing, I don't want to live over here ever again."

In his journalism lecture nearby Paul, at 31 years old, more alive, awake and alert than his class mates, was lapping up the information more attentively than anyone else.

"You cannot," the lecturer continued, "underestimate the role of the local newspaper in journalism. If you wanted to find out..." at which point a knock on the door stopped him, "...yes, come in!" he barked angrily.

At this point Brian Flanagan marched in, "Morning, Stephen."

"Brian, how can I help?"

Brian smiled and waved in a group of people which Paul did not take too much notice of as he was scribbling some more notes down. "We have some American students here interested in the teacher training college so those of you doing American studies can probe them for information for your course. Why don't you introduce yourselves?" he suggested to the visitors. Paul did not take in any of the student's names as they were mostly mumbled and heavily accented until the last one that was spoken the clearest, "Valerie."

"No," he thought, "it can't be?" The visitors were slightly obscured from his view by the hairy, slumbering student in front of him so Paul sneaked a look. "Oh, God, it's her!" His brain started to do somersaults at the sight of the gorgeous redhead from his past.

"As journalists of the future with a keen eye for local events and information," Stephen the tutor began with barely concealed sarcasm, "what would you recommend to our visitors to do while over here?" There was an embarrassing silence of indifference and no interest then a few mumbles and grunts.

"Lake District," said someone.

"Blackpool," said another.

"Yorkshire Dales," was another grunted suggestion. Paul allowed himself a smile and put his hand up, which Stephen spotted and was onto like a shot.

"Yes, Paul, always a pleasure to hear your thoughts and musings," which brought laughter from his class mates as Paul usually said nothing in lectures. Before speaking he glanced at Val who had her head down, arms folded and looked bored.

"I would recommend they go to a pub quiz," Paul began and he watched as Val's face registered the voice, then looked up and her mouth fell open as she realised who it was, "and if not a pub quiz what about a night of karaoke?" Paul's suggestion prompted laughter from everyone, including the American students, except Val who still looked shocked.

"Well," said Stephen, "Paul always has his finger on the pulse of the under-classes." which prompted more laughter from Paul's class mates and a sad look from Val.

Later, in the canteen, Michelle was just about to bite into an egg mayonnaise sandwich when Val appeared and her initial comment caused her to drop most of it down the front of her blouse.

"What is he doing studying here?" Val snapped.

"Who?" Michelle asked wiping at the mayo on her clothing.

"You know fine well who; Paul! It's like I've just been ambushed."

"Okay, I knew he was here, I didn't warn you as I just didn't think you would end up in any of his lectures, that's all. It's not like he is taking English."

"He's in the next freakin' room!" Val hissed, her temper as fiery as her hair. At this moment two of her students, Wendy and Brad, approached.

"Hey, Val, in that last lesson, that thing that guy said, Paul was it?" Brad began, causing Michelle to bite her lip to prevent her from laughing and Val to be even more angry looking.

"I think that was his name, yes," Val replied firmly.

"He mentioned something called a 'pub quiz'."

"Yeah, what is that?" Wendy asked.

"In pubs a quizmaster asks questions on general knowledge, sport, music, that kind of thing," Val began, "and if you win you can win prizes, usually cash or beer. The Brits love it for some reason." Wendy and Brad smiled.

"Cool!" said Wendy.

"Beer, I love beer!" added Brad. "Is there a quiz around here?" Michelle swallowed a mouthful of sandwich so as to answer quickly.

"The Flying Ashtray, our student union bar," Michelle told them, "they have one tonight which starts at eight thirty."

"The Flying Ashtray is still open?" Val asked in disbelief to which Michelle nodded.

"Great! Could we go Val?" Wendy asked and Val sighed.

"Okay, okay, we'll go, eight thirty," she said and the two students walked away smiling. Val turned to Michelle, "To keep me sane, please tell me you'll be there as well."

"I will," Michelle said and then when a thought struck her she added, "actually I've finished for the day so plenty of time to get ready." Val smiled but as she got up and headed for the exit she rubbed her head as a headache was coming on with all that had happened that day. Michelle left soon after, smiling to herself and planning mischief.

Walking along the corridor away from the canteen Val passed the library and saw Paul in there. She paused by the door and watched him trawl the shelves for the books he needed. Val allowed herself a smile recalling him in Waterstone's nearly three years before helping her choose a sports book for her Dad. After a while he found the book he wanted, sat at a desk and began writing down his notes.

"Excuse me," a girl's voice said quietly behind her, "can I just get by?"

"Sorry, of course," Val replied moving aside and then an idea struck her. "Before you go in," she pointed to Paul, "do you know him?" The girl looked and then smiled.

"Yeah, that's Paul, he's in my American Studies class," she confirmed.

"American Studies?"

"Yeah, he doesn't say much in class but when we are split into groups he makes us laugh. He's a nice bloke," Val smiled at the testimonial.

"Could you do me a favour? Could you ask him if he is going to the quiz at the Flying Ashtray tonight?"

"Sure, won't be a mo'," the girl went into the library and approached Paul's desk. "Hi, Paul."

He stopped writing and looked up, "Hi, Polly, you okay?"

"Yeah, I'm fine, I was just wondering if you fancied coming with some of us to the Flying Ashtray' tonight?" Paul looked puzzled.

"Think I'm a wee bit too old for a student bar," he said in a voice that sounded even older than he was.

Polly smiled, "No matter how old you are, you are still a student." Paul shrugged.

"That's true. So what's the occasion for the night out, then?"

"Quiz night, eight-thirty, being as you are so old you'll know loads more than us!" Polly laughed deliciously and tilted her head.

"Thank you," said Paul laughing, "I've not been to a pub quiz for ages but why not? I'll see you there."

"Great! See you later," and as Paul went back to his work Polly turned to Val, smiled and gave a thumbs up. Val smiled back, mouthed 'thank you' and went to round up her students.

Michelle made her way to the Flying Ashtray for six o'clock and found the place empty apart from a barman and a scruffy looking DJ in a striped beanie hat.

"Are you doing the quiz tonight?" Michelle asked him.

"Yeah, that's right," he looked at his watch, "bit early to come and get a quiz sheet, though."

"I know, I'll be doing the quiz later, but if I promise not to play this round, could you do a 'bits n pieces' type music round?" The DJ looked confused.

"A what?"

"Bits 'n' pieces, you play bits of music and the teams write down the artists whose song it is,"

"Right," said the DJ, "got you." Michelle handed the DJ an envelope and a CD.

"Envelopes got the answers in, CD has got the music," she explained.

"Okay, thanks," he said taking them from her. "And you promise you won't tell your team the answers?" Michelle nodded and smiled.

"As long as you bring in your English coursework tomorrow Curtis!"

"Okay, I will, I will."

Paul got home to the converted garage he lived in at Simon's and toyed with the idea of not going to the quiz. Then he thought about the bizarre reappearance of Val in his life.

*How odd.*

There was a knock on the door.

"You in, Paul?" it was Simon.

"Yeah, come in, mate," and in Simon came.

"How was school?" he asked laughing.

"Fine," Paul replied shaking his head, but smiling. "Actually, you will never guess who came into my class?" Simon appeared to be deep in thought.

"Idi Amin," Simon offered.

"No, not while I was there he didn't, no. It was Val." Simon looked puzzled.

"Val? American Val?" Paul nodded. "Hell, what's she doing back here?"

"She's brought some students over from the States to have a look around one of the colleges, should have seen them, there were some right bloody freaks!"

"What about Val?"

"Gorgeous as ever, bloody hell, I blew my chance there," Paul reflected. Simon came into the room and sat on the armchair.

"You might not you know, if she's here. How was she? Is she seeing anyone?"

"Never got the chance to ask her, they left our lecture hall after a few minutes." Simon nodded to take in Paul's information.

"So you don't know how long she is here for?"

"No idea."

Simon exhaled sharply and stood up, "Well, this calls for the pub tonight, then, get a clean shirt on, Paul, son."

"Can't do it tonight, Simon, I've been invited to the student union bar for a quiz night, of all things."

"Quiz night, Paul? No, we've been here before," and Paul laughed. "If you see her there tonight, by some crazy chance, are you going to try and talk her into staying?" Paul looked thoughtful for a moment.

"Nah, it'll just be good to catch up with her, that's all."

Val and her students made their way into the bar, the students wide eyed with wonder and Val sharp eyed looking for Michelle who finally appeared from the gloom.

"Okay, Val?"

"Do they never vacuum or polish in here?"

"Let's be fair, Val, I remember a certain red head not a million miles from me now who, in this very bar, once knocked over a pint of cider and as it swished around among all the crisps and fag ends, she hoovered up..."

"Alright, alright, point made," and they both laughed. The students got their drinks together and passed Val hers. "Okay, let's find a dark and quiet corner, then," and on the way she looked around for Paul. She could not see him but the girl at the library, Polly, was in and waved over to her.

A few moments later Paul entered the bar for the first time in his student life. "Oh, sweet Jesus, what is this place?" he asked himself.

"Paul! Over here when you've got a drink in," Polly called to him waving. Paul smiled back.

"Can I get you one?" he asked her.

"Pint of Guinness, please," and Paul headed to the bar with a surprised look on his face.

"A pint of Guinness? Bloody hell." Polly looked into the far corner of the bar and waved to get Val's attention. Once she had it she pointed towards the bar where Paul was paying for their drinks. Val smiled and waved back at Polly. Next to Val was Michelle and she spotted Curtis, the DJ, enter the bar and head to the DJ stand. He spotted her and winked and Michelle nodded and smiled back. Once at the DJ stand he turned the microphone on to a screech of feedback making everyone wince.

"Oops, sorry, welcome to the quiz, we'll get started in five minutes but first some more from The Fall."

At Polly's table Paul was introduced to her friends and he decided to dig and find out why after several weeks an invite on a night out suddenly appeared. "I know we are in the same class, Polly, but I was surprised you asked me along tonight."

"To be fair I wasn't coming along myself but when I was going into the library today a woman asked me to get you along here tonight so I thought I would join you."

"A woman? Which woman?" Paul asked taking a drink.

"Some red haired American sounding woman," Polly confirmed, much to Paul's surprise. After Val had been in his lesson he had not exactly fallen over himself to try to find her but it sounded like she was trying to find him. "To be fair, I'm not sure if she wanted me to ask you along to join her or me but here you are."

"Here I am," Paul agreed and as Polly took a drink and chatted to a friend he had a quick look around but Val was out of sight so he did not think she was there. More feedback prompted Curtis's return, "Okay, welcome to the Tuesday night quiz. First round is general knowledge; question number one," Polly picked up her pen.

"Good luck, everyone."

# 2010

We were out of the bath and Val was wrapped in a towel, padding around my lounge. I had dried myself off and wore an old football shirt and tracksuit bottoms. My front room seemed to amuse her, as every so often she would allow herself a smile or a little laugh at certain items. When she got to my writing desk she gasped and picked up the framed photo there.

"Your little lad Sean?" she asked.

I nodded, "That's him."

"What a sweetie, looks a bit like you." She put it back on the desk and made her way over to the sofa still taking in the room for a clue what to talk about next. I sat in the armchair, leant forward and waited. After a few moments she rummaged in her bag and produced my book. As she flicked through it I noticed she had highlighted certain lines and paragraphs, always the teacher. I bet she's a nightmare to have as a teacher, I thought, but I kept this to myself.

"This bit with the quiz when we took each other on?"

"Yes?"

"Apart from a few weeks at the quiz we never took each other on, we were always on the same team."

"I know."

"But what made you think of that?"

I shrugged, "Just with us being keen on pub quizzes I always thought that one day I might find myself in a pub, taking part in a quiz and on another team there would be you. Either that or I would enter a TV quiz show and be up against you."

"You've applied to be on TV quizzes then?" Val asked, placing the book in her lap.

"Yeah, I've never been on one, though." Technically this was true.

"I was meant to be on one once," Val continued, "Brainboxes, do you ever watch it?"

"Yeah."

*Know it well.*

"But when we were meant to be on, the team we were playing against got disqualified before we even started filming. We got a hundred pound each for our trouble but on the show we could have won so much more, thousands."

"Blimey, Val, that's awful."

# 2006

I nervously made my way through the TV studio with the contestant researcher of Brainboxes, Lauren, beside me. Sheepishly, we approached the floor manager and with good reason.

"Ah, Liam, isn't it?" he asked. "Underwater Bungee Jumpers team captain?"

"That's right," I confirmed, we shook hands and they were both clammy, mine with nerves.

"Great! You're here at last. Let's get you and the lads into make up then." He turned to walk away.

"Bit of a problem, Serge." Lauren piped up.

*Serge?*

He turned and came back, "What's that?"

Lauren looked at me so I explained, "Nuggett, one of the lads on my team, ran amok in the Chinese Embassy strip club last night and is in police custody."

"Ah, well, good job you have the reserve, then." Serge patted my arm in a friendly manner.

"That was the reserve." I told him. "Coley, one of the other lads, had a panic attack last night about being on telly and is in Hammersmith Hospital."

"Christ!"

"Another lad, Dom, never came back to the hotel last night. Another, Tim, missed his wife too much and went home on the first train this morning and the other lad, Bumble, is currently arguing with the security guard on the gate outside who refuses to believe he is called Pontius Alan Pilate."

"Jesus Christ! Right, well, I'll have to tell the other team they have won by default. Schoolteachers they are, come all the way from Stoke-on-Trent and had to get supply teachers in to cover for them."

"Hey, distance wise we've come further than that," I protested.

"But they haven't arsed up our schedule, son!" Serge looked at Lauren. "Get him out of here!"

# CHAPTER TWENTY-NINE

THE NIGHT AND THE QUIZ were rattling along and Paul was fitting in with Polly's friends in a rather haphazard way. They laughed at some things he said but he had no idea about some of the music groups and TV programmes they discussed. In the quiz they had completed the sport, current affairs, general knowledge and music trivia rounds and they were getting impatient.

"Should be finished soon," Josh, one of the team, suggested, "Curtis only usually does four rounds." To which all the others, except Paul, nodded to agree. A shriek of feedback and the quizmaster was back.

"Okay, people, four rounds down and all to play for," he announced. "As a bonus we now have a 'bits 'n' pieces' round." There was a murmur of confusion and interest. "Apparently, I will now play ten pieces of music and you have to write down the singer or group." He paused and there was silence as the information was absorbed. "Do you all understand that?" and the reaction suggested the majority did.

"God," said Val, "it's not like it's rocket science, is it?" and Michelle nodded.

Over on Polly's table Paul joked, "Anything after 1999 and I'll not have a clue!" and his team mates laughed. It turned out Paul did indeed have a clue as the songs seemed to fall into his lap;

- Valerie – The Zutons
- Valerie – Steve Winwood
- Valerie – Amy Winehouse
- Two Out of Three Ain't Bad – Meat Loaf
- Last Christmas – Wham
- It Started With a Kiss – Hot Chocolate
- Stop the Cavalry – Jona Lewie
- Without You – Nilsson
- Born In the USA – Bruce Springsteen
- French Kissing (in the USA) – Deborah Harry

Michelle had been busy downloading songs on her laptop after she 'finished early' as she told Val. She was actually in her lecture and had it on mute. As each song was played, to confusion all around, Val would occasionally glance in her direction to see her pull a face to suggest, "Well, fancy that." Polly handed in the quiz sheet and a few minutes later curiosity got the better of Paul and he collared the DJ at the bar.

"A'right, mate, Curtis, is it?"

"Hi, how are you?" Curtis asked.

"Fine, mate, fine, me name's Paul. That last music round?"

"Yeah."

"Some of the songs, well, they could have just been chosen based around events in my life."

"Right, I see," Curtis looked confused. Paul did not say anymore but his face was asking, "how, exactly?"

"I never put it together, my English tutor did it for me," he explained.

"I see, and your English tutor is?"

Curtis picked up his drink, "Michelle," he confirmed, and went back to the stand to continue marking. Paul allowed the information to wash over him and then realised why it was beginning to make sense. Just then he was joined at the bar by Val.

"Hi, stranger," she began and Paul turned to face her to gauge how the land lay. Val at least was smiling, "Come on Paul, hug it out!" and they did just that.

"Studying, huh?" she ventured at last.

"Yeah, I got made redundant from the book warehouse and with nothing else on the horizon thought I would go to the adult college,"

"My old adult college?"

"Yeah, saw your name was crossed off a few timetables and wondered where you were." Then they were quiet again as each struggled what to say next. There was then an interruption, more feedback.

"Okay everyone, marking is complete, back to your tables for the answers," Curtis announced. Val looked at Paul.

"I'd love to speak to you later, I have loads I want to say," Paul told her.

"Great, look forward to it," Val smiled and they headed back to their teams. Polly and her friends were gobsmacked that Paul got ten out of ten on the 'bits 'n' pieces' round.

"You forget that I am three hundred years old," he reminded them and they laughed. And then there was yet more feedback.

"Okay, everybody, brace yourselves, we have a dead heat which means one thing and one thing only, TIE-BREAK!"

"Woooooooooh," the teams shouted in mock excitement and with much laughter.

"The first team, from whom we need one team member only, is Polly's Parrots!" There was then a discussion around the table about who should go up.

"It's your team, Polly," said Paul, "so you should go."

"No, Paul, you've been brilliant all night, you should go." Paul looked around the table and there were nodding heads to confirm this was universally accepted so he rose from the table and headed to the DJ stand followed by cheers and applause, to which he waved back to thank them.

"Paul, was it?" Curtis asked and he nodded to confirm. "Okay, up against Paul we need a team member from the Yankee Doodle Dandies!" After a few moments from the other side of the DJ stand came Val.

"GO, VAL, GO!" her students shouted. Paul and Val smiled nervously at each other.

"Good luck," he said and she bowed her head, Paul thinking he might have seen tears forming in her eyes.

"It's Great Britain versus the USA! The Ryder Cup of quiz nights, if you will," Curtis began, to confused looks from Paul. "I will ask each of you questions and the first one to get one wrong will hand the quiz and the gallon of ale to the other team. Paul, your question first; what is the state capital of California?"

Paul's memory went to porridge and then came back. The first time he met Val at the quiz Jim had asked this question so she could get one right, but what was it? He began to think; everything in California was 'Los' or 'San' something. San, Los, San, Los. Then it came to him; Val was from San Jose, it must be San Jose.

"It's San Jose, Curtis," he said. Curtis pulled a face.

"Sorry, Paul, mate, it is in fact Sacramento." Val looked apologetically at Paul so he smiled and shrugged.

"Val, your question, you might find it tough as it's about sport.

Which book is known as 'The Bible of Cricket'?"Val looked shocked and recalled the book shopping trip.

"Wisden. Wisden is the bible of cricket!" she shouted.

"You are correct Val and the Yanks have won the ale!" As Val 'whooped' and joined her cheering team Paul quietly leant across the DJ stand.

"Michelle did the tie break questions as well, did she?" he asked Curtis and nodding to confirm it he replied.

"Yeah, mate, she did, she did," Paul smiled at him.

"Thought so." Paul felt foolish that he had been set up by Michelle. The drink he had consumed over the past hour or so made him paranoid and ashamed that he had been shown up by a woman. So, doing what men from north Lancahire had done for centuries in such situations, he decided to punch the nearest, innocent bloke in sight; and with that he rocked back and chinned Curtis sending him flying. There were gasps and screams of shock and disbelief. Paul rubbed his knuckles, surprised at how much it hurt and all around him was silence. He headed towards the door and on his way he shouted to no one in particular "Good night," and from the darkness some people called back.

"Night, Paul."

The night outside was cold and wild with a strong wind blowing off the nearby Irish Sea as Paul set off for home. He had probably got no more than fifty yards from the bar when he heard footsteps approaching in a run and braced himself fearing it was Curtis coming to hit him back. The person linked their arm in his, however, and said "Hi!" it was Val.

"Hi, yourself," Paul said.

"Christ your country is cold."

"Is that why you left?"

"On the top ten reasons I left it would probably be about number seven," Val confirmed, cuddling in more.

"And number one?" Paul asked thinking he could guess. Val shrugged.

"That would be you." Paul let out a sigh.

"Sorry, that doesn't make me proud, I wish you'd stayed. I made a bit of an arse of things, didn't I?"

"I helped things along a bit I think." As they walked along Paul glanced back towards the bar. "He won't be following you. Michelle is clearing up his cuts and bruises in the toilet."

"I'm not looking for him, what about your students, Val?" Val stopped and looked back.

"Oh, shit, I forgot about them!" then they both laughed and carried on walking away from the bar. Paul glanced at Val, delighted she was back in his life.

"Shall I call us a taxi? You'll be frozen," he suggested. Val shivered.

"I'm just getting used to it again, I'll be fine," and they walked at a quicker pace. They had reached the main road meaning they were a bit more sheltered from the wind and only a mile from the town centre when Paul stopped. At this relatively late hour cars were still passing by.

"Paul? What's up?"

"I went to high school at the same time as about a thousand other people. In my class were thirty people, some I got on with, some I did not. I went to college when I was 16 and again recently meeting about another thirty or so people. In my time at the book warehouse I worked with up to a hundred other people. Both my parents are dead and I hardly speak to my sisters. Of all the people who came into my life and left it I miss you the most."

Val was gob-smacked and her eyes filled with tears.

---

# 2010

"Liam, Liam, wake up! I've got to the best part," Val was shaking me to wake me up. My eyes prised open through the sleep and glanced at the alarm clock; three forty-five.

"You're still reading?"

Val kissed me, "I got to the part with the speech Paul made after the quiz night at the Flying Ashtray, is that what you thought about me?"

I sat up in bed, "Yeah, of all the people I lost or lost contact with it was you I wanted back in my life."

Val kissed me again, "Thank you, Liam." She flicked through the remainder of book in some confusion. "Still seems a fair bit left, though."

I took the book off her and placed it on the bedside table, "Finish reading it," she went to grab it back, "tomorrow, and you'll see a bit more of what I thought."

"Okay," Val kissed me.

"Goodnight." With that we snuggled back into the duvet and I turned off the light.

# CHAPTER THIRTY

## Life Changing Decisions

VAL WEIGHED UP PAUL'S ANNOUNCEMENT, "Are you drunk?" she asked with a little laugh then Paul smiled, put his hands on her face and began to kiss her passionately. When he stopped he smiled at her and whispered.

"I love you."

"Love you too. Can you picture yourself living in the States?" Paul looked delighted.

"Is that an invitation? I'd love to!" Then Val suddenly looked crushed.

"But Paul, your studies, what would you do about them," to which Paul shrugged.

"I'll just do my American Studies exchange year a bit earlier and see how we go," and Val smiled. "Also, the journalism tutor is doing me nugget in and I want out." Val hugged him and held him close.

"Don't throw it away, Paul. I'll get Brian to have a word with him."

Paul smiled, "Use your womanly wares on him?" he asked and laughed.

Val looked shocked, "No, you don't think so, do you?" Paul raised his eyebrows.

"You and older men."

"Hey!" Val playfully slapped him, "You're younger than me and I'm doing this for you." To which they both laughed.

"So, Mr Stevenson, you are leaving us, then, I hear?" Stephen, the tutor, asked when he collared him after American studies.

"Yes," Paul confirmed. He was sat uneasily on a desk in the lecture room. "I will be doing my American studies placement a year early and if it doesn't work out then I will be back here to carry on studying."

"If 'it' doesn't work?"

"Living with the woman I am in love with," to which Stephen nodded.

"Ah, the American redhead, don't blame you," Paul never replied. "The thing is you're the best student in that class."

"Why do you always pick on me in there, then?"

"If nothing else it focuses the minds of the rest of the class."

"Sorry but I want more from studies than helping you to teach," and with that Paul rose from the desk and left.

After the next term Paul was told he would have to wait a few months before he could start studying at USC so Paul and Val spent two weeks travelling around the U.S. Once they reached California, Val got her Dad and some of his friends in local government to arrange a green card for Paul to do some part-time work while he went back to England to sort things out.

In England, Paul arranged for the possessions he wanted to keep to be shipped over and put his affairs in order. He wrote a letter to each of his sisters; the one to Cheryl confirmed his new address, the one to Joanne, who he always blamed for the idea of him stopping with their Dad after their Mum's death, telling her he never wanted to see her again. The last two occasions he had seen her had been at each of their parent's funerals. Once in the States, Paul told Val what he had done with the letters.

"How do you feel, Paul, are you upset at all? Do you want to talk?" Val asked.

"No," Paul replied. "It's all sorted now, let's put a line underneath it, shall we? I've said what I feel and it's time to move on." While she thought he was being harsh towards Joanne she never said anything to that effect and offered him only her support.

Within the next few years Val continued in her position as a college tutor back at UCLA. Paul missed some things from home – Blackburn Rovers, his mates, English pubs – but filled his time with two part-time jobs; one at Starbucks and the other at an independent book shop. Students, female students, some of whom Val taught, came into the bookstore and told him they "just luuuuuuuuuurved" his British accent but he just smiled and told them, as a man nearing his mid 30s, to behave themselves. He didn't have the best jobs in the world but everyday he could not believe his luck that a gorgeous foreign woman like Val had fallen for him and that it had led him to live a new life here in the States. And Val…

Val introduced Paul to her father and as she had thought back in England while shopping for books, they did indeed get on. They went to the occasional baseball game together, which Paul tried to get into – at least the LA Dodgers wore blue and white like Blackburn Rovers - and Val sometimes felt left out. Work stretched her and when she came home to unload her problems on Paul she felt he was not intelligent enough and did not understand.

"Is that you, Val?" he called from the front room while watching CNN on one such evening. A smart, leather briefcase flying through the air into the lounge, missing his head by a whisker, told him it was. "Summat up, love?"

"The damned course work for the freshmen is turning into a pain in the ass," Val said, sitting on one of the sofas and rubbing her head. Paul moved towards the sofa, sat down next to her and made to hug her, "Don't Paul, just don't."

"Okay, okay," he said, getting up from the sofa and making himself scarce. He found solace in the kitchen and leant against the work top wondering if he had done the right thing in throwing in his lot with Val and moving over to the States. They had not dated before moving in together and he wondered, based on falling in love and the occasional sex session, had they rushed things? Back in England when Val fell out with Jim she could go to Michelle's house. She had no such outlet in the States as her Dad lived three hours away and to begin with she wasn't that close to any of her nearby work colleagues. Part of their garden fence took a hammering at the brunt of her moods. Paul completed his American studies diploma but gave up on education after it, which annoyed Val, also.

The phone rang at Paul and Val's home late one afternoon and Paul answered it as he was in on his own, apart from Flash, his Bassett hound, who had not yet mastered answering phone calls.

"Hello?" Paul answered.

"Hi, Paul, Michelle here, how are you both?" If nothing else Val and Paul getting together had brought Michelle back into their lives. She had calmed down a lot and on their good days, they both secretly thanked her for her role in getting them together.

"Oh, grand, splodge, grand, and you?"

"Aye, just fine, pet, just fine. Is our Valerie about?"

"No, no she isn't, late one at work, again, but I don't begrudge her, it's all going really well for her there."

"Great, get her to ring us before twelve midnight our time if she's not too late getting back, will yer?"

"No problem, Michelle, love, speak to you soon." Paul put the phone back on the stand and sat on the settee next to Flash tickling her ears, smiling. He then got a horrible feeling.

*Working late, again?*

At UCLA Val was sat at a desk in a lecture hall on her own staring intently at the laptop in front of her. She was trying to get her mind around some course work that was coming up for one of her classes but she could not. The reason for her lack of concentration suddenly entered the room.

"Valerie. Busy, are we?"

Valerie angrily turned to face the man who had just entered, "Erik, what do you want?"

The man made his way over to the desk and sat in Val's line of vision, "Last night, Val…"

"Last night meant nothing to me, Erik, so drop it."

"And Wednesday? How many late nights at work will your Englishman allow you?"

Val slammed shut her laptop, "I said drop it!"

"Come on," Erik argued back, "if your old man meant anything to you, we would not have been at it," he tapped his fingers on the desk, "on here, and at my place, like rabbits." Val looked into the distance at nothing in particular and wondered how she had got here, again.

*Did Erik have a point?*

---

# 2010

Valerie had gone to her hotel to have a think through things which I took to mean to sort things out with Barry. I chose the moment she was leaving to have a dig away at her for her future plans.

"Are you in England permanently now?" I asked her from my doorstep. She held her overnight bag coyly in front of her and raised her head.

"Yes, I'm done with travelling for now," she confirmed.

"For now, so you could go again?"

Val nodded, "Probably, not sure when."

Did I want to share my life with anyone other than Sean, again? I wanted to be here for him, not on the other side of the world. I decided to give Val a get-out.

"Carry on with the book and let me know what you think, okay?"

Val looked surprised, "Oh, okay, I will." I think it sounded like I was trying to get rid of her, possibly I was. I needed to think and Sean would be stopping with me in a few days time.

So I found myself sat at my desk working on what the next novel could be about, again, when the mobile phone rang with Val's name displayed.

"Hi," I answered.

"This bit in the States, with Paul realising Val had been working late, a lot: explain, please?"

"Well, it was just based on the fact that when we went to the quiz you were sometimes late after meetings at work and I just brought it in as an explanation about how her affair would start. It wasn't based on anything in particular you did, just what people come up with to explain their actions when they have affairs."

Val didn't reply immediately which I took to be her trying to take it all on board. "Right, I'll call back," and the call ended.

# CHAPTER THIRTY-ONE

LATER THAT NIGHT VAL MADE IT HOME as Paul was in the kitchen wrestling with pasta, the only thing he could cook and, as he was at home before Val most days, especially recently, they had eaten it a lot. Flash came to meet Val and she stroked and tickled the dog's ears. Paul was aware of this and appeared in the hall.

"Hi, Val, love, you got finished okay eventually? Tea won't be long, Michelle rang earlier," he said, and then disappeared back into the kitchen. Like all those years before, Val decided enough was enough and Paul, the good guy that he was, needed to know the truth.

"Paul, please come into the lounge, I really need to talk with you," she announced at the kitchen doorway and headed for the lounge. Paul looked confused for a moment.

"Okay, wait there," he turned the pasta down in case this took a while and made his way to the lounge. When he got there Val was sat on one of the leather sofas and looked worried.

"Val?" he asked sitting down to face her.

"The other night," she began strongly without hesitation, "at work when I told you I was working late I actually went to the home of a colleague and slept with him. It wasn't the first time. With how we got together and everything else before that when I was in England I thought it best to let you know this as soon as I could and not live a lie...

"So what are we going to do, Paul?"

There was that question again, just like Christmas Eve all those years ago in the Victoria, Val had thrown the decision back to Paul and asked "what are we going to do?"

"What are we going to do, Val?" he asked her back throwing his arms up in the air. He stood up from the settee and made his way to the bookshelf where all his books from home were. He took down a book about Blackburn Rovers, pausing to look at the photo of him and his sisters at Joanne's wedding which was among the gear he had shipped over and was on the shelf, flicked through the book and sat back down on the settee. Val stayed silent for a few moments but looked at Paul, wondering what was going through his mind. Was there a significance in the book he had taken down from the shelf and looking at the picture of him with his sisters?

"Paul, what are you thinking?" Val asked.

He snorted a laughed, "For one thing you haven't said sorry, yet. Why?"

"Would it help or make you feel better if I did?" Val asked.

"No, not really," Paul confirmed with a shake of the head. After a few moments he began to talk, "In England you were with Colin and left him for Jim. Then you fell for me when you were with Jim and asked if I wanted you to leave him. And now this! Is something wrong with you, Val?"

Val sighed. "I don't know, Paul, but if it's any consolation I haven't fallen in love with this man like I fell in love with you when I was Jim."

"When we moved in I thought I was the one for you but could this man be the one for you now, for life?"

"Doubtful," Val confirmed. Paul looked at the front of his book and put it down on the coffee table. Flash was looking at him as was Val, as if they were both waiting on his decision. Paul stood up and made his way past her to the front door.

"Paul?"

"I need to think," he announced over his shoulder, and left the house closing the door calmly behind him, rather than slamming it, which he thought might have given Val some satisfaction.

Paul walked aimlessly for about an hour turning over the events of the evening in his mind and soon found a bar not far from where he worked. There were only a handful of people in there and he made his way to a stool.

"What can I get you?" A bartender asked him as he passed.

"A draught beer please mate," Paul replied and the bartender weighed Paul up as he got him his drink.

"Are you English with that accent?" he asked.

"I am, yeah," Paul confirmed.

"Actor, are we?"

Paul laughed, "No, I work in a book store, and Starbucks."

"It's a long way to come for such mundane, dead end jobs. Could you not do those in England and free up some work for my fellow Americans?"

"Probably," Paul agreed, "I suppose you could say I moved here for love, and to study, but now I don't know." The bartender brought the beer over.

"Four dollars-fifty," and Paul paid with a five dollar bill.

"Keep the change, mate," he told him and then took a man size swig. He then paused to take stock of how his life had ended up and wondered what to do next.

"Hi, what are you doing here?" a voice asked. It belonged to a dark haired girl who came into the book store and was in one of Val's classes.

"Good question, sweetheart, I'm not really sure," he replied. She laughed. Paul knew her name was Laura only because Val had told him that one of her students had informed the rest of the class that she had spoken to a 'cute' – Val had almost spat the word out – British guy who worked in the Mega Death book store. Val didn't let on that this British guy was her boyfriend. The book store was suddenly full of giggling college girls who never actually bought any books.

"I've never seen you in here before. I'm Laura, by the way."

"Yes, I know and I'm Paul."

"How do you know my name?" she asked and then she gasped, "Stalker, stalker!"

"No, not a stalker, my," Paul paused, could he still call Val his girlfriend? "I know one of your tutors. Valerie Walters."

"You know Valerie? Gaaaaaaaawd, she's great," Laura sat on a bar stool next to Paul.

"Good, I'm glad you think so."

"How do you know her, Paul?" Laura asked dipping into a bowl of pretzels.

He looked at the clock behind the bar, "Until about an hour ago she was my girlfriend and I lived with her. Now, I don't know. I gave up a lot to come to the States to be with her and now?" Paul shrugged.

"Oh my God!" Laura exclaimed. She patted Paul's arm. "I'm so sorry."

"Not your fault, Laura." Paul took another man size swig of his beer and decided he might need another one soon. He found American beer weak and could drink it all night and tonight he might just do that. In the time he had been in America he had mainly drunk wine at home. "Another beer please, mate," he called to the bartender, "and can I get you a drink, Laura?"

"White wine spritzer, Paul, thank you," she accepted. Paul nodded at the bartender and he nodded back. "Are you going home tonight, Paul?" Laura asked him.

"Oh, I dunno, I haven't really thought that far ahead," he admitted. The drinks arrived and Paul gave the bartender ten dollars, "keep the change again, mate, thanks."

"You'll own this bar if you give me any more money," the bartender joked. Paul finished his last beer and picked up the next one.

"Say 'no' if you want but I live in an apartment around the corner with my friend, Connie, and we have a spare room if you want to stay there tonight while you try to work things out."

"Okay, cheers, nice one!" Paul said with a smile and took a drink.

"We also have wine," Laura smiled and turned to look over to a group of girls sat at the far end of the bar. "Connie, Paul will be stopping with us tonight, he's had a really tough time."

"Ok, hi, Paul!" Connie called back. Paul waved back and recognised her from the shop, also.

Back at home Val had thrown the pasta away and then paced up and down thinking and fretting as to what to do. After a while she picked up the phone and dialled a number.

"Hello?" a man's voice grunted down the phone.

"Jim? It's Val, how are you?" There was a moment of silence.

"It's five o' bloody clock in the morning and after nearly four years you decide to ring me now?"

"Sorry," Val said. "I have to explain why I left, you deserve to know."

"Okay," said Jim and he listened to how she had fallen for Paul and her actions that led to Paul forcing her to conclude she could not decide between either of them and that leaving to go back to the States was the only way to sort it and then she explained how she and Paul had met up again. Some of the things she decided to leave out, some of the public kissing, all of the sex. When she had finished Jim paused to take it all in.

"Well, I thought at the time you were both acting a bit oddly," he commented, "and now I know why."

"Do you blame Paul, or hate him now you know?" Val asked. Jim exhaled air loudly.

"No, not at all, the poor sod sounds like the innocent party in all this," he replied which they both laughed at. Then they were quiet, taking in the serious nature of it all.

"How are you, Jim, are you seeing anyone at the moment?" Val asked.

"Yeah, she's called Karen, and I am still DJ-ing but I've also got a part-time job as a sorter with the post office so all is well," he confirmed, "my kids have met Karen, they've grown up so much and I'm really proud of them."

"Great! I'm so glad. Take care, Jim."

"And you Val."

---

## 2010

Val rang me and asked if she could come back around to chat about the latest part of the book she had read. I was worried but when she arrived she hugged me and kissed me on the cheek but then in a very business like manner went into the lounge, sat on the sofa and dug the book out of her bag.

"This is what I think; I've just read the bit when Paul and Val split up after she revealed the affair with Erik and she rang Jim to tell him what had happened. Would you be able to make a go of it with me if I called Ian and told him everything that happened between us?"

I laughed, "Compared to the book, there would not be much to tell."

"Well, Christmas Eve is a carbon copy, the argument at Easter on my birthday, that's based on actual events, buying presents for fathers."

"But the shagging, we never got that far, then."

Val smiled, "We have now!"

"Yeah," I laughed, naughtily.

Val put her feet up on the sofa, went back to the book and quietly started to read.

# CHAPTER THIRTY-TWO

I MMEDIATELY AFTER ENDING HER CALL with Jim, Val wanted to call Michelle to pour her heart out about the latest Paul set back but as it was nearing five in the morning in England, she decided to do that the following morning, her time. There was a knock at the door and when she got there it was Erik.

"So this is where you live, then?" he asked as Val opened the door. "Nice! Shall we carry on where we left off?" Val slammed the door in his face and went back into the living room, crying.

The next morning Paul awoke and took a few moments to recall where he was. He got out of bed, got dressed and made his way into the kitchen. He appeared to be alone and this was confirmed by a note on the table;

"Paul! Great to have you stop last night, stay as long as you want but please buy wine to replace what you drank last night! We'll be at school until 3 this afternoon. L & C xx"

He read the note and then left the apartment to make his way back to his and Val's house. On the way there he did wonder if he would meet the other man or Val but only Flash was there.

"Hello, old girl, did you miss me?" he asked, stroking her ears. After a shower and putting on some clean clothes, Paul then made his way to Starbucks for the start of his shift. A glamorous woman in her early forties was the first customer he served and was looking at the drinks on offer.

"Can I have a Caramel Macchiato full foam semi whip low fat, please?" she finally asked a confused Paul to which he smiled.

"Well, I have no idea what that is but yes, yes you can," he replied and got the drink ready as best he could. While he was on with it he smiled politely at the woman who smiled back.

"Are you English?" she asked him.

"I am, yes," Paul confirmed.

"I love your accent, are you from London?"

"No, I'm from the north of England, Lancashire, just above

Liverpool," he advised and the woman nodded with a smile. Paul smiled too as this job was not very taxing and he had conversations like this all the time. His smile slipped a little when he noticed that Val had just come into the shop. He put the drink on the counter, "three dollars–fifty, please, love," he said.

"Would you like to go out for a drink sometime? Something stronger than coffee, perhaps?" the woman asked. Behind the woman Val's eyes were bulging out of her head and Paul tried not to laugh. He never had conversations like this, ever.

"Not now, no, I cannot, but thank you, thank you," he replied. The woman smiled, handed him five dollars and left the shop with her drink. Val came up to the counter and tried a smile but Paul thought she looked ill.

"You've been here before," Paul said to her.

"Course I have, Paul, I picked you up here last week," Val replied confused.

Paul shook her head, "No, I don't mean Starbucks, Val, I mean here, with you worried and looking ill, wondering whether a relationship is worth saving."

Val nodded, "That's true."

"Is it worth saving, Val?"

"Until recently I would have had no hesitation in saying yes, but after what has happened with me and Erik."

"Erik? Is that his name?" Paul asked and Val nodded to confirm.

"There is no doubt in my mind that I still love you Paul and I don't know why I found myself in the situation with Erik that I did but I did and here we are."

"Yeah, here we are," Paul confirmed with an ironic little laugh that he could not help.

"So, what are we going to do, Paul?" Val asked and Paul sighed and shook his head busying himself with a few tasks around the counter.

"Gawwwwd, I cannot believe you are going back to England, Paul! I'm sooooooooooo going to miss you." Laura had called into the book store and Paul had told her his news. "Will you ever come back to LA, even just to visit?"

"Not sure if I am going for good or just for a short while," he confirmed. "I made contact with an old friend of mine called Simon whose house I used to live in and I'm moving back there for a bit, to think about what I'm going to do next. What little stuff I brought with me will be in storage."

"You can stop with me and Connie whenever you want," Laura smiled and tilted her head in a sweet way.

Paul laughed, "Thanks, there is a big part of me that would really love to take you up on that offer."

Laura smiled but then looked at her watch and looked serious, "Oh, shoot, I've got a class to go to," she said and then she whispered, "with Val as the tutor." Laura bit her lip and felt bad at mentioning her name.

"Good!" Paul exclaimed, surprisingly, with a wicked thought entering his head. "I might see you later on this afternoon." He came around the counter and hugged Laura then kissed her on the lips and smiled. "I'll keep in touch, okay?" Laura nodded and left the store. Brad, the man who owned the store, appeared from the storage room behind the counter.

"If nothing else, when you go, perhaps I might get people in here who want to buy something," he complained. Paul smiled and then put two fingers up at him so Brad went back to the store room.

Later that afternoon Val was in the middle of teaching a class, "Okay, I refer again to Joseph Heller and Catch 22," she began, moving away from the board where she had just written some notes. She stopped at this moment after being distracted by someone tapping on the glass in the door. She was surprised to see Paul there and even more surprised that he was waving at Laura and Connie. They giggled and waved back. Paul then looked at Val and though he smiled weakly his eyes looked sad as he nodded at her and then made his way down the corridor. "I won't be a moment," Val told the class and headed for the door. In another class Erik was holding forth on some matter relating to the American Civil war when the door opened and Paul marched in.

"Can I help you?" Erik asked him in an irritated manner.

"Yes, you're Erik, aren't you?" he asked.

"I am," he confirmed and with that Paul punched him.

"Have some of that, you twat!" Paul announced as the class erupted in laughter from the men and gasps from the women.

"Paul!" Val shouted from the door. "What are you doing?" Erik was struggling to his feet and rubbing his jaw and it dawned on Paul that this man, who was bigger than him, could kill him, quite easily.

"Just cheering myself up before going back to the frozen north of England," he replied.

"You're going, then? Our relationship is not worth you staying to try and save it?" Val asked.

"Nah, it's not," Paul confirmed with a shake of the head.

"So the limey is going home, Val, that's fantastic," Erik exclaimed with a big smile. "Can we now carry on where we left off?"

"Shut the fuck up, Erik," Val hissed and left the room to go back to her class. Paul was stood there in Erik's class and was beginning to feel a tad foolish.

"Sorry for disrupting your class, mate," he said to Erik.

"I'd have done the same in your shoes," Erik replied rubbing his jaw again. Paul made his way to the door then paused.

"Take care of her," Paul said nodding down the hall towards the retreating figure of Val. "Try not to fail her like I did." Erik nodded and Paul made for the door stopping to wave at the class. "See you," he hailed.

"Bye, Paul," they chorused. He made his way back down the corridor and as he passed Val's room he stopped to look in and they exchanged warm smiles before he carried on walking.

## CHAPTER THIRTY-THREE

IN THE BACK ROOM OF A BUSY PUB in Blackburn full of expectant, hard-drinking football fans Paul was getting re-acquainted with Dan.

"I've missed having your company this last year or so, Paul."

"Cheers, mate," Paul acknowledged and they clinked glasses and got on with drinking and putting the world to rights.

"So have you got yourself a new job since you came back?"

"No, I just took up with my studies again, scraping by on what money I have left after selling my Dad's house," Paul confirmed taking a look around the pub, loving the fact it had not changed with it's old Rovers shirts and pictures of former players on the wall.

"Do you miss anything about the States?" Dan asked.

Paul looked thoughtful for a moment, "Just me dog," he replied eventually.

"That's not a nice nickname for Val, even mine of the school dinner-lady was better than that," said Dan. Paul almost fell for it but realised Dan was joking when he turned to face him.

"Nice one, Dan," he said, laughing.

At the match itself Dan was sat in another part of the ground to Paul but sent him a text at half time.

HAVE YOU SEEN THE MESSAGE ON THE SCOREBOARD?

Paul looked at the scoreboard where a handful of messages were coming along; TO LILLY, HAPPY 8TH BIRTHDAY, LOVE NAN AND GRAND-DAD. TO ANDY, HAPPY 10TH ANNIVERSARY, FROM YOUR WIFE, SARAH. TO HARRY, SORRY I CRASHED YOUR CAR, FROM TONY, YOUR BROTHER...

Paul read several messages like this and wondered what Dan had seen when suddenly;

PAUL STEVENSON, HAPPY BIRTHDAY!! PLEASE COME BACK TO L.A., MY WORLD IS EMPTY WITHOUT YOU AND I LOVE YOU, VAL x

Val never ceased to amaze him. For one thing, not having anyone in his life to buy him a present or a card he had practically forgotten it was his birthday. The man sat next to Paul had also read the message, "Don't know who that fella is but I'd be over there like a shot if I was him. It'd be warmer over there for a start and he wouldn't have to sit here and watch this shower of shite," he shivered.

"Fair point, mate," Paul said.

Back at the pub after the game, yet another defeat to a hotly disputed penalty, Paul was sat at his and Dan's usual table when Dan finally got back. "You've not gone home to start packing yet then, son?" Dan asked.

Paul looked bewildered and gave a little shrug, "Don't know what to do, to be honest. What would you do, if you were me?"

Dan laughed and came to sit next to Paul behind the pint he had bought for him, "Don't take this the wrong way, Paul, but most of the time I am really glad I'm not you and now is no exception. It's not my call, lad," he paused to look around the pub. "You've given all this up once before, can you do it again?"

Paul had arranged to meet Michelle for a meal at Rossi's to talk over what had happened and discuss his decision. It was Tuesday lunchtime and they were the only diners in there despite the 'happy hour' offer that was advertised in the window.

"Do you think I am crackers, Michelle, wanting to go back there and forgive her and try again?" Paul asked while wrestling with some spaghetti. Michelle put her white wine down to construct a decent reply.

"There's only really you who can answer that, Paul," she replied. "Did you get the spaghetti carbonara?"

"I did, I did," he confirmed, stopping to take a drink of Peroni. "I love her, I can't help it." Michelle smiled. "She cheated on me and I don't know why, what would make anyone want to do that?" Michelle shrugged. Paul stared into space then after a moment picked his fork up to try to tackle the spaghetti again.

"I'll go back, I'll not have a job, me green card has probably expired, I won't be able to study again, she's probably going to be shacked up with this Erik wanker making really tall Californian children together," Paul continued.

Michelle shook her head, "No, she isn't," she said.

Paul looked surprised, "Oh, have you spoken to her recently, then?"

Michelle nodded, "I have that, last Thursday, and she is really sad, she misses you and cannot believe you just left. Bizarrely she doesn't hate you for it and she thinks you were very strong and that you have grown."

"Oh," Paul smiled and got the spaghetti into his mouth, "finally!"

"When you get back I'll come over to see you both."

"I'll have to hope she'll have me back, first," Paul commented.

"She will!! So, when do you leave?" Michelle asked.

"Next Monday, I'm flying out from Heathrow."

"Not Manchester?"

"No, I've got something to do first."

Paul got out of a taxi and made his way to the front door of a semi-detached on a neat housing estate. The avenue was quiet, as it was late on a Monday morning. Paul knocked on the door and waited nervously. When the door was opened he smiled, "Hello, Jo, can I come in?" he asked his sister. She was holding an infant girl. "Hello, who's this?" he asked.

"She's your niece, Alice," Jo replied coldly, stepping a side to let Paul enter. He made his way into the lounge and sat down while Jo put Alice into her play pen.

"Tony at work is he?" he asked.

"Just left, if you'd have rung first he might have stayed."

"What for, to punch me?" Paul asked, remembering the letter he had sent. Jo shrugged.

"We understood your anger Paul, it was just not a nice thing to receive, especially when Cheryl was allowed to stay in touch. Heard they had a nice trip over, Universal studios, Golden Gate bridge..."

"When I get back over come and stop," Paul offered as an olive branch.

Jo looked surprised, "You're going back, then?" Paul smiled and patted the sports holdall next to him. "Doesn't look like you're taking a lot with you, are you not stopping?"

Paul laughed, "I'm not sure of the lay of the land or what sort of welcome I will get, so I might be back home in hours and back to square one." Jo smiled.

"I'm glad you came to see me. Can I get you a coffee?"

"Yeah, I'd love one, thanks."

## CHAPTER THIRTY-FOUR

EIGHTEEN HOURS LATER, another town, and Paul was getting out of another taxi and walking towards his old house. It had only been two months since he left and not much had changed. Someone had repaired the garden fence that took the brunt of Val's anger, possibly Harry, Val's Dad.

When he went back to England he had left his key behind so he had to knock on the door. He could hear a dog barking inside, Flash, his dog. It was late Tuesday afternoon in term time but Paul thought Val might have finished her classes by now, but he got no reply. Oddly her car was there. With nothing better to do he made his way to the bar where he had met Laura and Connie that time and when he entered the bartender recognised him.

"Hey, it's the English beer monster," he called, "you're back!"

"For now, mate, yes," he confirmed. They shook hands.

"Great! The takings will no doubt go up but for now the first one is on me."

"Thanks, mate."

Paul got into a drinking session and the bartender, Mario, kept him company as the bar got busier with students and low-paid workers, as Paul had been until a few months ago, coming in to unwind.

"I don't know if Starbucks will take me back," Paul said, to which Mario nodded, and Paul carried on. "I think I've burnt me bridges at the Mega Death book store with," Paul paused, "with, er, oh, Christ, what's his name, do you know him, Mario?"

Mario laughed, "I don't, Paul, he doesn't come in here."

"Brad! That was his name, evil fat bastard that he was. I'll have another, please Mario, mate," Paul downed his beer.

"Coming up, mate!" Mario replied to mimic Paul, with a laugh. As he got the drink ready Paul carried on talking.

"Did I ever tell you I was a big fan of the Doors?" Mario shook his head. "They were brilliant and Jim Morrison's picture is everywhere in this city, giving it Mr Mo Jo Risin', marvellous!" Paul was on the brink, weak American beer or no weak American beer, of going from merry to bladdered when from behind him he heard someone shreirk...

"Oh, my Gawwwwd! Paul, you're back!" Laura had arrived and threw her arms around him.

"Hi, Laura, how are you, love?" Paul asked patting her on the back and rolling his eyes at a grinning Mario.

"Heard about Erik and 'the punch', Gawwwd, you're like so the man, Paul, we all like kinda love you for that."

"I do me best, love, can I get you a beer?"

"Sure! Are you back here for good?"

Paul shrugged, "I'm not sure, do you know where Val is? I went to the house but she was not there, although I could hear Flash," Laura looked confused, "me dog, she was barking."

"Here's your beers, mate," Mario announced and Paul gave him some money, "keep the change, right?"

"Yeah, go on then, you cheeky sod!"

"I think she was on a college trip today, getting back later on this evening," Laura explained.

"Right, probably best I stay away tonight, then, I'm in no fit state to see her now. Can I crash at yours tonight, Laura?"

This suggestion seemed to please Laura who beamed, "Sure!"

Paul woke the next morning with a banging head and a mouth that felt like someone was squatting in it. "Was I drinking tequila?" he asked himself raising his head slowly. "And where?" he paused. "Oh, sod a dog," he was in bed with Laura, luckily a sleeping Laura. He found his watch in one of his trainers and checked the time; eight o' clock, or just after. Sneaking out of bed, so as not to wake Laura, he dressed and left the apartment. He reached his and Val's house but her car had gone so he had yet another full day to waste before seeing her.

He had wandered from shop to coffee house to some more window-shopping trying to kill time before going back to the house. He had even killed a few hours sat on a bench at the beach which in blustery March was not much fun. While heading for home he ran into Laura who was with Connie.

"Hi, Paul!" they trilled and they both hugged him.

"Hi, girls, been to college today?" he asked.

"No, we've had study time," Connie giggled, "so we haven't seen your Val." Laura began to laugh, also, but Paul just nodded.

"Did you stop at ours last night?" a confused looking Laura asked Paul.

*Oh, so I was that memorable, recalling that he woke alongside her, naked.*

"Yes, yes, I did," he confirmed.

"Where did you even sleep?" Laura asked.

"Sofa," he replied quickly.

"God, sorry, I never got you a blanket or nothing," Laura gushed.

"Don't worry," Paul responded with a wave of his hand and a shrug.

"Are you going to see Val tonight?" Laura asked him.

Paul nodded, "Hope to, just don't know what I am going to say to her or what I am going to do. She hurt me going with Erik, but…"

"But?" the girls prompted him.

"But," he couldn't finish the sentence so the girls nodded to show they understood what he meant.

"While you think it over can we get you a drink at Mario's?" Connie asked, to which Laura smiled and nodded enthusiastically.

"Okay, great idea, thanks, I can get the perspective of my problem from American womanhood then."

Val had finished work by four in the afternoon and had just got in the house and been met by Flash when the phone started to ring.

"Hello?" she answered.

"Valerie! Michelle here, how are you keeping?"

"Oh, fine, work's a little bit better, nicer hours currently," Val confirmed in reply as she reached the sofa, sat down and had Flash slump against her left leg.

"And how's the man settling back in?" Michelle asked with a giggle.

Val was confused; "How's 'the who' settling back in?" she asked.

"The man, how is he settling back in?"

"Which man?" Val wondered if this was a Geordie expression she had never heard in all the years she knew Michelle.

"Paul of course, there should be a below average height Englishman sat somewhere near you!"

"Paul's still in England," Val said.

"No! I had lunch with him last week and he was heading back to the States on Monday, he had seen your message on the scoreboard at the footie and was heading back."

"Oh," as Val had not heard from Paul since the birthday message she had arranged at Ewood Park she had put it to the back of her mind. "I was beginning to think he had not seen it."

"Well he did and once he knew how you felt he was coming back to see you and to try to talk things through."

A tear of joy rolled down Val's face which she wiped away. "But where is he, Michelle? There haven't been any plane crashes I've missed on the news, has there?"

"Not that I'm aware of."

"He's not been arrested for soccer hooliganism, running amok on the streets of Blackburn, Lancashire?"

"No, I haven't heard that he has."

"Then where the hell is he?"

The next morning Paul awoke with another hangover and a mouth like a glass blower's armpit to discover, "Oh, sweet, Jesus," he was in bed with a sleeping Laura, again, but they were with a, thankfully, also sleeping Connie. He again sneaked out of bed, got dressed and left.

The two girls had made their way to classes by early afternoon and it was with Val as their tutor. "Afternoon, all, how are we today?" Val asked breezily enough entering the room.

"Hi, Val," the class called back with varying degrees of enthusiasm and volume. Val set down her leather bag on the desk and started writing some notes on the board. Laura and Connie were sat near the front and were engaged in conversation with a couple of their friends. Val picked up on some snippets of the conversation.

"I was so wasted, again!" Laura announced as quiet as she could with having a delicate hangover induced head.

"Two nights in a row?" one of their friends gasped. Laura nodded to confirm.

"It was Paul's fault," Connie whispered, shooting a glance towards Val's back who stopped writing thinking it might make her hearing improve. "The English sure can drink! He's like some sort of beer animal."

Val spun around with a nervous looking smile, "I'm sorry, but is that my Paul you're talking about?" The girls looked guilty all of a sudden and blushed.

"Are we in trouble?" Connie asked quietly.

"He stopped with us last night, we think," Laura explained, "and the night before."

"And did he say why he hasn't come home, yet?" Val asked in quite a hard tone which caused the girls to fidget.

"He wasn't sure what to say to you or if you wanted him back," Laura explained and Connie nodded to back her up.

"We were trying to help him out with some advice," she added. "As American women, didn't he say?" Laura nodded this time.

Val dashed away from college after the lesson and headed to all the places she thought Paul might be; the Mega Death bookshop was locked up and had closed down according to the signs in the window. After walking for a few more blocks, the Starbucks Paul had worked at came into view and on the off chance he had got his old job back she entered it. There was a Hispanic looking man in his twenties behind the counter. Seeing Val he smiled broadly.

"Hi, there, what can I get you?" he asked.

"Is there just you working here today?" Val asked him, looking behind the counter, which confused the man.

"Just me, yes, now, what can I get you?" he asked again patiently.

Val's mind was racing wondering where else Paul could be, "Oh, nothing, nothing that you could get me," she replied.

"Val?" a voice called out from a corner table. Val had not noticed anyone else in there when she entered. It was Paul and he rose from his chair.

"How have you been?"

Val made her way over to him and threw her arms around him. She didn't sob but tears were rolling down her face. "Hang on a mo', Val," Paul said from among her arms, only slightly returning her hug. "There are things I think we need to talk about first."

"Okay, that's fine, I understand, shall we go home?" Val suggested.

"Nah, we'll stop here, it's neutral, like Switzerland." Paul went to the counter and ordered "Two half-whipped low fat demi-cappuccinos, please," from the Hispanic man, Joao, and then turned to face Val. "All that time I worked here I still don't know what that is. I could have given out loads of them wrong!" Val smiled warmly as she had missed his funny comments, although on this occasion she thought he was being serious. He brought the drinks over and sat back down.

"You hate living over here, don't you?" Val asked him after a moment of silence and a few sips of coffee. "Away from all your friends, Blackburn Rovers and the England cricket team."

Paul shrugged, "Hate's too strong a word, Val," he replied. "I love England but it's warmer here and it's where you wanted to live. It took me some getting used to but it is only what you had to do when you moved to England."

"Why did you leave me so quickly after the Erik episode?" Val asked.

"I was hurt but with how unhappy you had been recently I should have seen it coming," Paul replied. They each took another sip of coffee and let the silence take over.

"Are you coming back to live here?" Val asked, reaching out to take hold of his hand. "I miss you, and I love you." She smiled a tired smile.

Paul sighed, "I really do want to be with you, Val, but part of me worries that I will always have the 'Erik episode' as you called it in the back of my mind. I know I'm no picnic to live with."

"No, Paul," said Val. "How I was acting was no fault of yours."

"No?"

"No, I took too much on with the job and it took some getting used to and I foolishly took it all out on you. Please believe me on that."

"Okay."

"Would you be happier living somewhere else? Back in England, say?"

"Would you be?" Paul asked Val back.

"I'd be happier living anywhere if you were living with me," she told him.

"It's clear your work was making you unhappy and this led you to cheat," Paul suggested, to which Val nodded.

"Would it work if we moved to the east coast? It would be half way to England and halfway to California," Val suggested.

"Before we decide anything I need to ask and I think I am entitled to ask, Val; what of Erik? Is he still an issue?" Paul's voice was shaking a bit as he had to ask about him and say his name. Val paled a bit.

"He left the school, I threatened to report him to the principal," she explained.

"What did he do?"

"Nothing, just after being with me he was making passes at a few of the female students, including your friends Laura and Connie," Paul paled a bit himself as Val mentioned their names, "but they spurned him. Loyal, aren't they?"

"More loyal than you bloody were," Paul cut back.

"Yes, sorry, again," Val grimaced. "I think he saw a sexual harassment case looming." Val drained her coffee and seeing this Paul did likewise. Val put her hand in Paul's and smiled the warm smile he always loved. "Come on home, Paul. Now, please," she pleaded.

"Yes, I will, I miss Flash," he said.

"Oh, great, you're doing this for the dog!" To which they both laughed.

# 2010

"Wow! So they ended up back together again? Is this what you wanted?"

It was late, I wanted to sleep and Val had been reading all afternoon and into the evening. I knew what happened at the end of the book and decided it was time for cards on the table.

"I will tell you something before you read anymore, Val," I told her. She placed the book on the coffee table and waited. "I have missed you all these years, even just as a friend not as a possible lover, so I tried to find you on some of those social network sites. You were impossible to find."

"I was on one," Val told me. "Then I had creepy blokes from Yorkshire I went to school with mithering me so I removed myself from them."

"I sent you a few messages on one of them, did you get them?" I asked her.

"No," she shook her head. "Wish I had." I smiled.

"Well, I figured I might find you by contacting Michelle so I shoved a friend request in there, which I had to as she withheld it from view who her friends were, and when she accepted me I saw you weren't on there after all."

"We'd have fallen out by then," Val picked up the book and looked at the cover.

"What happened?" I asked.

"We had two massive, drink fuelled arguments; argument number one; we were on a night out in Blackpool and I got it in my head she had run into the sea to kill herself so the Coastguard engaged a helicopter to search for her, cost thousands to scramble they do, turns out she had gone home in a taxi. The second one; I jumped into my car to drive home to where I lived at the time, just outside Stoke and as I was getting on to the motorway a police car pulled me over and breathalysed me. Next thing you know I have a one hundred and eighty pound fine and a six month ban."

I slumped in the armchair, "Bloody hell, bet your dad loved that, being Old Bill."

"I've never ever told him about it," Val shrugged, "friends, huh?"

I sighed, "Okay, to follow up what I said, she accepted me as a friend and one night we had a natter on-line and agreed to go out for a drink"

# CHAPTER THIRTY-FIVE

## The Future - A Happy Ending

AS PAUL MADE HIS WAY home with Val, he had a vision of what the future might hold and mulled it over in his head. They were going to put the mistakes of the past behind them and move on. This is what he saw:

"Harry? It's Paul."

"Hi, Paul, any news for me?"

"Yes, you've become a grand-father again, baby boy, Jack. Mother and son are both doing well!"

"Beautiful, absolutely beautiful!" Harry gushed.

"He looks like Val, thankfully, and he's quite long so he won't be a short-arse like his Dad!"

Harry laughed, "Well, as long as that pleases you, Paul. Give my love to them both,"

"Will do, we'll see you soon. Oh, actually, while I think on, I need to ask you something, Harry,"

"Go on," Harry said.

Paul Stevenson, 35, had come a long way in the short time he had spent back in the States since coming back after the Erik episode. He took Val up on the offer to move to the east coast and they decided on Washington DC. Val was teaching in a high school and Paul had got an admin role at the British embassy where his work colleagues at least had some idea what football and cricket was all about. He was a happy man as he made his way back into the hospital and to Val's ward with a big smile on his face. When he got to her bed Val was looking lovingly at the infant in the crib next to her. She turned to face Paul.

"Did you ring him?" she asked.

"I did, he was delighted," Paul confirmed to which she smiled. "I've also rung my sisters, they all send their love. Do you want me to ring and tell your Mum?"

Val pulled a face which took the smile momentarily from her face. "Not just yet," she replied and had to force the smile back. She looked at their child and that brought the smile back to her face. "How did you decide on the name Jack?" she asked.

Paul smiled and replied, "It was my Grandad's name."

"Oh, I see, so it's a family name, then?" Paul nodded to confirm. "What about the middle name, Walker, what was that then? I read somewhere that the Scottish give their children their mother's maiden name as a middle name so do the English have something similar? Is Walker a family name too? It nearly sounds like Walters..."

Paul laughed nervously, swayed from side to side and grinned, "No, not really,"

"So, when Jack Walker Stevenson asks me in later years how he got his name, Jack was your Grandad's name and Walker?" Val pressed.

"Jack Walker was the father of the modern day Blackburn Rovers," Paul began to explain. "He was a steel magnate who pumped a fortune into the club, re-built the ground and helped us to win a championship," Paul sighed. "we owe that man a lot!"

Val groaned, "Paul! Oh, God, you've named our first child after something to do with Blackburn Rovers?" and then she laughed. "Why am I not surprised?" She smiled at the baby and then a thought struck her. "Jack Walker wasn't your Grand-dad then? We're not really rich, are we?"

"No, he wasn't and we aren't," Paul confirmed.

"Shame."

"Yes, isn't it? I might have got free tickets all these years."

Val smiled and Paul smiled too, "The choice of name might not surprise you but this might surprise you," he said.

"What?" Val asked confused.

Paul got down on one knee, "Valerie Walters, will you marry me?" Val was left open mouthed in shock and tears of joy rolled down her face. "I've done everything correctly, I even asked your Dad for his permission and bought this," at this point he produced a box with a ruby engagement ring in it from his jacket pocket.

"Oh, God, Paul, of course I will marry you!" They hugged.

"Oh, no, I'm going to have to make a load more phone calls," Paul pretended to complain.

"You bet. Where should we get married?" Paul's face brightened with an idea. "And not at Ewood Park, Blackburn, mister!"

"Spoilsport."

# CHAPTER THIRTY-SIX

## Ending 2 - Didn't They Almost Have It All?

THAT WAS THE DREAM as he looked into the future, something he thought might happen one day, but unfortunately for Paul this is what ended up happening:

"Harry? It's Paul,"

"Hi, Paul,"

"I've got some news for you,"

"I assume you are telling me I am a Grand-father again?"

"Yes, baby boy; Zac!"

"Marvellous!"

"Mother and son are both doing well, Grand-poppy!"

Harry laughed, "Wonderful, wonderful news, thanks for ringing and letting me know, Paul." Harry paused and it was a silence Paul did not want to interrupt. He could almost tell what Harry was thinking and after a long sigh he revealed his thoughts. "There is a part of me that still cannot believe you are not ringing me with this news as the child's father."

Paul Stevenson, 35, had come a long way in the short time since he went back to the States to make up with Val: he took Val up on the offer to move to the east coast and they decided on Washington DC. Val was teaching in a high school and Paul had got an admin role at the British embassy where his work colleagues at least had some idea what football and cricket was all about. He was a happy man and was enjoying his life until Val came home from work one day to reveal Erik had made contact and after initial resistance she had decided to give it a go with him after all. They had been having early evening meetings in hotels in the area for a few months now. And there was some other news; she was pregnant. Paul was back in England, again, within a fortnight.

This time Paul sighed, "Well, you know, you can never tell how life is going to turn out, 'H'. Val rang me and I was happy to help her out by letting you know the news to offer an olive branch."

"You're a good man, Paul," Harry told him.

"Too good sometimes," Paul offered back. "Shall I let her know you will ring her when she leaves hospital? It would mean a lot, seeing as she never made up with her Mum before she died."

"There's just something in me, Paul, that," Harry hesitated. "I still can't believe she hooked up with this Erik when he reappeared and left you again."

"Me and you both, Harry lad, but I'm back in England now and getting on with it. She's your daughter, give her a call."

"I'll think on it but I ain't promising anything, Paul. Take care, buddy."

"And you, 'H'."

That night Paul sought solace in the Prince of Wales with Simon and a few pints. They were mostly silent as they had caught up with most of Paul's recent news and had shared the dreams and hopes for the future, mostly Paul's hopes and dreams. Simon didn't deal in dreams. The pub had undergone a face lift since the 'glory days' as Paul termed them, the music was modern and ridiculous but it was still the Prince of Wales pub. It could still do with a bloody good clean.

"Well, it's good to have you back in blighty, Paul, old son," Simon said, patting him on the back. Paul smiled weakly back.

"What happens in here nowadays, then?" Paul asked looking around the pub.

Simon took a swig of his drink and smiled, "Not karaoke anymore, you'll be glad to know!" Paul laughed remembering his glorious night in there all those years ago, "They've actually brought the quiz back."

Paul went pale. "Oh, God, it's not Jim doing it, is it?" Since Val had rung Jim from the States he had not seen his former work mate and friend and didn't know if he wanted to.

"No, his sad mate Ken does it. Oh, look, there he goes now." Paul saw he was indeed heading towards the DJ stand. "Shall I get us a quiz sheet?" Simon asked to which Paul nodded. While he was away Paul looked around the pub once more and noticed it was still popular with students as well as locals. As Simon came back he noticed three student girls coming their way and they sat at the next table. Paul filled in the team name while Simon engaged the girls in conversation.

"Evening, ladies," he began. One of the three was giggling, another one glared back at him and the third had her head down.

"Oh, God, don't do this, Simon, we've been here before," Paul whispered. "Well, I have."

"Hello," the giggly girl replied.

"What are your names and where do you come from?" Simon continued coming over all Cilla Black on Blind Date.

"I'm Charlotte and I'm from Newport," the giggler began. "This is Amanda from Redditch," she was the one who was glaring and her face remained frozen despite her friend's cheery introduction.

"I'm never going there if they're all like that," Simon whispered and Paul smiled.

"And this is Candy,"

"Hi," the third girl said cheerily enough. Paul thought he detected a familiar accent. No, she can't possibly be.

"She's from San Jose, in America!" Charlotte confirmed her friend's exotic home town cheerily.

Simon raised his eyebrows and turned to face Paul jabbing a thumb in his direction. "No, don't," Paul pleaded quietly, shaking his head.

"Paul here knew someone from there," he could not help himself.

"Wow! Really?" Candy asked. Paul rubbed his forehead as he re-visited a nightmare.

"Yeah, he lived over there for a time, didn't you, Paul?"

Candy looked at Paul with interest, Simon smiled thinking he was doing his mate a huge favour, Charlotte giggled and Amanda still glared.

Paul sighed and got to his feet. "Sorry, something's come up, I've got to go," he announced and left quickly.

Later in the week Paul was walking through town after college. The sun was shining, it was early spring, he wore a quiet smile and his mind was clear; he could never see under what circumstances he would ever bump into Val again. He enjoyed his course work, his tutors were tolerant of his disappearances and re-appearances and his contemporaries in class, two a lot older, but the rest ten or so years younger, seemed to like him. The people milling around him were making their own way, the women passing smiled, the men passing nodded, no one knew him or bothered him. Or did they?

"PAUL!" a voice called out from behind him. He turned to face them.

"Hey, Michelle, how are you?" they hugged and kissed as friends would do.

"I'm fine, Paul, just fine. Heard you were back," she pulled a sympathetic face, not like the sympathetic face Val used to pull but a more squidgy Geordie face which sometimes let loose the occasional word from her home land. Paul smiled.

"Val had a kid, baby boy," he announced.

"Oh, right, right,"

"You didn't know?" he asked her.

"She rung me to tell me she was shacked up with this Erik character and," Michelle paused and looked around her, "I swore at her!" she gasped, grabbed Paul's hand and put her other hand to her mouth. Paul realised this wasn't mock horror. Michelle was shocked at her own behaviour.

*It had to happen some time.*

"Oh, dear," he offered.

"And we haven't spoken since."

"Blimey,"

"The cow, eh, doing something so horrible to someone as lovely as you," Michelle was looking into Paul's eyes in a really odd way. This was the sort of comment Val used to make about Michelle and it struck Paul as a really strange turn of events.

"Michelle?"

She pulled herself together, "Not busy are you? Shall we grab a drink?" She began to walk back in the direction Paul had just come.

"Sure, don't know when I'll be busy again," Paul replied. Michelle turned to face him, put her hands on his cheeks and kissed him.

"We'll have to see what I can do about that," she said and they headed off to the Red Lion.

"I once bought you a drink in here," Paul said. Michelle paused as she was entering the pub and looked puzzled.

"Did you? I can't remember."

"Good."

# 2010

It was the next morning, the sun was shining and it was getting warm. I had been inside pretending to work on my second book when she called out to me.

"Liam, I've finished it." I made my way to the back door to find her sat in the garden on the steps looking at the back cover of the book.

"Coffee," I suggested, "Or something stronger?"

"Coffee, please."

When I came out of the house with a coffee for each of us the book was on the steps beside her and she was looking into space. She took a drink and I waited for her to comment on the endings. She gave me a look...

"The two endings in the book with Paul and Val," I began, "is how I thought we would have ended up if we had hooked up; either happy ever after or together for a short while and then you found someone better." Val nodded to understand and I carried on. "The part with Michelle reflects the part that I made contact with her earlier than I made contact with you. She was in the pub the other night when you saw her as I had half invited her to join me and me mates for a drink. Turns out she was the only one I gave the correct pub to."

"Are you two shagging or, what?" Val asked, forthright as ever.

"No!" I tried to say it as firmly as I could and it was true. "You might have a shock if you talked to her now."

"Why?"

"For one thing she is the deputy head of a comprehensive school."

"Really?" Val gave a little laugh of disbelief.

I nodded, "She talks all posh, her Geordie accent has gone and she's like a young Margaret Thatcher."

Val looked shocked, "And that doesn't turn you on?" She raised an eyebrow, suggestively.

I laughed, "No, not really. She closed t'pit!" We both laughed at this point. Val then went back to looking at the book and allowed herself a smile.

"Will you sign it for me, Liam?" she asked holding the book towards me. I hesitated and weighed up what this gesture meant. If you were to end up living in the same house as someone, having a book in your possession written by them and signed by them would be a pretty strange thing to have. If on the other hand you were planning to disappear around the world again...

"You're not staying around here then?" I asked. She lowered the book slightly as stretching was getting tiring and in the same motion she lowered her head, possibly unintentionally as a reflex. Her arm must have ached as she put the book down and tried to smile.

"I'd like to think of it as a security blanket, a back up plan, a..." she paused as she wasn't selling this very well. "Who knows what our future holds?"

I put the cup down on the garden wall and walked a few yards onto my lawn, trying to think. After a short while I turned to face her, "Is this because of me making contact with Michelle?" She didn't reply but looked at the ground. "I told you why I did that, I was trying to find you."

"But, Liam, what she did to me," she protested.

"Was like a million bloody years ago. When I mentioned your name on the first night out I had with Michelle she visibly gushed about you, there was a tremendous amount of fondness, or love there for you. Do you not think it might be worth giving her call, meeting for a drink?"

Val stood up and marched towards me, "Has she put you up to this?"

"No, it was only with you reading the book and Michelle appearing at the end that I thought it best to bring her into the conversation. If there had been no book, if me and Michelle had not been out for drinks I would have asked you the other night if you had heard from her and left it at that. It was you I was interested in."

Val had her hands on her hips in a 'double-tea-pot' pose and stared at me. Without another word she turned, walked up the steps, into the house, through the front door and to God knows where.


Val told me later, she left my house more confused than angry and headed into town not sure what she was going to do. She realised that she had left her copy of my my book behind and wondered if I had signed it for her as she had asked. After a short while something I had said sunk in, so she headed back to the hotel where she had been staying and headed to her room. She got out her laptop and for the first time in years looked at her college alumni website. Of course, I never went to her college but I knew she went there. Were there any messages from me on her page?

The laptop was taking an age to log on, "Come on, bloody hurry up," she cursed it. Finally the site came up and her inbox had (4) next to it.

Message one; *"Hi! Hope this is the Val I used to quiz with. Liam here, it would be great to catch up"* – from October 2006.

Message two; *"Hello there, hope this is the correct Valerie Walters, it would be a strange old world if there was more than one of you. Happy birthday"* – my, God he remembered? – *Liam x* – from April 2008.

Message three; *"Hi, Val, I hear that you are teaching in India, that's awesome, if you are ever back in England it would be great to meet up and, as I see you are married bring the (very) lucky man along with you and you can meet my wife! We could go for a curry if you aren't sick of it by then, Liam"* – from August 2009.

Message four; *"Hi, Val, it's been so long. I'm sorry for being a cow, it is about time we hooked up again and got back to being friends, Michelle x* – from, blimey, last week!

She paused and let the messages wash over her. It seemed all her life was played out there in four emails.

# 1994

Monday night was quiz night and I had left Ian's DJ stand with a quiz sheet and made my way to where we normally sat. Tonight I was on my own and felt a little bit sad about that, a bit embarrassed, but anything was better than staying in and watching Monday night telly. As I took my seat before the quiz started, Ian was entertaining us with the likes of East 17 and the Urban Cookie Collective. Perhaps entertaining was not the right word. As I was writing my team name onto the quiz sheet - just my name, Liam - the attractive brunette I had noticed in the last few weeks tapped my arm.

"What's up?" I asked.

"Are you entering the quiz on your own?" she asked me with a lovely smile, suggesting she cared about me, a complete stranger. So I smiled a friendly smile back.

"Yeah, bit sad I know but it's better than being stuck in all night watching telly."

"So, are your mates not with you tonight?"

I shook my head and confirmed it, "No."

"What about your girlfriend, could she not have come down with you?" the blonde girl sat next to her asked. I pulled a face.

"Girlfriend?" I gave a little laugh. "Don't have one."

They both reacted with disbelief. The blonde girl gasped and the brunette exclaimed, "You don't have a girlfriend?" This prompted me to pull a puzzled face.

"No. Why do you think I should have?"

They went a bit quiet at this point, worried I think, that I might ask one of them out.

"Do you want to join up with us?" the brunette asked me after a moment of silence.

"Yeah, as long as you don't mind," I replied. The brunette turned and found her blonde mate nodding enthusiastically so this suggestion seemed to have met with her approval. I sat down next to them with a smile, this was possibly the best thing to have happened to me this week.

"I'm Liam."

"Val." the brunette girl confirmed. Val elbowed her friend who was looking into the near distance.

"Oh, er, Michelle, hi!"

---

# 2010

After Val left I sat in the front room with my feet up on the coffee table and my mobile in my hands. I was not sure how long I should leave it before ringing her, or texting her. Her copy of my book was beside me on the sofa and I picked it up to read the message I had written in it after she left.

*To Val, 16 years in the making, Liam xx*

Reading it again I wondered if she would turn up for it and I sighed, tossing it onto the table. After not seeing her for so long had I blown the chance to get her back in my life? We had kissed in the pub, talked on the phone, these were things we did before but we had also shared a bath and a bed, unlike our characters in my book these were new adventures for us.

# 1995

It was Saturday night and I was out with my middle brother, Steve, and our collection of mates so we numbered ten in total. We were in the Red Lion and after getting our drinks, tried to find enough square metres for us all to stand in together to talk bollocks and ogle women. The laughs were flying and the drink was flowing and then Steve tapped me on the shoulder.

"Aye, aye," he said to me, lowering his voice. When I turned to face him I was smiling and noticed he had a wolfish look on his face. "I've spotted a friend of yours!" I looked into the throng of people around us and initially failed to recognise anyone I knew.

"Who?" I asked a bit impatiently. He was laughing and my mood was now akin to a spoilt child being deprived of a Christmas morning present.

"Her!" he pointed again. "Isn't that the bird you used to do the quiz with?"

It was then I noticed Val talking to a lad I did not recognise and laughing. I had not seen her for a few months and she looked well. While she was never fat when we knocked about she now looked leaner. The lad she was talking to was a student type.

"Are you going over to say hello?" Steve asked.

"Am I hell!" I replied and we left shortly after.

Like most Saturday night's we found ourselves in Liberty's with the intention of being on the pull. I had been in there for a while and went to a little bar above the dance floor to get my next drink. Val was getting served and the only way I could avoid her was to turn and walk away. Stood behind her was a girl I had been introduced to once before who had gone to college with Val and Michelle. I noticed she clocked me and could see her brain ticking over trying to recall where she knew me from. Once she remembered me, if I had walked away I would have been rumbled so to the bar I went.


The only other times I had seen Val before this time, after we had fallen out, was when I had the devil in me and suggested to my mate Richie that we go to the quiz to wind her up. Two things worked against me; when we arrived she was not actually there and when Michelle saw me she gave me a friendly smile but did not speak. Also, I had recently been for an eye test and needed to wear specs for distances and I wore them out this night to get used to them, so I did not look particularly hard. Ian was his usual friendly self and I wondered if he ever had any idea what had happened.

Finally, towards the end of the quiz, Val turned up and went to sit with Michelle. She only noticed me when I went to collect our winnings from Ian. As I passed I heard someone comment, "Looks a wanker with those glasses on," but could not be sure who had said it.

A few months later I entered my favourite take-away place, Roosters, where I was such a regular that no matter how busy they were when I got to the front of the queue my food would be ready, nine chicken nuggets and fries was my junk food of choice at the time. On this night there were two more people in; Ian and Val. Ian spotted me, "A'right, Liam, lad," he said.

"Hi," I replied. Val turned slowly and gave me what I believed to be an enigmatic smile, she was either pleased to see me or she wanted to kill me, I could not tell. They left shortly after and Ian said "bye" on the way out, but Val did not.

So I found myself stood next to Val at the bar waiting to be served and after a short while she said, "Oh, hello!" I hugged her and from memory it was not returned but we chatted for a while, she told me her new body was due to early morning swimming sessions and she re-emphasised she wanted to remain friends. She told me that when Ian had asked where I was she said we had fallen out over her attempts to fix me up with Michelle. While I was pleased for the reprieve I never did go back to the quiz.

## 1996

I found myself in education of sorts for the first time since I had done a day release course just after leaving school, studying Psychology GCSE at a local college. It was the first step towards a failed attempt to become a sports psychologist. At the end of the first week I was in the Prince of Wales and saw that Ian was in. He told me Val had finished with him (did this mean she was single now!) and I was as sympathetic as I could be.

It was still late summer and when I joined my mates on the pavement outside I bumped into Val and Michelle. They were both very pleased to see me as shown by a massive hug from them both. I told them I was studying and what my hopes were for it. Val then invited me to stop over at her home in Blackpool, where she worked as a teacher, to go on a night out 'just as friends,' which was an odd thing to say, and I hoped something might come of it. The only way I could see it not working would be if she was already living with a bloke. In that instance I don't think she would have invited me. When I went to join up with my mates I realised I had still not got her address or phone number.

About a month or so later I bumped into her again and she was quite cold with me. I could not see the invitation of a night out being extended this time, especially when she said at one point, "we would have been good friends if it wasn't for one thing" and she raised an eyebrow as if to say 'and you know what that is.' I didn't know. I made my excuses and left. The only time I saw her after that was when I saw her car parked outside the Prince of Wales pub and wondered if I would bump into her that night and realised she was sat in the driving seat. I knocked on the window and when she opened it I realised Ian was in there with her and I could not really broach the subject of a night out so after a few minutes I was off to join up with my mates. That was 1997 and until now that was that.

# 2010

Until Val rang again or until I worked up the courage to call her, the search for inspiration for the second book continued and as I based my first book on some life experience I got an A4 pad and wrote a few ideas down. Could I turn my drinking memoirs, rejected by every publisher and literary agent, into a work of fiction? I brought the details up onto my PC and changed a few names that I had not already changed. I wasn't going to fall into that trap again! It was while I was making a start that the landline rang and if nothing else at least I knew this was not Val ringing.

"Hello?" I answered.

"Hello, Liam, I have some news," the clipped tones on the other end of the phone signified it was Michelle.

"Oh, really, what's that?" I asked.

"Well, I think you could guess, Valerie rang me," she replied.

"Ah, yes, we had run into each other," I sheepishly confirmed.

"Liam, I am so pleased."

"Great, when Val and me were chatting I said it was about time you were friends again."

"Not that, well, that pleases me also, I am pleased that you two might get it on." This stopped me in my tracks.

"We might?"

"She said there was a chance, Liam and if I was you I'd give her a call, test the water."

"I will."


In the next few days I didn't get the chance as I had Sean stopping with me and he took up all my time. I didn't even work on the next book. On the morning of the day Sean was being collected by Fiona, my ex-wife, my agent rang me.

"Liam, Tom here," he began.

"Hi, Tom."

"The publishers are leaning on me for a few chapters of the next book. They took a huge gamble on you, well, on both of us really and so far no one has been going crackers for Who's Going To Drive You Home."

"Actually, Tom, I have been putting a few things together, I've got me son with me at the mo' but I'll get something over to you this aft'." I fired back.

"Okay, look forward to it."

Such is the nature of my new occupation that as I was preparing the chapters and synopsis to forward over to Tom he rang me again. He sounded quite cheerful.

"Liam! Tom here, again."

"Ah, Tom, glad you rang, I'm just getting the chapters together that we talked about, and any minute now I'll..."

"Forget that for the moment, I ring with some good news. I have had a film company on called Stage Door Inc. Heard of 'em?"

"Name rings a bell," I replied but to be honest I did not have a clue.

"They had one of their guys pick up 'Who's Going To Drive You Home?' to read on a train journey and they loved it and can see a film in it. I've fixed up a meeting next week and they are keen to meet you. Ever written a screenplay, Liam, lad?"

I laughed, "Not a successful one, no."

Tom cackled down the phone, "Well, come and meet them and see what they want. I'll ring to confirm the details in the next few days."

"Nice one, cheers, Tom," and when I hung up I was smiling broadly. Imagine someone making a film of my work.

The call distracted me and I had got behind so I was still tidying Sean's things up when there was a knock on the front door. As I came out of the front room with toys in my hand I could see through the glass that it was Val. My heart skipped a beat as I was pleased it was her and also because I did not ring her as Michelle had suggested, I wondered if she was going to be mad. When I opened the door she was smiling so that was a relief at least.

"Hey you, how have you been?" she asked.

"Fine, thanks, and you?" I noticed she was looking at the toys. "What's up?"

"Oh, God, sorry, is Sean here with you? I could come back."

I glanced at the toys, "Oh, er, no, no he isn't, he was today but has gone now, I was just tidying up. Come in, come in." She followed me up the hall into the front room and I put the toys in a box already over spilling with them. Before being offered the choice, she sat in the armchair and was still smiling but it was almost beginning to look a bit forced, "Do you want some wine?" I asked.

"Actually, I'm starving, do you fancy ringing out for a take away?" she suggested. "Then I'll have some wine."

"Yeah, certainly, do you fancy pizza?" Val nodded so I rummaged through a draw in the kitchen for the menus and brought them in.

An hour later we were sat in the lounge ploughing our way through delicious pizzas; I had ham and mushroom and Val had plumped for something called a Rambo Flamethrower which seemed bloody hot. We hadn't really talked much since she arrived and conversation was nil as we ate away, apart from a few appreciative "Mmm" noises. There were only a few slices of 'flamethrower' left when Val wiped her hands on the kitchen towel and fixed me a stare, thankfully accompanied by a grin. "Can I ask you something?"

"Sure," I replied.

"Why did your marriage end?"

"Show you mine if you show me yours."

Val looked aghast, "I'm sorry?"

"Why have you and Barry split up?"

"We haven't officially."

"So where is he?"

"He got the offer of a job back in Nottingham, where he's from, and left me up here to think what I wanted to do." Val picked up a slice of pizza, looked at it and then put it back. "When I was in India teaching he didn't work. He had the chance to help out at the school I was working at or even for some of the UK companies over there but he didn't fancy it."

"So what did he do all day?"

"Fuck all; drank, smoked and acted like a complete twat."

I stood up and went to the kitchen to fetch the wine and two glasses saying, "Do they do college courses in that?" Val laughed. She took a drink of the wine and I finished the last slice of my pizza. "Do you want my last one too?" she asked but I shook my head.

"So was it the fact he was acting like a twat the reason you were arguing the other night and might split up?" I asked her. Val took another drink and looked embarrassed.

"Okay, cards on the table time, when me and Barry first started going out he suggested we go to a quiz at the local pub near where we lived and when I got a few questions right he asked me if I went to a lot of quizzes and I told him about going to the quiz at the Prince of Wales. From there I mentioned Ian and you. He was fine at that point about you both but in our first month in India we were in Goa and a lad walked into the bar we were in wearing a Blackburn shirt. I mentioned I knew a Rovers fan and asked if he knew you and when Barry asked if Blackburn Liam was also pub quiz Liam he got it into his head that I had not got over you and was still obsessed with you."

"I see, blimey," was all I could say at this point. Val ran her hand over her forehead, took a drink and carried on.

"It had not been brought up for about a year or so and everything looked fine. We came back here for a few days once we were back in the UK just because I went to uni here but that night I saw you in The Sun we had another row. He tricked me by asking if you still lived around here and when I said I thought you still did he went mental thinking I had been looking you up on the internet and that was the only reason we had come back." I looked into my drink.

"Was that another reason you were not on any social network sites then or answering your messages?" I asked her.

Val nodded, "I have seen the messages now. I even got a recent one from Michelle and we have been out for a meal together, that was good."

"Great, she had rung me to let me know, but that's brilliant."

Val smiled, "So go on, you and... your wife."

"Fiona."

"Fiona, right. Where did it all go wrong?"

# 2009

It was a Saturday and I had been into work to do a bit of overtime. If every working day was like this it would be bearable; no phone calls from irate policy holders or brokers, just all paperwork. As I arrived home I was hit by the aroma of food being cooked and headed to the kitchen.

"Hi!" I said to Fiona's back as she slaved away with her elbows in pans and food.

"Oh, hi, you're here, great. I ran into Tina at Morrison's and invited her and Dave over for dinner tonight." Tina was an old friend of Fiona's but Dave I did not know.

"Who's Dave?" I asked.

"New fella," Fiona informed me.

"Oh, so she's finally binned Mark, then?" Mark was Tina's husband and a waste of space. He drank and hadn't worked for many years. We thought he hit her about. When sober he could be quite charming and very funny which meant that Tina always struggled to get out of there.

"If you get Sean's coat on, me Mum will be here soon to collect him, he's stopping over so we can, you know, have a night of it." Fiona smiled. It was some time since we had had a 'night of it'.

The food was delicious, Fiona was a demon cook and Tina and Dave were good company. We live in a very small town and I did not know him but he seemed to know me and weighed me up when he arrived. After the meal we were in the front room and we started talking generally. Tina's conversation soon came around to Mark and while the subject matter was obviously still raw she spoke strongly and Dave seemed supportive. She mentioned how she was continually charmed by Mark and for so long could not leave him no matter how bad things got.

There was a brief lull in the conversation just after Tina said that as Mark was her first big love she found that the hardest thing to forget. "You can't use that as an excuse not to look for happiness somewhere else, though." I opined. Dave gave a snort of a laugh.

"Yeah, right mate," he said. I stopped in my tracks and looked at him.

"Er, I'm sorry?"

"I bet if that bird from the quiz came knocking on the door you'd be off like a shot," Dave said and leant back in his chair allowing himself a satisfied smile.

"Which bird from the quiz?" I asked him, wondering how he knew.

"Which bird from the quiz?" Fiona asked me. There was silence for a moment and all was confusion apart from Dave still smiling.

"How did you know about her? Who are you?" I asked.

Dave was still smiling suggesting he was enjoying this, "My brother had a front row seat of your little fling with her at the Prince of Wales. Her boyfriend never knew what was happening but he did and when I rang him tonight and told him whose house I was coming to he told me all about it."

There was silence as everyone let the information wash over them. Dave never gave any timescales of when this happened but by the look on Fiona's face, she had decided that this had happened some point in the last few weeks, or days. After a short while Tina turned to face Fiona. "Do you think Mark will ever ring me again?"

# 2010

Val listened to what happened and her face did not portray any emotion. She waited for me to conclude the story. "It led to a lack of trust and honesty and she had the impression that I still held a torch for you," I concluded. "And by Christmas last year I was out of there."

Val leant forward and put her glass of wine on the coffee table, "And do you, Liam?" she asked. "Do you still hold a torch for me?"

It was early September 2010 and I had a productive day at the PC updating my drinking memoirs to make it into a fictional novel. Also, I worked a bit more on the screenplay which had the working title 'Missing You'. After I logged off I dashed upstairs, had a quick wash and put on a clean shirt. I came back downstairs and before leaving the house, sent a text.

From my home I walked to the end of the street, crossed over past the DIY store and headed down the canal footpath. After five minutes I was at a pub called, with no originality, The Water's Edge. I made my way to the bar, ordered a bottle of white wine and caused confusion by asking for two glasses and two menus. With the early evening basking in late summer sunshine I sat outside to wait for her. Within ten minutes she came along the footpath from the car park.

"Great, you're here. I had hoped you got my message."

"I did, yes, and thanks for inviting me."

"For you," I said passing her a glass of wine, "and I got menus if you fancy something to eat from here."

"Liam, you're spoiling me!" she gushed.

"And how was your first day back at school, young lady?" I asked studying the menu.

"Fine," she replied, funnily enough the exact word Sean uses to describe every day at school.

"Did you remember the apple for teacher?" She paused as the wine glass was halfway to her mouth.

"I am the teacher, you fool!" and we both laughed. Once our laughter stopped she looked serious for a moment. "Have you heard from Val yet?" I grimaced.

"Email from her this morning," I confirmed.

Val and I had started going out for the two months since we had bumped into one another. We took it steady which was difficult as she moved in to my house so we were effectively living together. I thought this was going to be it, that after missing our chance first time around we were going to be together. Then one evening when she was on her laptop I innocently asked her what she was looking at, to be cheerily told it was a site advertising jobs teaching English as a foreign language overseas. It was a sentiment I did not share. Within a fortnight her bags were packed again and she was on a plane to Cambodia.

"I really thought she was back for good once you had hooked up again."

"So did I, but there you go," I replied with a shrug, lowering my head. Michelle took another drink and looked along the canal and turned back to face me.

"How long will she be gone for this time?"

"No idea, no idea." Michelle placed her right hand in mine.

"Sorry, Liam, I really am," and I forced myself to smile back. Michelle smiled at me, lowered her head and looking shy she moved around the table to sit alongside me.

"You know, if you need me, I'm here for you Liam," and at this point she kissed me, on the lips, for several seconds.

"As like a girlfriend type person?" I asked when we broke apart.

"Yes, why not?" and she laughed.

I smiled. I couldn't think of a reason why not.

*Other novels from Empire*

# THE CARPET KING OF TEXAS

## PAUL KENNEDY

**"TRAINSPOTTING FOR THE VIAGRA GENERATION"**
**SUNDAY MIRROR**
**"DRUG-TAKING, SEXUAL DEPRAVITY... NOT FOR THE FAINT HEARTED."**
**NEWS OF THE WORLD**

This shocking debut novel from award-winning journalist Paul Kennedy tells the twisted tales of three lives a million miles apart as they come crashing together with disastrous consequences.

Away on business, Dirk McVee is the self proclaimed "Carpet King of Texas" – but work is the last thing on his mind as he prowls Liverpool's underbelly to quench his thirst for sexual kicks.

Teenager Jade Thompson is far too trusting for her own good. In search of a guiding light and influential figure, she slips away from her loving family and into a life where no one emerges unscathed.

And John Jones Junior is the small boy with the grown-up face. With a drug addicted father, no motherly love, no hope, and no future, he has no chance at all.

The Carpet King of Texas is a gritty and gruesome, humorous and harrowing story of a world we all live in but rarely see.

ORDER THIS BOOK NOW FOR JUST £6
WWW.EMPIRE-UK.COM